# BEFORE THE LIGHTS GO OUT

A THRILLER

# JAFE DANBURY

https://www.JefePress.com
**Ordering Information**
Quantity sales: Special discounts may be available on quantity purchases by corporations, associations, schools, and others. For details, you can contact the publisher and author at:
**jefepress@yahoo.com**
**jafe.danbury@yahoo.com**

**ISBN 978-1-7333440-5-0** (print)
**First Printing, December 2025**
Printed in the United States of America
This is a work of fiction. Names, characters, locations, and incidents either are the products of the author's imagination or are used fictitiously. Any resemblance to actual persons, either living or dead, businesses, companies, events, or locales is entirely coincidental.
**Cover concept and interior photos by Jafe Danbury**
**Cover design and formatting by Damonza.com**

## PRAISE FOR WORKS BY JAFE DANBURY:

*The Other Cheek: Boy Meets Girl. Girl Beats Boy. Just Your Typical Love Story…*

*Leaving Phoenix* (Book 1 in the PHOENIX Series)

*X* (Book 2 in the PHOENIX Series)

*So Much Forever* (Book 3 in the PHOENIX Series)

Praise for JAFE DANBURY'S debut novel
### *THE OTHER CHEEK:*

*FINALIST, "Best First Novel" category, 2020 Next Generation Indie Book Awards*

"This read to me as a desperately written burn book no one was supposed to read, how real and honestly it was written, absolutely sucked me in with the emotional rollercoaster that was this man's life. Such a page-turner with how flawlessly this book flowed. My only wish was that I could read this book over for the first time. You won't be disappointed if you read this book. Bravo!"

~ BECCAH, AMAZON REVIEW

"Jafe Danbury is a superb writer, riveting my soul to every turned page… Oprah Winfrey must interview Jafe on her Super Soul Sunday program. Everyone should read this superbly written story."

~ ELAYNE SILVA-REYNA,
AUTHOR OF *WOLF DREAMER OF THE LONGEST NIGHT MOON*

"Jafe's page-turner is a first-class read I would recommend to everyone fascinated by the extremes of human tolerance and abusive behavior."

~ R. Goodwin, Goodreads

"An intense, sometimes-brutal novel about acknowledging and escaping an abusive relationship."

~ Kirkus Reviews

"Yes, this is a story of domestic abuse, but there is also a deeper meaning. It is also a story of hope, a story of making it through to the other side, a story of 'the other cheek.'

I stayed up past my bedtime reading this one... that doesn't happen often. This book definitely comes from the author's heart, and I totally respect him for putting his story 'out there.'"

~ M. Ammons, Goodreads

# PRAISE FOR *LEAVING PHOENIX:*

*GOLD, "Mystery/Thriller" 2023 Reader Views Literary Awards*

*FINALIST, 2022 IAN Book of the Year Awards*

*GOLD, 2022 Reader Views Award*

*FINALIST, 2022 Readers' Favorite Book Awards*

*GOLD, 2021 Literary Titan Book Awards*

"Wow! What a phenomenal book! I don't have many 'favorite books,' but this one has been added to my very short list! I had such a hard time putting it down, but I did have to sleep and interact with my family, LOL."

~ Travel Thru Books

"This novel is likely to earn strong reviews by word of mouth. Now is precisely the time for this novel. It is intense and often gripping to read, but it is also highly satisfying as you put yourself in the shoes of a young woman who must unravel her past and face a dark truth. Jafe Danbury displays a well-crafted treatment of tone and pacing, as well as a well-fleshed-out protagonist that you will truly care about. Danbury kneads the tension slowly, allowing Phoebe to accumulate resilience and intelligence as she gets closer to the truth. A must-read for any lovers of suspense and mystery, *Leaving Phoenix* is a heart-pounding and profoundly suspenseful novel that reaches an enormously satisfying arc."

~ Readers' Favorite Book Reviews

"A tense and involving tale of a young woman seeking revenge and finding a family."

~ Kirkus Reviews

"Danbury is a master storyteller. Phoenix's life is nothing short of a miracle, and the intricate plot he lays out for his main character traces her life from conception through her fearless resolve to find her mother's killer at any cost. Phoenix is a phenomenal main character and is a picture of strength and determination. The relationship she is able to form with her grandfather after two decades with her adoptive father is touching and quite amazing. In addition, her willingness to relive the past is truly a testament to her incredible strength of character."

~ Literary Titan

"A well-edited story alive with striking images, sharp dialogue, and the pain and promise of self-discovery. Deep character development and welcome lighthearted moments lead the way in keeping the pages turning. The mystery is believable, and the characters are lovable with well-thought-out character arcs and a relationship to story development. Any mystery fan who loves a mostly fast-paced narrative with a splash of romance will find this is a rewarding addition to to-be-read lists."

~ Book Life Reviews, Publishers Weekly

*WINNER, 2024 Book Excellence Award: "Suspense"*

*FINALIST, 2024 Independent Author Awards: "Thriller"*

*FINALIST, 2023, Readers' Favorite Awards*

"Jafe Danbury's construct of a potentially horrific story takes the reader through a major roller coaster of fear and trauma that breaks through with a surprising resolution. The plot trajectory was so fascinating that I could barely put down my cigar while reading (my favorite combination of activities). Many thanks to Jafe for such an amazing journey through the PHOENIX series! I'm very much looking forward to Book 3!"

~ C. TALLEN, GOODREADS

"I love the fact that Phoenix's story has continued. While it's a traumatic subject, it was handled gracefully and with heart. The characters are so very well written and they're down to earth and relatable. My favorite part is the music references. Gave me ear worms where some of the songs wouldn't go away. Mr. Danbury has a true gift for writing and I'm excited to hear that there's going to be a third book to this series!"

~ L. A. WILCOX, GOODREADS

"Jafe Danbury's thriller, *X*, sinks its claws into you from the beginning and doesn't let go, using multi-perspectivity to keep you in its grip. With surgical precision, this author stitches together a series of heart-pounding events that keep the pages turning feverishly late into the night. You're left breathless as the plot plunges into shadowy danger, ratcheting up the vitalizing suspense with exquisite timing. *X* will leave your pulse racing and your heart aching. You'll find yourself holding your breath as Phoenix and her family confront impossible choices. Phoenix's family has fierce love that burns like a torch, lighting their way through the darkest moments. The bonds between them are unbreakable, even as sinister forces threaten to tear their world apart. Jafe Danbury's ruthless, unputdownable thriller is not easily forgotten."

~ TAMBI SMITH, GOODREADS


"A sensitive topic handled very well. As the second in a new series, this one definitely came out swinging and never stopped! Such a sensitive topic but handled with a lot of care and discretion, great foundation and now the series is twisting and turning in a way I can't stop reading. I love the way this author writes. I can envision the people and backdrops in every scene as well as hear the soundtrack he lays. Looking forward to the third installment!!"

~ COLLEEN CURTIS, GOODREADS


"Jafe's writing skills reached new heights in this one. He fearlessly tackled a sensitive subject, one that I find very hard to think about, let alone read, and knocked me right out of the literary stratosphere. I also want to applaud Jafe's gift for description. Seriously, this guy knows how to paint a vivid picture with words. Every scene, every detail, it all just deepened my adoration for his writing. Bravo and a loud cheer, Jafe, you seriously outdid yourself!"

~ M. OLIVER, GOODREADS

"An Unforgettable Sequel That Leaves You Breathless!

*X* catapults readers back into the gripping world of Phoenix and Curt with heart-stopping intensity. Jafe Danbury once again proves his skill as a master storyteller, weaving a tale of relentless suspense and gut-wrenching emotion that will leave you on the edge of your seat from start to finish.

As Phoenix and Curt find themselves facing every parent's worst nightmare, the stakes are higher than ever, and the tension is evident with each turn of the page.

Sharp and gripping as ever, Danbury draws readers into a world where danger lurks around every corner, and nothing is as it seems!"

~ MANDY S., GOODREADS

"Danbury's expertise in crafting a riveting tale shines through, making *X* a book that's difficult to put down. His flair for suspense keeps readers on the edge of their seats, continually urging them to turn the next page. For its engrossing plot, well-rounded characters, and gripping narrative, *X* comes highly recommended as one of the most remarkable reads in recent memory."

~ LITERARY TITAN

## PRAISE FOR *SO MUCH FOREVER:*

*WINNER, SILVER MEDAL, Crime Fiction, 2025 Readers' Favorite Book Awards*

*FIRST PLACE WINNER, Fall 2024 The BookFest Awards*

*WINNER, 2025 International Impact Awards*

*WINNER, 2025 Book Excellence Awards*

*WINNER, 2025 Maincrest Media Awards*

"Jafe Danbury has arrived! This book was a WILD ride! *So Much Forever* is the incredible third book in Danbury's PHOENIX Series, and in my opinion it's his best yet. Packed with enough action and adventure for a lifetime - the story takes place over only 10 days - and what an intense 10 days they are! Murder, kidnapping, drugs, murder, trauma, (did I mention murder?)… Danbury leaves no dramatic stone unturned. I was captivated from the first chapter to the last and gasping in shock throughout. With this thriller, I think it's safe to say that Jafe Danbury has arrived. I can't imagine what he has for us next… because how would it top this? Recommended."
~ CHARISSA COSTA, CHARM CITY READERS

"This is the third book in the PHOENIX series, and while I absolutely adored *Leaving Phoenix* and *X, So Much Forever* truly takes the cake. It has all the elements I crave in a thriller—tension, twists, and deeply layered characters—plus some unexpected surprises that took the experience to another level.

Jafe's ability to craft such a gripping narrative is incredible. I found myself laughing, gasping, and even cheering at various points. A few moments had me literally on the edge of my seat, completely immersed in the story. I had to remind myself to let out the breath I had been holding.

What sets *So Much Forever* apart for me is its darker tone, which I know many of you will appreciate. The story delves deeper into the shadows than the previous books, adding a rich layer of complexity to the series. Jafe's writing is as sharp as ever, drawing me in with every carefully chosen word. He's a master storyteller who knows exactly how to ensnare his readers, making it nearly impossible to put the book down.

*So Much Forever* is an outstanding read that I didn't want to end! Move this up on your TBR!! Five incredibly high stars from me!"

~ LEIDY C., GOODREADS

"The emotional depth of the characters, especially the portrayal of survivors grappling with their trauma, added a powerful layer to the fast-paced plot. Overall, *So Much Forever* is more than just a thriller—it's a story of resilience, family, and the fight for survival. It's a gripping, fast-paced page turner that will stay with you long after the final chapter."

~ OM SEN, GOODREADS

"A famous author once described the secret to writing a great thriller: 'When your character's in trouble, you need to get him into even more trouble.' Well, the Martinsens are certainly having a run of deadly bad luck as the mayhem strikes their family again in Jafe Danbury's third novel in the PHOENIX series.

Thoroughly researched and highly descriptive, Jafe's narrative flows smoothly throughout the book. His characters are totally believable, and we always hope that the good in them will triumph over the evil in their antagonists.

I'm a fast reader, which often leads to disappointment when I finish a book too quickly, usually in a day or two, but this chunky offering from Jafe kept me totally entertained for twice the usual time. You can read this novel as a stand-alone, since Jafe skillfully weaves the back-story into this third book in the PHOENIX series, but for full enjoyment, I recommend also catching up with his previous books, *Leaving Phoenix* and *X*.

A fantastic read from this rapidly emerging and maturing writer."

~ REG G., GOODREADS

"The world Danbury crafts is vivid, and the tension doesn't let up for a second. I could almost see the action unfold like a movie. The life-or-death scenario Phoenix faces had me holding my breath, and I found myself rooting for her through every twist and turn.

Phoenix, Curt, Rose and company are back with a vengeance. In book three, we are introduced to a serial killer who will stop at nothing to get what she wants. Be prepared for nonstop action and breathtaking scenarios.

Superb plotting and writing contribute to making this a must read. Although this can be read as a standalone, do yourself a favor and read the exciting thrillers *Leaving Phoenix* and *X*, books one and two, first, to enjoy the full impact of *So Much Forever*.

Definitely a five-star read. Well done, Jafe Danbury!"

~ CAROL N., GOODREADS

"A fast-paced page turner with sequences that are the stuff of great cinema."

~ DANA LARRABEE, AUTHOR

"One should really use the camera

as though tomorrow you'd be stricken blind."

~ DOROTHEA LANGE

To my family, on both sides of the pond.

# BEFORE
# THE
# LIGHTS
# GO
# OUT

# CHAPTER ONE

## BOTHELL, WASHINGTON
## THURSDAY, DECEMBER 11
## 6:10 AM

THE LAST VESTIGES of the family's leftover Thanksgiving bounty were fighting for space on the sparse Formica countertop of the cramped kitchen. It had all the appearance of a failed Tupperware party.

A family of three certainly didn't justify the need for a seventeen-pound Butterball, nor all the boilerplate accoutrements, but the friends they'd invited cancelled at the last minute, the couple citing nasty flareups of bronchitis (his) and Crohn's (hers), leaving the Dunkels with enough food for a small army.

Even the best of feasts will grow tiresome when you've had nothing but the same thing for a couple of weeks, and today's sandwiches would be the last of it. If Reagan was feeling thankful for anything, it was for the fact they could move on from the burnout of the traditional meal's leftovers.

Besides, being a German, it wasn't even traditional to her, but she played along.

Cranberry sauce? Meh. She much preferred a good red cabbage with apples. And she had never understood the fixation on turkey. She found it to be dry and tasteless. Never mind that millions of starving people around the world would literally kill for the giblets she'd casually tossed in the trash. Third World problems weren't on her radar this morning, nor any other. This was Seattle-adjacent Bothell, not Somalia, but perhaps they were sister cities.

Reagan Dunkel scraped the last globs of mayo from the now-empty jar and spread it equitably across the six slices of dark, whole wheat bread laid out before her on the breadboard, while Fynn busied himself with a stack of documents on the kitchen table.

His attention was laser focused as he thumbed through the pile, verifying that the color-coded page markers clearly indicated where the signatures were to go. And there were several.

Satisfied, Fynn placed his good Cross pen atop the stack and joined his wife. He gave her a peck on the cheek as he surveyed her construction project. "No cranberry sauce on mine, bitte."

"I know. We're out of the good mustard," Reagan said, yawning widely as she held up the empty vessel of his favorite, the dark one with the seeds. "You want this instead?" she asked, indicating the school-bus-yellow plastic squeeze bottle of French's.

"Um, no," he shuddered. "Danke. Extra stuffing, though, if there's enough. And dark meat, bitte."

"Yep, this'll finish it," Reagan acknowledged as she configured the turkey pieces, laying a foundation for the generous scoops of stuffing she was now mashing down atop of it all. Next came a leaf of the now-wilted, week-old iceberg lettuce before she firmly pressed the top piece of bread atop it and sliced the sandwich diagonally. With some effort she coaxed it into the too-snug zipper bag.

Another yawn, this one bigger. She was really dragging this morning and not sure why. The last time she remembered feeling this groggy was the knockout punch from an *Apfelwein* hangover in the twelfth grade–a mistake she'd only made once.

She shook her head in an effort to rid it of cobwebs, trying to remember if they'd consumed any alcohol with dinner the night before, but she realized they hadn't. Nor all week, for that matter.

*Weird.*

Fynn poured her a second cup of coffee and handed it to her. "Looks like you could use this," he said, glancing at his watch. "Want me to check on Steffi?"

"Right here," their soon-to-be-sixteen-year-old-daughter interjected as she entered the kitchen, fresh from the shower. Her hair was tucked beneath an impressive, Marge Simpson-esque towel beehive that made her look a foot taller than her height of five-foot-one. Her gaze was locked onto her iPhone screen.

She wore a trendy, aftermarket sweatshirt emblazoned with the Rolling Stones' tongue logo–a band several decades removed from her radar, but the image looked cheeky enough to be considered cool–paired with her severely thrashed Levi's that looked like she'd survived a bear attack.

Reagan looked over her shoulder and spun around, alarmed at her daughter's state of unreadiness. "Honey, we need to leave in fifteen minutes! Come on now... dry your hair. Chop chop!"

"We're way early," Steffi countered.

"Normally, yes, but I'm taking your dad to the airport after we drop you off. We talked about this. C'mon...."

"'Kay," she replied, rolling her eyes as she liberated her still-damp, shoulder length, orangish mane. "No stuffing on mine; it's gross," she muttered as she exited down the hall.

Fynn consulted his watch a second time, which didn't go unnoticed by his wife.

"Got your passport?" Reagan murmured, taking a sip from her mug.

He checked his sport coat's inner pocket and confirmed such. "Yeah."

"Tickets... documents?" she queried as she closed the remaining two sandwiches, nudging them into their baggies. She placed the sans-stuffing one, along with an apple and a bag of Cool Ranch Doritos, into Steffi's backpack.

"Tickets... in my pocket. Docs just need your signatures; they're on the table. There's signature flags where you need to sign. Just take a couple of seconds."

Reagan blew a long strand of blond hair from her face and began washing her hands, taking a moment's pause as she noticed a dark discoloration, a latent, charcoal-colored stain of some sort on the underside of her right thumb. None of her other digits were similarly affected and she shrugged it away as she scrubbed it mostly clean. She quickly rinsed the now-empty containers before returning the condiments back to their stations in the refrigerator door.

As she closed the fridge, she paused, her hand remaining on the handle.

"What is it?"

"Nothing," she replied through a sigh, looking around the countertop.

"You sure?"

"I don't know where I left my phone," she clucked, scurrying about the kitchen like a chicken searching for a piece of corn.

Fynn watched her for several seconds, tracking her movements before putting her out of her misery. He smiled and pointed to the white Samsung device sitting in the middle of the off-white countertop. Right in front of her. "You mean this one?"

Reagan stared down at it. She could cry, but she hadn't budgeted time for it this morning. "Yeah. That one...."

She pocketed the phone and plopped down onto the wooden dining chair, scooting in closer to the paper stack while grabbing the ballpoint pen. "Where do I sign?" she asked, her tone indicating a combination of frustration, fatigue, and fogginess. "I wish we didn't have to rush through this at the last minute."

"I know... the orange flags there," Fynn said, pointing to the first one. "Uh, want me to get your glasses?"

"No time for that treasure hunt; I misplaced 'em yesterday. Good thing I see the optometrist later," she said softly as she squinted and signed on the first line. "As long as I'm not buying a timeshare or something. I trust you." Fynn watched over her shoulder as she made her way through the stack of pages, affixing her signature to each.

"Great," he said as she signed the last page. "Here, I'll put these in my folio while you nudge Stef along. I've just got to close my suitcase, then I'm ready to go."

Reagan handed him the pen as she rose from her chair. "Stef and I'll be ready to go in ten minutes."

"Okay." Fynn watched as she disappeared down the hall, toward the sound of the hairdryer, calling out as she went. "Stef!"

With great ceremony, Fynn slowly turned the barrel of the pen, fully retracting its ballpoint before pocketing it and vigilantly rechecked each page for any missing signatures.

Especially on the final three pages, to which he gave extra scrutiny as he straightened the stack and slid it into his zippered folio.

As he grabbed his sandwich off the counter and tucked it into his small carry-on duffle, the phone vibrated in his jeans pocket, indicating a new message. He quickly retrieved it and, after a glance, thumbed in the briefest of replies:

> *Yes.*

# CHAPTER TWO

## EVERGREEN HIGH SCHOOL
## KIRKLAND, WASHINGTON
## THURSDAY, 6:55 AM

THE RED FORD Focus hatchback joined the armada of other vehicles jockeying for position alongside the curb closest to the school's office building. The rain was coming down in sheets, and umbrellas burst open everywhere as students exited their family cars, navigated puddles, and made the mad dash for the front entrance.

"Tell me you brought your umbrella, Stef," Reagan said, adjusting the speed of the wipers.

"I forgot," Steffi replied sheepishly.

"Honestly…" Reagan sighed, shaking her head in disbelief as she made eye contact with her daughter via the rearview. "We live in Bothell–Bot *Hell*, where it rains… like, what… a hundred-sixty-five days a year?"

"I know… I forgot it 'cause we had to leave so early. It's okay. I've got my hoodie."

A Subaru Outback flashed its indicator and began its quest for the exit, opening up a spot. "Honey, you can–" Fynn said, gesturing to their opportunity.

"Okay," Reagan said, turning the wheel and inching forward. "I just don't want you catching a cold, honey," Reagan continued, maneuvering curbside and setting the parking brake. She turned her head toward the rear passenger and smiled. "Don't forget, I'm picking you up at 1:40. *Sharp*. Minimum day today. Watch for me; we can't be late, okay?"

"'Kay," Steffi replied, leaning forward and wrapping her left arm around her stepdad's shoulder in the briefest of insincere half-hugs. "See you... have a safe flight."

"Thanks, honey. Love you," he replied with little emotion behind it.

"Yep." The rear door popped open. Steffi squeezed out, slammed the door, and disappeared into the downpour.

"Ay-yi-yi," Reagan muttered as she checked her mirrors, threw the wipers into overdrive, and pulled away.

"She's your daughter," Fynn said as he checked in with his watch and clutched his folio.

"Please stop... and we're fine on time."

From Kirkland, the schlep to Seattle-Tacoma Airport was typically thirty-five minutes, give or take, under perfect conditions, but the combination of morning commuter traffic, an accident on the I-5 South, and a flooded "fast" lane had been enough to agitate Fynn to no end. He tapped his foot nervously as he craned his neck to see around the large delivery truck in front of them.

"Could you please relax?" Reagan pleaded, straining to see through the downpour. "It's only 8:20. You're flight's not until... what, 11:00? Eat your sandwich, why don't you? You skipped breakfast, you're grumpy, and they won't be serving you anything for... a while."

"They advise passengers to arrive three hours beforehand. Especially international. Fuck," he uttered, fishing out his sandwich without further argument.

The offending truck changed lanes, revealing the exit to SEATAC, a quarter mile ahead.

"See. We're fine."

"Mm... finally," he mumbled through his mouthful, spewing a projectile of stuffing.

Reagan checked in with her mirrors and took the offramp, trying not to obsess about the glob of Stove Top goo polluting the center of her windshield.

It felt like threading a needle in the dark as Reagan barely managed to wedge the Focus between two large SUVs parked alongside the Lufthansa passenger drop-off area at Terminal 1. They'd left her precious little wiggle room and her car's backend was sticking out into the lane a bit, just enough to elicit a smattering of rude honks.

It's a good thing she hadn't tried a proper parallel parking maneuver because her peripheral vision was dicey, making that feat nearly impossible of late. This morning's parking attempt could best be classified as *skew* or *oblique*, and far from parallel.

With a little effort, Fynn pried his six-foot-two, athletic frame from the tight space, clutching his carry-on satchel tightly while Reagan hopped out and opened the rear hatch-back to retrieve his suitcase.

"Let me get that, Ray," he said, using his nickname for

her as he reached past her and extracted the large, hard-sided case. He set it down on its four wheels, extended its handle, and hoped he wouldn't get dinged for any extra weight.

"Call me when you land… or at least text me, depending on what time it is," she said, reminding herself he had a brief layover in Paris before arriving in Hamburg.

"I will."

Another couple of blaring horns got her attention, punctuated by a glance from a decidedly impatient security guy who gestured her along with his clipboard. Reagan nodded her understanding.

"Okay… got everything?" she asked her husband. "Checked the front seat area?"

"I'm good," he confirmed, clutching his carry-ons as he leaned down nearly a foot to kiss the top of his wife's head. "Thanks for the ride. I'll let you know when I'm settled."

"Safe flight, honey. And good luck with the meeting. I think we're making the right choice."

"Yep," he replied distractedly. "You and Stef going to be okay?"

"We'll be fine," she managed, just as somebody began mercilessly blasting their car horn, which went on for the better part of ten seconds. Reagan spun toward the source, returned the glare, and responded appropriately. "Yeah?! Well Merry Christmas to you, too!"

This got a chirp from the security dude's whistle, accompanied by more stink eye. He began walking toward them, his hand on his radio.

"'Kay….bye, honey. Love you," she said, craning her neck to meet Fynn's gaze.

"You too," he said, flashing a half smile before pivoting

toward his luggage and wheeling away briskly. Reagan gave the security guy a thumbs-up as she climbed into her car and pulled away.

As Fynn got to the terminal's entrance, the doors automatically opened and, seeing a trash receptacle, he paused to fish something from his jacket pocket and casually tossed it inside:

Reagan's glasses.

# CHAPTER THREE

THE RAIN WAS starting to dissipate some, and Reagan dialed down the interval of the wipers as she scanned the boulevard for the Starbucks they were to meet at.

She had only been to this one once before, and it had been over a year ago and with the same person. The coffee giant had more than ninety locations in Seattle alone, but this was the only one she'd ever set foot in. She was old school, frugal to a fault, and perfectly happy with her decades-old Mr. Coffee machine at home.

But this was where her BFF, Amethyst, had recommended they meet this morning, and the location was only a block's walk from the gallery she operated.

As Reagan braked for a stream of pedestrians at the cross-walk, she finished the last bite of her sandwich when the unmistakable green logo came into view, a half block ahead on the right. She glanced at the clock on her display, which indicated she was right on time. As she pulled ahead and neared the front of the store, she noticed her friend was as well.

Amethyst, or "Ames," as Reagan called her, stepped

around a sidewalk puddle and, head down, briskly headed for the entrance. The fact that she was wearing her usual rose-violet rain hoodie, along with a matching umbrella, made her easy to spot amongst the crowd.

A friendly tap of Reagan's horn got her attention and Ames looked up from under her rain hood and waved, to which Reagan reciprocated as she pulled into the parking lot.

Amethyst was pulling off her purple knit gloves and staring at the menu board when Reagan entered. She smiled warmly and initiated a quick hug with Reagan, during which time three more customers fell into line behind them. "Hey, Ames. Good to see you."

"Likewise, Ray Gun!" she replied, employing the nick-name only a bestie could get away with. "Thanks for coming out, Twinner," she added, shaking her blond permed curls back into shape. Unaware she was even doing it, Reagan fol-lowed suit, shaking out her nearly identical doo as well.

About a year before—in fact, the same day of their previous Starbucks rendezvous—Reagan had complimented Ames on her perm, citing how she couldn't seem to find a stylist to do anything with her own straight, blondish locks. So, Amethyst being Amethyst, she surprised her with a joint spa day at her favorite salon, and the "twinner" look was born.

At 34, Reagan was two years her friend's junior, but they'd both been blessed with a youthful appearance that belied their years. They didn't dress similarly, Ames being the more fashion-conscious and color-coordinated of the two, while Reagan favored her casual loose-fitting sweatshirt with jeans or the occasional corduroys and her Merrill hiking shoes.

Their like-styled hair framed their faces similarly and,

combined with their compact five-foot frames, they could probably pass themselves off for twins, thus Ames's affectionate moniker for the sibling she'd never had. The only difference: Ames's galaxy of freckles.

"No problem. We missed you guys last week," Reagan said, shivering as she pivoted toward the blast of cold air coming from the door as a couple more customers entered, joining the growing line. "Man, this place must have a license to print money," she continued. "I haven't seen a line like this since I took Steffi on Space Mountain at Disneyland."

"Yeah, it's always like this."

"Jerry over his bronchitis?"

"Just about. Finished his antibiotics. He was bummed to cancel on Thanksgiving with you guys. We both were."

"No worries, Ames. You guys had a quiet Thanksgiving at home then?"

"You could say that," Ames said with a laugh. "A couple of turkey TV dinners, binge-watching a season of *NCIS: Hawaii*… how sad is that?"

"Aww, that *is* sad. So, how's your—what is it? Colitis?"

Amethyst scrunched her face in embarrassment, certain that at least a half dozen patrons were now privy to her delicate condition and possibly even reconsidering their mochas.

"Sorry," Reagan whispered, equally embarrassed.

"Um, a bit better, thanks," Ames whispered back as the customer in front of them stepped aside and proceeded to the other end of the counter. "Know what you want?"

"Me? No, not really. I mean, a coffee I guess," Reagan replied, completely out of her element. The menu was extensive, and the board was fuzzy and of no help to her.

"Good morning. What can I get started for you?" the

barista asked cheerfully. Amethyst went first as she launched into her boilerplate go-to order in a lingo that Reagan found completely foreign. "Hi. Venti white chocolate decaf soy mocha, no whip. And I'll take one of those spinach-and-feta egg-white wraps, plus some of the potato-and-cheddar bites."

"Terrific choice. And your name, please?"

"Ameth–" she began before changing to something spella-ble. "*Ames.* Thanks."

"Okay, Ames," the barista said with a smile as she pulled out her Sharpie and began annotating the drink cup. "Any-thing else for you today?"

"Yes, whatever my friend's having. And put it on my tab," Ames said, turning to Reagan. The line was quite long now, and the natives were getting restless. "Know what you want?"

She didn't. Not even close. In the effort to save face–and an hour—Reagan simply blurted her response to the barista: "Uh, just a coffee," she said, her reply punctuated with an awkward smile.

"Which size would you like?"

"That biggest one. Like my friend's. But you can add a couple of espresso shots to mine, please," Reagan managed, surrendering to an impressive yawn that got Ames's attention.

"Good call on the add shots there, Twinner."

"Okay, venti coffee of the day. Room for cream?" the barista asked.

"Yes, lots of room. Name's Reagan… like the president."

The twinners had been lucky to score a small table in the back, furthest from the door. Every time a customer came or left, a cool blast of air served to remind patrons it was December in Seattle.

Amethyst bit into her wrap and took her time chewing, studying Reagan's face as she did. Her friend appeared distracted, tired, and a bit uneasy as she quietly sipped her double red-eye coffee.

"Hey," Amethyst said, adding a cutesy wave to remind her she was still there.

Reagan looked up, making eye contact. "Hey."

"You okay?"

"Hm? Yeah. Sure. Just really, really tired this morning," Reagan said, taking another pull of caffeine.

"Didn't sleep? How come?"

"No. I mean, yes, I slept. I think. I'm just... kinda foggy."

"You didn't order any breakfast, Twinner. I'm sitting here, gorging myself. You should've ordered something. You want part of this?" she asked, gesturing to the wrap.

"I had a sandwich on the way. I'm good," Reagan replied, flashing a weak smile.

"If you say so," Ames said, popping a potato cheddar bite. "Oh!" she exclaimed through a mouthful. "Sorry, almost forgot. You're probably wondering why I called you for this little meeting today."

Reagan set down her coffee and shrugged.

"One of your pieces sold yesterday!"

"Wait... what?"

Ames's raised eyebrows and goofy grin told her this wasn't a joke.

"Seriously?"

"As a heart attack. Yeah! Another of the darker, moody, black-and-white studies you're known for. Customer was a new client, said he wanted it for his office. Congratulations, Ray Gun!"

"Wow… was it one of the ones from the Northwest Collection? The fishing boats, or–?"

"Nuh-uh," Ames began, popping the last bite in her mouth, "one of the others. From your older collection, one of the Germany photos you took. The guy asked if you had any more like the one he bought. Guy loves the trains, I guess."

Reagan took a long sip of her coffee and wasn't quick to reply. When she did, it was soft, and mostly to herself. "One of the train ones… huh."

"I'm telling you, I'd love to renew your exhibit at the gallery, Ray. Showcase some new pieces, host another event. Reintroduce you to a new audience. Your stuff is so freaking fabulous, Twinner. Tell me you've got some more stuff at home you just haven't shown me yet," Ames said hopefully.

"I don't know. I'd have to go through my files and my old negatives. I'll have a look."

"Promise?"

"Promise. I'll have more time to focus on that after Fynn's trip."

"Okay. Mm," she said, pausing for another sip. "So, when's he going?"

"Today. Now. Just dropped him off at SEATAC on the way here."

"Wow. Got ya. You couldn't go with, huh? I mean, Christmastime in Germany? What could be better?"

"Not a vacay opportunity, I'm afraid."

"Must be tough keeping tabs on the biz from this side of the pond, right? I can't imagine."

"Too many moving parts. It's become extra stressful lately… unnecessarily so, really. Truth be told, it hasn't helped our relationship."

"Sorry, kiddo. Still thinking of selling it at some point?"

"Not thinking. *Doing.*"

"Get out!"

"Yep. Fynn's been resistant for quite a while; he's wanted to expand it, not liquidate it."

"But?"

"But I reminded him it had been my parents' business, and they'd willed it to me, so we've operated it the way they had wanted it to be run all these years. They'd never been comfortable with his grand ideas of growing the operation exponentially through imports."

"They'd had that business a long time. Like before you were born, right?"

"Yeah. I mean, my father started out as a young man, like eighteen years old, working the fishing boats on the Baltic. He married young and he and my mother set up a small stand in Kiel, selling white fish and *Räucheraal*–sorry, smoked eel– along with *fischbrötchen* sandwiches with pommes-frites. Simple."

"Sorry, I still can't stand fish. Just the smell of it makes me gag," Ames said, shuddering as she wiped her mouth. "But then they were in Hamburg, right?"

"They were; they made the move several years later. Theirs was always a small-but-successful fish market, offering fresh local fish to local patrons and a few markets around Kiel and, later, Hamburg. More business came with the new location, and they supplied fresh fish to additional markets and some grocers, along with running a busy lunch counter for the locals. Mama and Papa were perfectly happy with their little *Fischmarkt*. They hired about a half dozen employees. Heck, I even worked that lunch counter when I was old enough to and, shortly after I met Fynn, he became part of the operation as well."

"Ah. I was going to ask about that," Ames said, draining her beverage.

"Yeah, we both worked it for a while, in Hamburg. Enough to know the ins and outs, anyway. My parents had more than enough customers and established supply chain, and now a sizeable income, and they were perfectly content with that business model."

"But Fynn had other ideas."

Reagan took a long pull from her cup, nodding.

"He was all gung-ho, driving my parents nuts with his crazy ideas of expansion and, more recently, hounding me with grand schemes of importing Alaskan pollock, salmon, cod, even live lobsters!"

"Lobsters? Seriously?"

Reagan nodded. "I had to put my foot down, tell him no. It's too much, not to mention a questionable practice to introduce live specimens from outside the region. We don't need that level of chaos or risk, plus it's across the frigging pond." Reagan paused to down the rest of her coffee. When she came up for air she added, "Plus, I've got plenty of money."

"Wow, so... ?"

"So, Fynn's meeting with some bankers and potential buyers this week in Hamburg. Papers are all drawn up and," Reagan said, pausing to look at her watch, "currently sitting in his lap at thirty-something thousand feet. I mean, I inherited the business, and I should have the last say in how it's run. And how the torch is passed."

"See? Aren't you glad I rescued you from all that?"

Reagan nodded her appreciation. "It was hard, leaving. Especially…" Her voice trailed off.

"I know…." Ames put a comforting hand on her twinner's. "We don't have to talk about that."

With her free hand, Reagan rubbed away a tear and looked up, attempting a smile. "So…."

"Yeah… *so*. I guess congratulations are in order," Ames said, smiling as she clinked her now-empty cardboard cup against Reagan's. "Cheers!"

"Prost!"

# CHAPTER FOUR

I T HAD BEEN great hooking up with Ames, and Reagan vowed to touch base the following week, once she'd had a chance to peruse her photo files in search of any new material worth considering. They both agreed that another gallery event would be amazing, and just the thought of it had Reagan buzzing. That, and a little help from the espresso shots.

Her eyes felt like two burn holes in a blanket as she navigated the aisles of Trader Joe's. They stung, struggling to establish any semblance of depth of field, and no amount of rubbing them had succeeded in wiping away their strain and fatigue.

*Where the hell did I leave my glasses?*

Reagan had almost an hour to kill before she had to pick up Steffi, and she needed to grab some provisions, being as they were now fresh out of turkey and all that.

She grabbed some organic grapes, a couple of the good Mexican mangos–only because they were on sale–along with three bags of spring mix salads. In the baked goods aisle, she regarded the pecan flavored Danish Kringle pastry. It was too sweet for her own taste, but Steffi loved it, so Reagan grabbed one for her, along with the almond-flavored one she herself loved, adding both Frisbee-sized confections to the cart.

As Reagan wheeled to the end of the aisle, she pivoted her cart left and, in the process, bumped into an elderly woman's elbow with enough force to dislodge the basket of fruit she'd been carrying, launching oranges and apples in several directions.

"Oh, how clumsy of me! I'm so sorry, ma'am! Are you okay?" Reagan asked, kneeling down to assess the woman's condition.

The frail woman rubbed her elbow and flashed a sour expression as she regarded the spilled produce she'd carefully selected. "Why don't you watch where you're going?" she admonished as she picked up a nearby orange and returned it to the basket.

"I sincerely apologize… my fault. Are you hurt?"

"No, but you should really watch where you're going," she clucked.

"You're right. Here… I'll get it, ma'am," Reagan said as she set about collecting the fruit, returning it all back to the basket. "There…."

Collecting the basket from her assailant, the woman shook her head and walked away. Reagan let out a sigh and muttered to herself. "Scheisse."

Reagan exited the store and looked both ways before proceeding to her car. She had established a routine out of necessity in recent months, having once stepped out in front of a minivan driven by an individual with sharp reflexes. She hadn't even seen it coming.

*Look left... right... left again... right... left once more... okay.*

With her groceries stashed in the rear hatchback, save the bag with the almond Danish on the passenger seat, Reagan stowed the cart to the designated area and pulled away from the lot.

She had forty minutes before she was due to pick up Stef, and she'd rather get there early and wait than play pole position with all the other moms.

As she made her way onto the busy boulevard, she gripped the wheel a little tighter. Even though it was daytime, and the rain had stopped, she didn't feel as comfortable driving in brisk traffic as she used to. And, after dark, all bets were off. She'd mention this to the new optometrist.

Reagan reached over into the bag and pinched off a small portion of the almond Kringle, bringing the confection to her nose. The store only carried this version at Christmastime, and she savored its almondy, almost-Marzipan-y aroma before stuffing it into her mouth. *Oh, my gawd....*

As Reagan savored the residual icing and licked it from her fingers, a blur of motion came from outside her periphery, getting her attention, but entirely too late. She stepped hard onto the brake, skidding helplessly, and a brief moment later the Focus made violent contact with the Jeep Cherokee that had entered the lane directly in front of her.

In that split second, Reagan had managed to reduce her speed considerably before impact, but the remaining momentum was enough to drive her bumper and front end into the rear of the Jeep, resulting in a loud and jarring crunch and thrusting her torso painfully into her seat belt and shoulder restraint.

Reagan pounded the steering wheel angrily, taking in the damage to the Jeep's rear hatch while noting that her own airbag hadn't deployed. She put on her turn indicator, made eye contact with the other driver, and patted her chest in a gesture meant to express apology.

"Great frickin' job, Reagan!" she cried, admonishing herself as she and the other driver pulled their vehicles to the shoulder.

The Jeep's driver exited first and began making her way to the rear of her vehicle as Reagan climbed out to meet her. "I'm so sorry, ma'am. I didn't even see you come into–"

"Dammit," the woman said as she inspected what would certainly be thousands of dollars in repairs to her rear end. "I just bought the car a month ago and now it's going to be in the shop for God knows how long... you didn't see my blinker?!" she asked, looking at Reagan now and trying to contain her anger.

"I... honestly... did not see you coming into my lane, ma'am. I was on my way to pick up my daughter, and I was going the speed limit. I don't know–"

"Let's just trade insurance information. I've got someplace I've got to be too. *Dammit.*"

# CHAPTER FIVE

## EVERGREEN HIGH SCHOOL
## KIRKLAND, WASHINGTON
## THURSDAY, 1:42 PM

S TEFFI WAS STANDING curbside, in her appointed place and at the agreed upon time. She shifted her backpack to the other shoulder and let out a sigh as she watched the time displayed on her iPhone's home screen advance to 1:43.

A familiar sounding beep got her attention, and she looked up as her mom's Focus limped up to the curb. With its now-wrinkled hood, askew front bumper, and a new crack extending across the windshield, the beater hatchback looked beaten.

Reagan made eye contact with her daughter before burying her face in her hands. She listened as the passenger door opened, a body plopped into the seat, and the door closed. She didn't need what came next.

"What the hell, Mom?"

"Steffi, please don't start."

"No, really. What happened? I mean, are you okay?"

"I'm okay, thank you," Reagan said, turning toward her daughter. "Besides my pride, which is severely mangled right now, I'm... fine. The car, not so much... jeezus."

"Can we just go? This is embarrassing and I don't want my friends to see me."

"That's what you're worried about, what your friends might think?" Reagan replied, pulling away from the curb and exiting the school driveway.

"Sorry, Mom. It's... I'm supposed to take my driver's test next month. I don't–"

"It still drives. It just looks like hell. Here, let's get you some more practice," she said, pulling over the curb in what was now a residential section. "C'mon, you can drive to our eye appointment."

"Yeah?"

"Yeah," Reagan said, climbing out and walking around to the other side. Her left shoulder felt like she'd suffered a kick from a mule. As they clicked into their seatbelts and Steffi finished adjusting the mirrors, Reagan looked at her daughter and added, in as comforting a tone as she could muster, "Thanks for being on time, honey. Um, take a right at the stop sign."

# CHAPTER SIX

## VISUAL EYES OPTOMETRY
## BELLEVUE PROFESSIONAL PLAZA
## THURSDAY, 2:05 PM

REAGAN AND STEFFI were seated across from each other and were the only ones in the tiny waiting area. Stef was glued to her iPhone, and her earbuds were stuffed into her ears.

Reagan was oblivious to anything else in the room as she studied her daughter's face. Stef was growing up so quickly and seeming to look more like her father each day. Same cleft in her chin, the ginger hair. She would be driving on her own soon. Her little Steffi....

These facts combined to freak her out just a little, and her thoughts drifted to having just been involved in a fender bender an hour before. She hadn't even seen the Jeep.

She had been dreading this eye appointment for some time and hoped this new doctor would be better than the last one. Today would be her much-belated second opinion, having had a less than great experience with the last guy a couple of years back. Had it been two years or three? She wondered if her eyes had changed much.

She knew they had to have.

She made a mental note to call her insurance agent and obtain a couple of estimates to get the frigging Focus fixed.

She didn't love the car, and recently she'd been getting notices in the mail about a "lemon law" that might pertain to it, but, other than a couple of transmission hiccups, it had been mostly trouble-free. For her purposes it had been fine so far, and it was paid off. She sure didn't want another car payment, and she was pissed at herself for getting in an accident.

*How will Steffi take her driver's test now? Crap.*

"Mrs. Dunkel?"

Reagan turned to the source and looked up to see a young, twenty-something woman standing there, smiling at her.

"Uh, yes. I'm Reagan Dunkel. My daughter, Stefanie, is here too. We both have appointments."

"Great, I see that," the assistant replied, glancing at her clipboard. "I'm Jenny. Would you like to go first or your daughter?"

"Honey," Reagan said, hoping Steffi would hear her above the ear buds. When she got no reaction, Reagan waved her arm and gestured for her to remove the devices from her ears.

"What?" Stef asked, slightly annoyed before noticing the other woman.

"Stefanie–*Steffi*–can go first," Reagan said, forcing a smile as she turned back to her daughter. "Honey, you can leave your electronics with me. Please follow this nice lady and they'll get you started on your eye exam. I'll go after you."

"'Kay," Stef said, powering down her phone. She stood,

handing her mother the device as she pocketed the earbuds and proceeded down the hall.

Reagan set down the last of the magazines on the end table. She'd suffered through three *People* magazines and a months-old *Newsweek*. She looked at her watch. It had been over forty minutes.

She rocked her foot nervously and let out a sigh, dreading the inevitable. A moment later, Steffi walked up to her, her outstretched hand indicating she wanted her phone.

"Hey, honey. Everything go okay?" Reagan asked, handing it to her.

"I guess," Stef replied with disinterest as she wedged the buds back into her ears and took her seat.

"Reagan, we're ready for you now," Jenny said.

"O-kay then…" Reagan managed as she stood and sent up a futile, silent prayer on her way down the hall. Not that it would do any good, she figured, as she was agnostic on her best day, and a short putt from being full atheist.

Jenny's face materialized from behind the optical exam apparatus Reagan's chin had been resting upon. Reagan's neck was killing her, and she wondered if she might have whiplash.

"You can scootch back," Jenny said as she tapped some notes into her computer. "Now I'm going to have you scoot a couple feet this way so I can measure your intraocular pressure–sorry… your eye pressure. It's a check for glaucoma and we'll be blowing a little puff of air into your eyes."

"Good times. I've had it done before, no worries."

"Great. Okay, now I'll adjust the tonometer for your height. Chin on the rest, please. We'll start with your right eye… I'll raise this up a little, and… there. Now, please open your eyes wide and stare straight ahead. Holding still. You'll feel a little puff of air. And, ready?"

"Mm-hmm."

*Puff!*

Jenny consulted with her computer monitor to make sure she'd gotten the desired result.

"Great. Now we'll do the other eye. Same way… looking straight ahead… and…"

*Puff!*

Another couple of keystrokes at the computer revealed she'd been successful. "Great. Now did you want to get your pupils dilated today or have an Optomap scan?"

"An opto-what?"

"Optomap. It's an alternative to pupil dilation for those who wish not to have that done. If you'd prefer that we don't dilate you, the camera digitally scans an image of your retinas. Takes detailed pictures of the inside of your eyes that you'll get to see and discuss with the doctor."

"I definitely don't want to get dilated. I'm driving home after this appointment."

"Understood. Just so you know, there's a forty-dollar additional fee for the scans."

"Fine."

"Okay, I'm going to ask that you wheel your chair over

here a little," Jenny said as she made a couple of adjustments on the white imaging machine. "A little closer… there."

Reagan couldn't help but think how much the apparatus resembled those "Stormtrooper" helmets from the *Star Wars* movies, only a bit bigger. This thing was closer to the size of a wine fridge, but a space-age one, like the astronauts might have if they were allowed one up there.

She stretched her neck forward, her forehead pressed against the cool plastic and her chin resting in the optimal position on its bar. It wasn't comfortable, but it was better than the dilation option, she figured. As long as it wasn't a guillotine.

"Comfortable?"

"Um… I guess," she replied, trying not to chuckle at how absurd the question sounded.

"Perfect. Right there. Now, we're going to start with your right eye. I'll adjust the height here a little. Better?"

"Sure."

"Let me bring this into focus for you. Do you see the little farmhouse there? Across the field?"

"Farmhouse? Yeah. Kinda."

"Good, now, when we start the program, I'm going to have you use the clicker here," Jenny said, handing her the small handheld device, "and you'll push this button whenever you see the white dot appear."

"Got it. I did this a few years ago, but I think it was, like, a hot air balloon, not a house."

"Quite possible," Jenny replied, stepping away and taking a position behind her monitors. "Ready?"

"Ready as I'm going to be, I guess."

"Okay, we'll begin."

Reagan let out a slow, deliberate breath through her nose. She kept her forehead and chin pressed against the huge apparatus as her right eye strained to focus on the distant farmhouse. It looked like it was a million miles away. She gripped the remote clicker, squeezing the life out of it in her sweaty hand, her thumb poised on its button like a contestant jacked up on a buttload of energy drinks and playing for her very survival in a round of *Final Jeopardy!*

She awaited the first white dot to appear in her field of view. *There!* She clicked the hand controller button as the first dot faintly flashed, not far from the little house. A moment later, she thought she saw another, in a different spot, again close to the house. *Click.*

A few, seemingly long moments went by where Reagan refrained from clicking a response. "Are we done?"

Jenny studied the monitors. "No, not quite, please keep watching and responding," she said, clicking her computer mouse. "I'll let you know."

Reagan's concern level was slightly elevated. She didn't want to fail the test and figured a few lucky button clicks might improve her score. At intervals about two seconds apart, she began jamming her thumb on the device's button, randomly responding to dots unseen, in hopes a few of them might hit paydirt. This was worse than the Whack-A-Mole game she'd played at the carnival.

*Click. Click. Click!*

Jenny made a few keystrokes on her computer keyboard and stepped from behind her machinery. "We're going to switch eyes now," she said, gently adjusting Reagan's head position so that her left eye was properly aligned with the eyepiece. "How's that?"

"Okay, but the focus seems a little off."

"I'll adjust that," Jenny said, dialing in the electronics. "Sharper now?"

Reagan strained to discern the slight level of improvement. "Yes," she said, a white lie.

"Great, we'll do it as before," Jenny said, resuming her position behind the monitors. "Clicking when you see a white dot."

"They're kinda faint," Reagan replied, half statement, half complaint.

"I know... okay, head still. And... we'll begin."

Three seconds went by. *Click.*

Then another five seconds... ten....

"I think it might be broken," Reagan said.

"Please keep watching and try not to talk. Head still, please."

Reagan fired off a couple of random clicks as before, but not in response to any stimuli. *Fuck it. Click. Click. Click.*

Another twenty seconds went by before Jenny keyed in a few commands and stepped around to face the patient and collect the hand controller. "All done," she said, flashing a half smile that belied her thoughts.

"Did I pass?" Reagan asked, wiping her sweaty palms on her jeans.

"You'll have a chance to discuss the tests with the doctor shortly. You'll also get to see the images we took. I think you'll find the technology is pretty amazing."

"Oh, um... how'd my daughter do?"

"The doctor will share his findings with you," Jenny said, switching off the machine. "If you'll excuse me for a moment, I'll see if he's ready to see you."

# CHAPTER SEVEN

TEN MINUTES INTO Dr. Gruber's exam, Reagan had already determined that this new optometrist was a bit of an asshole. He seemed to lack any degree of bedside manner, foregoing any attempts at pleasantries, and had all but barked his prompts for where to look during his inspection. *Definitely German.*

Reagan's neck was sore, having been stretched beyond its tolerances, yet she remained perfectly still, her face pushed against yet another optical contraption—this one a metallic gizmo, more old-school, and decidedly medieval looking. The room was dark, and an unseen hand waved a very bright flashlight, taking turns stabbing each eye.

Add to that, the doctor's breath smelled like he'd fired down an onion-laden double buffalo burger for lunch. She wondered if he'd paired it with a side of buffalo chips. His face was mere inches away from hers and she held her breath, trying not to gag.

"So," he started, the sound of his chair's metallic wheels meeting the floor's linoleum as the distance between them increased. He stood, flipping on the wall switch, restoring the fluorescent room lighting. Reagan blinked several times as the room came back into semi-focus.

The doctor made no attempt at a smile behind the graying, poorly trimmed mustache. "Did you bring your old glasses with you?"

"No. I didn't," she answered, risking the oxygen. "I can't seem to find them," she added, the heat rising in her cheeks.

"I see. And you say your last eye exam was…" he began, pausing to consult his notes, "*three* years ago?"

Reagan didn't like his tone, as it conveyed judgment, and she didn't need it today. If he continued to lay any on her, she might just have to comment on his horrendous combover and worst-case halitosis.

"Yes. About. I've been kind of busy."

"That's a long time between visits…"

*Gawd… please make it stop.*

"… especially since your eyes can change quite a bit during that time."

*No shit, Sherlock.*

"And you have difficulty seeing in the dark. You checked that box on the form."

"A bit. Yeah. I don't know. Doesn't everybody?"

This didn't deserve a response, apparently, as he shuffled the few steps to his desk and plopped into his chair. He began futzing with the computer.

*Click. Click. Click.*

Reagan cricked her neck back into its natural position and looked straight ahead, squinting in an attempt to read the framed diploma on the wall. She couldn't make out any of it.

The doctor's breathing sounded labored.

*Might want to throttle back on the buffalo burgers there, Doc.*

"I'd like to show you some images," he said, clearing his throat. *Click.*

"Okay...."

"I'll put them up on the big screen there so you can better see them," Dr. Gruber said, as the forty-two-inch monitor in the corner of the room populated with icons and a photograph of what looked like a round, gelatinous mass with a few red striations running through it. It looked a bit like a petri dish of goo, or maybe a grape somebody had smooshed.

"Is that my eye?"

"It's an eye, but not yours. This is a file photo for reference. What you see here is a digital retinal image of a typical, healthy human eye."

"Pretty amazing tech there," Reagan said, genuinely impressed with the advances in the optometry world. "Eyes are the window to the soul, they say."

No response from Doctor Loquacious other than, "Mm."

"What's that red, stringy stuff there?"

"These... are the retinal veins and arteries inside the eye," he responded, like a bored substitute teacher. "Again, this is a normal, healthy, human eye."

He made a couple of mouse clicks, and a new image opened in its place. This one looked decidedly different, and his silence hung in the air for several seconds.

"And this?" Reagan dared ask.

"This... is your eye. Your right eye."

Reagan stared at the image on the screen, trying to remember how the previous photo had looked. The "healthy" one. She was no doctor, and her eyes might not be the greatest, but even she could tell that this image, paired with the hesitation in his words, spelled trouble.

"This is… from today?" she asked, knowing full well it had to be.

"It is, and–"

"Gawd… and can you show me the first one again, please?"

"Sure," he replied. A couple of mouse clicks later, the photos were displayed side-by-side. "Again, the healthy eye, the reference eye, is on the left. Yours is–"

"The one with all the black shit polluting it, apparently. Sorry, doctor, but what the heck? Was the camera lens dirty?"

"The camera's lens is working as it should. Those… black clumps… are called bone spicules–they're pigment deposits."

"Pigman?"

"Pig*ment*. The retina here," he began, indicating it with the cursor, "is comprised of two kinds of cells, the rod and the cone cells. Essentially, the rod cells are the ones that influence how you see light. They help to diffuse glare as well as help make it possible to see properly at night."

"And the other ones?"

"The retina's cone cells affect how you see and differentiate colors. So, together, the rod and cone cells make it possible to navigate changes in light and properly process the colors you see."

Reagan let out a sigh, afraid to ask the next question, but it had to be asked. "And the black things–you called them pigment deposits?"

"Yes."

"What do those mean?"

"To put it bluntly, the pigment cells of your retinas are dying."

"What do you mean, dying? They can't be actually–"

"Dying. Like, a slow death. The bone spurs, the black stuff there, is the debris that forms as the cells die off. Kind of like a graveyard."

Reagan slowly brought her hand to her mouth as she studied the image with renewed intensity. The black debris was pervasive and impossible to ignore. It was everywhere and becoming all she could see.

The doctor continued speaking, but his voice seemed to fall into to the background as she processed this damning information. This would explain why she had trouble with some colors but, more importantly, why her peripheral vision had been going to hell and why she'd been having a devil of a time seeing anything in a darkened environment.

She heard his voice slowly fade back in.

"What we're seeing here, and it's progressed in both eyes, is an advanced degree of what's called Retinitis Pigmentosa, or RP. You mentioned that your peripheral vision was becoming severely challenged, which the Optomap test verified. Your field of vision has become limited to a very narrow range, in the central region."

"So…"

"Based on your age, the rapid pace of the degeneration, and your genes–you mentioned your mother had troubles with her eyesight at a young age?"

"Yes, I remember her having issues and bumping into stuff, but what's that got to–"

"You're going blind," he blurted out with all the sensitivity of a mechanic diagnosing a faulty water pump."

"Fick mich," she swore softly in her native German,

almost panic-laughing as she fought for breath. "No, really… was zum Teufel!" *What the fuck!*

The doctor rubbed his own eyes. He didn't take well to cursing, and her attempts to bury it in German didn't escape him. Patients second-guessing his diagnoses was another non-starter. Instead of responding to her, he performed another mouse click, and an entirely new image appeared on the monitor.

"Sorry for my language, it's just that–"

"Not what you wanted to hear, I know."

Reagan took a few moments to recover from the shrapnel of the truth bomb. "What did you mean when you said *blind…* ?"

"Just what I said. Based on your remaining field of vision, which is down to about ten degrees, and the rapid degeneration of your retinal cells, you may have anywhere from two to three years before–"

"Before what?!" she interrupted.

"Before you're completely blind."

Reagan shook her head, refusing to hear it. *This guy's no better than that last asshole doc.*

"Not. Possible… I refuse to believe that! I'm young. I'm… I'm a fucking *photographer*, for Christ's sake!"

"Your reaction is understandable under the–"

"What about Cadillac surgery, vitamins… ? They have to be, like, treating mice for this stuff, right? What's the cure?"

"*Cataract* surgery wouldn't help. Intensive vitamin regimens may slow things down a little but there can be undesirable side effects. There's currently no cure for this disease and, if one is eventually developed, it would still be many years out."

"I'm. *Not*. Going. Fucking. Blind."

"We can't change the facts, I'm afraid. As we sit here today, you are already legally blind. As in, you will no longer be allowed to operate a motor vehicle. You'll need to find somebody to take you wherever you need to go. No driving. Effective immediately. I'll be referring you to a retinal specialist in Seattle who can arrange for resources such as braille training, and other support services. They can arrange transportation if necessary."

Reagan's limited field of vision was trained on his lips and whiskbroom mustache as he spoke these words, each a dagger in her heart. The rest of the office had disappeared from her tunnel vision view, his words muffled. A few moments went by. What he said next brought her back to reality.

"It's a hereditary condition, I'm afraid. You likely had RP passed down to you, genetically. Probably from your mother, even if she hadn't been properly diagnosed."

"What do you mean? How's that possible? My mother had eye issues, yeah, but… I mean, my daughter's fine."

The doctor paused, taking a slow, deliberate breath before responding.

"Your daughter is beginning to show early signs of this disease as well, I'm afraid."

"Den Mund halten!" *Shut up!* "She is not!"

The doctor pursed his lips and highlighted the image with the cursor.

"Sorry for my language, it's just that–she's only fifteen. There's no way…" Reagan said softly, wiping away a tear as she studied the new image. It didn't look nearly as bad as the previous one–her own–but it didn't look completely healthy either. There were pockets of black specks populating it.

"What's this a picture of?"
"This is your daughter, Stefanie."

# CHAPTER EIGHT

THE FOCUS'S HEATER was churning out plenty of warmth, yet the air in the car was frosty and quiet, buried in an avalanche of things unsaid.

Steffi had programmed their home address into her phone's nav system, and she snuck glances down at the screen as the robotic voice guided her directions. Neither human said a word, and Reagan gazed out her window, focusing on nothing but the grayness that was everywhere. They were almost home, but she took little comfort in that.

"In one thousand feet, stay in the right lane and take the exit to Kirkland Avenue," the virtual guide said, prompting Stef to turn on her indicator and change lanes accordingly.

Reagan turned forward, her attention drifting back to sad realities. Steffi was an excellent driver, she noted, realizing she herself was now useless–and *illegal*–to be an authorized copilot.

Steffi negotiated the turn admirably and switched off the nav. She knew the rest of the way. "Nice job, honey," Reagan said softly, dreading the conversation that would come later.

"Thanks," Stef said, checking in with the mirrors as she

pulled onto their street. A half block ahead, on the left, their one-story, gunmetal-blue-shingled home came into view. "Do you want me to park in the driveway or... ?"

"The garage," her mother answered without a moment's hesitation. She didn't need the nosy neighbors asking questions about the car's damage.

Hell, she didn't need any of this.

Reagan carried in the last of the groceries and closed the door with her foot. She placed the bag on the kitchen counter, next to the others, and began emptying them. "Can you help me put things away, honey?"

"Yeah," Steffi replied, pausing to plug her phone to the USB wall charger.

"I got you this," Reagan said, flashing a half-smile as she handed her the pecan Kringle.

"Ooh, yum. Thanks, Mom," Stef said as she started to break the seal on the packaging.

"Ah-ah... that's for dessert. C'mon, let's finish here and I'll get dinner started.

"You are cruel, Mother."

"Yes, I am. I'm horrible," Reagan replied quietly, fully believing the self-assessment.

Reagan pushed things around on her plate, her fork more a bulldozer than eating utensil. She'd managed all of two bites over twenty minutes and had tasted neither.

The stroganoff was the quick version, from a box: just add

water, milk, and brown some burger. It wasn't bad, and Stef loved it, but the weight of the day had snuffed out Reagan's own appetite. Maybe forever. She didn't even have an interest in her almond Kringle, which spoke volumes of her preoccupation with impending doom.

Steffi finished her last bite and wiped her mouth on a napkin. "It was good, Mom," she said, bussing her plate to the sink and retrieving her precious pecan pastry from the pantry on the way back to the table. "Want me to bring yours over?"

Reagan shook her head. "No, honey. Thanks."

"'Kay," her daughter muttered as she retook her seat and breached the seal on her favorite thing in the world. "It's starting to feel like Christmas a little," she said, a childlike smile surfacing as she took her first bite.

"Good, honey," Reagan replied, her mind on a million things as she reciprocated with a facsimile of a smile. She continued watching her daughter who, in the bliss of this innocent, fleeting moment, looked more five than almost sixteen. Steffi closed her eyes as she savored the holiday-time confection, as yet unaware of the tunnel of darkness ahead.

Reagan set down her fork and tossed back the rest of her glass of chardonnay.

*Christmas. Gawd.*

# CHAPTER NINE

AS SOON AS Stef had retreated to the sanctity of her room and her ever-present earbuds, Reagan finished the dishes, as well as her bottle of chardonnay.

More rain was forecast for the morning, and she was already beginning to feel her life starting to suck more, chipping away in incremental chunks. Her crippled car was stuck in the garage, and her own wings were now clipped–forever–banished from ever operating a motor vehicle again.

Oh, and she was going *blind.*

*FUCK!!!*

A phone call to the mom of Stef's homeroom BFF, Vickie, saved the day, as she had kindly offered to shuttle Steffi to and from school until the holiday break, which was coming up. The girls had the same after-school schedule twice a week, as they were both on the junior varsity volleyball team, so it wasn't a problem, she'd assured her.

Reagan assembled what would be the morning's half-pot of coffee and made a couple of mental notes to call her insurance agent, then make inquiries about repair estimates.

Depending on how all that went, she'd decide whether or not to call Ames as well.

As she returned the coffee canister to the pantry, her fingers ran along the surface of the Formica kitchen countertop, pausing as they arrived at a discolored divot in the surface. It was one of several like scars, spaced at intervals, from the little tealights that had served as her nighttime guides for much of the past year. Until she'd nearly burned the place down. At least they matched the similar crop circles that ran the length of the hardwood hallway floor.

It had been a rookie mistake not to place the aluminum-housed candles into proper tealight holders, thus the circular burn marks. And Fynn had given her ample needling for her carelessness in letting them burn through the night that one time.

After careful consideration, she'd retired any and all candles, instead resorting to a less-flammable alternative: the rope lighting she'd found at the local hardware store.

It now served as her beacon, and even though it looked like a tacky-as-hell discothèque embellishment, it illuminated her pathway, extending from the kitchen, through the living room, and continuing all the way to the bedrooms at the far end of the hall.

She fumbled for the kitchen light switch and turned it off, the only glow now coming from the runway lights guiding her approach.

*Reagan, this is Tower. You are cleared for landing.*
*Roger fucking that, Tower.*

Reagan took considerably extra time brushing her teeth, not due to some new conscientious dental routine, but instead because the mirror and its lighting afforded her an opportunity to closely scrutinize her *officially* now-defective eyes.

Her pupils still presented as the beautiful hazel pools Fynn had once fallen in love with and, other than the tinges of red caused by the fatigue of enduring the Day from Hell, the whites of her eyes appeared normal as well.

The whiteness, she knew, betrayed what was going on behind the scenes. She pictured an internal firing squad, shooting indiscriminately, and the silent screams of her retinal cells as they were assassinated, dying off, one by one, the cruel evidence piling up like a couple cords of firewood, their heaped ashes filling the fireplace.

Reagan spit her foam into the sink, turned off the spigot, and verified her nightstand light was lit before switching off the main light and making her way to the bed that beckoned. It seemed a mile away. She verified her alarm was set to make sure Stef got off to school with a decent breakfast. *And an umbrella!*

A quick glance at her phone told her Fynn hadn't checked in yet.

In all of the morning rush to get him to the airport, she hadn't had a chance to make the bed, but she took note that Fynn had made his side. It was something that annoyed her– and not just a little–as it could be construed as judgmental, or maybe just laziness. Either way, it had been getting under her skin more than she realized and she'd have to mention it. He was a bit anal that way.

As she slowly lowered herself into the prone position, something she'd looked forward to all day, she paused, her head stopping just above the pillow. There, on the pillowcase, appeared a small, odd-looking smear, like a charcoal-colored ink stain of some kind. She shrugged, flipped the pillow over, flicked off the lamp.

Her head sunk into the cool, dreamy, fluffy down. What was left of her functioning mind briefly flashed upon the stain she'd seen on her right thumb that morning. A long time ago....

*Weird.*

# CHAPTER TEN

## FRIDAY, DECEMBER 12
## 9:12 AM

S LEEP HAD BEEN elusive, and on the night Reagan needed it most. She had tossed and turned in an effort to switch off the relentless stream of mental images, vivid imaginings of her precious retinal cells being murdered, their body count rising as they stacked up into their random, black piles of death. Evidence of a cruel and relentless slaughter underway within her very eyeballs.

*Eyeball genocide.*

It was the stuff of a horror film. And she hated horror films.

She gripped her fifteen-ounce coffee mug with both hands and took another sip, hoping the caffeine from this second cup might kick in at some point. The first cup, useless. She'd managed to get Stef out the door in time for her ride, along with her peanut butter sandwich and a bag of Flaming Hot Cheetos. She'd also made certain she had her umbrella.

A phone call to Stuart, her insurance agent, had followed,

and arrangements were made for an adjustor to come by the house to assess the damage to her vehicle. She was dreading the dollar amount, not because she couldn't afford it, but more a feeling of being pissed off at herself for this unnecessary and unplanned expenditure. And her rates would probably go up now. An unforced error.

On paper, she was an excellent driver, never even having had a ticket. Not a single accident. Well, until yesterday. And yesterday she got her frigging wings clipped.

Her mind went to the song "Fun, Fun, Fun" by the Beach Boys, and she changed the chorus in her mind to *"till her daddy takes the* Focus *away." FUCK.*

Reagan picked up her cellphone and viewed the message on her display again. The one from Fynn. He'd texted in the middle of the night, and it'd gone unnoticed during her little horror movie-thon:

> *> Made it. Beat up from the flights. Couldn't sleep on the plane. Crying baby behind me. Baggage being delivered to hotel sometime today, I hope. Don't ask... going to bed. Check in with you later. ~ F.*

She was tempted to text back with some snark about being sure to make his side of the bed when he wakes up, but she thought better of it. Instead, she went with:

> *> Sorry you had a rough flight. Get some sleep. Good luck later. Let me know! ~ Ray*

Reagan powered down the phone, grabbed her coffee, and disappeared down the hall. She wanted to be showered and ready for the adjustor who'd confirmed he'd be there "between ten and two." At least it had stopped raining for the time being.

The four-hour window was shrinking. Reagan had showered, dressed, and been ready for the adjustor since 9:45, just in case. It was now 11:15. She shook her head as she pushed away the remainder of her almond Kringle, licked the icing from her fingers, and got up from the kitchen table.

A noisy swarm of questions and concerns were buzzing in her brain and vying for her attention. Her twenty-seven-inch iMac stared back at her from its little table at the end of the counter. *Might as well use the time constructively.*

She spent the next hour doing Google searches for *Retinitis Pigmentosa,* hoping she might unearth some nuggets of encouragement, breaking news of the latest and greatest treatments and miracle cures, or anything she could find that might disprove the prognosis of doom the eye doctor had lain on her yesterday.

There was none to be found, and the more she clicked on links pointing to the hereditary nature of the disease, the more hopeless she felt and the angrier she became. *Thanks a lot, God!*

She clicked out of the search window and, after another glance at the clock, opened up her Music app and the iTunes store. She selected New Playlist, renaming it something apropos to her current mindset, with a little help from the seventies band, War: "Slippin' into Darkness."

"Let's get this pity party started, Reagan!" she barked at the screen as she commenced listening to samples, dragging and dropping, and building an eclectic mix of songs that fed her despair. She honestly couldn't remember the last time she'd downloaded any music files–probably not since college–mainly because she had long been a bit of a purist and an aficionado of vinyl, but... *desperate times.*

A knock on the door snapped her back to reality and, looking up at the clock, she saw that it was now 1:44.

And she'd managed to purchase upward of thirty songs.

"Coming!" she called out.

# CHAPTER ELEVEN

REAGAN WAITED UNTIL the nosy neighbor across the street had collected her mail and gone back inside before backing the damaged vehicle from the garage for the adjustor's inspection. Somehow, it looked even worse than it had yesterday.

The man was young, maybe thirtyish, and he appeared to be Japanese. Maybe Polynesian. He was pleasant enough, and he had a warm smile but was all business once he opened the program on his tablet and began inputting his findings. Reagan knew nothing about cars, with the possible exception of how to wreck them. The adjustor was crawling around, checking a hundred areas of the car she would never have guessed might be affected.

"All done here, ma'am," he said, his head finally reemerging from the underneath the front bumper as he powered down his device. "Good news is we don't have to total the Focus."

The way he pronounced it, it almost sounded like *Fuckus*, and Reagan had to bite her lip. It was too perfect, and she decided it was going to be her new name for the car going forward. She might just have to rebadge the logo accordingly.

"I'll send this information to your insurance agent this afternoon, and he'll be contacting you with the findings and to see if you wish to get a second—"

"I don't. I mean, I'll go with your estimate, thank you. I just want to get this fixed as soon as possible. Thank you."

Reagan pulled the car back into the garage, waved to the looky-loo neighbor watching from her kitchen window across the street, and lowered the door.

A glance at her wristwatch reminded Reagan that Vickie's mom would be delivering Steffi back home any minute. She went back inside and began clearing the iMac's search history.

The sound of a car door slamming got Reagan's attention, and she powered down the iMac. A moment later, she heard the car zoom away as Steffi walked in, closed the front door quietly, and set down her backpack.

"Hey, honey. How was your day?" Reagan asked, turning to face her.

"Okay," Steffi replied, unconvincingly. Her face looked a bit drawn. She pulled up her hoodie without making eye contact, continued down the hall, and disappeared into her room, closing the door behind her.

"Everything okay, baby?" Reagan called out after her.

"I guess," came the weak response from behind the door.

"Can I fix you some cocoa?"

"No!" Steffi replied sharply before amending it. "No, thank you... just tired."

"Okay, honey. You can take a nap if you want. I'll wake you in time for dinner."

This got a muffled response. "'Kay...."

Reagan let out a sigh and picked up her phone to mute the ringer so as to not disturb Stef. An icon alerted her to a new message, and she clicked on it. From Fynn.

> *Still haven't delivered my suitcase. Phone charger and power pack are in my checked bag. Phone's about to die. Will check in when I can. At least got some sleep! ~ F.*

Reagan thumbed in her reply and shook her head as she hit send.

> *That makes one of us. ~ Ray*

She thought about calling her twinner. She needed to talk to someone or she was going to blow a gasket. Her thumb hovered over the call button, but she didn't want to disturb her at work. She could at least text her, she decided.

> *Hey, Ames. You're probably slammed but I at least wanted to check in. Still thinking about what we talked about. Will dig around my photo files when I can. BTW, I had the mother of shitty days yesterday... too much for a text. Call me later if you get a chance.*

> *~ Ray Gun* 🖤

She thought about adding *Happy Friday* to it, but there wasn't much to feel happy about, so she hit Send. *Keeping it real.*

Steffi was in her baggie sweats, her feet in mismatched socks when she emerged from her room and shuffled toward the kitchen.

"There she is," Reagan said, trying to muster cheer neither one of them was feeling. "I was just about to knock on your door and tell you I ordered Chinese from that new place you like."

"'Kay," Stef managed.

"Glad you got some rest, honey. I could hear your little snore from here."

"I snore?"

"Yes. Well, sometimes. But it's cute... not one of those chainsaw snores like... Fynn's."

Steffi took a seat at the table and rubbed her eyes. "Do we still have Gatorade?"

"We do. What flavor would you like?" Reagan asked as she approached the fridge.

"Not sure what flavor it is, but do we have the blue one?"

"Yep," Reagan replied, pulling one from the crisper drawer and handing it to her. "The blue one pairs well with sweet and sour pork, which should be here any minute."

No response: the attempt at humor was lost on Steffi. Her expression was blank, and Reagan could tell something was off. "What're ya thinking about, kiddo? Things okay at school?"

"Mostly," Steffi said softly. "Crap day in P.E."

"Oh? How so? Anything you want to talk about?"

Steffi's eyes came around and met her mother's. "Volleyball

today, and I missed three volley shots I usually make. Shots I *always* make. Ones I've never had a problem with. *Ever.*"

"I'm sorry, honey. That must've been tough."

"Coach said he'd keep an eye on me during next practice, but...."

"But what, honey?"

"If I keep making errors, he may have to bench me for the JV team," Steffi said as the waterworks started flowing.

Reagan put her arm around her daughter's shoulder and drew her into a hug. Her own tears began trickling down as she replayed the eye doctor's comments from the day before. Thanks to her cursed DNA, Steffi, too, would become a card-carrying member of the RP Club. She just didn't know it yet.

# CHAPTER TWELVE

T WO EMPTY KLEENEX boxes and an hour and a half later, they were still seated at the kitchen table, along with eight now-cold, still-unopened to-go Chinese food containers.

To say the discussion had been very difficult would be a gross understatement, and the news was beyond devastating for Steffi. Reagan had tried her best to broach their joint prognosis with sensitivity and tact, as she herself was still processing it all, and the conversation had devolved into a heaving-shoulders, bawling, quivering mess for them both.

Reagan had never given much thought to the saying, but she was now faced with its truth: "Denial ain't just a river in Egypt." Her eye exam three years ago should have clued her in and, had she actually listened to her doctor, it would have hinted at an inconvenient truth.

She and her daughter silently entertained a series of worse-case thoughts, each more depressing than the last.

Stef thought about her sports scholarship dream that seemed to be slipping away. And so much for the idea of ever being attractive to boys—the whole white cane deal would eventually make that a non-starter. She honked her nose into the tissue. She sounded like a Canadian goose.

Reagan's dream of being the next big deal in the photography world was now toast. Plus, she could no longer even drive a car. Her very independence had been pulled out from under her, instantaneously. And, most importantly, how could she take care of her daughter?

She snapped open another fortune cookie and tossed the unread paper aside before jamming the snack into her mouth. She was afraid to look at the fortune because hers had already taken a huge hit, plus it would probably read: *Blind leading the blind means both are lost.*

# CHAPTER THIRTEEN

THE UNEATEN FOOD, all eight boxes of it, had been stashed in the fridge, and mother and daughter had both crawled into Reagan's California king bed.

They were curled up together, with Steffi's head tucked under her mama's chin. Reagan buried her nose in her daughter's scalp, taking in the aroma of her floral shampoo, as well as subtle notes of something else—something only a mother could pick up on: hints of that newborn baby smell she'd cherished nearly sixteen years before. Another tear rolled down Reagan's cheek.

Steffi was snoring the cute snore. Reagan kissed the top of her baby's head, trying to remember how many years it had been since they'd done this. To the best of her recollection, she figured it had to be at least ten, and probably after Steffi had not been picked for the lead in the kinder play.

Reagan stared up toward the dark cottage cheese ceiling she couldn't see but knew was there. It was the same with the night sky in recent years, as she missed seeing the fields of stars she knew had to be twinkling above her.

She had never mentioned this to anybody, and she tried

to pass it off as light pollution or Seattle cloud cover. Still, there were those occasional clear nights, and she knew the stars hadn't been unplugged. Her mind went back to that river in Egypt: *Denial.*

The room was dark, save the blurry nightlight across the room. With Steffi asleep on her left arm, Reagan endeavored not to wake her as she reached for her cell phone on the nightstand. The display told her it was 10:10, and there were no new messages from Fynn.

*How the hell can they lose his luggage?*

As she pondered that, along with a myriad of pervasive dark thoughts, she tried to stay awake. She wondered, if she were to close her eyes, might she awaken to a world of permanent darkness, having seen her last sight? The very thought gave her shivers, and she pulled the blanket higher onto both of them.

## REVERB HARD ROCK HAMBURG
## SATURDAY MORNING, DECEMBER 13
## 07:15, CENTRAL EUROPEAN TIME (CET)
## (FRIDAY, 10:15 PM, PACIFIC TIME)

The hotel room was still quite dark, thanks to the blackout curtains, with only a hint of daylight sneaking through their edges. He'd slept like a rock. A hard rock.

Fynn's open suitcase sat atop the folding luggage rack, next to the long dresser that also served as a stand for the forty-six-inch television. He picked up his fully charged cell-phone from the nightstand and checked the time, noting the girls were probably sound asleep at home.

His stomach grumbled, his thoughts going to getting a good German breakfast of eggs and decent brats. He knew just the place, as he frequented it when he was in town; it was only about a half-mile walk from the hotel. He grabbed the remote and called up a news channel, muting the TV's volume before it could wake up the companion sharing his bed.

The weather stats scrolled across the bottom of the screen telling him he wouldn't need his umbrella this morning, but it would still make for a brisk walk.

Fynn turned toward the blanket-shrouded shape next to him, giving it a nudge. When he got no response, he pushed his thumb upward on the remote's volume knob, drowning the blissful silence with the sound of power tools, as the news had cut to a splashy commercial for *Bauhaus*, Germany's equivalent to Home Depot.

This elicited a groan, followed by a stir, before they rolled over onto the other side.

Another nudge from Fynn. This one less gentle. "Hey! Move your ass. It's breakfast time."

"Danke schön!" Fynn called to his host, waving as he stepped back out onto the street.

He wrapped the wool scarf around his neck. It was still brisk out, but he liked it. He found it invigorating. He was also feeling infinitely better having checked the breakfast box off his list. He looked at his watch, which he'd set to the local time upon landing the day before: 9:20.

He'd dined solo this morning, his partner claiming stomach issues. Oh, well.

Sure, he could have opted for the hotel's buffet breakfast, but it had been a long trip across the pond, and Fynn had been absolutely craving the *Bauernfrustuck*. The owner/chef of this tiny café made it special for him whenever he came in, as it wasn't on the regular menu.

Prepared in a skillet, *Bauernfrustuck* was a hearty German "farmer's breakfast" comprised of chopped potatoes, a whisked mixture of eggs, milk, and basic spices, to which bite-sized pieces of grilled brat were added. The mixture was stirred and cooked for several minutes before being sprinkled with a good cheese and some chives. It surely must have satiated many a farmer. It sure worked for him, anyway.

As he started down the block, Fynn racked his brain to remember which foster mother had first prepared it for him, and in which home he'd enjoyed it. The third, he decided, and it was probably the only thing he'd enjoyed from his childhood.

He'd been hard-pressed to find anything as good in Seattle, though several chain restaurants offered their own competing versions of skillet breakfasts. Still, not the same.

*Too bad Reagan never learned her way around a kitchen. Aside from boiling water for Steffi's mac and cheese.*

Fynn shook his head, dismissing the thoughts, and stopped to liberate a cigarette from its pack. He fired it up and took a deep drag as he quickly did the mental math, knowing it was still the middle of the night over there. The nine-hour difference worked in his favor at the moment, but he knew he'd have to check in with a proper phone call in a few hours.

In the meantime, he was unincumbered and had all the time in the world. The sun hadn't shown itself yet today, and it might not at all, but the air was crisp and his energy electric, so he resumed what would be a thirty-five minute stroll toward the *Fischmarkt*.

He had to make sure things were in order for tomorrow morning's anticipated crowd. This included the proper showcasing of the brand-new items.

The thought put a pep in his step.

# CHAPTER FOURTEEN

REAGAN TOSSED FITFULLY as her internal horror movie played out; it was even more vicious than before. Her eyes fluttered open as she struggled to discern the strange vibration she was now hearing. Her senses were slowly coming back, including the sensation that she was now spooning with her daughter, still sound asleep.

She turned to the nightstand and found the vibration's source; her phone was vibrating with an incoming call. She turned to grab it and cleared her throat as she anticipated it being Fynn.

But it wasn't.

She squinted at the display, which indicated it was Amethyst calling her back.

"Mm… hey, Ames," she said softly.

"Aww, did I call you too early, Twinner?"

"No. No, it's all good. Just having a slower than usual morning here. Thanks for calling back," Reagan replied as she slowly spun around, her feet finding their slippers.

"Sorry I didn't call you back last night. Got your message late; I had a gallery dealio."

"That's what I figured. Sorry about my message. Must've sounded pathetic to—"

"Stop. What're friends for when one needs to share, right?"

"Yeah, truer words…" Reagan said, crossing over to the bathroom and taking a seat on the porcelain throne. She closed the door so as not to wake Steffi.

"So, what's going on, Ray Gun? I sensed a darkness I don't usually get from you."

"A darkness… yeah, I guess you could say that," Reagan replied, the irony of the reference sinking in. "Hey, um—and you can totally say *no*, Ames—but are you available to meet up for a coffee or something. I mean, if—"

"Totally on board with that, Twinner. You're my priority today. Where and when do you wanna meet up?"

"Well, that's the thing. I'd… kinda need a ride.…"

## COZY COTTAGE CAFÉ
### 9:25 AM

Amethyst had picked her up at the house, Reagan having arranged a hangout day for Steffi and her friend Vickie at home.

The Cozy Cottage Café was an until-now untried breakfast place about a mile from Reagan's house and, thankfully, the vibe was living up to its name. Plus, the food was rocking it.

Reagan poured even more syrup onto her already-soggy slices of French toast as Ames watched in amazement, swallowing a bite of her own Denver omelet before she spoke.

"That's it. Waterboard that evil bread," she said with a chuckle. "Make it give up its deepest secrets."

Reagan stopped the flow and set down the glass dispenser. "Gawd. Drowning my sorrows. Sorry."

"Nothing to apologize for, Twinner. Seriously, sometimes you've just got to slather on the maple product to make things right. I get it, girl."

Reagan looked around to see if anybody else was watching the spectacle. They weren't. She cut into it with her fork and delivered a drippy bite to her mouth. "Gawd."

Ames dug into her country potatoes, which she'd similarly tortured with ketchup. "So. What's up, Ray?" she asked, stabbing a chunk of potato before spearing a piece of breakfast link to make the perfect shish ka-bite. "Please."

Reagan wiped her mouth and let out a sigh, her eyes darting around but not focusing on anything. They finally came around to Ames's and they locked in. Reagan's tears were forming in their corners, as if awaiting permission to launch. "I'm...." It was all she could get out.

"You're... *amazing*," Ames said, finishing for her. What else are you?" she asked, setting down her fork so she could rest her hand upon her friend's.

"I'm..." she managed, two fat tears rolling down her cheeks. "I'm... *shit*. Sorry. I'm... going...."

"Where are you going, sweetie?"

"BLIND!" she blurted, louder than she'd intended.

The tiny café went silent, save the sound of several forks

clinking to rest onto their plates. Reagan paused, sensing the attention their table was now getting.

She took a deep breath, leaning in closer as Ames gently squeezed her hand and nodded as if to say, *it's okay.*

Reagan glanced down at their joined hands. She could feel the warmth Ames was generating. She looked back up at her friend as she whispered the words that even she couldn't believe were true.

"I'm going fucking blind."

# CHAPTER FIFTEEN

METHYST'S HAND WAS still sitting atop Reagan's, slowly caressing it as she listened raptly to every one of her best friend's trials and concerns. They had been sitting like this for more than two hours now and, other than their coffee cups, their dishes had long ago been cleared away.

Ames's tears had been flowing as well and, between them, they were all used up. Their server, Janet, had been awesome, and continued to be, refilling their coffees repeatedly while exercising tremendous sensitivity. She hadn't even brought the check over, wanting to give these two friends all the time they needed.

"Gawd, Twinner," Ames said softly as she shook her head. "It's all too much for one person to handle," she continued, rubbing her fingers across Reagan's hand again. "And I'm so sorry to hear that Steffi might—"

"Not might. *Will*... she *does* already. Not like mine yet, but... We *both* got tested yesterday. Just a matter of time before... sorry for my language, but this is so fucked up, on so many levels, Ames," Reagan said, expecting a new wave of tears, but they were on backorder, like they'd decided they no longer wanted to participate.

"I know. Yeah… nothing short of cruelty, this," Ames said softly. She shook her head, still unable to fully process it all. "And Fynn knows, right?"

"He knows I've been having… challenges… but I don't think he fully knows the prognosis. I mean, I haven't told him. He's in the freaking fatherland right now, and we haven't had a chance to talk."

Amethyst looked out the window for a few moments as she absorbed everything. She turned back to face her BFF. "Hey. Look at me, Ray. Tell me the truth because, as your bestie, I've got to know."

Reagan's eyes locked into Ames's. "Okay."

"Tell me, as you're looking at me, right here, right now… what do you see?"

"What do you mean? I see my bestie–"

"No. I mean, I *know* that. Thanks. You're my bestie, too. What I want to know is, *what* do you see? Exactly. Like, what is your… field of view in this moment? Describe it in detail. Please."

Reagan stared at her from across the table. Her expression was blank, but she understood the assignment. "I see, clearly, your face. Your head, your shoulders…."

"And?"

"And… *nothing*… other than a blurriness," Reagan said softly, her hand going to her mouth, hoping she hadn't spoken to loudly. "As if I'm in a darkened room, or at night… next to nothing. It's a tunnel, Ames," she finished through a whisper. "And it'll only get worse, until…."

Amethyst shook her head, refusing to believe that her

beautiful, young best friend–who also happened to be her favorite photographer–may be damned to a life of complete blindness.

"Thank you, Twinner, for your honesty. Dammit, this sucks, but..." she paused to punctuate her statement with a resolute smile, "I'm on your team, and we're gonna win."

Reagan's mouth formed a tight line as her eyes attempted to convey a smile. She nodded her head in a deliberate bob reminiscent of one of those fifties-era, red drinking-bird toys.

"I know. Thank you."

"Count on it, Twinner. So, Merry Christmas!" Ames said, trying not to explode in laughter at the absurdity of it all.

"Happy Holidays! *Not!*" Reagan blurted in similar fashion. She turned her compromised gaze to the window, watching a stream of carefree people happily scurrying about their normal activities, many carrying what looked like gift bags, as they joyfully prepared for the most important of holidays, all while an unsolicited inner Andy Williams voice reminded her that it's the most wonderful time of the year. But not for her; he was lying.

The reality of that impending event crashed into her like a second avalanche. She hadn't even factored in all that goes with that, and it was just her and Steffi. "Christmas... Gawd."

Ames squeezed Reagan's hand firmly, bringing her back to the moment. "Twinner. Listen very carefully because I've got what just might be the best idea in the long history of best ideas."

Reagan's attention locked back in. "Yeah?"

"Yeah. Definitely."

Reagan scrunched her face. "Lay it on me then. The

suspense is killing me–which in itself might be a good thing right now," she said through an awkward chuckle.

"Okay. So, hear me out. We have our prognosis, right? I mean, to the degree that science, and the medical *experts* can determine at the moment, right? And, who knows? They aren't always right. But, for the purposes of what I'm about to say, let's assume they are right. Again, there may be some experimental shit coming down the pike with lasers, or stem cells, or pig eye transplants, or whatever...."

"Cut to the chase, Ames, please."

"Okay. So, is your passport current?"

"Yeah. Why?"

"What about Stef's?"

"Her passport?"

Ames nodded.

"Yeah. I mean, it should be. We had to cancel a family trip to Germany about five years ago because Fynn got sick. It would've been her first trip back there. But yeah. It's current. So?"

"So... you need to consider what I'm about to say very carefully because this is perfect," Ames said, barely able to contain her excitement.

Reagan scrunched her face, going with it as she awaited the whole, big, *Best Idea in the World* reveal. She nodded. "Lay it on me."

"Okay. Here it is. Dig it: *This* is the time. Right fricking *now*. While you can still–I hate to even say this–while you can still get around. While you and your precious Steffi can experience life as sighted persons, taking in new places–together–cementing visuals in your minds, making memories, and taking those killer *pictures* of yours!" She paused to breathe, but also to gauge Ray's level of engagement.

"Huh…" Reagan replied, nodding thoughtfully as she absorbed the enormity of Ames's proposal.

"Right?! I mean, seeing all the beauty that there is to see! Absorbing it all! Before…."

"Before… ?" Reagan asked.

"Before the lights go out."

# CHAPTER SIXTEEN

BY THE TIME they'd finally relinquished their window table, it was close to noon. And their server, bless her, had picked up their tab.

They might not have solved all the world's problems–not by a long shot–but not for lack of trying. They'd each hugged Janet on their way out the door, thanking her for her wonderful service, and for her incredible kindness in comping their meal. Ames had left a *very* generous cash tip that actually exceeded their tab, and the girls promised they'd come back to see her, and their new favorite place, the Cozy Cottage, soon.

Amethyst had cleared her schedule to hang with Reagan and suggested that, since it was a nice day out, the two of them poke around some of the cuter local shops on the block.

Ames picked out several flannel shirts for her hubby, a few exceedingly cute-but-pricey dog toys for her sister's Corgi, and a couple of secret purchases for her bestie when she'd had her back turned. She'd had everything wrapped on the spot, happily toting her two large gift bags as she stealthily studied Reagan's joy level.

Reagan appreciated the gift of time with her friend, out in

the wild, in an attempt to salvage any semblance of her trampled-upon Christmas spirit. For a couple of hours, Reagan was able to focus on things other than her current plight, and it was the first time she'd felt anything even close to the same zip code as *joy* in a long time. She actually smiled on more than one occasion, which Ames found heartening.

Reagan had found a cute coat for Steffi, a matching beanie, and the new Uggs her daughter had mentioned wanting because Vickie had a pair. She picked out a ribbed turtleneck sweater for Fynn, along with a new Cross pen from the stationery store. Unlike Ames, she decided she'd wrap everything at home, later.

"Look at you! Atta girl," Ames said with a broad smile. "See? You need to get out more."

"I can't remember how long it's been since I last did this, Twinner. I mean, going out to actual brick-and-mortar stores and all."

"Good for the soul sometimes."

"But not good for my credit card," Reagan chuckled.

"You don't have to worry about that. Remember? I'm just glad to see you enjoying yourself."

"Thanks," Reagan replied warmly.

"Hey, do you mind if I duck into that shoe store across the street for a few minutes?"

"Not at all. Go for it. There's a couple more shops I want to check out on this side. I'll find you."

Ames materialized onto the sidewalk nearly thirty minutes later, having added two bags of shoes to her bounty. Reagan was sitting on a bench, just outside the shop, when Ames found her, her eyes closed, her face tilted to the sun. She wore a hint of a smile, and she appeared to be listening to all the sounds going on around her.

"Ray...."

"Hey...."

"Wow, I'm so sorry I took so long in there. It was a target-rich environment, you know what I mean. How'd you make out?"

"Good. I think I'm just about done with all my shopping," Reagan replied, standing, and collecting her own bags.

"Okay. Me too! Let's put all this stuff in the car."

Reagan was actually glad Ames had spent extra time in the shoe place because it had allowed her to stealthily scope out the nearby jewelry store.

She hadn't expected to but had been lucky enough to find *the* most exquisite gift for her bestie. The three-piece amethyst pendant and earrings set was beautifully crafted in a teardrop shape, and in a supernatural shade of violet—the most beautiful quartz she'd ever seen. Prong-set in fourteen-carat yellow gold, it had been the most extravagant purchase she could remember making. Ever. But her friend was worth it. She couldn't wait to give it to her at Christmas.

As they reached her top-of-the-line, burgundy Porsche Cayenne, Ames set down her bags and chirped the remote to activate the rear hatch. It proved a tight fit due to the Corgi-sized gift crate taking up the rear seat, and after they had stuffed all the bags inside, Ames closed the motorized hatch. She turned to Reagan with a mischievous smile.

"One more stop before I take you home."

The locally cut Douglas fir was perfectly shaped and, being five foot tall, it meant Reagan would have no trouble reaching the treetop to embellish it.

Amethyst helped Reagan bring it through the front door and, after moving a wooden apple box of LP records out of the way, they propped it up in the corner of the small living room.

"Yes... some Christmas spirit is what this place needs. Seriously, Ray, this should help you and Steffi get through your holiday funk a little better, right?"

Reagan stared at it as she drank in the aroma that only a freshly cut Christmas tree can provide. "I'd all but forgotten how great that smell is. The old, wannabe plastic tree is definitely staying in its box in the garage this year! Maybe forever. Thank you, Ames," she said, leaning in for a long hug.

"Don't mention it, Twinner. It's no big thing, but sometimes it's the little things that end up being the big things, n'est-ce pas?"

"Indeed."

"You have an angel to put on top of it?"

"Nah, I don't believe in 'em. Maybe I'll stick a rubber Halloween bat up there. Might be more appropriate, y'know, with the whole blindness theme this year?"

"Glad you haven't lost your twisted sense of humor. Okay, I'll leave you to your tree and your stuff," Ames said, gesturing to the gift bags they'd already brought in. "I've got to scoot and feed my sister's dog. And then my human. If I don't beat him home, I'll find him sitting at the kitchen table holding a knife and fork, waiting. I swear, the guy is amazing in a lot of ways, but God forbid he ever learn to use a can opener and a microwave. Anyway...."

"'Kay. Thanks for… everything, bestie," Reagan said, her smile not worn off yet.

As Amethyst turned to exit, she peeled the sticky note off the front door. "I think this is for you," she said, handing it to Reagan, who took a moment to read it:

*Having dinner at Vickie's.*

*They're bringing me home.*

*I have my key.*

*XO*

"Gives me time to stash a few things," she said, waving as Amethyst stepped onto the porch. "Say hi to Jerry."

"Will do, Twinner!"

# CHAPTER SEVENTEEN

DINNER HAD BEEN leftover Chinese, paired with a red Gatorade. Dessert, the remainder of the Kringle.

Reagan stepped out into the garage and flicked on the light, taking a moment to give her car some stink eye before turning her attention to the shelving units that lined one wall.

The three large, plastic bins labeled *XMAS* were stashed atop the tallest shelf in the garage, which meant Reagan had to figure out the procedures involved with adjusting the weird, orange, metal extension ladder contraption Fynn had bought at the hardware store a month before.

She missed the simple, traditional–and foolproof–wooden ladder, and her hubby had made an executive decision one day while she was out, because it was one of those must-have *As Seen on TV* products, and it looked cool.

Reagan had never been considered mechanically inclined, and she swore a blue streak as she fumbled with the heavy ladder's metal hooks, pulling them out from the existing holes that corresponded to the apparatus's closed-and-locked position. She figured she needed to add at least a couple of feet in height and, after ten minutes of trial and error, and a couple of pinched fingers, she'd finally solved what amounted to a Rubik's frigging ladder.

"Pain in the ass," she muttered as she slid the ladder closer against the shelf unit and began ascending the rungs of death. "Wouldn't that be something, to die this way, after all the other bullshit going on?" she asked herself. She briefly considered stepping up onto the very top of the ladder but decided to heed the bold warning sign, a step lower.

One of the long bulbs in the garage's fluorescent light box was dimmer than the rest, flickering in protest as it threatened to expire. The lighting wasn't optimal, and Reagan glanced down to check her footing before reaching out, her hand grabbing the near handle of the first bin.

"Come to mama...."

She slid it toward herself and managed to grab the bin securely by both handles. After a moment, she dared a glance to the floor. *Now, how the hell do I get this down to the ground?*

The answer came to her in the form of a sound, as she heard the front door slam, followed by a familiar voice. "Mom? Are you home?"

"In the garage!"

The tree was secured into the classic red and green tree stand—the medieval looking one with the three thumb screws that sink into the flesh of the tree's trunk—where it would sip its last meal of tap water.

Mother and daughter sat crisscross on the floor as they regarded their handiwork, looking for any blank spots in need of an ornament. "Great job with the lights, honey, and good call on the blinkers."

"Thanks. I like this way better than the plastic tree. The old one smelled like plastic... and dust."

"Well, I have to agree with you," Reagan said, breathing in the sweet, Christmassy smell.

"And I'm glad we found the handprint ornament you made for me in Kinder. That's my favorite because it's from my favorite daughter."

"Only daughter," Steffi laughed. "You done with the gold paper?"

"Yeah," Reagan said, passing her the tube of gift wrap. "Who're the CDs for?"

"Vickie. Got her some wristbands too. For volleyball," Steffi replied, pulling the last of the paper from the long tube.

"That was nice of you," Reagan said as she chose a roll of paper in a snowflake design and pulled Amethyst's jewelry box from its bag.

"Ooh, that must be for me," Steffi said with a chuckle.

"Mm, 'fraid not, kiddo."

"Who's it for then?"

"My friend, Ames. She's done a lot for me, and I couldn't resist getting her something nice," she said, opening the flip box to show Steffi.

"Gawd, Mom. Is she your friend, or... your secret lover?" she teased as she secured a piece of tape to the last flap of Vickie's gift paper. "Seriously, that's nice. She'll friggin' love it."

"I hope so." Reagan smiled as she cut a small piece from the paper roll. "If you want something else to wrap, there's a turtleneck there, for Fynn. It can be from you."

"'Kay," Stef said as she grabbed a roll of green wrap. A moment later, "Mom?"

"Yeah, honey?" Reagan replied. Steffi had stopped what she was doing and was looking directly at her.

"What's... it like?"

"What's what like, baby?"

"You know… your eyes. What's it like… like, what do you see?"

Reagan set down the scotch tape and considered her response. The question had been direct, but not impolite. Her daughter deserved a good answer, especially since she would likely be facing the same level of handicap at some point. Reagan picked up the empty tube and handed it to her.

"What–?" Steffi began, taking hold of the cardboard tube, momentarily confused.

"Take that, now put it up to your right eye. Close your other one," Reagan instructed.

"Like a telescope?" Steffi asked, bring it up and peering into it.

"Yes… or a tunnel."

Steffi squinted into the small hole of the three-foot-long cardboard tube. She looked like a pirate as she moved it around, regarding the flashing lights of the tree before landing on her mother's face at the other end.

Her mother's mouth was drawn into a line, and her eyes showed a level of motherly concern she'd never seen before, the expression telling her all she needed to know.

Steffi shook her head, not wanting to believe it, but she knew her mother would never lie to her. She slowly lowered the tube, dropping it to the floor as they both leaned into each other's arms, locking into a quivering hug that might even register on the Richter scale.

# CHAPTER EIGHTEEN

## HAMBURG FISH MARKET
## ALTONA, BY THE ELBE RIVER
## SUNDAY, DECEMBER 14
## 06:55 AM, CET

TO SAY THE Hamburg *Fischmarkt*, or Fish Market, had been around a while would be an understatement.

Since 1703, this local institution has been a magnet to shoppers coming for the fresh fish offerings, and even the spectacle of the fish auctions, if one chose to witness that. The large marketplace always opened for shoppers on Sundays: in the winter months at 07:00, while in the summer months it opened two hours earlier.

Shoppers would come by the hundreds, even thousands, and the crowd was guaranteed to include a mix of both early birds and the night owls returning from a late night of dancing or even stumbling home from the red light district. Either way, the owls often nursed their hangovers as they stood along the water's edge, enjoying a medicinal meal of a steaming hot cup of coffee in one hand and a fresh fish sandwich in the other.

To the uninitiated, early bird and night owl alike, the thick aroma of fresh seafood might be off-putting, but it was a small price to pay for having access to some of the best fresh seafood available in Germany.

During the years he and Reagan had assisted at her parents' booth here, Fynn had always found it amusing that she resorted to wearing a neck scarf she had generously spritzed with her strongest perfume in order to counter the stench. Cursed with a very active gag reflex, it was the only way she could get through the day.

Fynn shook his head as he remembered those days as he too had spent many a day working the booth of the family business. He barely even smelled the fish, really, as—for him—being exposed to it on that level was akin to working in a florist's shop and becoming unaware of the roses' fragrance. Besides, he equated the smell of fish to *money*, and now there would be much more of it.

His nostrils flared as he took in a deep breath and looked at his watch: 06:59. The other vendors watched the clock as well, while sneaking glances of the competitors' booths. It looked like a good crowd gathered outside. Fynn counted down the seconds; then, as the market clock's minute hand clicked ahead to the top of the hour, he winked at his three associates, giving them the green light to pull away the draped sheets and wax paper that shrouded the display of offerings.

Fynn closely watched the faces of the crowd, and the other vendors, as their collective jaws dropped at the big reveal. His impressive display featured not only the expected local fair but also something very new: fresh imported Alaskan pollock, salmon, and cod, perched atop their beds of ice and each adorned by a small, decorative American flag on a stick.

Plus, there were the two large tanks of live lobsters, front and center, which had the effect of magnets as the crowd was collectively pulled closer.

"Seht her, Hamburg! Frische Hummer aus Maine!" declared Fynn, the ringmaster.

*Behold, Hamburg! Fresh Maine lobsters!*

## MEANWHILE . . .
## REAGAN'S HOME
## BOTHELL, WASHINGTON
## SATURDAY, DECEMBER 13
## 10:02 PM, PACIFIC TIME

What had started out as a quiet evening of decorating the tree, enjoying cocoa from their Christmas mugs, and wrapping gifts together, had ended up being another highly emotional night for Reagan and Steffi.

Their prognoses were still very fresh in their minds, and it would continue to be a lot to process going forward. For Steffi, especially so, in light of the answer she had received to her question. The truth bomb, courtesy of a look down the end of the cardboard tube: the glimpse into that very dark, future rabbit hole that had absolutely devastated her. She'd crawled off to bed shortly after. Her mother's.

Reagan switched off her nightstand lamp and gently

kissed her daughter's forehead. Steffi was lights-out, the kiss prompting her to roll over to her own side as she continued snoring the cute snore. Reagan wished she could do the same.

She stared into the black void, wondering why she still hadn't heard anything from Fynn. What had initially been a source of concern was now morphing into a slow boil of anger. In the event she didn't receive either a call or a message from Fynn by morning, she made a mental note to call their longtime head employee, Hei Li.

In an effort not to disturb Steffi, Reagan carefully flipped her own pillow over to the cooler side and began lightly tapping her head onto it, rhythmically, as she commenced counting herself down to slumber. She wasn't picturing fluffy sheep, however. Instead, she was envisioning her retinal cells again, falling to their messy deaths, surrendering one by one onto their black piles. Inside her frigging eyeballs!

She'd lost count after 240-something and succumbed to the pitch-dark abyss.

# CHAPTER NINETEEN

## SUNDAY, DECEMBER 14
## 6:42 AM, PACIFIC TIME

REAGAN FLIPPED OVER to her other side, her limbs spasming as she gasped loudly, her eyes fluttering open as she fought to emerge from the foggy nightmare place. She reached over to the nightstand and grabbed her phone: *Quarter to seven... gawd.*

And no new messages. *You bastard.*

She rolled back over, reaching her arm out, only to find the bed otherwise empty. Steffi was anything but an early riser, and it wasn't a school day.

"Stef?" she called out, her scratchy throat barely cooperating. She tried again, this time a bit louder. "Steffi?" Several moments went by with no answer. "Probably went back to her bed," Reagan muttered as she clumsily extracted herself from the mound of blankets, stepped into her slippers, and shuffled into the bathroom.

Five minutes later, Reagan stepped into the hallway, shoving her phone into the pocket of her gray Terry robe. The rope light runway was still illuminated. She stopped outside Steffi's bedroom door, listened, then slowly turned the knob and peeked inside. The bed hadn't been slept in.

She followed the runway to the other end, which led to the kitchen and the back patio area. She was careful not to bump her hip on the sharp-edged hall table, one she'd collided with countless times before. She had the bruises to prove it.

Reagan could smell coffee as she approached. She trained her attention to the patio, where she could see Steffi sitting in one of the Adirondack deck chairs, her knees tucked in close to her as she clutched her coffee and stared out at the bare, gray trees in the distance.

Reagan selected the tallest mug from the cupboard and poured herself what appeared to be some industrial strength java. It was jet black and bordered on yesterday's burnt offering from a gas station's dirty coffee pitcher. She allowed herself a very generous pour of Bailey's Irish Cream to lighten it a few shades. Half & Half wasn't going to cut it today.

She opened the slider and stepped out onto the patio, resting her free hand atop Steffi's shoulder and staring out at those same trees. Other than a few unseen birds conversing, it was a blissful silence, one that would assuredly be shattered later by a neighbor's gas lawnmower.

"Hey, Mom," Steffi said, almost whispering.

"Hey, baby," Reagan replied softly, squeezing Steffi's shoulder. "Been up long?"

"A little while... I made coffee."

"Yes, I saw that, thanks," Reagan replied, gesturing with her mug.

"Came out kinda strong."

"Mm," Reagan said, finishing her sip. "Rocket fuel. That's why they invented Bailey's."

Somewhere, out amongst the tree line, the birds were having words, getting their points across before the humans fired up their obnoxious Toros.

"What're you thinking about, sweetie?"

"Nothin'."

"Mm… well, mind if I join you out here and think about nothin' too, for a little bit?"

"Nah. That'll be okay," Steffi replied softly, her puffy, red eyes looking at her now.

"Thanks," Reagan said as she lowered herself into the other Adirondack and braved another sip. *Needs more Bailey's.*

A moment later, the birds, spooked, vacated the trees en masse and flew away to safety at the unmistakable roar of the Toro. And another, maybe a Craftsman.

"For God's sake, it's not even seven o'clock!!" Reagan called out to the inconsiderate neighbors. "It's *Sunday!* You should all be at friggin' church!"

This got a chuckle from Steffi. "I love you, Mom."

Breakfast was toaster waffles, scrambled eggs, and the Mexican mangoes Reagan had splurged for the other day. *Just before crashing the car.* She shook her head, thinking about the unresolved repairs, making a mental note to have it towed to the body shop first thing Monday.

She rinsed the syrup off the plates, mindful to avoid using the hot water as Steffi was in the shower. Vickie had called during the meal, asking Stef if she wanted to go to the mall. With her mom volunteering to chaperone, it hadn't taken much in the way of pleading to get an okay from Reagan. Besides, she enjoyed the idea of having the house to herself today.

She had some important stuff to do.

And some calls to make.

# CHAPTER TWENTY

REAGAN STOOD UNDER the stream of lukewarm-at-best water Steffi had left her. She needed to have another talk with her daughter about her thirty-minute hot shower routines and remind her of the fact that the family shared one water heater.

Just as she finished whipping her shampoo into a rich lather, the water's temperature suddenly dipped, plummeting to a level of frigid cold that would cause any Eskimo to swear a blue streak.

"Oh! My! Gawd!!! *Jeezus!* Stefanie Dunkel, you are so *freaking* grounded!!" Reagan shrieked as she danced spastically under the cold stream to rinse out the product.

If the rocket fuel java hadn't adequately done its job, the glacial waterfall sure as hell had. *Good morning!!! Arggh!*

Twenty minutes later, someone had mercifully killed the engine on what she hoped was the last of the offending gas lawnmowers. As to not jinx the restored Zenlike silence, Reagan waited a full three minutes before uttering her response quietly to the universe. "Thank you." *Om.*

She came in from the patio and closed the slider just as she heard her phone beckoning from the kitchen table. She snatched it up, fully ready to lay into Fynn, but saw it was Hei Li, returning her call. In two seconds, Reagan glanced at the clock and did the mental math, figuring it must be 19:15–the equivalent of 7:15 PM–over there. She'd always loved how Hei Li had told her how to pronounce her name: *Hei Li, it rhymes with uke*-lele!

"Hei Li, Guten Abend!" *Good evening!*

"Hello, Guten Abend, Reagan! Sorry I'm just now calling you back. I didn't get your voicemail until after dinner because my phone was on the charger. How are you?"

"Me? I'm... okay, *danke*. I feel bad about troubling you with this, but as I'd mentioned, I still haven't heard from Fynn since he left. He texted me once, saying he'd arrived, but his luggage hadn't, and his phone charger was in it, and... well, that was *Thursday*. I was just wondering–"

"Oh, yes! Yes! It went great!"

"Excuse me?" Reagan replied, walking back over to look out the slider. "What... went great?" she asked as she pinched the bridge of her nose.

"The Fischmarkt! This morning! It went amazing!"

"I'm sorry; I don't follow... what was so extra amazing about it, Hei Li?"

"The American lobsters!! The Alaskan salmon, the fresh cod... we sold out of all of it, very quickly! It was *wunderbar*!!" she replied, beaming her exhilaration across the pond.

Reagan's expression slowly went slack as she processed this news, picturing the scene as Hei Li had just described it, while envisioning her husband secretly pulling the levers from behind the big curtain. She closed her eyes and, through her nostrils, took in the mother of all slow, deliberate breaths.

"Miss Reagan? Are you still there?"

"Mm. Yes, Hei Li. I am."

"Isn't this exciting?! We're expecting a double shipment for next week, I believe!"

"Very exciting," Reagan said in a soft, measured tone. "So, Fynn was at the market this morning? And he told you about this... this next big shipment?"

"Oh, yes! He was so excited, and–"

"Did you notice if he had his phone with him, Hei Li?"

"His phone? Yes, I saw him using it a couple of times. Would you like me to tell him you called?"

"No!!" Reagan replied more adamantly than she'd intended. She quickly caught herself, softening her tone as she continued. "No, no... thanks. Please don't mention that we talked. I'd like to hear Fynn's excitement when he tells me all about the big day himself. Okay?"

"Okay."

"Promise me."

"I promise," Hei Li replied.

"Thank you."

"Was there anything else?"

"No, no, there wasn't. It was nice talking with you, Hei Li. Thanks for calling me back."

# CHAPTER TWENTY-ONE

REAGAN FINISHED HER last lap of the kitchen, having risked wearing out the cheap linoleum as she blew off a bit of steam. She was properly pissed as she plopped down into her chair at the tiny computer nook.

She powered up the iMac and punched in her password: *WWRD*. As she watched impatiently for the icons to populate the twenty-seven-inch screen, she dug deep, trying to give her husband the benefit of the doubt. She tried to think of any reasonable explanation for Fynn's lack of communication, but she kept coming up empty.

A quick check of her email inbox found nothing from Fynn. There were a series of emails from the retinal clinic her eye doc had referred her to, but she'd check those later. Or maybe even send them to spam; she'd decide later. She didn't have time for this blindness shit right now.

She had bigger fish to fry.

Reagan picked up her phone and stared at its screen. She refused to call Fynn; he'd have to call *her*. But she could sure as hell text him again.

> *> WTF, Fynn? Did you forget how to use your effing phone???*
>
> *I'm home - all day. You need to call me. I don't care what time.*
>
> *And before you meet with the bank on Tuesday!!*

She signed off with a flippant—yet not entirely non-factual—moniker:

> *~ Sightless (but not clueless) in Seattle*

Reagan heard the turntable's stylus bouncing around quietly as it drifted aimlessly in the dead wax zone—the area on a vinyl record between the end of the last track and the label—at the end of side one. She stared at the screen, counted to ten, and threw caution to the wind as she clicked the *Buy Now* button on the shopping site, hoping Steffi would approve of her choice.

*She'd better, I just spent an hour researching the damn things.*

"Merry Christmas, and you'd better not lose these ones," she muttered as she rose from her chair and attended to the regimen involved with playing side two. After a careful cleaning of the vinyl surface with a solution and her soft cleaning brush, she poised the needle over the first track and slowly lowered it into the first groove, savoring the initial kiss and pop.

Reagan cranked up the volume a few notches as German

vocalist extraordinaire Caterina Valente launched into another whimsical number, "Tipitiptipso." This album, a 1958 release, was a favorite of hers as it was one of several she'd rescued from her parents' collection after they had passed, and it conjured happier memories of her childhood in Kiel.

As an only child, she could have inherited all of her parents' belongings, but navigating their estate from across the pond, she'd allowed the lion's share of the furnishings to be sold at auction, opting instead to keep the things that meant the most to her: their best German Christmas ornaments, the extensive record collection, and her father's turntable.

Her father had been the audiophile in the family, and he had long appreciated the virtuosity of Caterina Valente, especially since she spoke fluently in six languages and–even more remarkably–could sing in eleven. There wasn't a note she couldn't hit. A true nightingale, and with more voices than a mockingbird.

"Tipitipitipso…" Reagan sang along as she crossed to the kitchen and poured out the vestiges of what looked more like sludgy black motor oil than this morning's special attempt at coffee. She made a mental note to have a clinic with Steffi on the proper coffee-grounds-to-water ratio later.

Reagan almost never had coffee in the afternoon as it interfered with her sleep, but she'd all but forgotten what a good night's sleep even felt like. Besides, a caffeine boost was in order while she awaited Fynn's call, so she grabbed the cannister of store brand French roast from the pantry shelf. It felt atypically light, and a glance inside confirmed it was nearly empty–not nearly enough to make even a small pot. *Steffi.…*

"Looks like it'll be black tea today, Reagan," she muttered to herself as she got out the stepstool in order to reach the small box on the top shelf. She sniffed the box, not sure what the shelf life was for tea leaves, but at least it was the good stuff she'd bought at her favorite tea shop in Kiel on her last visit there. However many years ago that was.

Reagan filled the tea kettle to the top from the sink's filtered water spigot and placed the vessel atop the gas stove's burner. As she ignited the burner, a ping alerted her to a message on her phone. She hustled over to the workstation and snatched up the device.

"It's about time, Fynn. What the–" she muttered, seething that he'd been too spineless to actually call back.

But the text wasn't from him. It was from Steffi.

> *Hey, mom. OK if I have dinner at Vickie's? I'm invited. Pls? I'll be home early. I got U an xmas present.* ☺

Reagan allowed herself a half smile. Her response was immediate, but contingent.

> *Fine with me. Pls be home by 7. School night... I got you a Christmas present too.* ☺

She hit send and sighed with relief that she'd be able to work uninterrupted now, while also dreading what she might be conjuring up.

Reagan clocked back in at her "office," closed out any evidence of the earbuds storefront and purged the history of today's little Christmas gift spree. She wouldn't be doing much in the way of shopping this year, but she at least hoped to maintain an element of surprise.

Her mouse cursor drifted down to the bottom of the large screen, hovering over the icon of the *Photos* app in her dock, while her mind hovered over her twinner's strong suggestion that she revisit her old image files in hopes of inspiring the next great gallery show.

She hadn't allowed herself to go back into those older files in quite some time, fearful of the feelings associated with the nightmare that had played out over a decade before, in the *Hamburg Hauptbahnhof,* the Hamburg Central Station.

Taking a deep breath, she closed her eyes and, upon reopening them, clicked on the long-avoided file folder simply marked with the two initials: *HH*

It might as well have stood for *House of Horrors* because it was her Pandora's Box.

There were a couple dozen thumbnail images in the file, all taken the same day. *That day.*

Reagan grimaced as she clicked on the first thumbnail, liberating it as it sprung to life, its larger, fully realized version filling a good portion the oversized display. The image before her was one of many she had digitized from her original 35mm film stills, back when she was still shooting that format and before she had gone fully digital.

These had been shot on her Nikon using a fast, 400-speed Kodak black-and-white stock she'd been experimenting with, called TMax 400. Its high sharpness and high contrast properties had lent itself to the handful of images she'd been coaxed to enlarge to display size, one of which had just sold. Other than a handful Reagan had submitted to the gallery–all dramatic shots of the locomotives–she hadn't revisited any of the others.

The tea kettle screamed from the kitchen, its whistle immediately transporting her back to the squeal of locomotive brakes, the station, and the horror that had played out there.

# CHAPTER TWENTY-TWO

REAGAN TOOK A sip of her black tea. It had cooled to room temperature, but she thought nothing of it, her eyes never leaving the screen.

She was relatively pleased with three more images she had unearthed–possible gallery considerations once they had been edited a little–and she felt comfortable sharing them with Ames. After all, there appeared to be an interested buyer. She made copies, added her watermark to each, and dragged them over to a new folder on the desktop. She quickly labeled it: *MAYBE*.

Reagan's pulse began to quicken as her attention returned to the remaining thumbnails, the dozen or so she had casually snapped after her hero shots of the trains. Shots of the platforms, the travelers, and...

Her parents.

Stefan and Ulla Licht, sixty-two and sixty, respectively, had been at the station to see her off that day a dozen years ago. After all, their daughter was embarking on her first trip across the pond, to *America*, having been invited to intern and work as an assistant to a photographer whose work she greatly admired.

Stefan and Ulla had never made the pilgrimage to the States but dreamed of one day visiting California. Neither of them had any interest in the tourist traps like Disneyland or Hollywood. No, their desire was to visit, of all places, the Reagan Library in Simi Valley, having been enamored by the fortieth American President ever since his famous address at the Brandenburg Gate, overlooking the Berlin Wall, in June of 1987.

So enamored were they that they named their only child after him. Their daughter had eventually come to like her name, though it had been a source of ridicule in primary school. She wore it as a badge of honor and considered herself lucky she hadn't been named after Cleveland.

Reagan's father, Stefan, had showed little emotion that day at the station, his face settled into an almost-frown, as was his way. Their only daughter was hanging up her apron and pursuing another interest outside of the family business. And in another country.

His bride, Ulla, exhibited a softer expression that belied her similar feelings. Ever since childhood, Reagan had always loved her cameras, and Ulla knew that one day her passion would take her away from the seafood stalls. She was happy and excited for her daughter's opportunity, yet she held back the tears that were right below the surface. America was so far away.

The opportunity afforded Reagan had come about after a chance encounter with a young woman, an American art grad a couple of years older than Reagan, who had recently seen some of her work at a tiny gallery in Kiel and expressed a keen interest.

She had introduced herself to Reagan, telling her she had just completed her studies in Frankfurt while living with her parents, both United States Air Force, who were stationed at the Rhein-Main Air Base there.

Reagan had immediately taken to her, as her new acquaintance seemed almost like a sister. Plus, the gal had the most intriguing name. "Amethyst. Like the purple quartz!" she'd offered, playfully.

Amethyst explained that she had recently been hired to help open a new gallery in the States. Washington State, on the West Coast, to be exact. She wanted to show the owner some of Reagan's work, and the rest was history.

Things had happened fast. The only Seattle-bound flight Reagan had been able to secure on short notice was out of Frankfurt International and on a red-eye that evening. So she had opted to save what little money she had by taking the train to Frankfurt from Hamburg, about a four-hour trip.

Reagan's excitement that day was tempered by other emotions as she snapped a series of candid photos of her aging parents' faces as they all gathered on the platform. Using her long lens, she had captured just how weathered they both looked: the decades of sun, salty air, and the stresses of the family business had taken their toll. Her mother's dark sunglasses and her wooden cane only hinted at the undiagnosed troubles she had with her vision.

Reagan's new husband, Fynn, was there too, holding her three-year old daughter, Stefanie, a child she had out of wedlock with a smooth-talking dockworker who had bailed as soon as he learned of her pregnancy.

Reagan's marriage to Fynn had been more out of

convenience than true love. She was a single mother with a young child. He was the charming, handsome, repeat customer at the Fischmarkt who came by the family's booth at least three times a week. Stefan had always regarded him suspiciously, not sure if the young man was more interested in his daughter or the Fischbrötchen, fish sandwiches he always ordered.

Another smooth talker, Fynn had inundated her with his charm and confidence, plus he seemed to like her young daughter. Six months later, she and Fynn were married in a civil ceremony, one her parents did not attend.

Tears welled up as Reagan weathered the memories. She clicked on the next image, the first of a series of shots she had taken of the group on the platform, through the window, from her vantage point on the train.

In this photo, her parents were standing there, track-side, stoically marking the moment as their daughter's train prepped for departure. Fynn stood just behind them, young Steffi in the crook of his arm as he waved. Steffi waved as well. A handful of other well-wishers stood there too, but the crowd was small at this hour.

Reagan clicked on the next image, then the next. There were only subtle differences in them as they had been taken seconds apart, almost like frames of a movie. One young couple was reacting to their baby who must have been crying from the nearby stroller. Another couple was waving to the train. Another person, seemingly older and expressionless, wearing a ball cap and dark wraparound sunglasses, sat in a wheelchair with a blanket across his legs.

Reagan clicked on another image, taken moments later.

She knew this to be so because she noticed the perspective had changed slightly, as if her train had just begun its departure. In the photo, her parents remained where they had been, but the young couple with the stroller was no longer visible. Fynn was no longer waving; his head was turned, his attention seemingly more on the empty tracks of the adjacent platform behind them now.

Another mouse click revealed the next image, Reagan tracking the subtle changes that only the photographer would notice. This time, Steffi's face was buried in Fynn's chest. Her daughter had been especially tired that morning, Reagan remembered, having had a feverish, sleepless night.

The next photo was much the same with a couple of small variations. Fynn was looking over at the man in the wheelchair, and the man seemed to be looking back, his head turned toward him.

*Click.* Reagan advanced to the next image, her pulse quickening while her hands became clammy. Fynn had stepped several feet away in this photo, his back to the camera as he held Steffi.

*Click.* Fynn had stepped out of frame in this next shot. Her parents had turned away as well, their backs turned to camera now, as if to follow Fynn.

*Click.* The last image in the series now filled Reagan's screen. Her family was no longer visible. There was one anomaly that stood out in this photo, however.

The wheelchair man was also gone, but the wheelchair remained!

# CHAPTER TWENTY-THREE

REAGAN NEARLY COLLAPSED from her chair, her irreparably broken heart having been mercilessly ripped from her chest now a second time. *Gawd, if we only knew when we're saying our last goodbyes!*

She resumed breathing, though rapidly now, her free hand clamped to her mouth as she enlarged the image and moved her cursor around to focus on its nuances. Zoomed in as she was now, the image's grain increased exponentially, but its resolution still provided adequate detail, thanks to the film stock she'd used.

Frame-by-frame, her focus kept going back to the mystery man in the wheelchair. Were he and Fynn interacting in some way, or was she just reading into things?

She rubbed her fucked-up eyes and crooked her neck until it made a popping sound of relief, only now allowing herself to revisit the fragments she remembered from that day.

The memories of which she'd suppressed all these years.

She hadn't learned about what had transpired at the Hamburg Hauptbahnhof until later. Much later.

Reagan's phone had lost its charge on the train while enroute to Frankfurt, as she'd forgotten to charge it during her shared sleepless night while attending to Steffi's fever the night before. And the eleven-hour flight across the pond, going through customs, and the taxi ride hadn't helped her keep up with current events.

It wasn't until she had retrieved her phone's charger from her suitcase, upon arriving at her friend Amethyst's apartment in Seattle, that she had gotten her first alerts to an emergency.

Amethyst had rushed into the guest bedroom at the first sounds of Reagan's screaming, holding her quaking friend as she cursed God and the universe for so cruelly taking her parents from her.

Fynn had left her over a dozen voicemails and even more texts, pleading for her to call him back, as there had been "a horrible accident."

Hamburg Police had later filled in some of the blanks, as it was determined Stefan and Ulla Licht had somehow fallen onto the tracks as another train approached on an adjacent platform. They had been killed instantly, and a couple of witnesses had claimed they thought they saw somebody push them, though they had been unable to provide a description.

A third person, a young man, had reportedly fallen victim to a similar unprovoked attack, though on another set of tracks at an adjacent platform a few moments later. The third victim had survived, though he had suffered the loss of both legs. Even though delirious with pain, he had somehow managed to describe his assailant as a foreigner, of Arab persuasion.

A wide net had been cast as it was assumed this same assailant was responsible for both attacks, but the case had never been solved. No arrests had ever been made, and the tragic loss had forever changed her.

She would have no way of knowing, as change can be incremental and almost imperceptible, but in those horrific moments over a decade ago, Reagan's world had begun its slow plummet and spiral into darkness.

The memories seared her like hot pokers now, her tears cascading as she wailed like a wounded beast, surrendering to, and cursing, the dark place.

# CHAPTER TWENTY-FOUR

## REVERB HARD ROCK HAMBURG
## MONDAY, DECEMBER 15
## 01:00, CET
## (SUNDAY, 4:00 PM, PACIFIC)

S UNDAY HAD BEEN a very long day but a hugely successful one. There had been much to celebrate, with a lavish room-service dinner, the best wine on the hotel's menu, and a dip into the Asbach brandy.

Fynn was propped up in bed in the darkened hotel room, naked underneath the sheets, his post-coital state of relaxation ruined as he stared at his cellphone screen, its clock displaying the newly minted hour. He lit up a cigarette.

His partner was lightly snoring, which he found annoying. He always had. Fynn reread the message for what had to be the hundredth time, ruminating on how and if he should respond.

> *WTF, Fynn? Did you forget how to use your effing phone???*

*I'm home - all day. You need to call me. I don't care what time.*

*And before you meet with the bank on Tuesday!!*

*~ Sightless (but not clueless) in Seattle*

He sure as hell wasn't going to engage in that clusterfuck of a discussion at this hour. Besides, how would he explain things? This was... *wirklich beschissen* (really fucked up)! And he was at a loss of how to buy more time until his bank appointment on Tuesday.

Fynn took a deep drag on his cigarette and dropped it into the half-filled water glass on his nightstand, the tobacco's ash sputtering as it joined a dozen other soggy butts floating in the blackened liquid.

*Scheisse!*

Shit!

He closed out the message app and opened a search window for Lufthansa. Several clicks, some mental math, and ten minutes later he reached over and poked his lover. The snoring stopped, a sleepy groan replacing it.

"Mm."

"Hey... wake up."

"Mmm..."

Fynn poked again, harder. "*Aufwachen!*"

"Mm?!"

"I need you to do something," Fynn barked, yanking away the covers. "*Jetzt.*"

*Now.*

# CHAPTER TWENTY-FIVE

**REAGAN'S HOME**
**BOTHELL, WASHINGTON**
**SUNDAY, DECEMBER 14**
**4:40 PM, PACIFIC**

UNPLANNED TEARS, STEMMING from ripping off the scabs of long-repressed memories, had resulted in Reagan's unscheduled nap. It had been short, but deeper than the Marianas Trench.

It took several moments for her to reorient herself as she emerged from the fog of her horrific nightmare, the vivid imaginings of her parents' demise refreshed. She was all cried out, for now, and she didn't remember how she'd ended up on the living room loveseat.

Reagan slowly got up and shuffled to the kitchen, pulling out one of the blue beverages from the refrigerator drawer and took a long pull from it as she stared out the window. The bare trees in the distance blended in with the rest of the gray afternoon, the only color coming from the next-door neighbor's newly installed Christmas lights.

*Christmas. Gawd….*never mind herself; she couldn't care less at this point.

*What kind of Christmas is it going to be for Steffi?*

Reagan louvered the kitchen blinds closed, blocking out any references to the once joyous holiday, and plopped back into her computer chair. She woke up the iMac.

Her eyes felt like two burn holes in a blanket, and she bumped up the font several sizes as she opened up her email account. She began composing a new message to Ames, attaching the three photo files from the *MAYBE* folder.

> > Hey, Twinner. Rough day here, but I've been going through some of the old pics, per your suggestion. When you come up for air, please check out these three (attached).
>
> They're raw—not edited or anything—but... whatcha think... maybe??? Any potential?
>
> Let me know your thoughts, even if you think they suck. Thx!
>
> Oh, and I'm thinking about what you said the other day! TTYL!
>
> ~ Ray Gun xo

Reagan's finger hesitated over the mouse button for a moment, and she hit send.

A quick glance at the kitchen clock assured her she still had time before Steffi got home. She exited her *Yahoo!* account and opened a fresh browser window, letting out a huge sigh as she made her declaration:

"Let's do this!"

# CHAPTER TWENTY-SIX

NINETY MINUTES LATER, the whirring of the inkjet printer was joined by the distinct sound of a key slipping into the front door's lock. Reagan quickly exited the computer's browser, stashed her now-molten-hot Visa card back into her wallet, and powered down the iMac.

It was getting dark, and she flipped the wall switch on, illuminating the runway lights just as Steffi walked in.

"Hey, Mom," Steffi said, closing the door behind her. She had two large shopping bags in tow, indicating a successful day at the mall. "Got the coffee you wanted, too," she added, pulling out the can and handing it to her mother.

"Hallelujah… thanks, baby. I'll pay you back. So, how was dinner?"

"It was okay, mostly," she replied, carrying her bags to her bedroom. "We had lasagna, which was good, but the veggies blew."

"Oh?"

"Yeah. Vickie's family loves kale, apparently. I think it's nasty. Tasted like something from the Devil's grass catcher!"

"I think you described it perfectly," Reagan said with a

chuckle. "Put your stuff away and give your favorite mama a hug."

"'Kay, be there in a minute," Steffi replied as she rifled through the giftbags, stashing a few small treasures in her bottom dresser drawer.

Reagan had worked straight through dinner; it hadn't even crossed her mind to eat anything.

She scooped generous portions of a new, as-yet untried ice cream into two bowls and topped them with inordinate amounts of Ghirardelli caramel sauce from a squeeze bottle. An avalanche of chopped walnuts followed, before the spiral shots of aerosol Reddi-Wip.

"Yay, Mom!" Steffi chimed as the bowl was set in front of her. "What are we celebrating?"

"Celebrating? Oh, nothing in particular. Just thought we both deserved a treat," Reagan replied, taking her own seat and licking some whipped cream off her finger. "Okay with you?"

"Always okay," Steffi said, shoveling in a large spoonful and closing her eyes. "Oh, my gawd... what is this? It's insane!"

"Yeah? I'll check the name on the carton when we're done, but it was something like Moose Track Chocolate Caramel Avalanche or something. Sounded good. Glad you like it. I promise, there's no kale in it!" she said, laughing at the thought.

They both savored the treat in silence for several minutes, Steffi finishing first and licking her bowl like a dehydrated dog in a heatwave. "Mm... get this one again, Mom."

"Will do," Reagan replied, taking her time with the final

couple of bites. Steffi watched her closely, sensing something, but not sure what.

"How was your day, Mom? Sorry, forgot to ask earlier."

"My day? It was okay, I guess. Got some things done on the computer, arranged for the insurance company to have the car towed to the repair shop tomorrow. Having ice cream with my baby," she said, punctuating the last with a smile.

"'Kay," Steffi responded softly. She wasn't completely satisfied with her mother's answer, though. "I got your Christmas present today."

"You didn't have to get me anything, honey. Thank you, though. You're sweet."

"I know... but I wanted to, and I've been saving my allowance, so...."

Reagan smiled again, taking her time and deliberately scraping the vestiges with her spoon and licking every morsel. The bowl looked almost squeaky clean enough to return directly to the cupboard, and she noisily dropped the spoon into it with great ceremony. She looked up at Steffi and smiled broadly. "I got your present today, too."

"Yeah? Cool," Steffi replied, starting to surf her phone.

"You ready?" Reagan asked.

Steffi looked up from her device, clearly confused. "Ready for what?"

"Christmas!"

"*Christmas...* yeah, almost, I guess."

"Well, come on, hand me your bowl. We're opening presents!"

Steffi handed her the bowl. "Mom, it's not even close to Christmas yet! You're not high, are you? Hello? I've got another week of school, and–"

"Doesn't matter. Meet me at the Christmas tree in fifteen minutes," Reagan said as she set the bowls in the sink.

Steffi pushed in her chair, giving her obviously stoned mom one more look before heading down the hall.

*She's definitely high.*

Steffi had put on her jammies, puppy slippers, and a robe. Reagan was dressed similarly, with the exception of her fleece lined moccasins.

Steffi sat cross-legged near the skirt of the Christmas tree while her mother ceremoniously flipped the wall switch, activating its array of blinkers. "There... that's more like it, right?" Reagan asked, digging deep to approach a modicum of festivity. She had something to sell, and she'd never been particularly good at bullshit.

"Yeah, Mom," Steffi said, still baffled. She'd at least had time to do a hasty wrap job on a couple of things and stuck them under the tree.

"So," Reagan said, adjusting a crooked ornament.

"So, what about Fynn? Won't he be home for Christmas? I was going to give–"

"Well, you can give it to him when we see him, how's that?"

"Yeah. But when–?"

"Okay, now I want you to keep an open mind. Can you do that?"

"I guess," Steffi conceded. "Wassup?"

"*Wassup* is we're going on a little trip, you and me," Reagan said, a new level of excitement evident in her expression.

"But you said the car's going to the shop tomorrow. How–?"

"We won't need a car. Don't worry about the car."

"Okay, please elaborate then. I'm not good at Twenty Questions," Steffi said with a sigh.

"Fair enough," Reagan said, plucking an oversized Christmas card envelope that had been hidden in the tree's branches. "Here, honey. It's from Santa," she added, handing it to Steffi.

The envelope was too thick for just a card, Steffi noted, and it was addressed with her name.

"Go ahead, open it," Reagan said, flashing a nervous smile.

Steffi shrugged as she slipped her finger under the flap and ran it along the sealed seam. When she got to the end, she stopped and looked up. "I only got you something small, Mom."

"Honey, I will cherish whatever it is you got me, I promise. I still have the ceramic ash tray you made me when you were five, and I don't even smoke," Reagan assured her, adding a chuckle. "Go ahead."

Steffi reached in and pulled out what appeared to be a bifold printout, several pages long, with a staple in the top corner. As she extracted it, something else fell out. It was a little smaller and wrapped. "What the–?"

"Okay, now open the wrapped part first, honey."

"Kay…"

As she did, she paused at the sight of something familiar, yet unfamiliar: her passport. "What the heck, Mom? You got me a passport?"

"No. You already had a passport; you just haven't had an opportunity to use it since it was renewed."

"And... are we going to Hawaii or something?" she asked, her face lighting up a little.

"Hawaii, erm... no. Besides, you don't need a passport to go to Hawaii. It's still in the United States."

"I know that," Steffi replied, slightly embarrassed. "Where then?"

"What's it say? On the papers there?" Reagan prompted, hoping the gift she'd just spent thousands on would be well received. Also, it was non-refundable.

Steffi scanned the first page, noticing it was an itinerary with what looked like flight numbers and times, and... a destination. "What the hell?! *Germany?!!* Mom, are you kidding me right now?" She looked up at her mother, whose grin told her she wasn't. "We're going to friggin' Germany!!"

"We are! You haven't been there since you were three years old, honey. You probably don't even remember anything about it, but it's where you were born. And it's where I was born. And it'll be good for us to experience it together—" Reagan caught herself before she said the quiet part out loud. *While we can both still see.*

"Mom, that's rad. I mean, I guess it is. When, like... next summer?"

Reagan smiled, and shook her head slightly, a prompt for Steffi to read on.

"It says... Tuesday... December... *16th!* Mom! That's, like, *two days* from now! What about school?! There's no way... Mom, we can't–!"

"We *can*. It's fine, honey. I'm calling the office first thing in the morning. Your vacay starts right now. You can sleep in tomorrow, then we'll start packing! We can open our other things tomorrow. Let's go to bed; you can sleep with me."

Steffi looked up from the documents, her mouth gaping as she continued to process the event. She'd scanned the papers a second time, searching for any indication that this was a prank, but there hadn't been any. This was legit.

The enormity of the day's events had left Reagan with nothing left in the tank. She yawned like a lion, switched off the tree lights, and proceeded down the lit runway.

"Merry Christmas, honey," she said as she reached the end of the hall. "And don't forget to turn off your alarm clock before you come to bed."

# CHAPTER TWENTY-SEVEN

LUFTHANSA FLIGHT LH 492
OUTBOUND FRANKFURT
MONDAY, DECEMBER 15
12:55, CENTRAL EUROPEAN TIME (CET)

THE DISTANT CITY had faded from view, and the aircraft was approaching cruising altitude. The earlier hop, from Hamburg, had been a brief one, with the layover being longer than the actual flight. He was tired as he settled in for the longer stretch—the one across the pond.

There wouldn't be anything to see for a long while. Clouds were boring, and this next leg would be an insufferable ten hours before arriving in Vancouver.

Thankfully, that layover would be only an hour before the connection to Seattle.

He lowered the window shade before reclining the Business Class seat. If there was any saving grace to this hastily arranged trip, it was that he'd scored a bulkhead seat.

Because he needed the leg room, and lots of it.

# CHAPTER TWENTY-EIGHT

REAGAN HAD SLEPT fitfully, but she was resigned to the fact it was going to be the new norm.

Her recurring nightmare had taken on new levels of horror, with her twisted imagination conjuring up new worst-case visuals to portray the cruel slaughter of her dying retinal cells.

Last night's version had even represented a sinister Pac Man character, complete with gaming sounds, its steely sharp teeth gobbling up everything in his path, with the helpless retinal cells being no match for its speed or voracious appetite. It had ruined her.

After considerable tossing and turning, she surrendered to the Pac Maniac at 4:00 a.m., emerging in a cold sweat and finding it impossible to sleep any further. She'd quietly gotten up at 4:15, while allowing Steffi to sleep in for as long as she needed to.

Reagan availed herself to the rare first shower opportunity, guaranteeing herself some actual hot water for a change. She used Steffi's bathroom so as not to disturb her.

By 5:00 she was already into her second cup of coffee as

she planned out what needed to be a productive day. She had two hours to kill, so she banged out two loads of laundry.

At 7:00, she called the school office, notifying them of her daughter's planned absence. The school attendance clerk said she would notify Steffi's instructors and that they would email her with any assignments she might be missing.

Reagan's next agenda item was to call Vickie's mother, advising her she wouldn't be needing any rides this week, thanks... and Merry Christmas!

Laundry was folded. She'd dusted the whole house, save Steffi's room. The fridge was purged of perishables, with the exception of a brand-new carton of milk she'd take a chance with, and she spent a good hour watering her collection of Hoyas.

The tow truck picked up the *Fuckus* before ten. Reagan was motorin'!

Two medium-sized, soft-sided suitcases had been brought in from the garage and were awaiting their payloads. Reagan knew she would have to advise Steffi on what to pack and, more importantly, what not to.

Steffi emerged from the bathroom and shuffled down the hall to the kitchen, where Reagan was in the finishing stages of a bacon and cheese omelet. She looked up at the clock: 11:35.

"Good afternoon, honey."

"Hey," Steffi managed through a yawn. "Mm... really? Wait, it's not afternoon."

"I know. Just kidding. Hey, you needed the sleep," she continued. "Dish yourself some of the blueberry pancakes. What kind of juice do you want?"

"Blue, I guess," she replied, pulling out her chair.

"*Juice*, babe."

"Orange."

"Can you grab it out of the fridge, please? I'll have the same." Reagan said, sliding the eggs from the nonstick pan onto an awaiting platter.

"Sure," Steffi said as she retrieved the large vessel.

Reagan surveyed the table, noted the missing syrup, and grabbed it from the pantry as Steffi filled their juice glasses. "Okay... I think we're good. Have a seat, honey."

"Did you call my school?"

"Yes, honey. And Vickie's mom," Reagan replied before taking another bite of her pancake. "Everything's taken care of."

Steffi took a sip of her juice and, looking over the top of the glass, stealthily studied her mother, waiting for the other clown shoe to drop. Her gaze shifted to the two suitcases in the corner of the room. "I don't know what to pack. I don't know what kind of weather–"

"Not to worry, sweetie. I'll help with that, okay?"

"I guess," Steffi said, pushing her empty plate aside. "Can I be excused?"

"I don't know... *can* you?" Reagan replied, wiping her mouth and revealing a half smile.

"Please don't bust my balls right now, Mom."

"Steffi. I'm not trying to–do that. I'm just...."

"Fine. *May* I be excused, please?"

"Of course, honey. Just leave your dishes. I'll take care of 'em."

"'Kay. I'm gonna take a shower," she said softly as she pushed in her chair and headed down the hall. "And I'll save you some hot water!"

"Already took mine, but thanks for being considerate," Reagan replied.

"Yep."

Reagan finished handwashing the dishes, mindful not to just stick them in the dishwasher as she normally would have. She shuddered at the thought of coming back from Germany, only to find a stinky science project inside the KitchenAid.

The doorbell rang and a peek through the window indicated the UPS guy had come early.

"Yay," Reagan muttered as she brought the package inside and ran the scissors along the tape on the unnecessarily large shipping box. After digging through volumes of brown packing paper, she retrieved the two tiny items, one containing Steffi's gift. *Really?*

"We're gonna need more conditioner, Mom," the voice bellowed from down the hall.

"Okay, thanks," Reagan replied, as she hastily wrapped both boxes and placed them under the tree. Her cellphone was ringing from somewhere. Her cheeks bellowed and she let out a sigh as she scurried about the kitchen, then back to the living room, relying more on her sense of hearing than her kaleidoscopic eyes. The ringing was coming from atop the fireplace mantle.

She snatched up the device on the fourth ring. "Hey, Twinner!"

"Hey, Ray Gun! You okay?"

"Yeah! Yeah... why?"

"You just sound a little out of breath a little. Did I call you at a–?"

"No, no... perfect time, thanks," she said, crossing

through the kitchen and stepping out onto the patio. "Lots of moving parts right now."

"Sounds like it. Hey, sorry for the delay. I had a full morning with the electrician, but I just got your email, and *yeah…* I'm digging what you sent! I definitely think those shots have potential. How long before you can show me edited versions? This week?"

"Well, that's the thing…."

"Your voicemail kind of left me hanging last night, but it sounded like you were… c'mon, spill it, Twinner! Did you… do… what I think you did?"

Reagan put her hand to her mouth and just nodded excitedly for a few moments, as if Ames was right there with her.

"Ray? You still there?"

"Yes! Sorry. I can't believe it myself, but *yes*. I was thinking about–you know–what you had said. And you're right. Steffi and I are leaving tomorrow, for freaking Germany! Gawd!"

"Oh, my God….that… Twinner, can I just tell you, I am so friggin' proud of you right now!" Amethyst chirped, punctuating it with a happy laugh. "You will have the absolute best time!"

"I hope–I mean I just sprung this on Stef last night. It's a lot for her to process."

"Now, did you say you were leaving tomorrow? Like *tomorrow* tomorrow?"

"Yeah. I know, I'm crazy, but it's like you said. It's now or never." Reagan said, adding a disbelieving giggle.

"And you scored seats?!"

"I've never, ever done this, but yeah. Got lucky and, well, it's a week before most people are traveling… and the only two seats available were in First Class!"

"Shut up. Are you serious?"

"As a heart attack, yeah! I won't even tell you how much they cost–I probably could've bought a new car for what I paid–but I've been pinching my pennies my whole life, and I'm biting the bullet on this one. I know it was impulsive; I just hope I'm not being stupid, y'know?"

"I just want to reach through the phone and give you a big twinner hug, girl. You're so doing the right thing! Now, tell me one thing."

"What's that?"

"What time am I taking you to the airport tomorrow?"

Reagan had spent the better part of an hour helping Steffi select the necessities for the trip.

A check of the weather app on her phone had confirmed that it wasn't currently snowing over there, but that could change at any moment. It was December.

One warm jacket, one scarf, one knit beanie... one pair of jeans–and with no holes in them! Two sweaters. Six pairs of socks, eight pairs of undies, four bras. Four tee shirts, but not the Rolling Stones one.

"We'll do laundry at some point, so we'll be fine."

Steffi had a worried expression as she stared at the nearly full suitcase sitting atop her bed.

"What's the matter, honey?"

"I still haven't found my earbuds," she replied, looking like she might cry.

"C'mon. We're done in here," Reagan said, zipping the

case and lifting it down to the floor. "What do you say? Let's take a break and finish opening our Christmas presents."

Steffi pulled her new off-white jacket from the gift box and stood up to try it on. It was not only a perfect fit, but she also loved the faux fur collar and the embellishments. "Oh, my God, Mom. I love it. Totally goes with the Uggs. Can I bring it?"

Reagan smiled as she watched her daughter take a slow spin. "Of course, honey, but you'll have to leave the other coat home then."

"Duh!" Steffi said with a laugh. "Definitely this one."

"Here," Reagan said, handing her another, slightly smaller box with the same wrapping. "This goes with it."

"Yeah?" she replied, her grin widening as she took the box. It took her all of ten seconds to rip away the wrapping and open the box, revealing the matching beanie. Her eyes went wide.

"Bitchin', Mom!"

Reagan smiled, letting the language slide as she regarded her daughter's joy. "You like?"

"I *love*. Thank you, Mom!" Steffi said, initiating a hug.

"I'm glad, honey."

Steffi disengaged from the hug and looked at her. "I only got you the one thing, Mom."

"Honey, I love the camera keychain. It's my favorite gift ever, not counting the ashtray you made," Reagan said with a warm smile. "Thank you. Oh, and you have one more thing to open."

"Mom...."

Reagan retrieved the small box that she'd buried within the tree's branches and handed it to her. "Go ahead, open it."

Steffi smiled as she shook her head. "This better be the last present… you spent too much on me, Mom."

*You have no idea.* Reagan chose not to elaborate on the several thousands of dollars she'd forked over for the plane tickets and instead answered with a shrug and a motherly smile. She watched as Steffi liberated the box from its Grinch wrapping paper.

"Earbuds! Rad, Mom!" Steffi exclaimed, almost jumping out of her Uggs as she hugged her mama. "You're the best."

"I hope you like 'em. These ones are a little different than your old ones."

Steffi explored the description on the outer box. "What does it mean, 'AI translator earbuds'? Like, different languages?"

"Apparently lots of them. I can't tell you how to use 'em, but yes! You can read the owner's manual while I pack my clothes."

"Rad…."

# CHAPTER TWENTY-NINE

W HILE STEFFI WAS busy in her room playing with her new electronic gadget, Reagan took the opportunity to survey her own clothing choices.

She stared down at the suitcase on her bed. She knew she had to abide by the same rules she'd given her daughter. She removed the third sweater she'd packed and nodded. Aside from her toiletries, she was good.

Steffi's earbuds had reminded her of one thing, though. She wasn't even sure if she still had it, but she had to look. But where?

Reagan went back out to the garage, which seemed cavernous now that the car had been towed away. The ladder was still out, and she positioned it against the rack she wished to explore. As she perused the annotations on the boxes, the one simply marked *MISCELLANEOUS* seemed like a good choice, as it was likely a catch-all.

It wasn't heavy, she noted, as she carried it to the floor and unfolded the box's top flaps.

"Oh, my gawd," she muttered as she carefully extracted

the item on top. It was one of her favorite vintage playthings from her own childhood, the original Wooly Willy toy!

She had always enjoyed the simple, classic toys—the ones that didn't need batteries—and this one still stood the test of time. Its simplicity, not unlike the Etch-a-Sketch, fostered a child's creativity while offering countless variations of play.

Reagan stared at the goofy cartoony face of its mascot character. It featured a bald man, smiling, and with a red clown nose. The face was sequestered behind a clear plastic housing that also contained a measure of black iron powder.

She pulled the red "magic" magnetic stylus from its holder and began dragging the black powder around but, instead of *creating* a wacky hairdo, eyebrows, and facial hair like she always had, she found herself pulling the black iron powder directly onto Willy's eyeballs. She'd done it without thinking about it, almost like it had Ouija Board powers. *There...* *Retinitis Willy.*

She shook the powder away, returned the magic pen to its holder, and shuddered. The next item in the box appeared to be an old school yearbook, but she didn't recognize it as one of her own. Closer inspection revealed it to be one of Fynn's, from his *Abitur* of secondary school—the equivalent of twelfth grade, or senior year in American high school.

Fynn had never been much of a sharer. That applied not only to his emotions, but also his past. She knew a little about it—at least the part about having been bounced around various foster homes as a youngster—but not much else. She'd never seen this yearbook before.

Curiosity got the best of her, and she began thumbing through the book. She at least needed to see his photo, she decided, before moving on to the rest of the box. She found his school photo easy enough. Even at this age, he had clocked in at a tick over six-foot tall and he had been gifted with a beautiful smile, that is, before his perfectly aligned pearly whites would later surrender their luster to decades of cigarette addiction. His hair was fuller and blonder.

A continued thumb through found a few more photos of Fynn, though they were candid ones and part of a yearbook collage of upperclassmen and friends on campus. In all of the photos with Fynn, he seemed joined at the hip with another lad who always stood next to him. He looked to be several inches taller than Fynn and he too presented as athletic, though a bit lanky. He appeared to have a darkish birthmark on his face, sizeable enough to register in the photos. Reagan struggled to remember what they called that over here... *port wine stain?*

She closed the book and extracted the next thing, another yearbook. But from Kiel University. *You never told me you attended Christian-Albrechts-Universität!* "What else haven't you told me?" she muttered as she opened its cover and began leafing through it.

"Okay, Fynn Dunkel, show yourself," she whispered. Another cheesy class photo gave way to a full three-page pictorial of the *Leichtathletic-Mannschaft*, or track and field team.

Again, Fynn's smile and lean, athletic build made him easy to find in the group photos. There were also a few action shots of Fynn running the track, grabbing the baton in relay races, as well as clearing the hurdles with apparent ease. Interestingly, she noted, Port Wine Stain Guy was there, standing right next to Fynn in the team photos. It was almost like they were conjoined twins, though this guy didn't share his smile.

Reagan studied the black and white photos, wondering

how she had ever ended up with the smiling young man portrayed here, her now-husband. Her asshole-now-husband-who-wasn't-calling-her-back. *Fucker!*

She slammed the book shut and set it aside. *What was I looking for? Oh, yeah!* She reached into the box and felt around, her fingers wrapping around the object of her desire. She pulled it out and regarded the rather ancient-by-today's-standards piece of technology: her Apple iPod Nano 2G music player. It was only about three inches long by maybe an inch wide. It felt so small, even in her tiny hand, and she marveled at the compact, silver toned device that had once been her go-to music player a couple of decades before.

"Gawd, please tell me the charger cable's in here too," she said, reaching back in the box and feeling around. Something felt familiar. She pulled it out and realized she'd hit paydirt.

"Yes!! Oh, thank you, thank you, thank you...."

Her mission accomplished, Reagan quickly returned the books and Wooly Willy to the box and replaced it on the shelf before turning off the garage light and going inside.

She had an iPod to charge and a playlist to install.

# CHAPTER THIRTY

## SEATTLE-TACOMA (SEATAC)
## INTERNATIONAL AIRPORT
## MONDAY, DECEMBER 15
## 5:40 PM, PACIFIC TIME

TIRED AND PISSED that the Vancouver connection had been delayed, this put him into Seattle later than advertised and was making his already-long day longer. His stomach growled as he stood in the queue for customs.

He'd wisely skipped the whole baggage claim craziness by only bringing his cross-shoulder bag. This wasn't one of those trips where one would be bringing gifts for the grandkids or needing multiple changes of wardrobe. He was packing light. Very light. This would be a quick in-and-out.

Passport in hand, he tried to anticipate what he hoped would be brief questions. He had never been accused of being loquacious, especially after a long, impromptu trip across the pond and seated one row ahead of a screeching baby. He needed sleep.

The couple in front of him thanked the official and wheeled their multiple suitcases away as the stone-faced agent waved him forward. *Showtime.* He did his best to muster a smile as he approached the booth.

The agent watched closely as the man presented his passport and made eye contact, adding a hint of a smile. The agent consulted his screen, comparing it against the passport data and photograph. He thumbed through the passport pages, making note of its stamps and dates traveled. He looked up.

"Business or pleasure?" he asked, watching for any ticks in the traveler's demeanor.

"Pleasure," the man said. "A brief hunting trip," he volunteered.

The agent studied him further, taking note of the unusual birthmark extending across the man's right cheek. It rather resembled the "boot" of Italy, he thought. Being Italian himself, he would know.

He gave the passport photo another moment's scrutiny, deciding that it matched the man standing in front of him. His height appeared to match the six-foot, six-inches listed as well. He stamped the document and handed it back to him.

"Enjoy your stay. Next!" the agent called out, gesturing to the family of four next in line.

"Danke. Thank you," the tall man replied, stashing the passport and zipping his shoulder bag. He walked away with a slight limp as he scanned the array of signage until he saw:

*Rental Cars.*

## MEANWHILE...
## REAGAN'S HOME

With the aid of an adapter, Reagan had her vintage iPod connected to the iMac and was beyond pleased to find the tiny device held a charge and was still functional. It was only a two-gig player, but that was plenty for her purposes, and her old, wired ear buds were still bringing it. They'd be fine for the long flight, she decided. Besides, she didn't want her phone cluttered with music files.

The tiny, archaic device had an even tinier—and decidedly difficult to read—monochromatic display screen, which she remembered being a challenge to see even when her vision had been good. Reading the tiny one-inch display now was next to impossible without the aid of a magnifying glass, but she'd make do.

As she finetuned her playlist selections, she monitored them on the computer with the new set of earbuds she'd bought herself—identical to her daughter's new ones. Steffi was the tech in the family and had already paired them, dialing their settings for both her mom's iMac and cellphone.

*These are pretty wonderful! Merry Christmas, Reagan!*

She had finished purging dozens of old music files from the pod, wondering how she had ever thought them to be cool jams twenty years before. *"Behind These Hazel Eyes"... really?* She dragged it to her trash folder.

"And, last but not least," she muttered as she dragged the

final file of her new playlist to the folder destined for her iPod. *Thirty songs should be enough for now.* She relabeled the playlist and sent it to her tiny music machine: *Before the Lights Go Out*

"Mom! What's for dinner?" Steffi called out from her room.

"I don't know… grilled cheese and soup, okay?" Reagan replied with reciprocal volume.

"Yeah… when're we eating? I'm starved!"

Reagan exited her Music app and shook her head, her stress level evident by her answering in German, "*Gib mir eine Minute, aber geh mir nicht auf die Nerven!*"

She got up from her chair and began digging in the pantry, retrieving a can of Cream of Tomato. When she closed the pantry door, she was surprised to see Steffi standing right there, her earbuds stuffed in her ears and wearing a huge grin.

"What?"

"Mom!" Steffi said, fighting for breath. "I'm pretty sure you just said, '*Give me a minute, don't bust my balls!*'" she managed as she doubled over laughing.

"Gawd… guess I'd better watch what I say now," Reagan said, appreciating the humor.

"These things are effing amazing, Madre!"

# CHAPTER THIRTY-ONE

REAGAN HAD NEVER taken a big interest, nor delight, in cooking, but she managed to hold her own. One thing she shined at, however, was her grilled cheese sandwiches. At least in Steffi's estimation. They were Michelin quality.

Her "secret" didn't seem particularly noteworthy, Reagan thought, but she enjoyed them almost as much as her daughter did. Fynn had never fully appreciated the components she used for them, so she'd long ago stopped making them for him. And if he wanted tuna fish, he had to make the nasty thing himself.

She always used the same fresh, locally made sourdough, a combination of medium Wisconsin cheddar with her favorite Trader Joe's pepper jack and just the right amount of time on the griddle with unsalted butter. And, of course, it paired best with the Campbell's.

Steffi dipped the second half of her sandwich into the soup, staining the bread a rich orange-red, before taking another bite. "Still the best combo ever, Mom."

"Mm… I agree, honey," Reagan said. As she was starting

into her second half, the doorbell rang. She set down her sandwich, looked at her watch. "Hmm?" she murmured as she peaked through the blinds and opened the door.

"What is it, Mom?"

"FedEx," she replied, picking up the overnight box and returning to the table. "Wasn't expecting anything," she mumbled to herself as she inspected the sender's Seattle address. She shook the box, which was very light in weight, and heard something slide around inside.

"Christmas present from a secret admirer, Mom?" Steffi teased.

"Highly doubtful," Reagan said as she scored the packaging tape with her dinner knife. She reached inside and pulled out a plastic bag containing a metallic, tube-shaped item that appeared to be folded into four equal lengths, each slightly over a foot long. "What the–?"

As she liberated it from the plastic, the pieces began falling into their natural places, as they were connected, and there was something that looked akin to a white marshmallow on the end of the last piece. At the other end, a rubberized handle, and a small strap.

Steffi made the connection first and set down her sandwich, her appetite quelched by this cruel piece of buzzkill, a tangible reminder of their shared future. "May I be excused?"

"Sure, honey," she answered absently as her daughter left the room. Reagan's fingers slowly wrapped around the rubberized handle, and the cane's red stripe immediately clued her in, as did the business card that had fallen onto the table.

From the Retinal Clinic.

"Jeezus... gawd...."

Reagan lay awake in the darkened bedroom, the only offer of light coming from the nightlight next to the door. She stared at her open suitcase, which sat atop a folding luggage rack along the wall, the nightlight bright enough to illuminate some of its contents, especially the white marshmallow tip of her new "gift" from the clinic.

She turned onto her other side, silently cursing her condition and any god that would allow this to be happening to her daughter as well. She put her arm around Steffi, who was doing a variation on the cute snore, and kissed the top of her head.

The alarm was set for 3:45 a.m., and they had a big day ahead of them. Reagan closed her eyes. After a few minutes, she surrendered, only to find herself in the darkest alley in Lala land and engaged in battle against the evil Pac Man monster, her only weapon a flimsy marshmallow-tipped cane.

# CHAPTER THIRTY-TWO

EXTENDED STAY AMERICA
KIRKLAND, WASHINGTON
ROOM 111
MONDAY, DECEMBER 15
11:22 PM, PACIFIC STANDARD TIME

THE DISCARDS WERE sequestered into two piles: the greasy skins with however-many herbs and spices, and the considerable bone heap. He preferred his chicken naked, and he found the highly spiced skins an abomination. He sucked the last bit of dark meat off a thigh bone and added it to the collection.

Aside from the untouched coleslaw, which he also abhorred, the skin and bones were all that remained from the ten-piece family meal deal, and he had no family.

Ekkehard Hase stared at the carnage and briefly entertained a decades-old memory of his brief time living with his third foster family. It had been in a small home on a rural property, and the older couple were probably well-meaning when they assigned the then ten-year-old with a few farm chores.

One of his duties had been collecting the eggs from the dozens of chickens they had in their coops. An easy enough assignment and one he fully understood. He just allowed a bad impulse to run things off the rails, however, and when they discovered over thirty dead chickens, each with their necks broken—and a few even missing their heads—he was sent back.

Ekkehard chuckled at the memory as he washed down the last bites with a long pull from his bottle of Beck's Pilsner. He unleashed an impressive belch and finished wiping the grease from his hands with one of the meager hotel towels.

It was his first time on this side of the pond, and the time change was kicking his ass. He knew he had to get some sleep to ensure he was thinking clearly; he couldn't make any mistakes.

His visit at Extended Stay America would be quite brief, which was fine with him.

Brushing his teeth seemed like too much trouble, plus he hadn't packed a toothbrush. He confirmed his phone alarm was set for 04:00, then read the text message and punched in a quick reply:

> Verstanden. *Understood.*

# CHAPTER THIRTY-THREE

## REAGAN'S HOME
## TUESDAY, DECEMBER 16
## 4:05 AM

"COME ON, HONEY. Time to get up," Reagan said as she nudged Steffi for the third time in twenty minutes.

"Mm. I'm up…" came the garbled response from beneath the covers.

"No, you're not. Let's go… aufstehen!" *Get up!*

"'Kay," Steffi replied with sleepy annoyance. She sat up and rubbed her eyes. "Can I have the first shower?"

"Only if you promise you'll leave me some hot water," Reagan said as she folded her pajamas and placed them in the suitcase atop her frigging cane.

"I will."

"Good. Now, chop-chop!"

## SAME TIME
## EXTENDED STAY AMERICA
## ROOM 111

Ekkehard Hase soaked in the bathtub. He wasn't one for showers, even when home, and he had his own reasons for that. He had dialed in his water temperature to his preferred range, which was north of 40 degrees Celsius, and draped a soggy washcloth across his face as he lay back.

One thing that was good about getting up at 04:00–and probably the only good thing–was that you got first dibs on the hot water before other guests.

He allowed himself a brief, five-minute soak before flipping the tub's drain open and swinging his legs over the side of the porcelain tub. As he sat on the edge, he took great care in toweling himself dry before grabbing the prosthetics he had propped up against the sink.

He attached them to what remained of his limbs, long ago severed just above the knees, and carefully rose to the standing position and his full height. He towel-dried his hair, put on yesterday's shirt, and checked his watch.

He wouldn't be enjoying the continental breakfast this morning as he'd be checked out an hour before it even started.

# CHAPTER THIRTY-FOUR

REAGAN DID A quick sweep of the house, making sure all windows were closed and locked, that there was nothing left in the fridge that would be turning bad, and that all the house trash cans were emptied to the big ones outside.

She cursed herself for not having assembled a pot of coffee the night before, especially since she'd never needed it more in her life than right now. There was no time for that now. She washed her hands at the kitchen sink and started at the sound of a knock on the front door.

"Stef! You about ready?! We gotta go, kiddo!" she called down the hall on her way to answer the door.

"Yeah! Coming!"

Reagan swung the security bar out of the way, turned the deadbolt and opened the door to see the most welcome of sights. Amethyst was standing before her, beaming her huge grin and, perhaps even more welcome, holding a cardboard drink tray with three venti Starbucks coffees.

"Hey, Twinner," Ames said. "Your shuttle service is here," she added with a laugh.

"OMG, Ames, you have no idea how happy I am to see you right now... and if that's what I think it is in those cups, I... I just want to kiss you!" Reagan said, taking great care as she relieved her of the drink tray and stepped aside. "Come on in. Steffi should be out any minute."

The sound of luggage wheels clacking across the faux wood tiles confirmed that as Steffi approached. "Hey...."

"Hey, Steffers," Ames said, using her affectionate nickname for her favorite fifteen-year-old. "Big adventure, right?"

"Yeah. I mean, I guess," she replied, reciprocating Ames's hug. "Thanks for driving us," she added before noticing what her mom was holding. "Is that–?"

"It is. They're all the same: Venti caramel soy lattes with an added shot and no whip. Take your pick–except mine's the one with the lipstick on it," Ames said with a chuckle.

"Righteous," Steffi said as she grabbed one. "Mom, can we have waffles?"

Reagan finished a sip of her coffee and tilted her head in answer to her daughter's goofy query. "We're leaving in... ten minutes. So, no on waffles. Grab a granola bar if you want–in fact, grab me one too, please. Ames, you want any–?"

Amethyst took a sip of her coffee, waving off the offer as she added a fresh red smudge to the lip of the lid. "I'm good, thanks. Could I use your restroom though?"

Reagan stepped aside. "You know where it is, second door," she said as she watched her friend scurry down the hall.

"Brush your teeth?"

"Yep," Steffi said, her eyes closed as she savored the caramelly goodness.

"Phone? Charger? Earbuds?"

Steffi's thumbs up told her she had everything.

"I've got your passport with mine... tickets... chargers... iPad," Reagan said to herself, rattling off her own inventory before she turned to Steffi, finding a half-smile to match her half-excitement. She wanted to salvage Christmas for her daughter and in smaller measure, for herself. There was a lot on the line, and Steffi didn't know the half of it. They needed this, and it was going to be perhaps their best chance at reconnecting their mother/daughter loose ends.

"We're going to have fun, hon. You'll love revisiting Germany, now that you can fully appreciate it. You'll see."

"I know," Steffi replied after downing the last gulp. "Okay with you if I have the window seat on the way over?" she asked, selling it with a smile.

Reagan kissed her forehead, then looked into her eyes as she answered. "Of course."

# CHAPTER THIRTY-FIVE

## REVERB HARD ROCK HAMBURG
## TUESDAY, DECEMBER 16
## 14:30, CET

FYNN PLACED HIS coat back onto its hanger in the closet and loosened his necktie as he paced around his hotel room. He ran his free hand through his hair, trying to contain the level of upset from his voice as he talked with the banker. They closed at 16:00, and it was cutting things too close. *Dammit!*

"Nein. Nein problem... danke. Ja, zur selben Zeit... Mittwoch dann. Auf Wiedersehen."

He hung up the phone and launched it into the bed pillows with a velocity akin to a big-league pitcher's best fastball.

He'd had to reschedule his appointment with the banking officials, pushing it back yet another day—to *Wednesday* now—as he waited for receipt of certain confirmations coming from Stateside. There was a lot on the line and a few variables he needed to have handled before he proceeded with the next step. He screamed his frustration to his reflection in the mirror. "Scheisse!!" *Shit!!*

### SEATTLE-TACOMA (SEATAC)
### INTERNATIONAL AIRPORT
### INTERNATIONAL DEPARTURES
### TUESDAY, DECEMBER 16
### 5:45 AM PACIFIC TIME

The burgundy Porsche Cayenne jockeyed for position, competing for a spot with the other early birds, before eventually pulling curbside at the Lufthansa departure zone. Ames engaged the parking brake and unlocked the electronic rear hatch. Somewhere, the sound of an airport security person's shrill whistle chirped. The day was young but shaping up to be a stress fest.

"Sheesh… where's everybody going this fine morning?" Ames asked as she climbed out.

Reagan exited as well, helping Steffi out while making sure neither had left anything behind. They joined Amethyst at the rear of the vehicle where she had already pulled out the first suitcase. "Here, let me get that," Reagan said, reaching past her to heft the second suitcase. "Oomph," she muttered as she wrestled it to the curb and set it on its wheels.

"Mom," Steffi said, pointing to the approaching security person.

"I know. We're going as fast as we can," Reagan said,

making sure the security guy was privy to their efforts to get the hell out of Dodge.

Amethyst came around and gave them each a hug. "Have the absolutely best time, you two! I'm so excited for you," she said, pausing to reach into the pocket of her overcoat. "And, just a little something for each of you," she added as she handed them two small, identically wrapped boxes, plus another. "Merry Christmas."

"Aww. You didn't have to get us anything, you brat!" Reagan said, kissing Ames's cheek, then pausing as she realized the error of her ways. "Shit! Ames, I totally forgot to give you your Christmas present! It's at the house!"

"No worries, Twinner! You're sweet," Ames replied with a smile. "I can get it after Christmas, when Jerry and I get back from Telluride. He's already there, with family. I'll be joining him there."

"No..." Reagan whined, thoroughly disappointed in herself. Another sharp report came from the security guy's whistle and Reagan flashed him a scowl before turning back to Ames. "Look, here's my house key," she said as she liberated it from her sparse keyring. "Please, please pick up your gift. It's wrapped and has your name on it. Under the tree. I'm such a dork. When do you leave again?"

Ames waved to the security guy before turning back to Reagan. "Tomorrow. Listen, I'll pick it up on my way home, after I leave here. Okay? You're so sweet, and I love you for it."

"Promise?"

"Promise! Now, before they throw my fine ass in jail, you guys get inside and be on your way!"

"Okay! Love you, Ames," Reagan said, leaning in for one more quick hug before stepping back to the curb.

"Love you more, Twinner. Now don't forget to text me when you land, Ray Gun!"

Reagan nodded and smiled as both she and Steffi waved and wheeled their bags inside. Ames watched as the sliding doors swallowed them up before she turned to the guy with the whistle. He was making his way toward her and looked like he might be ready to blow a gasket.

As she climbed back into her car, she rolled down the window and took a deep breath as she turned to the man, disarming him with a smile he probably wasn't accustomed to.

"You're doing a fine job. You have yourself a very Merry Christmas."

The man relaxed his grip on his whistle, and a small measure of his stress seemed to diminish, if just for a moment. He watched as she pulled away from the curb and disappeared into the growing sea of cars.

He honestly couldn't remember the last time anybody had ever wished that for him, or extended him any pleasantry whatsoever, and a hint of a smile found his face for a couple of seconds before the next volley of car horns ruined it.

# CHAPTER THIRTY-SIX

EKKEHARD HASE DID one more visual sweep of the quiet neighborhood before unwrapping the culinary curiosity that was to be his breakfast. The food was cold, which was to be expected since he'd purchased it the night before and left it in the car overnight, anticipating the need.

The photo on the drive-thru marquee had looked appealing enough, so he'd ordered a "number seven" accordingly. He found it odd that anyone would name such a sandwich a "Mick Crib." At least, that's what he thought he'd heard the order taker call it.

The Chevy Volt the rental company had saddled him with had wholly inadequate legroom for his tall frame and his prostheses were hugging the steering column. It was okay though; he would only be needing the car for a couple of more hours. Hopefully less.

He peeled back the paper and regarded the strange thing in his hand. Its appearance suggested a partial mammalian ribcage of some sort and based on its size, perhaps belonging to an alpine marmot, maybe a coypu. He couldn't be sure;

God knew he had mutilated many a mammal in his youth, and just for fun. He didn't care about its source at this point; he was starving. He sunk his teeth into the sloppy barbecue. *Amerikaners.*

He polished off the sandwich with gusto and washed it down with the remainder of his orange juice. As he checked in with the rearview mirror to wipe the sauce from his mouth, he noticed a vehicle entering the street behind him. He awkwardly reclined the seat as a purple SUV approached, slowing as it reached the house across the street from him.

It pulled into the driveway, and Ekkehard could now see that it was a Porsche. *Not bad.* More noteworthy, however, was its diminutive driver, who was exiting the vehicle and walking briskly toward the front door. It had been about a decade, he figured, but it was her.

"Guten Morgen, Reagan," he whispered to himself as he watched his mark pull out a key and enter, leaving the door slightly ajar.

With some effort, Ekkehard extracted his legs and exited the vehicle, closing the door quietly behind him. Checking his surroundings, he crossed the street.

He wouldn't have much time.

Amethyst made her way into the kitchen, the heels of her leather, knee-high boots announcing her location on the linoleum. She paused and smiled at the school photo on the fridge of Steffi spiking a volleyball for a game winner. Another photo, next to it, was of Reagan and Fynn, taken years ago at the family fish market.

There weren't much in the way of Christmas decorations, at least in the kitchen, Amethyst noted, but that changed when she entered the living room and saw the tree, the three stockings hanging from the fireplace mantle, and a handful of wrapped gifts.

She bent down and inspected each, each of which were addressed to Fynn, except one, its inscription unmistakable. She stood, holding the box, smiling as she read its annotation:

*Merry Christmas, Twinner! (Open me now!!)*

She briefly considered just taking it with her to open later, but she abandoned the thought once she saw the explicit instructions. "If you say so," she muttered, smiling as her fingernails breached the taped seams of the festive paper.

As the wrappings fell away to the floor, she at once recognized the name of the shop, its gold-embossed logo prominently centered on the front of the navy blue, felt-lined box. There had to be some mistake; Reagan didn't shop at such places, and this place wasn't cheap. "Nuh-uh...."

The box was fairly large, at least necklace sized, she noted, and she shook her head as she opened its hinged lid to find the most beautiful gift she had ever received.

"Are you *crazy*, Twinner?" she murmured as she lifted the vibrant purple quartz jewelry from the gift box. She had never seen such exquisite amethyst, and her eyes immediately welled with tears.

"Anything for me?" a man's voice asked from somewhere behind her.

Amethyst started, spinning around to see an exceedingly tall man staring down at her. She blinked away tears as she tried to focus on him. He was smiling oddly, had a strange mark on his face, and had spoken with an accent. It definitely wasn't Fynn.

"Who–?" was all she managed as she reflexively took a

step back and tumbled into the tree, knocking it over before she landed awkwardly amongst the presents. She opened her mouth to scream but the intruder was too fast. His arms shot out, grabbing her with lightning speed and strength as he tossed her like a rag doll, headfirst over the couch and toward the kitchen.

Amethyst landed hard on the linoleum, at the base of the counter, and frantically tried to crawl around the corner as she began hyperventilating, praying a neighbor would hear her desperate screams. "HELP! HELP ME!! PLEASE HEL–!!" she managed before the lanky man grabbed onto her right ankle and pulled her back across the floor.

"Hush now, Reagan," he hissed, as he considered his next move. *Make it look like an accident*, he'd been told.

"What–?! Wait… I'm not Reagan!" she cried out, flipping onto her back to better see her attacker. "I'm not–!" she pleaded, her adrenaline and clarity of thought having fully kicked in.

"Of course you're not," Ekkehard mused, his gaze going to the nearest window. There didn't seem to be any activity or rescue party. "You think I'm stupid, is that it?"

"No… no… no, I don't think you're stupid. I think you have me confused with somebody else. Please let me go. I won't–"

"I know you won't," Ekkehard replied menacingly. He shifted his grip to her neck and lifted her, standing her against the kitchen counter. Amethyst's hands grabbed at his arms unsuccessfully, unable to pull them away. She flailed, her hands reaching around for any kind of potential weapon, but she only managed to sweep two cannisters to the ground, followed by a blender, which crashed noisily.

"What do you want?" she asked, her bottom lip quivering.

"I want… you… to die," the tall man said, lowering his face to her level, now only inches away. Amethyst turned away, finding the demon hideous. And his breath… it smelled like ass.

She tried to kick him but couldn't; he was leaning against her, pinning her legs against the counter. Her arms reached behind her, frantically grabbing at a whole lot of nothing, until her right hand touched upon something. It at once felt familiar, and she could feel that this monster was slowly squeezing the air out of her.

"That's it," he whispered as his enormous free hand gripped her jaw, directing her to face him. "Go to sleep now."

Her eyes went wide as the implement she'd found came out of nowhere. Ekkehard bellowed like a bear as the better part of Amethyst's weapon found him, its six-inch blade sinking into the fleshy part at the back of his shoulder, near the base of his neck. "Du schlampe!!" he screamed out, his grip on her throat loosening as his other hand removed the kitchen knife and tossed it across the room. "Du schlampe," he hissed, an insult even she recognized. *You bitch!*

He grabbed the kitchen towel, pulling it from its ring by the cabinet, and pressed it against his wound while grasping Amethyst by the arm and launching her, with all his might, headfirst into the iMac screen, sending it—and her—crashing lifelessly to the floor.

Ekkehard took a few shaky steps over to where she lay, awkwardly bending down to assess her state. He turned her over onto her back, noting the trauma to her blood-spattered nose and cuts on her forehead from her impact with the computer screen. Her eyes were closed and her mouth hung open.

Somewhere out on the street, a dog's barking interrupted his inspection. He quickly pulled out his cellphone and snapped his victim's photo as proof, before rolling her back onto her belly. *Make it look like an accident.*

He wasn't sure about that; it looked more like a tornado had come through. But one thing he was sure about: he had to get the hell out of there.

# CHAPTER THIRTY-SEVEN

**LUFTHANSA FLIGHT 419**
**LEAVING DULLES INTERNATIONAL AIRSPACE**
**ENROUTE FRANKFURT INTERNATIONAL**
**TUESDAY, DECEMBER 16**
**6:30 PM, EASTERN STANDARD TIME**

THE AIRCRAFT HAD reached cruising altitude and Steffi turned her gaze from the window to the smiling flight attendant, who was setting a napkin and a warm cookie on her tray table.

"What would you like to drink, miss?"

"Oh, wow. Um, do you have Gatorade?" Steffi asked, removing her earbuds.

"Mm, I'm afraid we don't have that, but we have several juices," the woman replied, adding a warm smile. "We have apple, orange, pineapple, tomato, cran–"

"Apple, please."

The attendant nodded, smiled, and turned her attention to Reagan. "And for you, ma'am?"

"A white wine, if you have it, please," Reagan answered, smiling back. She was unaccustomed to this level of service. First Class was already showing itself to be a far cry from their first leg–in economy, and on another airline–out of Seattle.

"We have a nice chardonnay," the attendant confirmed.

"Perfect."

"We'll be around with your selections in a moment."

"Thank you," Reagan and Steffi answered in unison.

As the cabin attendant moved on to the next row of passengers, mother and daughter turned to each other and smiled. "What do you think? Nice, huh?" Reagan asked.

Steffi nodded excitedly. "Cookies and a hundred movies? I could get used to this."

"Yeah. Well, don't. The cookie alone was probably a thousand dollars," Reagan replied with a chuckle. "Ooh, I almost forgot," she said, digging into her personal bag and retrieving the gifts Amethyst had given them that morning. "Here, let's open these two together; they look similar," she added as she handed Steffi the one with her name on it.

"Cool," she said, shaking it once before tearing into the paper. Reagan did the same and they looked at each other, nodding as they opened them synchronously.

"No friggin' way," Steffi said with a muted gasp. "Did you get the same thing as me?"

Reagan stared into the small, two-inch square box and felt her eyes moistening as she pulled out the beautiful broach. It was in the shape of a camera, and bespeckled with an abundance of gorgeous Swarovski crystals. She turned to Steffi, who was having a similar reaction to her own gift, a Swarovski crystal covered volleyball.

"Your friend's so nice, Mom," Steffi said. "I love it."

"Me too, honey. Yes, she is. That was very thoughtful of her."

"Yeah. Wait, wasn't there another thing from her?"

Reagan pulled the remaining gift from her bag and read the inscription. It was to both of them and there was a longer inscription on the tag.

"What's it say?"

"'Just for fun, if you get bored on the long flight across the pond,'" Reagan said, reading it aloud. "Here, you open it," she added, handing it to Steffi.

Steffi made short work of the wrapping and liberated the playing card-sized package, not sure whether to laugh or to cry.

She held it up to Reagan and, a moment later, they both had an awkward laugh at the deck of UNO cards, its raised bumps indicated they were the National Federation of the Blind Braille Edition. "Oh, my gawd," Reagan muttered as she watched Steffi remove the plastic wrap.

"I'll deal," Steffi said.

The unfamiliar space was murky, making it difficult to determine what time of day or night it was. A shaft of late afternoon sunlight provided a hint as it peeked from behind a cloud and squeezed in through a nearby window. A neighboring pool of light spilled across the linoleum floor, and it was coming from the next room. It seemed to be blinking.

Amethyst was completely disoriented.

The image was fuzzy at best, especially considering there

was a cocktail of blood, sweat, and tears clouding her vision, but it was definitely a photograph on the floor next to her. And as it slowly came into focus, the face became familiar. It was of Fynn, though decades old. She found it curious that it would be lying on the floor, and even more so that she would be.

A low groan escaped her as she struggled to regain consciousness. Her eyes slowly blinked open, though she could feel the left one was but a slit and wouldn't be cooperating further. As moments of awareness began streaming in, they all seemed to be telegraphing variations on a theme: just how many areas of her body were in acute pain.

*Where am I? What the hell happened?*

Amethyst took her time rolling onto her side, her tongue recognizing the distinct taste of blood as she licked her puffy lip. She had difficulty breathing through her nose, her nostrils caked with dried blood.

Her back and much of her torso were screaming, and as she regarded the mess she was lying in, her memory began to function again.

Under her shoulder lay the remnants of a shattered iMac monitor, its terminally damaged screen streaked with blood. She was laying on a bed of office supplies and computer accessories, plus shards of metal, plastic, and glass. Various fridge magnets and miscellany were strewn about, evidence of the struggle that had ensued.

She tested her voice, but all that squeaked out was raspy and weak. "Twinner?"

*Holy mother of God.* She felt like she'd been T-boned by an eighteen-wheeler, but she knew otherwise. It had been a man—more like a monster—and a tall motherfucker.

Her hip vibrated. By the time she was able to liberate the iPhone from her pocket, whatever incoming call or message had alerted her had ended. The phone's cracked screen indicated several messages awaited her, but she was too out of sorts to open them.

Instead, she dialed 911.

## MEANWHILE...
## EXTENDED STAY AMERICA,
## SEATTLE

Ekkehard Hase sat on the edge of the bed, a scowl etched on his face. He was none too pleased about having to extend his stay after all, his hand forced by a flat tire on the way to the airport, resulting in a missed flight. And another rental car. He had specified a vehicle with more legroom, a Chevy Suburban this time.

His current digs were still twenty miles from SeaTac International Airport but, to be on the safe side, he didn't want to chance a second night at the other one. And he'd paid cash.

He took a pull from a bottle of Beck's and massaged the stumps of his legs as he watched the local news for any reports of a murder in Bothell. So far there hadn't been any.

Ekkehard had spent the better part of an hour cleaning his knife wound and applying the first aid ointments and dressings he'd procured from the pharmacy down the street.

It still hurt like hell, and he'd given up hope on the ibuprofen ever kicking in.

He polished off the remainder of his dinner—the second of two additional "Mick Crib" sandwiches he'd picked up on the way. He decided he rather liked them now, even if he couldn't distinguish their source material.

Another glance at his phone. Nothing, though he wasn't surprised his text hadn't been acknowledged yet, considering it was nearly 04:00 in Hamburg. The photo hadn't been pretty, but it was clear enough evidence to validate the completion of his task.

Ekkehard wiped the residual sauce from his mouth and decided against getting up to brush his teeth. He could do that in Frankfurt. Besides, after the day he'd had, he felt more hammered than a schnitzel.

After setting his phone alarm for 03:00, he switched off the TV and pulled the bedding over him. It might be early, but not for him. He wasn't going to miss his flight this time.

# CHAPTER THIRTY-EIGHT

## LUFTHANSA FLIGHT 419

THE CABIN WAS dark, save the *Fasten Seatbelt* signs and the little strips of dim runway lighting along the floor. They were a far cry from her own rope light runway at home.

Reagan's comfort level was severely diminished as she considered the need to get up and use the lavatory. It wasn't the facilities she feared. It was the effect her tunnel vision was having in such dim environs, and she was alarmed by how bad it was. Her peripheral vision was non-existent in the dark.

She took note of the aircraft's position as it was graphically presented on the video screen, showing they were over the North Atlantic, somewhere mid "pond" and below was the ginormous island of Greenland.

A quick glance over at Steffi verified she was fast asleep, having consumed a rather gourmet meal of beef tenderloin, Caesar salad, and a selection of cheeses. She'd also consumed two inflight movies, as well as three cookies.

She didn't want to disturb her, so she quietly unbuckled her own seatbelt and slipped her bare feet into her Sketchers.

As she rose from her seat it took her a moment to get her sea legs–or air legs—and she gripped the headrest for stability. Most of the other passengers were asleep, she noted, with the exception of a couple of apparent business warriors fixated on their laptops.

The first-class lavatory was only about fifteen feet from her seat, thankfully, and she couldn't imagine the schlep down the length of the dark tube to one of the aft lavatories in coach. Her destination's tiny, illuminated sign indicated it was vacant.

"Here we go, Reagan," she muttered, hoping the self-pep talk might help her resolve as she stared at the runway lighting and put one foot in front of the other, taking her time. The short distance felt more like a 5K hike, and she was relieved when she felt the latch for the lavatory door and squeezed herself inside.

Reagan squinted as her eyes adjusted to the relatively bright lighting in the small space. She attended to the mission at hand, washed her hands in the rudimentary basin, and stared at her reflection in the mirror, hardly recognizing herself. She blamed the bags under her eyes on exhaustion, but she'd never noticed just how much she was starting to look like… her mother.

"Hallo, Mutter," she whispered, shaking her head as she opened the folding door and made the trek back to her seat.

It was going to be a very, very long day ahead. She hoped she could at least get *some* sleep and, upon buckling back in, she had a date with the Advil PM in her pocket.

She pulled out her trusty iPod and stuffed in her wired

earbuds. The first song on her pity party palooza playlist was already cued so she hit the play button.

# CHAPTER THIRTY-NINE

## HAMBURG
## WEDNESDAY, DECEMBER 17, SOMETIME...

F YNN'S FACE WAS still burrowed in the overly soft hotel pillow. It was the droning of a vacuum cleaner down the hall that had awakened him.

His crusty right eye creaked open, and he slowly got his bearings in the still-darkened room. Daylight was creeping in along the edges of the window's blackout curtains, and he propped himself up on his elbow to consult the clock radio's display.

He shook his head in an effort to clear some cobwebs, because clearly it couldn't be...

### 06:35

"Was zur Holle?" he managed, his voice gravelly and his thinking muddled by the half bottle of Asbach he'd consumed the night before. He'd not only slept through breakfast, but also lunch, and he still hadn't heard any updates from Ekkehard! Or had he?

After three attempts, his hand found his phone on the nightstand and he sat up, stuffing a pillow behind his back as he powered up the device. He cursed himself for having somehow silenced his ringer and notifications. A moment later, his message app indicated he'd received two texts.

He blinked rapidly, several times, as if his eyelids could magically wipe away the effects of too much good brandy, but he knew from experience this hangover could only be helped by a twenty-minute shower, followed by a pot of strong coffee, some eggs, and breakfast potatoes to soak up the alcohol.

The texts were both from his lover, he noted. Fynn took a deep breath, knowing full well that everything they had worked toward all these years was riding on this.

His and Ekkehard's closeted life went all the way back to when they'd both been taken in by the same foster family, when they were both adolescents. Neither had understood their individual impulses prior to that, and it didn't take long for the two of them to explore them—together. One day, after a few months of secret rendezvous, their foster father had caught the boys kissing in the chicken coop, resulting in both their reassignments, individually, to two other foster families.

Their secret relationship continued, though clandestinely, as they spent much time together in after-school activities, mostly involving sports—and especially track and field, where Ekkehard had proven himself a standout sprinter. They were always the last two to leave the locker room and rumors floated around.

Fynn's and Ekkehard's childhoods had mirrored each other's, as they had each been born into poverty and into loveless families. It had been during their years together in secondary school that they had vowed to succeed in a business, some-how, and to create a life together.

Fynn had seemingly found the answer when he discovered the Lichts' family business, and his marrying their daughter had been the way to get his foot in the door. For years, his ideas, his grand plans for expansion, were shot down by the owners, Stefan and Ulla, and he had resented it. They were a barrier to his success, and it had become necessary to eliminate that barrier.

Thus, the *accident* in Hamburg.

It had been an unfortunate necessity. And the execution of said accident had resulted in some serious collateral damage, the loss of Ekkehard's legs, on another platform, while making his escape that day. He and Ekkehard had maintained their story of witnessing another assailant being responsible for all three victims that day. The truth was their little secret, and they managed to adapt to Ekkehard's handicap. It changed nothing as far as they were concerned.

So, with Reagan being the Lichts' sole beneficiary, a clear path had presented itself.

Fynn's marriage, and establishing a coparenting scenario for Steffi in Seattle, had been a necessary charade as he helped run operations, splitting time in Hamburg, while his *wife* pursued her dream of becoming a successful photographer in America. He supported her dream, even if she didn't seem to support his.

She controlled the finances, made the final operational decisions in what had been her parents' business. She had control over the accounts, and the fish market belonged to her. She was sitting on a large amount of money, and she could afford the time it took to build a name for herself as a photographer.

But that was all changing.

It would all be his now to run as he pleased, and he and his partner could finally get married, be legitimized, and realize the dreams they both had vowed to achieve.

It was happening.

*Make me proud, Ekkehard.*

Fynn opened the first message, which consisted entirely of a photo file. It didn't need further explanation. His eyes widened and his foggy brain cells screamed for clarity of understanding as the image filled his phone screen.

The surrounds were immediately familiar, yet the family kitchen's computer nook was in shambles. Much more alarming was the main subject, the woman sprawled face-up against the carnage. Her bruised face bloodied with spatter with gashes across her forehead, it was obvious the struggle had been violent.

Even though he had expected the outcome, actually seeing the lifeless body of his wife in this way proved difficult. His gag reflex was kicking in, and he shook his head and closed his eyes. Upon reopening them, he stared harder at the image.

Her wrecked nose is what got his attention, because there was something else that couldn't be explained away by the blood spatter. With trembling fingers, he zoomed in on her face. And his worst fear at once confirmed. *Sommersprossen!! Reagan doesn't have* freckles!!

Fynn's immediate reaction was involuntary as his stomach projectile-purged its foul contents, spilling brandy and remnants of last night's pepperoni pizza across the bed's comforter.

Ekkehard's hastily rescheduled flight had resulted in his seat assignment in steerage. His prostheses were jammed against the seatback in front of him and he cursed his luck at being wedged between an obese man, who had already claimed their shared armrest as his own, and the smelly teenaged boy whose greasy hair indicated he hadn't showered in days. Add to that the screaming baby in the row behind him.

The seasoned flight attendant was all business as she passed through the cabin for a final time. With no attempt at a smile, she leaned in to remind Ekkehard to power down his device and stow it for takeoff. He nodded his compliance. There wasn't a signal anyway, and he hadn't heard a response back from Fynn.

He stashed the phone in his zippered shoulder tote and turned toward the window, sneaking a peek past the smelly boy as the plane began its slow taxi toward the runway.

Unbeknownst to Ekkehard, the message he'd been expecting finally snuck into his inbox. It would remain unchecked for several hours, not until he made his connection at Washington Dulles, but its message would be abundantly clear:

> *> Du verdammter Idiot! Was Hast du getan?!!! Das was nicht sie!!!!! Ruf mich an und steig nicht in das!!*

> *You fucking idiot! What did you do?!!! That wasn't her!!!!! Call me NOW and don't get on the plane!!*

Oops.

# CHAPTER FORTY

STEFFI'S FOURTH INFLIGHT movie had just ended, and she pulled off her lame airline-issued headset. She pulled up her window's shade a couple of inches and the sunlit clouds, in concert with the wafting smell of breakfast service, clued her in that they were probably getting close.

She nudged her mama gently. Reagan was lights-out from her sleep med and still wearing her headset. "Mom," Steffi said softly and, getting no response, picked up the antique music player and squinted at its tiny display. It was a song she'd never heard of before, but most of her mom's music was: "Can't You See" by Marshall Tucker Band. *What the hell, Mom?*

"Mom!" she whispered more urgently, nudging her again. "Mom, I've gotta go pee. And they're serving breakfast. Wake up."

"Mm?" Reagan mumbled. "What?"

Steffi reached over and gently removed the headset. "Mom. Good morning. Breakfast is coming, and I've got to climb over you. Be right back," she said as she unbuckled and squeezed past her.

"Okay," Reagan said to herself, punctuating with a yawn. She reached across Steffi's seat and raised the shade slightly, unprepared for the daylight. "Whoa."

The flight attendant's announcement served as a wake-up call for several passengers. The cabin crew was beginning a breakfast service, she advised, and the flight would be arriving in Frankfurt in approximately two hours.

Steffi squeezed past her and buckled back in. "I'm starved."

"Me too," Reagan said, smiling, as she stashed her electronics and raised her seatback a bit. She was groggy, but grateful she had managed a little shuteye. She figured three cups of coffee should help, and she smiled as the first cup was placed on the tray table in front of her.

Steffi's apple juice was delivered as well, along with each of their meals consisting of a tiny omelet, a German-style brat, breakfast potatoes, and a roll with cheese.

Reagan turned to her and smiled. "Having fun yet?"

"Yeah. This is pretty rad, Mom."

# CHAPTER FORTY-ONE

## FLUGHAFEN FRANKFURT MAIN
## FRANKFURT AIRPORT
## WEDNESDAY, DECEMBER 17
## 09:40 CET

S TEFFI HAD BEEN tasked with helping navigate the two of them through the bustling international terminal, first to the proper baggage claim area, then customs, and now to the rental car area.

It wasn't her familiarity with the airport–far from it; she hadn't been here since she was a youngster–but instead, her vision was less compromised than her mother's, thus she could better pick out the signs. Thankfully, they were easily distinguishable as they were in both German and English.

Customs hadn't been an issue, but it had taken a bit of time. Reagan and Steffi stood at the car rental counter, their wheeled luggage nearby, as they waited for the agent to return with the final paperwork.

Reagan had prearranged the vehicle when she made the

flight reservations, and she hadn't been exactly forthcoming with the minor detail of her recent diagnosis of being legally blind. The thought was crossing Steffi's mind as they stood there, but she said nothing.

The rental agent returned to the counter carrying a multi-page contract, which she turned toward Reagan. She appeared to be mid-twenties, and her blond hair was gathered in a ponytail. She flashed a smile before she explained which boxes needed initials. Her English was impeccable.

"Okay, here we are. You said you wished to add the extra damage coverage, and that you would be the sole driver. So, please initial here… and here. The vehicle will come with a full tank of gas, and it is a hybrid. An MG crossover SUV."

"Sounds good," Reagan said, initialing both boxes. She winked at Steffi as the agent separated their copy of the documents, folded them, and stuffed them into a paper folio.

"Okay, you are all set. The shuttle can be found just outside these sliding doors, and it will take you to your vehicle. Thank you so much and have a pleasant visit."

"Thank you… er, danke," Reagan replied, as she grabbed the handle of her suitcase. She turned to Steffi. "We need to hustle, hon, c'mon."

The ten-minute shuttle ride had provided the time for Reagan's urgent phone call to the bank in Hamburg, as she expected they opened at 10:00. It was the same institution her parents had had a longstanding relationship with, as well as the one she continued to run the family business accounts through, even if long-distance.

She'd had the foresight to bring her iPad with her, having

transferred several financial documents over to it, as well as her photo files from the iMac.

She was speaking with a senior accounts manager she wasn't familiar with, yet he assured her they would place the requested freeze on the accounts, effective immediately.

"And, very importantly, please confirm that you will not, under any circumstances, unfreeze these accounts without my express authorization and until further notice from myself."

"Very well, Frau Dunkel. I have seen to it, and we will await further instructions until you personally come into the branch. Again, my name is Otto Becker, and you can ask for me. Was there anything else we can assist you with today?"

"Nein, danke. I appreciate your discretion and prompt attention to this matter. You can reach me at this number, and via message or email. Danke schön."

"Bitte schön. Auf Wiedersehen. Goodbye."

Reagan let out a sigh she'd been carrying from the other side of the pond. "Scheisse!"

*Shit!* Steffi didn't need her translating earbuds to understand that; she'd heard her mother say it often enough at home to get the meaning.

"There. I think that's it," Steffi said, pointing out the window to the red MG hatchback. As the shuttle came to a stop and the doors opened, she asked, "Think you'll be okay driving? I mean, you know... based on what the doctor said?"

Reagan turned to Steffi, her smile meant to reassure.

"Not sure, honey... but *you* will."

# CHAPTER FORTY-TWO

THE SUN HAD come out, thankfully, and Reagan felt it best that she be the one to navigate their way out of the busy airport traffic and through the first few roundabouts. Had it been nighttime, all bets would be off. She decided they would have to limit their travel to daylight hours.

Her phone both vibrated and chimed an alert from its perch on the console.

"Oh, it's Fynn, Mom! Want me to answer?"

"No!! Sorry, *no*, honey. Don't touch it. Let it go to voicemail!"

"Ooo-kay..." Steffi replied, turning her gaze forward as they navigated the first roundabout. The phone's vibration stopped, indicating the caller had left a message.

"Sorry for sounding sharp, honey. We just don't–" The sound of Steffi's phone vibrating interrupted her.

"Mom! He's calling on mine! Do I just–?"

"Ignore it. Yes. Please."

As they exited the roundabout, which took them on a road with less intense traffic, Steffi turned to her and asked the million-dollar question. "Mom! Does Fynn even know we're friggin' coming?"

Reagan turned to her and shook her head slightly, offering the thinnest of smiles. "No, hon, he doesn't."

"I mean, what the hell? It's almost Christmas and we just flew across the whole world, and we're not going to hook up with your husband? With my stepdad? At Christmastime? That's messed up."

"It probably sounds strange, honey, I know. But...."

"But *what*? Are you guys okay? I mean, tell me you're not getting a friggin' divorce. You aren't, right?"

"No, honey, nothing like that," she said, patting Steffi's knee. She added a smile, hoping it would help sell what she was about to say next, as Steffi hung on the pause.

"We... just... don't want to ruin the surprise!"

## EVERGREENHEALTH MEDICAL CENTER
## EMERGENCY CARE
## KIRKLAND, WASHINGTON
## WEDNESDAY, DECEMBER 17
## 5:25 AM, PACIFIC TIME

The attending nurse inspected the dressings on her patient's cheek and forehead, as well as the one on her left eye, which remained swollen shut. The surgery had gone well, and Amethyst was in recovery, having had her broken left arm, collar bone, and three ribs attended to. She'd received several sutures, as evidenced by the bandages taped to her face.

The nurse had seen every kind of trauma in her twelve years here, including patients involved in car wrecks, and for some reason she had always had the hardest time seeing victims of assaults. Probably because she herself had escaped a violent marriage in her early twenties.

She checked the patient's vitals, scanned the monitors, and quietly keyed in an annotation to the data base. Drawing the privacy curtain, she turned to leave, but a groan came from behind her and stopped her in her tracks.

She spun on her heels and slowly pulled the curtain back along its curved track.

"Good morning, Amethyst," she said quietly, offering a nurturing smile. "Such a beautiful name. I'm Betty, your attending nurse today. How are we doing? Are you experiencing any pain?"

"Mm…" she replied, her voice raspy. She licked her dry bottom lip, which remained swelled. "Thirsty."

"Here, let me get you some water," Betty replied, grabbing the small water bottle and inserting a straw. She handed it to Amethyst, who grabbed it with a shaky hand. "Got it?"

Amethyst nodded weakly. "Thank you."

"Do you know where you are?"

"Hospital," Amethyst answered softly, choosing not to respond with the other alternative: *Duh*. "Where is–?" she began, still groggy from the anesthesia and getting her first glance at the cast on her arm. "What–?"

"You're at Evergreen. Your arm was broken in two places, as was your collar bone. Three of your ribs were cracked, and we've attended to several lacerations and bruises. Your surgery went well, and your husband was notified. I understand he was able to book a morning flight out of Telluride; he should be arriving here in a few hours."

"How did I get here?"

"I believe a neighbor called it in, yesterday, after seeing your vehicle sitting in the driveway with the door left open. But somebody else called it in as well."

"Who?"

"You did. Your 911 call got the paramedics and police dispatched to the house. They found you in the kitchen, and you arrived here by ambulance."

"God, I must look like... mm... can I see–?"

"A mirror? Yes, but you're pretty banged up. Are you sure you'd like to see?"

Amethyst handed her back the water bottle and shook her head resolutely. "Please."

The nurse pulled out a handheld mirror from a drawer and gave it to her. "You've been through a lot, but you will heal. It may take several weeks, though."

Amethyst held the mirror in her one good hand and slowly turned it towards her. The immediate reaction to her reflection was a combination of shock and horror. She fought back her gag reflex and let out a weak gasp, her shaky hand laying the mirror down on her stomach as the tears welled up.

"My God," she muttered as memories of the events that caused this damage began rushing in. "I look like an effing train hit me."

"I'm so sorry," the nurse offered, taking her hand, stopping short of sharing her own experiences of being beat down by a maniac. "The police asked me to notify them when you came out of surgery and were in recovery. You think you might feel up to talking to them? Perhaps you could provide some information about your assailant? That can be a big help. Would that be okay?"

Amethyst took a long moment to consider this. Her assailant was still out there, and she feared the monster's return. Also, this savage had mistaken her for Reagan, and he could be looking for her. She picked up the mirror again and took a longer look at the evidence of his brutality.

She stared hard at her reflection. The face looking back at her was battered, and barely recognizable, yet her one good eye was staring back with an intensity of emotion that had supplanted any fear.

She lowered the mirror and slowly nodded, turning to nurse Betty as she answered resolutely. "Absolutely," she said, her lip quivering as she assessed her growing anger. *I would be more than fucking fine with that.*

The nurse returned the mirror to the drawer. "Good. I'll let them know," she said with a tight smile.

Amethyst cleared her throat and turned to her. "One more thing?"

"Name it."

"My cellphone."

# CHAPTER FORTY-THREE

FYNN MOPPED UP the remaining yolk with the help of a thick slice of good bread. In addition to the half loaf of Weisbrot, he'd polished off four over-easy eggs, two wursts, and an extra-large portion of potatoes.

He finished his cup of coffee–his fourth–and seemed to have cured his hangover but not his anger. He woke up his phone again and checked for any missed messages.

*Nothing from Ekkehard.*

*Nothing from Steffi.*

*And nothing from Reagan. Dammit!*

Fynn wiped his mouth, balled up his napkin, and tossed it on his plate. He pulled out a wad of euros and dropped them on the table as he got up. His nod to the owner didn't include his typical smile.

Exiting to the street, he fired up a cigarette and took a deep drag.

*Surely Reagan knows about Ekkehard's visit to the house by now.*

*Does she suspect anything further? Was she the one who had the accounts frozen?*

*Where the fuck is Ekkehard!?*

After three drags, Fynn angrily tossed his ciggie to the curb and stormed away. He decided on a briskly paced stroll to the Fischmarkt to check on things, and to think things through.

He had a big shipment due to arrive Friday, and a big payment to make on delivery, and he couldn't have Reagan fucking things up.

Reagan drove conservatively, keeping to the right lanes as much as possible, while monitoring the sun's position in the sky. Jet lag was hitting Steffi hard; her eyes were closed, and her head rested against the window.

As the crow flies, the drive from Frankfurt to Hamburg is slightly over three-hundred miles and could be made in about four hours, in normal traffic, and with normal eyesight. They would have to find a place to stay before they lost daylight, Reagan decided, because all bets were off once it got dark. She wouldn't be able to see her own hand in front of her face, let alone operate a motor vehicle.

Her right thumb was especially fidgety, and she ran it back and forth along the top of the steering wheel, threatening to wear out its faux leather while she processed her thoughts. *How did Fynn manage to initiate new documents with the bank without my knowledge and consent? Did he think I wouldn't find out? And how–?*

As Reagan chewed on those questions, she noticed her nervous habit and stared at her metronomic thumb. That's when it came to her, her hands tightening, white-knuckled as she strangled the wheel.

*That stain on my thumb that morning... Fynn notarized bogus docs... using my thumbprint... while I was sleeping... and I fucking signed them!*

"Fuck!" she screamed out, braking hard as she exited to the side of the road and came to a stop. She pounded the wheel. As Reagan turned to her disoriented passenger, Steffi's wide eyes and expression made it abundantly clear her daughter was staring back at a crazy person.

"What the hell, Mom!?"

"Sorry, honey. Gawd... I–"

"You *okay*? Did we... hit a *dog*, or something?"

"No, no, nothing like that."

"What, then?"

"Um, just a little stressed. I know; how 'bout we switch places, and you can drive for a little while? You mom needs to look at the map."

Steffi tilted her head as she continued to look at her quizzically, and not without concern. "Mom, I'm not licensed to drive in America, and... we're in effing *Germany*. What if we–?"

"It'll be fine, I promise," Reagan interjected. "We'll be getting off this road in a few kilometers, at the next roundabout, and we'll find us some food and a place to stay for tonight. Okay?"

"I guess," Steffi replied under her breath as they each got out and swapped seats.

Steffi took her time readjusting the mirrors, tweaking the seat back, and getting acquainted with the instrument panel before switching on her turn indicator and pulling back onto the road.

As they got up to speed, a warning chime and flashing indicator got Steffi's attention.

"Mom…" she said, turning to her passenger as if addressing a child.

"Yeah, honey?"

"Seatbelt."

# CHAPTER FORTY-FOUR

REAGAN MULTITASKED AS she watched for road signs and concentrated on the phone glued to her ear.

She was listening to the voicemail for the seventh time, the one Fynn had left a couple of hours before. She closed her eyes, her blood reaching boiling, as she listened to his performance, his lies, and the faux concern and love dripping from his message.

*"Hey, honey... so sorry I missed your call. I guess I should say, calls—plural. Apologies, no excuse, but with my lost luggage and not having my charger, I've been... anyway, sorry. Just wanted to check in to see how you and Steffi were doing at home. I miss you. Things are going well here, and everything should be—"*

That's where the signal had been lost, and the message truncated. But she knew the end of that sentence. At least she imagined it: *"... and everything should be fucked for you once I get control over everything. Love you."*

She exited the voicemail app and looked up, pointing to the sign. "Next exit, babe."

"'Kay," Steffi replied, her fifteen-year-old-driving-without-a-license-in-frigging-Germany game face intact.

"You're doing great, honey. Proud of you."

Fynn inspected the two additional lobster tanks that had just been delivered. They were well constructed, had been water-tested for integrity, and their thermostats and filtration calibrated.

Another large, industrial refrigeration unit had also been added, and things were shaping up for Sunday's splashy reveal. He draped sheets across the new equipment to preserve stealth.

Their longtime suppliers of fresh local fish would be making their usual deliveries on Saturday, but all he could think about—and *obsess* about—were the two additional shipments, each sizeable, coming in from his new import partnerships.

And they would be needing payment upon delivery.

There was an unresolved problem with another partnership that still festered, that of his incommunicado lover/assassin, Ekkehard. If he had exercised more care and not been so hasty, he would have offed the right person, and not her best friend by mistake.

As a result, there remained risk, and lots of it. Fynn needed to close some loopholes, and quickly.

His phone chirped an alert, snapping him out of his preoccupation. It was a text, and from Ekkehard. *Where the hell have* you *been?!* His jaw clenched and the vein in his temple swelled as he read its contents:

> *Sorry. Missed your message. Didn't get it until after I boarded connecting flight.*

*You got the photo, yes? Was there a problem? Didn't understand.*

*I arrive at Hamburg tonight. Will call when I land.*

*Ich liebe dich.* 🖤

*Love you?!* Fynn's fury had reached a volcanic state. He spun on his heel, erupted in a guttural roar, and was about to catapult his phone into smithereens against the cement when he stopped short, having just noticed his employee, Hei Li, watching him. She quickly looked away, pretending not to have noticed, as she resumed washing out a smaller lobster tank.

Fynn held up his device and tried to save face with a smile. "Stupid phone! Sorry."

Hei Li faked a smile in return and nodded, but she remained unconvinced.

Fynn walked over to her and rested his hand on her shoulder. "Thank you for getting things organized today, Hei Li. Good work. I'll be at the hotel if anything comes up, okay?"

"Yes."

"Danke. Tschüss," Fynn said, flashing an insincere smile.

"Tschüss," she replied. *Bye.* She watched as he hoofed it out onto the street and disappeared down the block.

# CHAPTER FORTY-FIVE

PARKHOTEL BERGHÖLZCHEN
HILDESHEIM, GERMANY
WEDNESDAY, DECEMBER 17
16:25, CET

THE THREE-PLUS HOUR drive had seemed like an eternity, especially for Steffi, and Reagan was relieved to have found a room here, and before dark. Any port in the storm.

The only room available had been a junior double, with one double bed, which would be just fine. They were lucky to get it, especially since this was a spontaneous stop, without a reservation, and in the Christmas season.

They had showered, changed into fresh comfy clothes, and were glad they had brought their jackets with them as they sat at their outdoor table on the hotel restaurant's front terrace. Having a dedicated restaurant, as well as breakfast in the morning, meant they wouldn't have to venture out, especially after dark.

Reagan took a sip of her exquisitely dry German Riesling, admired the blooms in the terrace's flowerboxes, and studied the sky. The last remnants of sunshine were bidding adieu as the clouds began shifting to the gray tones.

She hoped it wouldn't rain tomorrow for the drive to Hamburg. Even if it did, the drive would only be a couple of hours, but she remained concerned about any reduced visibility, and she was making things up as she went.

Reagan wasn't intimately familiar with Hildesheim. Far from it, having only visited the region once, in her teens, while on a day drive with her parents. Still, some of the local landmarks had left impressions with her all those years ago, including the architecture of Church of St. Michael and St. Mary's Cathedral, among others. She had found churches rather fascinating back then, as her parents had been religious and brought her up that way. But that was before the cruel turn of events that resulted in her parents' tragic deaths, and before she had subsequently decided there could be no God that would allow such things.

There was also Hohnsensee Lake, and she wished she could show Steffi the Thousand-year Rose, which was also known as the Rose of Hildesheim. It was noteworthy, and aptly named, because it was believed to be 1,000 years old and the world's oldest living rose. Dedicated to the Assumption of Mary, the massive bush had almost completely taken over the apse of the Hildesheim Cathedral. Even though she was no longer a churchgoer, Reagan remained impressed by the rose bush. It was a true anomaly and she considered herself one as well.

As this unscheduled overnight stay wouldn't allow for

any sightseeing, perhaps there might be time to include a sightseeing stop on the way back, she thought.

*There might not be another chance.*

"Whatcha thinking about, Mom?" Steffi asked, taking a sip of her apple juice.

"Mm," Reagan murmured, setting down her wine glass. "Just flashing back on a few things from when I was about your age. I stopped here once, in Hildesheim, with my mama und papa—my mom and dad. It's a nice place and I hope we can see some of it. We just can't right now. Perhaps on the drive back. We'll see."

"That's fine," Steffi said, liberally spreading a pat of butter on a fresh brötchen and taking a bite. "These rolls are way better than what we have at home."

"I think you'll find that just about everything tastes better over here, sweetie," Reagan replied, smiling as she caught the server's attention for a refill of her glass. She turned back to Steffi. "How's your goulash?"

"Oh my God, Mom... I thought that Dinty Moore stew was, like, the world's best, y'know, but this—what's it called? *Ghoul...* ?"

"*Goulash*, but spelled without an *h*, so as not to be confused with anything demonic," she said with a chuckle. "Glad you're enjoying it, sweetie. I've always loved that dish, too."

"You should make this at home. Total gamechanger," Steffi replied, her eyes twinkling as she prepped another forkful.

"I'll have to do that. Wait... please, hold that bite. You're so adorable right now. Let me snap a quick picture, honey," Reagan said, digging out her phone. "Don't finish it yet."

"Better hurry, then," Steffi teased, lowering her fork as her mom futzed with the camera.

"Marking the moment, hon," Reagan said, framing the shot. "Okay!"

Steffi scooped up an impressive forkful of the stew and posed with the bite, her mouth open and smiling.

"Smile... say... *schnitzel!*"

"Schnitzel!" Steffi parroted, waiting for permission to land the bite as her mother snapped several photos. "Can I just eat it now?"

"Yeah," Reagan said, taking reciprocal delight in her daughter as Steffi chewed and smiled. "Let me see those before you post anything," she said, wiping her mouth.

"I'm not going to post them–they're just for us," Reagan assured her just as the server, a charming college-aged girl with the most beautiful blond ponytail, returned with a Riesling refill.

"You can just leave the bottle," Reagan said. "Danke schön."

"Bitte schön," the girl replied with a bright smile, her ponytail dancing a waltz as she walked away.

Reagan set her phone on the table and took a bite of her own dish of delicious sauerbraten–a sliced, tenderized rump roast marinated in a unique gravy of aromatic spices–which was plated with spätzle noodles and some of her favorite red cabbage.

"I've been missing this," she said with a mouthful.

Her phone chimed.

She grabbed the device and stared at it, briefly thrown off by the different ringtone, but noticed it was a *What's App* call–an app she reserved for international calls–and its caller ID:

*Amethyst!*

"Wow! Excuse me, honey... gotta take this–it's Amethyst!" Reagan said, setting down her fork.

"Go for it," Steffi replied, giving her a thumbs-up and redirecting her focus to the plate in front of her.

"Twinner!!" Reagan enthused, hoping the long-distance connection would be a clear one. A few seconds went by without hearing anything back. "Ames! Hey... you there?" Crickets. "Amethyst, if you can hear me, let me know... otherwise I'll hang up and try–"

She was interrupted by an utterance, a voice on the other end that was faint, labored, raspy. Definitely not her young friend. Reagan was just about to hang up when she heard someone clearing their throat, then loud whispering her name, or a version of it.

"Ray Gun...."

Reagan's face went slack, and even Steffi could tell something must be wrong.

"Ames? Gawd, Ames... is that you? Girl, talk to me. Are you okay?! What's... ?"

"It's me... or what's left of me," Amethyst managed. "Listen, I'm a bit rough, but I need to tell you something and you need to listen very carefully. You listening?"

"Yeah, sweetie. I'm listening, I'm here... gawd... talk to me," Reagan replied, her eyes locking into Steffi's.

"First," Amethyst began, clearing her throat again, "thank you for the beautiful necklace," she said, her own cough interrupting her.

"Oh, my gawd... you're so welcome, Twinner. It was just–"

"Hear me out, Ray!" Ames interjected urgently, "I think you might be in danger, girl."

Reagan pushed her plate away, her brow furrowing. "What do you mean, *danger*? What makes you think that?"

Steffi pushed away her plate as well; she was locked into the one side of the conversation she was hearing. "Mom?"

Reagan tried to wave away Steffi's concern. "It's okay, honey," she whispered, before rising from the table and walking toward the other end of the terrace. "Ames? What's happened?"

"Your place, at least the kitchen, is kinda messed up, honey. And I got kinda messed up with it."

Reagan's imagination and concern were stirring up a vivid cocktail. "What the–?! How... bad... is it?"

"It's mostly your computer and some of the–"

"Ames!" Reagan barked, not loudly, but more sharply than intended. She lowered her voice a notch so as to not disturb the diners at the other tables. "Sorry, Ames. Listen, I don't care about the effing *computer*... how bad are *you*? *That's* what I'm concerned about. Tell me, please, what happened? Because I'm starting to freak out a little here," she pleaded.

"I'm okay. I will be, anyway, they tell me. I'll spare you too many of the details, but let's just say it's best we aren't on a video call, if you know what I mean."

"Gawd," Reagan gasped, her free hand wiping away the onset of tears. "So, you're not calling from Telluride."

"'Fraid not. Slight change of plans... I'm at Evergreen emergency. Jerry just flew in; it's fine."

"Jeezus... your Christmas...."

"It is what it is... listen: the police were at your house, Twinner, and I got to take my first ambulance ride, so that part was fun at least," Ames managed, her laugh morphing into a cough.

"Ames, you need some rest. We can talk more later when you're–"

"No!" Amethyst demanded, her voice finding the strength to convey her urgency. "I need to tell you right now. The guy who did this? He thought I was *you*, Ray! This was meant for *you*, and I just happened to be there!"

"What makes you think that? I mean, it could've just been a burglary you interrupted, right? Maybe—"

"Wrong, Ray. I'm telling you: this guy—and no insult to guys—he was one tall-ass, evil, ugly motherfucker! And he had this messed up birthmark—or maybe a burn, I don't know, but it looked kind of like the boot of Italy, or something, on his face!"

This stopped Reagan cold.

An Arctic-level chill ran up her spine and the fine hairs on her arms stood at attention. What little was left of her blurry-at-best, rapidly declining peripheral vision seemed to ramp up its decay rate a thousand-fold in that moment as she pictured the assailant Ames had just described.

Her immediate surroundings faded away as she let her tunnel vision focus on one random thing: the streetlamp across the street that that had just blinked on. Its timing coincided with her own lightbulb moment.

She knew without a shadow of a doubt who it was.

And who had to have sent him!

"Ray? You there? Ray!"

"Yeah… I'm here," Reagan replied numbly.

"Sorry to be the bearer of bad news, Twinner."

"I'm the one who's sorry, Ames. Gawd. I promise you this guy will pay for what he did to you. Count on it," Reagan said, seething at the thought of the unprovoked and misdirected violence leveled against her bestie. There would actually be *two* guys who would be paying for this.

A few moments of silence hung out there until Ames weighed in again. "Hey, Ray, so my nurse is here to check on me now. Before I go, promise me one thing."

"Anything, Ames. I promise."

"Just… watch your back."

# CHAPTER FORTY-SIX

## PARKHOTEL BERGHÖLZCHEN
## THURSDAY, DECEMBER 18
## 03:05, CET

F OR REAGAN, SLEEP hadn't come, and she resigned herself to the fact that it wouldn't be arriving for the foreseeable future.

She had hoped the extra bottle of room service Riesling might help take the edge off her flurry of raging thoughts, but it hadn't.

Thankfully, Steffi was doing a variation on the snore, her sweet head tucked into the nape of Reagan's neck. Reagan stared into the fuzzy black void where she knew the ceiling to be, while a plethora of doubts was running through her mind, questioning everything.

Could the man she'd married a decade before really be a monster? Could he be behind the recent evils that were unfolding? If so, had he *ever* loved her? Had he really orchestrated the deceit with the bank, with trying to abscond with the assets, and the very business her parents had built?

Reagan's restless feet kicked at the covers as she visualized the scene Ames had described and, worse, the violence and suffering inflicted on her. By the tall man.

Ames's warning circled back: *Watch your back.*

Her active mind flashed back to the images she'd found in Fynn's yearbook, and she visualized the sasquatch standing next to him in virtually every group photo. They had been joined at the hip then, he and Fynn, which meant they probably–definitely–were now. Her thoughts went to another series of photos.

*Jeezus.*

As gently as possible, Reagan extracted herself from beneath her sleeping child and guided Steffi's head onto her pillow. She pulled up the covers and tucked her in.

Reagan got up, felt around for her carry-on bag, and pulled out the iPad. Upon powering it up, she noted its full charge and, using its bright screen as a nightlight, she carried the device with her to the chair in the corner of the dark room.

*I have to fucking know!*

She rubbed her aching, tired eyes and opened up the Photos app. She went directly to the *MAYBE* file and the photos she'd recently added for later consideration.

She had to revisit the Hamburg horror once more.

Returning to the decade-old images she'd taken from the train, just before its departure, Reagan studied the series of photos with renewed scrutiny. Her lip quivered as she regarded the faces of her parents while they stood innocently on the platform, watching their only daughter, whose train was about to leave the station and she for a new life in America.

They looked so innocent, so loving, Mama and Papa. They could have no possible idea that, in a matter of moments, their lives would end in the worst of ways, as they were pushed onto the tracks of an inbound locomotive on an adjacent platform.

She remembered seeing the Zapruder film in her teens. It had been taken before her time, but it was regarded as the most critical visual evidence documenting President Kennedy's assassination in Dallas, that November of 1963.

Like countless others—conspiracy theorists, students of history, and the morbidly curious alike—Reagan had viewed the grainy eight-millimeter film footage taken by eyewitness Abraham Zapruder that fateful day, studying it, frame-by-frame, back-and-forth, to discern the exact moments the American president's mortal wounds were inflicted in horrific fashion by a sniper. Or snipers.

She was doing much the same now with her own photos, and her interest was laser focused on the mysterious man in the wheelchair, with the ballcap, and a blanket across his lap. He sat there, expressionless, a scant few feet removed from her parents, from Fynn, from young Steffi on his shoulders.

She progressed two images ahead, zooming the image a little when she came to the frame of film she'd captured where the wheelchair man and Fynn turned to each other.

*Was that a moment between them? A signal? Who is that guy?*

The slightly down angle, combined with the bill of the ballcap, made it difficult to see his face. She moved ahead to the next image. *There!* She zoomed in and magnified the image. The angle of his head was different, upturned ever so slightly, but providing a better glimpse of the face below the brim. Reagan isolated just his head now, going full frame with it on her tablet. There was considerably more grain as a result, but one thing became abundantly clear:

*This fucker has the mark on his face!!*

# CHAPTER FORTY-SEVEN

THE SCREENSHOT HADN'T been optimal, but she'd attached it in a text to Ames anyway. She hadn't elaborated with any context, only the briefest of shorthand: *Tall guy?*

Reagan took a sip from her third cup of coffee and was just beginning to feel its effects. She set down her half-eaten brötchen and glanced at her smartwatch display: 06:40

She had hated to rouse Steffi so early, but at least *she* had slept well and was enjoying her traditional German breakfast. Aside from the early-bird, middle-aged couple at another table, the terrace restaurant was quiet at this hour. The skies were a rather dark, ominous gray.

Reagan's sleep-deprived and highly caffeinated mind was reeling from her all-night epiphanies. If she was correct, and her gut told her she was, she could not only identify Ames's assailant but also tie him—and her snaky spouse—to the plot.

It also put the tall man and Fynn both at another scene, under the guise of strangers, and the likely merchants of her parents' deaths at Hamburg Central Station.

Reagan felt her pulse quicken and her face flush as she

pushed away her breakfast plate. The eggs, the cheeses, the marmalades, all untouched. She had no appetite this morning, with the exception of one for vengeance.

"Almost done, Stef?"

"Yeah, I guess. Why do we have to leave so early, though? Is Hamburg a long drive?"

"No, not really a long drive–maybe a couple of hours–but we don't want to get caught up in the rain if we can avoid–"

The first fat rain drop hit the table, interrupting her thought, but making her point for her.

## THE SPECIAL CONNECTION
## FISCHMARKT HAMBURG ALTONA
## THURSDAY, DECEMBER 18
## 11:35, CET

The Special Connection cafe's shingle advertised *Coffee, Food & Love*. Fynn had come here for the coffee and the food. Sitting at the table, alongside Ekkehard, he wasn't feeling the love right now.

He stared out the window, silently watching umbrella-laden shoppers dodge the puddles that were forming. The rain had started coming down in sheets and he hoped for better weather for Sunday's Fischmarkt. It had to be.

The small cafe was a delightful spot, an easy walk to the nearby Fischmarkt, and a favorite with many locals. The homey decor included hanging plants as well as flower arrangements on the tables, making it a welcome place to enjoy their wonderful winter menu, for breakfast or lunch.

Ekkehard, having not eaten since the final meal service on his flight, noisily gorged himself on one of the breakfast specials, the "Walking on Sunshine," which consisted of scrambled eggs on sourdough bread with melted cheese and a tomato cream cheese. He'd paired it with an order of their special tahini-infused pancakes, served with a berry compote and crème brûlée sauce.

Listening to Ekkehard forage reminded Fynn of his youth, when one of the foster families he'd briefly lived with had assigned him the job of feeding the pigs. The sounds coming from his left had completely killed his appetite; he had barely touched his hot banana bread or the cinnamon porridge, both of which he loved.

Fynn's anger continued to fester like a boil, his level of discontent evident in his scowl, as he and Ekkehard sat at the long, wooden bench table that faced the large view window. The seating arrangement suited his current mood right now, as there were several stools set along the length of the table, and on only one side. Fynn couldn't bear to look at Ekkehard at the moment. Not after his colossal fuck-up at the house. He'd already spent an hour chastising him on the ride from the airport.

He stubbed out his cigarette and immediately lit another. When he spoke, he chose a measured tone. His gaze remained on the goings-on outside, and there was precious little eye contact.

"Are you about done shoveling your fucking food, or can I order you something else?"

Ekkehard slowly set down his fork, considering the offer,

but deciding against it. He was still wincing from the earlier verbal beatdown. He wiped his mouth, shook his head, and stared straight ahead. "I'm finished."

"Mm…" Fynn grunted, directing his cloud of smoke upward before he continued. "Let's hope we're not *both* finished after that clusterfuck you caused."

"I said I was—"

"Sorry? Sorry, yes, I'm sure you are. Now the question we need to answer is what do we do now?"

Fynn pivoted on his stool, facing Ekkehard, who looked like he might cry because he had no answer for him. Fynn ground out his cigarette, took in a slow, deliberate breath through his nostrils, and placed his left hand on Ekkehard's knee. "I think we both know a mistake has been made, Ekkehard, and I can tell you feel bad about it. All we can do now is… damage control. Come on," he said, pulling a wad of euros from his pocket and peeling off several. He set them down atop his banana bread and picked up his umbrella. "Let's check on things at the Fischmarkt."

# CHAPTER FORTY-EIGHT

I T HAD BEEN slow going in the deluge. The windshield wipers, even on their highest setting, were inadequately prepared for the intensity of rain that had been leveled against them for the past few hours.

As they entered the Hamburg city limits, Reagan directed Steffi to pull over at the first available gas station. As they pulled under the canopy and alongside the pump island, the percussive sound of raindrops pounding the MG's roof stopped but continued pummeling the canopy overhead.

Steffi had never driven in such conditions and as she turned off the engine she commenced breathing again. "Scheisse!!" she blurted. "Sorry, that's the only German word I know–and I got it from you, Mom... *shit!*"

"Scheisse is right. That was brutal, and pretty scary, I know. You did great, honey."

Steffi turned to look at her mother, appreciative for the acknowledgement. She mustered a half-smile and let out a sigh as she watched her get out and wrestle with the umbrella.

"I'm going to top off the tank real quick, hon. Let's switch seats; I think I can handle the city driving okay if the rain–"

As if a faucet had been turned off, the rain abruptly stopped. The resultant silence was deafening.

"–lets… up. Wow," Reagan said, shrugging her shoulders and beaming a smile at Steffi through the windshield as she closed the umbrella. "Ta-da!"

Steffi climbed out, her amazement evident. "Let's hope your magic holds up, Mom!"

### 15 MINUTES LATER . . .

Hei Li nervously chewed on a cuticle as she watched the repairman.

The tech grunted as his wrench fought for space inside the bowels of the large reefer unit. He had been called to do an emergency replacement of the compressor on their largest industrial refrigerator. The compressor was not only the heart of the refrigeration system, he'd advised; it was also going to be the most expensive.

Choosing not to get service wasn't an option, however, not with the weekend's shipments coming in.

Hei Li wasn't sure if Fynn was coming in today but, considering her boss's mood lately, she hoped the repair could be completed soon, just in case. She had called Fynn at the hotel the afternoon before, advising him of the faulty unit's need for repair and he'd begrudgingly given her the greenlight to call the tech. It was his reaction to the bill she feared.

Her phone vibrated in its hip holster and, expecting it might be Fynn, she answered on the second ring. "Hallo?"

"Hei Li!"

Not expecting the caller's voice to be female, she peeked at her display.

"Reagan?!"

"Yes, yes... hi, Hei Li! Everything okay with you?" Reagan asked.

"Uh, mostly. I mean, I've got a repairman here fixing the main refrigerator right now, but... yes. *Alles gut.* It's nice to hear from you. What's up?"

"Listen, Hei Li, quick question: Is Fynn there right now?"

"No, he's not. I'm not sure if he's coming today or not. He told me last night he had to go to the airport and *might* come in later, but... did you want me to tell him you–?"

"*No!* No... no, thank you. Please *do not* mention that I called you. Okay, Hei Li?"

"Uh, sure. No problem," she replied, her curiosity kicking in. She turned her back on the repairman and walked to the rear of the stall. "Is everything all right?"

"Okay, yes... well, it *will* be. It's very important, Hei Li, that Fynn doesn't know you and I talked."

"Got it."

"Thanks. I want to keep it a surprise...."

"Keep what a surprise... if you don't mind my asking?"

"That I'm here... in Hamburg."

"Wait! You're *here?!* Oh, my God, Reagan... I can't wait to see you. Where are you staying? Can I pick you up, or... ?"

"No, I have a rental car, thanks. I'll find a place. Listen, since the day's still young, I think I'm going to take my daughter someplace special while the weather's decent."

"You brought Steffi with you?! That's fantastic. Where are you taking her?"

"Going to do an excursion to Lübeck. I want her to experience the café at Niederegger for a taste of the best marzipan."

"Oh, I haven't been to Lübeck in years, but Niederegger is still the best. She'll love it!"

"Would you like me to pick you up something, Hei Li?"

"No, no, danke. You two have a great day. And watch the weather... they said it could even snow up north, but I'll believe it when I see it. Call me later, bitte. I can't wait to see you, Reagan."

"I will. Okay, tschüss!" Reagan promised as she signed off.

"Tschüss!" Hei Li said, smiling as she ended the call and holstered her phone. She turned around to check on the repairman but was met with an unexpected surprise–actually two surprises–standing just a few feet away. Her jaw slackened as her gaze travelled up to the very tall man and her boss standing next to him.

"Ah, yes... Lübeck," Fynn said, a sinister grin spreading across his face. "Reagan always loved the marzipan."

# CHAPTER FORTY-NINE

CAFÉ NIEDEREGGER
MARKET SQUARE, LÜBECK
THURSDAY, DECEMBER 18
14:55, CET

REAGAN'S STINT BEHIND the wheel had been uneventful and blessed by three factors: the lack of rain; the fact that the seventy-kilometer drive was, for the most part, a relatively straight shot, traveling northeast; and Steffi monitoring her side mirror during lane changes. Even with the construction delays on Nordkanalstrasse and the A24, they'd made it in a couple of hours.

Finding street parking anywhere near the market square was another matter, and they had happened on a spot about a kilometer's walk from their destination: the world-renowned Café Niederegger.

Reagan hadn't elaborated on their planned "lunch stop" here and she couldn't wait to see her daughter's reaction to it. Her own excitement was palpable, as it had been over a dozen years since her last visit to this magical place when she had dragged her then-new fiancé, Fynn, there for a day trip, her parents volunteering to babysit their young granddaughter for the day.

Fynn's reaction to the café had been lukewarm, she remembered, and he'd never developed a taste for marzipan in any form. *That in itself should've been a red flag!*

So much had changed since then and most of it in the last week! Reagan shuddered to think of Fynn now, but she wasn't going to let her contempt for him diminish her and Steffi's experience.

As they neared Breite Strasse, Reagan's nostrils flared as she took in the lovely aromas of roasted almonds and fresh mulled wine. The sights, sounds, and smells of Christmas were in the air as she and Steffi approached the bustling energy of *Lubecker Weihnachtsmarkt*– Lübeck's Christmas Market–in the square around the town hall.

As they turned the corner, Steffi stopped in her tracks and she regarded the magical scene. Reagan smiled, watching her daughter's reaction as she took in what amounted to the picture-perfect Advent backdrop.

Steffi stared slack-jawed at the beautifully decorated Christmas trees, the otherworldly displays of lights, and the food vendors. There were all manner of Christmas arts and crafts booths spread throughout the market square where one could buy anything from traditional Christmas tree decorations to toys and regional products and gifts.

"Mom... oh, my God. It's... *Christmas*! It's like... stepping into a snow globe!"

"What do you think?" Reagan asked rhetorically. It was impossible to repress a smile here, and she was feeling every bit of wonderment Steffi was. It was the same transformative experience she'd had when she first visited the Christmas markets with her parents in her own youth.

The crowds meandering through the market square's Christmas village were enjoying their mulled wine, gingerbread, and roasted nuts. The holiday spirit was contagious, the experience nothing short of magical, and there seemed to be a smile on every face, young and old.

Steffi pointed at the impressive blue-green gables that adorned the top of the massive Gothic brick structure, its backdrop against which the market was situated. "Mom, what's that place? Was that, like, Hitler's bunker or something?"

"No, honey. Nothing like that," she answered, suppressing a laugh. "*That* is a very old and famous building called the Rathaus. It's one of the largest medieval town halls in Germany, and it's… gosh… probably about 800 years old."

"Wow… that's even older than you!" Steffi teased with a laugh.

"Hey, now."

"*J.K.*, Mom."

Reagan shook it off, glad to see Steffi's sense of humor returning. "You ready?"

"Can we get some gingerbread? Smells amazing!"

"Mm… we're kind of saving our appetite, honey."

"For?"

"You'll see."

"Okay. Can you take my picture first?"

"Absolutely," Reagan said, pulling out her phone, the photographer in her searching for the best angle. "Take a couple of steps to your left."

Steffi shuffled accordingly. "Can you get the big Christmas tree in the picture?"

"The tree, yep. Okay, say *marzipan!*"

"Marzipan," Steffi chirped.

"Okay, stay right there. Let's take a quick selfie of us both," Reagan said, joining her daughter and adjusting the phone's position for a low angle shot to accommodate the tree. "Say, *käse!*" *Cheese!*

Steffi parroted her once again, smiling for the cheesy shot. A wind gust wrestled with her scarf, and the temperature seemed to be dipping. "Brrr!"

Reagan could see the gold and red NEIDEREGGER LÜBECK marquee just ahead. She was already salivating. "C'mon," Reagan said, putting her arm around her. "Let's get this party started!"

As far as Reagan was concerned, I. G. Niederegger Café was her personal Disneyland and, in her estimation, *the* happiest place on the planet. She hoped Steffi would find it to be as well.

It was a study in sensory overload—in a good way—and as Steffi stepped inside, she couldn't believe what she was seeing. The rows of glass display cases were resplendent, featuring a cornucopia of colorful and sumptuous confections where one could purchase an extraordinary variety of delicious marzipan creations "to go."

But Reagan and Steffi weren't going anywhere. Except

upstairs, to the main event: the divine café dining room. But first, they had to run the gauntlet.

The gift shop area was unequaled as well, featuring table after table of every kind of marzipan creation imaginable, including an incredible array of nougats, pralines, torts, and every manor of clever gift items and endless assortments. It made it virtually impossible to keep one's euros in their pocket, and Reagan could feel them burning a hole in hers.

"Mom! Look!" Steffi squealed, holding up an ornate gift box with a heart-shaped window that displayed its assortment of individually wrapped heart-shaped marzipan treats. "I think these are dark ones, right? Can I get this for Vickie? She loves dark chocolate, and I'm sure she's never had marzipan! Please?"

"Of course, honey. But let's get it after lunch, okay? We need to score a table. We'll pass through here again on the way out, I promise."

"'Kay," Steffi replied as she set it back on the table. "Do they serve marzipan in the café?"

Reagan smiled knowingly. "If memory serves…."

The hostess beamed her best smile. "Your table is ready. This way, please."

Steffi couldn't believe her eyes as they slowly made their way along the long glass display cases, each featuring the freshly made offerings of the day. She had read Roald Dahl's classic numerous times as a kid and seen both movie treatments of it, and what she was seeing right now felt akin to having won a Wonka golden ticket.

This was a seemingly endless array of exotic cakes, each more sumptuous looking than the last, and it was virtually impossible not to rubberneck all the way to their window table.

Reagan was pleased to find the dining room to be unchanged from her last visit. At this time of day, the large windows provided ample illumination and alleviated some of her visibility concerns.

"Holy marzipan, Batman…" Steffi uttered as they reached the table. "I already saw, like, five things I want, Mom!"

"Well, let's maybe narrow the five down to two, if you can," Reagan said with a smile as they took their seats. "I'm sure I'll be getting a couple as well. And we can share tastes!"

"That works."

"Please don't ask if they have Gatorade, though. They won't, so you should probably order the *apfelsaft*, which is—"

"Apple juice."

"Very good," Reagan replied, just as their hostess arrived.

"Guten Tag. Good afternoon, my name is Heidi, and I will be serving you," she said, her accent charming and her English excellent. "Have you decided on anything to drink?"

"I'd like the apfelsaft, bitte," Steffi said, winking to her mother.

"Sehr gut," the server replied, turning to Reagan. "Und Ihnen?"

"Kaffee Marzipan mit Likör Niederegger, bitte," Reagan said without hesitation. It was her favorite beverage here.

"Sehr gut, danke," Heidi said with a smile to both as she left.

"Did you order coffee with liquor in it?" Steffi asked teasingly. "Go, Mom!"

"I did. Don't worry, though; I won't be getting drunk on one coffee." *Though I wish I could.*

"Can I try a sip?"

"Mm… we'll see. C'mon, let's go pick out our desserts!" Reagan said, not needing to sell the idea as they sprang from their chairs.

It had taken some doing but Fynn finessed the rental Saab into a spot that had just been vacated by a Smart car.

They were only a couple of blocks from the Market Square, he figured, because he could see the turquoise-y gables of the Rathaus, which he knew was adjacent to where Reagan had told Hei Li they'd be going. That being said, he knew stealth would be needed.

He reached beneath his seat and grabbed a nondescript gray knit watchman's cap and put it on. Reagan had never seen him wear one, so it should work, he figured. He turned to his legroom-challenged passenger. "You should probably change your… shoes."

"*Was?*" *What?* Ekkehard replied. "I didn't bring any others."

"I anticipated the need and brought them for you. They are in the rear compartment," Fynn said, pushing the hatchback release button on the dash as he watched his passenger exit the vehicle and walk around to the rear.

Ekkehard lifted the hatch to its highest position and ducked his head in to pull back a wool blanket, revealing a zipped duffel bag. The bag was familiar to him, and as he carried it back to the car, he immediately clued in to Fynn's reference for changing his "shoes."

As he plopped back into his seat, he set the bag on the ground, but within arm's reach.

"We don't want to give ourselves away now, do we?" Fynn asked, the question rhetorical, as he watched his partner unfasten the Velcro fasteners running up both seams of his trouser legs, giving him better access to his metal prosthetics. Upon removing them, he set them on the floor behind their seats.

Ekkehard pulled the cloth liners from his residual legs and took a full minute to rub the stumps as Fynn looked around for any looky-loos. Seeing none, Fynn nodded, watching as the now-not-so-tall man reached into the duffle and pulled out a fresh set of liners, along with his other "shoes," which were of a completely different design, composition–and length–than his others.

These "blade" prosthetics were designed for and used mostly by competitive runners, something Ekkehard had some experience with. He hadn't worn these in some time, however, as he didn't do much running these days, but he understood Fynn's specifying them today. The woman would not expect to see him here today and, if she had expected to, it would be the taller version of himself. These, specially made for him, would lower his lofty profile by well over half a… foot.

Ekkehard took care as he pulled on the fresh set of cushion liners. Slipping them on–inside out–onto his stumps, he slowly rolled them up to prevent any wrinkles or trapped air pockets, in preparation for the prosthetic.

As the next step required having his legs out straight, Ekkehard turned and swung his stumps out the door, much to the horror of a three-year-old boy who was passing by with his mother. Ekkehard offered the lad a twisted smile, but it only served as further fodder for the boy's nightmares to come.

Upon slipping on the blade prosthetics, Ekkehard slowly rolled the suspension sleeves all the way up. Their vacuum style mounts aided its adhesion to his residual legs and, once he stood and took a couple of steps, the resultant pressure squeezed out any remaining air.

The carbon fiber running blades were constructed of multiple layers of carbon fiber, fused together, which made them light, strong and highly elastic. The "C" shape blade, acting as a foot, mimicked a "running on toes" running form, compressing by body weight and returning to its original shape as he pushed off of it.

Ekkehard shifted his weight on each leg, bouncing slightly, as he got acclimated to his "C" legs. He refastened the Velcro on his pants, rolled up the cuffs a bit, and nodded to Fynn, signaling he was good to go.

Fynn smiled, happy to see his partner using the blades today. They had been a costly investment a few years back, and he enjoyed the irony that his wife had unwittingly paid for them as a buried line item on his Fischmarkt expense report.

Fynn exited the vehicle and walked over to his partner, who now stood a few inches shorter than he. He reached out and caressed Ekkehard's cheek. "Lass uns gehen." *Let's go.*

# CHAPTER FIFTY

REAGAN TOOK A sip of her exquisite Kaffee Marzipan and savored the subtle Likör infusion. She regarded her and Steffi's identical plates. She hadn't intended to, but she had ended up ordering the exact same two desserts. *No need to share.*

Each wedge of cake was three layers high, one with chocolate and marzipan cremes, and the other an exotic marzipan tort, beautifully adorned with a seemingly impossible array of fresh fruits. It looked like something out of a Technicolor movie.

Steffi took a bite of the fruit one and moaned with delight. Her mouthful got in the way of her diction, but Reagan was able to decode the joy behind it. "Ohmygawdthisissoamazing."

Reagan snapped a candid photo with her phone and set it back on the table. She closed her eyes and marked the moment. Nothing was going to spoil this experience.

Her phone had other ideas, however, as it vibrated an alert. She picked up the device:

*1 New Message.*

Steffi wiped the corner of her mouth. "Who is it, Mom?"

"I don't know, honey," she replied as she went to retrieve it. It wasn't another call from Fynn, thankfully. It took her a moment to recognize the number before realizing that this was a message from Ames.

Its one-word reply to Reagan's earlier query about the Tall Man was accompanied by a photo: a selfie, taken from what appeared to be a hospital bed. It took Reagan several moments to recognize what she was seeing, as the battered and bruised, stitched-together face of her bestie stared back at her. The one word reply supplying confirmation:

> *YES!!!*

Steffi set down her fork, trying to get a read on her mother's expression. Something had shifted. "Everything okay, Mom? Who was it?"

Reagan set the phone back on the table, screen side down, and slowly turned to her. She didn't want to lie, so she didn't. "My friend... Ames. She... had an accident. She's in the hospital," she answered softly, all the previous joy sucked out of her.

"Oh, no. I'm sorry... is she going to be okay?"

Reagan half nodded as she replied, shell shocked as she turned her gaze to the window. A few snowflakes were beginning to spiral down outside but she didn't react to them. "I think so. I hope so...."

Steffi patted her mama's hand. "I hope so too." She followed her mother's gaze to the window and her eyes widened. "Hey, it's starting to snow, Mom! How beautiful is that?!"

"Like being in a snow globe," Reagan said, doing her best to smile as she referenced her daughter's earlier comment.

Reagan's thoughts were swirling in her head like so many snowflakes, creating a blizzard of concerns, but she didn't want to panic her daughter.

A shiver ran down her spine, and she threw back the remainder of her kaffee. She signaled to the server for another as she processed the thoughts that confirmed her worst nightmares.

*The Tall Man did that to Ames, thinking it was me… he killed my parents! And that fucker is Fynn's best friend!!*

"You should try the fruit one, Mom. It's bomb."

"Mm… thank you, I will," Reagan replied, reemerging in the moment as Heidi set another kaffee on the table. "Danke," Reagan said to her. She picked up her fork and cleaved off a chunk, not really savoring the bite as she chewed on her thoughts.

The snow was coming down harder outside now. And so was the reality of their danger.

# CHAPTER FIFTY-ONE

S TEFFI PAID FOR the gift box of dark chocolate marzipan, surprised by the few small coins she received as change from the euro bills her mother had given her. "Danke."

She walked over to her mother, who was staring out the window at the marketplace. The sky was already darkening, and the snow flurries were picking up substantially.

"Here," she said, offering her mom the coins.

"You keep those, honey. Souvenirs of our trip," Reagan said, mustering a half smile somehow. "Good thing we have our jackets and scarves but wish we'd worn proper snow boots." She pulled her knit cap from her jacket pocket and put it on. Steffi followed her lead. "Somebody shook your snow globe, babe."

"It's pretty."

"And pretty cold. Here," Reagan said, adjusting the scarf on Steffi's neck and pulling up her jacket's hood. "You ready?"

"Yep."

"Okay, stay real close."

Fynn stood at the entrance to the market square, squinting at the falling snow. The merriment of the Christmassy scene completely escaped him. He'd just seen a couple of women exit the Niederegger gift shop together, but with their heads down, and their hoods—plus the snowfall—it was difficult to tell if it was them. "We need to get a bit closer," he said, pulling the cap over his ears.

A moment passed without a response, and he looked over his shoulder, only to find Ekkehard ten yards behind, struggling a bit with his blades in the snowy street. Fynn motioned for him to hurry, his gaze returning to the two women he'd spotted and the flurry between him and them. Ekkehard arrived, a bit out of breath, and Fynn turned to him, pointing.

"There… I think it may be them. Kommen!" *Come on.*

"Brats," Ekkehard muttered, his mouth watering as they passed a sausage vendor.

"Not now, Dummkopf!" Fynn hissed, swatting the back of his head.

Any remnants of the afternoon's sun were now extinguished, leaving only a gray canopy and snow flurries that had just decided to blow sideways. Several people were disappearing into nearby shops, as most seemed surprised by the atypical weather shift, while others—the ones wearing proper boots and winter gear—soldiered on and plodded through it with firm grips on their cups of mulled wine.

Reagan's concerns were rapidly multiplying as she tried to navigate the vendor booths and get her bearings. Soon it would be dark, very dark, and the snow showed no signs of letting up.

Also soon: she wouldn't be able to see *anything*.

She made sure Steffi's arm was linked around hers as she tried to navigate their way. She thought she could make out the pointed gables of the Rathaus, but she wasn't sure. Her already limited field of vision was severely diminished with these added variables. And they had at least a kilometer to go in order to reach the car, if they could find it.

"You okay, babe?"

"Um…" Steffi muttered, her frozen fingers struggling to grasp the giftbag.

"C'mon, we need to find our way out of this crap."

Steffi's response was most unexpected yet provided some welcome levity as she launched into singing a favorite carol. "It's beginning to look a lot like Christmas…"

Reagan tried to hide her concerns as she chimed in, "…everywhere you go!"

Fynn and Ekkehard had closed some distance and now only trailed the two hooded figures by ten yards. This had helped considerably, especially since their marks were now singing and Fynn recognized the voices. He turned to Ekkehard and nodded confirmation, then motioned for him to stop.

Reagan brushed the clumped snowflakes from her face as she stopped to get her bearings. Steffi did as well, and as she looked up, she got a good look at the Rathaus gables. "This is where we came in, Mom," she said, pointing. "We need to go this way… I'll lead, okay?"

Reagan nodded and gave Steffi's arm a squeeze. Her baby

was growing up, and she was grateful she was also stepping up to take charge. It was the future-blind leading the blind, and in these conditions, she conceded the navigation to her daughter.

They turned the corner, exited the market square, and proceeded on the kilometer's death march to the car. Steffi had experienced snow before but never on this level, and she tried not to second guess herself as they slowly made their way down the street. They were being punished by flurries, since conditions had been quite different when they first arrived.

"I think we have... maybe... four or five blocks on this street, then we take a right, where the car is." *I think.*

"You're our eyes right now, honey. I trust your instincts," Reagan said, loud enough to be heard over the wind gusts. "Maybe this stuff will stop soon," she added optimistically.

"Yeah... *that* would be nice," Steffi called out. "Come on, I've got you!"

The girls were on the move again and Fynn gave his partner a nudge as they followed suit. *They must be heading toward their car.* He picked up the pace slightly, as he didn't want them reaching their vehicle before they could be intercepted. If they did, it might prove impossible to find them again.

Fynn put his right hand into the pocket of his coat, taking comfort in both the respite from the cold as well as the feel of the Walther PPK/S .22 caliber pistol's grip. Its low profile, smooth ergonomics, and ten-round magazine had made it attractive, and being an unregistered piece had sealed the deal with the street seller.

He hoped he didn't have to use it, but if the need arrived,

he would, to protect his interests. If the Walther was good enough for James Bond, it was good enough for his purposes.

"They're heading to their car, I'm sure, but also toward ours. We need to get there first," Fynn said as he noticed the street adjacent to the sidewalk had recently had its snow pushed to the curb. He pointed to the area with the lighter snow deposits. "Time to see what those shoes can do! Stay to the other side of the street and try to get ahead of them—without being seen!"

Ekkehard nodded, preparing himself for the run by unzipping his jacket a little, allowing for both arm movement and heat dispersal. "I go now."

"Go. I'll be coming up behind them and will find you. Do not let them get past you!"

"Ja," Ekkehard said as he pushed off toward the clearer pavement, dodging a couple of motorists and eliciting their beeps in the process.

As he watched his partner sprint off and disappear into the darkness between the streetlamps, Fynn couldn't help but flash back to their younger days together on the track. Ekkehard had been unbeatable then, and he was in his element now, he knew.

The rules of engagement had been made clear during their drive here, and Fynn could just imagine the look on Reagan's face when Ekkehard caught up to them.

# CHAPTER FIFTY-TWO

**I**F REAGAN EVER fully recognized the full degree of her handicap, it was right now. She had ignored the signs for the longest time, denying the existence of a problem as she made physical adjustments to her environment in order to function, while refusing to accept the diagnosis. And the long-term ramifications.

Until right this moment.

She was as good as blind here in the dark, the last vestiges of her vision reduced to a small window—a narrow tunnel—and with zero peripheral awareness. If that hadn't been the case, she might have had some awareness of the man who had been running alongside them on the other side of the road.

"Another block, I think, Mom, then we turn right… down the street where the car is!" Steffi called out above the wind as she squinted through the blowing snow. This was a test for her senses as well, and she suddenly found herself wondering about her own limitations. Still, she had to take charge in this situation. "Hang on."

"Sorry… I'm not much help right now," Reagan replied, wanting to sit down and cry, but that wasn't an option. "All I can see is that streetlamp down the block. I'm sorry for getting us into this. You must regret ever–"

"Stop it, Mom!" Steffi retorted, cutting off the negativity spigot. "We're coming up on our turn, next corner, and–" She came to an abrupt stop and shrieked in pain as she grabbed her ankle. "Yowch!! *Gawd*!!" She buckled awkwardly onto the sidewalk.

"What is it?! What happened?!!" Reagan called out as Steffi's arm slipped out from hers.

"My *ankle*!! I stepped on a bottle or something and... *fuck!!* I twisted it!! *Dammit!*" Steffi cried, the acute agony evident in her voice.

Reagan had never really heard her daughter curse on this level and knew it had to be bad. Her mama bear instincts kicked in as she knelt down to assess the ankle, but only by touch. "Oh, no... let me see, honey...."

"Mom, you can't... just give me... a couple of minutes. *Ouch*!!"

"But—"

"But *nothing*, Mom!" Steffi hissed through gritted teeth. "Mom, please–go stand under that awning over there," she said, making sure her mother saw exactly where she was pointing. "I'll... be able to... *hop* the rest of the way, but give me a moment. This hurts like a mutha!!"

"Okay, I'm sorry, baby! But are you sure there's nothing I–?"

"Mom!!!!" Steffi roared. "Get out of this weather for a second. I'll be okay!"

Reagan turned, focusing her meager vision on the small awning she'd been directed to. She guessed it to be about thirty feet away, which seemed like an eternity, but she had precious little depth perception to properly gauge it.

Reagan reluctantly took slow, deliberate steps in that

direction, eventually reaching the three steps that led to a small landing and the door of the closed shop. The awning was small and offered little protection.

Grabbing the railing, she made her way to the topmost step, regretting the snow, while cursing the disease that was rendering her utterly powerless to do anything about their predicament.

She blew warm breath onto her frigid fingers, listening for any sounds from her injured daughter. She no longer heard her moaning in pain, thankfully. She waited another minute or two before she called out to her. "Steffi? Talk to me… how's the ankle? Are you okay?!"

The silence was deafening, which only made her near blindness feel more debilitating.

"Steffi?!" Reagan called out, louder now. Only the wind replied. "Stef!!! Stef-fi!!?" *Did she fall? Is she unconscious?!*

Reagan's panic officially kicked in. She couldn't clearly see the spot where she'd left her daughter, and the snowflakes were invading her eyes. She swatted them away as she descended the steps back onto the powdery sidewalk.

"Where are you?!! *Stefanie*!!!" she cried out, doing her best to retrace the way back, navigating through her own private, kaleidoscopic tunnel. As she got to what she thought was the spot, she found only disturbances in the dusty snow. There appeared to be something else laying at her feet and she bent down to pick it up.

A heart-shaped gift box of marzipan chocolates.

# CHAPTER FIFTY-THREE

"*STEFFI!!!!!*"

Reagan's next-to-useless eyes went wide, her head jerking left, right, and behind as she scanned the dark as through a low powered telescope. Other than the blurry headlights of a couple of passing cars on the street, she couldn't make out much of anything.

She let the candy box slip through her fingers and made no effort to retrieve it.

"Stefffffi!!!" Reagan wailed again, getting no response and no attention from anyone. She had no sense of direction out here, and no landmarks, other than the distant streetlamp she'd seen earlier. She had to head toward that, as it was in the direction they had been going, and her daughter had marked their position:

*Another block, then we turn right, down the street where the car is.*

She had to try. She had to find her baby. "Stef...." Her mother bear roars had left her weakened, her pathetic cries reduced to whispered pleas nobody would hear.

As she trudged forward, she paused every few seconds, muttering Steffi's name, her throat now beyond raw. She followed the sidewalk until the curb stopped, indicating a cross street.

*Then we turn right, down the street where the car is.*

Several cars passed by in front of her, their blurred lights streaking past. She could hear them better than she could see them, and she frantically waved her arms for help, her efforts ignored. Nobody would stop for the crazy lady.

She turned right, onto the new section of sidewalk.

In their haste to get to the café earlier, she hadn't really made note of where she'd parked the MG. But then, she hadn't planned on this. *Any* of this.

With zero peripheral vision on this darkened block, she had to turn and face each parked car, assessing their shape and their make and model. They each had at least some layer of snow on them, making it all the more difficult to discern the vehicles' colors as well.

She knew hers was a hatchback. And it was red.

Reagan approached a car that appeared to be the approximate shape and size of hers and began fervently brushing away its snow. "C'mon!!!" She stopped when she saw that it wasn't her red MG and was instead a green Volkswagen. "Dammit!!"

Three cars ahead, she discerned another possibility. *Definitely a hatchback!* She once again began wildly swiping away the snow, this time revealing a black Mercedes. "Scheisse!!!"

Reagan stepped back onto the sidewalk and screamed up at the very sky that was dumping a world of misfortune on her. "God!! I don't even believe in you—not *at all* anymore—but you don't get to do this to me!! You don't get to do this! You can take away my eyesight, you can take my business from me, hell, you can even make me freeze to death out here, but you cannot—you *will* not—take my daughter from me!! You hear me?! Not my Steffi! Not the one thing left in this world that matters to me, you got it?!!" She paused her rant just long enough to swipe away at another snow-laden vehicle. "What kind of god would let—?"

*A red... MG! An effing red, beautiful MG hatchback!!*

"Woo-hoo!!! Please," Reagan pleaded, retrieving the remote key fob from her pocket and trying it. The headlights, though mostly buried, flashed weakly, and she heard a most welcome chirp. "Thank you, God!!" she cried out, surprised to hear herself even saying those words as she opened the door and poured herself into the driver's seat, slamming the door shut hard.

Things went eerily quiet. The buffeting winds were silenced by half, leaving only the sound of her heaving breaths. "Okay... okay... okay...."

Reagan stabbed her palm against the horn button, holding it there for half a minute as the tinny horn beeped its meager SOS. *Maybe Steffi can hear it!* She released the button and listened, hoping to hear her baby's voice cut through the silence, but it didn't come.

The hesitant ignition fired up on the second try, and she strapped on the shoulder belt.

Reagan couldn't make out anything beyond the steering wheel, so she engaged the windshield wipers, choosing their most powerful speed. As the layer of snow pushed off to the margins, the problem remained. She didn't know which way to go and, even if she did, she couldn't see much at all. Her thoughts were racing, but her heartbeat was in the lead.

She cranked on the heater, knowing full well it would take

several minutes to kick in with any warmth. She pounded the steering wheel.

"Give me something to work with, God! If you're even friggin' there!!"

An approaching car's headlights washed over her, and she held her hand over her brow as she squinted through her tears. As the vehicle passed, things went quiet again. She had nothing to go on, and she knew it.

She felt a weak vibration coming from somewhere. Deep in the thermal layers of her coat, she heard the muffled sound of her phone ringing. "Jeezus!" she cried, as her hand desperately clawed its way into the depths of the pocket, her fingers only making contact with the device on the third ring.

The display clued her in first.

"Hei Li!! Hei Li, gawd, am I glad...."

A voice interrupted her. "Mm... no, not Hei Li... and not God...."

Reagan recognized the man's voice immediately and she choked down the urge to vomit.

"Where... where the *fuck* is my daughter, you spineless son of a bitch?! *Where*?!!!" she bellowed into the mouthpiece, her raw vocal cords doling out what little remained of her voice.

"Now, now... is that any way to start off our conversation, Ray? Goodness." Fynn's voice smoothly dripped its poison into her ear. Reagan clamped her eyes shut, her teeth grinding at the sound. She yanked down the zipper of her coat because it was quickly getting hot in the cab, a combination of the car's heater and her now-boiling blood.

"What the fuck, Fynn! Where is she? Steffi is off limits, you sorry son of a—"

"Ooh, hey. That hurts, especially coming from my *wife*. Wow. Hey, I've got an idea. How about we start again, shall we? Maybe... I don't know..." He kicked into a mocking, sing-song-y voice. "*Hey, honey! Merry Christmas! Steffi and I wanted to surprise you, and–*"

"Give it a rest, Fynn! I asked you a question! Tell me where my daughter is, damn you!"

"First things first."

"Yeah? *Yeah*?! What's the first thing, asshole? Steffi's *hurt*. That's the first thing!" she screamed, her body quaking. She turned down the heater, while making no effort to wipe away her tsunami of tears.

"Steffi is... fine. Okay?"

Reagan listened for elaboration, but it didn't seem to be coming. "Where did you take her?" she asked, her voice calmer than she felt. "Let me talk to her."

"We'll get to that."

"We'll get to that, my ass! Let me talk to her... *now*. Let me hear her voice, Fynn!"

Reagan listened to dead air for the better part of thirty seconds before she got a response, and it wasn't from Fynn.

"*Mom*?!!" Steffi sobbed. "Mom!!"

"Steffi?! Steffi!! *Steffi*... are you okay, baby?! Where did they–?"

Steffi's voice was cut off as the phone was yanked from her. Fynn's voice came back on the line, interrupting Reagan. "Nice try, Ray. There. You got your proof, okay?"

"Listen, Fynn–"

"No, *you* listen, and very carefully, Ray, because time is of the essence, not only for Stef but for all of us. And you aren't exactly in a place to bargain right now, are you?"

A long moment went by without a response. "Are you listening?" he asked.

"I'm listening," Reagan said, sniffing as she wiped away the mess. "What is it you want? And... why the hell are you calling from Hei Li's phone? Did you lose your charger again?" she asked sarcastically.

Fynn's voice was soft, his diction impeccable as he addressed only the initial question.

"What I want, Ray... actually, what I *need* is for you to get in touch with the banker you spoke with the other day. You need to explain your *mistake*. You need to remedy the mess you created, Reagan, and... God, I hate to repeat myself, but I will, just to make sure we're crystal clear on this—*first* thing tomorrow morning. Friday morning at ten, Ray. In person, at the branch. Remove all restrictions, and *any* holds on the accounts, effective the moment you meet with them tomorrow. *At ten.* Are we absolutely clear on what I'm saying here, Ray?"

"*Why*, Fynn? What compelled you to go behind my back, like, like the venomous snake you—obviously—really are? Huh? Do you, like, owe money to an effing *cartel*, Fynn? Is *that* it?"

When it was clear his answer wasn't forthcoming, she probed further.

"How long have you been planning to screw me over, to screw your stepdaughter over, to effing rip away my business—my parents' business—for... for... *what*, you greedy bastard?! Did you think I wouldn't find out? Did you really think—?" She stopped herself.

The silence at the other end was chilly, then he responded. "Did I think what, Ray?"

"Hamburg."

"What about it... Hamburg?"

"Think about it," she answered firmly. "Think about it, and chew on it, you fuck. We'll talk about it tomorrow, after I've gone to the bank and when we meet–you and me–and once you've returned Steffi to me."

"Dammit, Ray–"

"We'll talk in the morning. I'll call you, at this number. And don't forget to charge your fucking phone."

*Click.*

# CHAPTER FIFTY-FOUR

REAGAN SAT BEHIND the wheel for another hour, turning the engine on, then off, then on again in order to run the heater as needed while she waited for a break in the weather and processed her thoughts.

A glance at her smart watch confirmed her suspicion that it wasn't late; it only felt that way because she was utterly exhausted–physically and emotionally. Reagan cursed her predicament and the fact that she was feeling powerless to do anything about it while her daughter was in jeopardy.

She hoped Steffi wasn't in too much pain from her ankle sprain–if that's what it was, and she had to trust that Fynn would muster the modicum of moral character to keep her safe for now.

In the meantime, Reagan had to keep herself safe as well, for both of them.

Her eyes were strained beyond their limits, while their droopy lids threatened to surrender and call it a night. Knowing she couldn't miss her ten o'clock meeting with the banker in the morning, she set her now fully-charged phone's alarm for 07:00, just in case.

Some quick mental math reminded her that she probably had a ninety-plus-minute drive back to Hamburg, and the bank, and that was only if the weather improved significantly. But the way it was looking now, all bets were off.

One thing she did know was that the multiple cups of marzipan kaffee she'd enjoyed earlier were vying for her attention now; she had to pee. Reagan shut off the engine, popped open the door, and climbed out into the falling flakes. The snow was coming down a bit lighter now, she noted, as she assessed the situation and looked around for a stealthy place to squat.

The vehicle parked behind hers was a small cargo van and the space behind it presented her best opportunity to do the deed she hadn't done in the wild since that *apfelwein* party in the twelfth grade.

Reagan waited for a set of headlights to pass and disappear around the corner before she got down to business. The relief was immediate and intense, and she wasted no time getting reassembled and back into the warm car.

As she got herself situated, Reagan resigned herself to having to spend the night here, curbside, hoping for a better weather window in the morning. She locked the car doors, zipped up her coat all the way, and pulled up the hood.

Reagan's fingers fumbled along the edge of her seat until she found the button to recline it for the all-nighter ahead. As the seat's motor slowly whirred, she surrendered to the relative comfort the makeshift bed provided. As her eyes closed, she murmured a prayer to the god she was convinced didn't exist.

*God, please take care of my baby.*

## FRIDAY, DECEMBER 19
## 07:02, CET

It took a couple of minutes, but the source of the incessant beeping eventually became familiar.

Reagan grimaced, her face scrunching as her crusty eyes struggled to take in her surroundings. She licked her lips; her mouth tasted a bit nasty.

It immediately became clear that she wasn't home, nor was she nestled snuggly in a comfy hotel bed. She turned off her phone's alarm as her muddled thoughts sought clarity.

She was laying back, reclined in the torturous driver's seat of a rental MG, and her body was hating her for it. "*Jeezus... Gawd,*" she groaned, arching her achy back as her eyes tried to focus. She whirred the seatback to the upright position and turned on the ignition, firing up the heater and deploying the wipers.

Reagan squinted out the windshield, focusing to the best of her ability, not expecting to see much. She caught her breath. Either she'd gone completely snow-blind or something had changed outside—significantly.

It proved to be the latter.

The snow had stopped. Some early-bird pedestrians were walking the sidewalks, and cars were traversing the drivable streets. There was even evidence of a sunrise in the making.

"Oh, my gawd... thank you!!" she declared, alarmed at how much she sounded like the creature from Steffi's favorite childhood movie, *E. T.* Her stomach growled but she couldn't think about food right now. Her thoughts flashed back to Steffi, to her injury, and to the threatening conversation with the viper whom she shared a name with. She momentarily struggled to remember what day it was, then it hit her.

"Friday. At least it's not the thirteenth."

For a fleeting moment, Reagan considered retrieving her toothbrush from her luggage but quickly decided against it. She could brush her teeth later. Right now, she had to take advantage of this good weather window and, somehow, get her ass to Hamburg before ten.

# CHAPTER FIFTY-FIVE

## HOTEL HANSEHOF
## HAMBURG, GERMANY
## FRIDAY, DECEMBER 19
## 07:11 CET

A BEAM OF SUPERBRIGHT morning sun punched through the opening in the drapes, stabbing Steffi in the eyes as if from a laser. She blinked several times and rubbed her face in an attempt to become oriented, but she was in a fog from the sedative Fynn had slipped into her Döner sandwich for the drive from Lübeck.

She didn't remember much, but as she turned over in the twin bed, her ankle loudly complained, serving to remind her of the evening's events.

As Steffi looked around the room, she noticed the rumpled linens on the queen bed next to hers, providing another quick flash of recognition as she remembered being more than a little creeped out by the sight of her bastard stepdad sleeping in the same bed with the ugly asshole–the one with the weird mark on his face and the freaky feet.

She could hear water running in a basin; it was coming from the bathroom across the room. With its door open, it was situated only a few feet from the main door that exited to the hallway, and she quickly surmised she wouldn't be able to make a dash for it, especially with a wobbly wheel.

Steffi pulled back the covers and tested her foot as she stood. It still hurt, but it definitely wasn't broken and probably not fully sprained. She'd suffered worse on the volleyball court and hoped she could shake it off soon. She hopped over to the window and snuck a peek through the drapes.

A few buildings looked slightly familiar, she thought, but then everything over here seemed to look the same. In the distance, she saw sparkly reflections coming off a body of water.

Steffi turned away from the window, looked toward the bathroom to gauge any activity, and picked up a laminated card from the nearby nightstand.

*Hotel Hansehof, Hamburg. Breakfast available. Fish Market, a ten-minute walk.*

The sound of a razor tapping against porcelain got her attention and she quickly returned the card to where she had found it. She sat back on the bed, her thoughts racing. *Where's my phone?*

Steffi scanned the nightstand, then carefully slid open the drawer. Nothing but a Bible and a condom. On the nearby chair lay her jeans, folded, next to her shoes. She looked down to her feet and only then noticed she was wearing unfamiliar pajamas.

*Somebody fucking undressed me! Shit!* She wondered which one of them had, and both prospects were beyond creepy.

A loud cough came from the bathroom, which was immediately followed by an impressive fart. The sounds coming from the bathroom indicated it wasn't Fynn. In all her years living under a roof with him, she'd never heard him fart like that.

She ran her fingers through her hair. *Think, Steffi!* As she brought her arm down, she noticed something that might be useful. She was still wearing her smart watch. Could she get a message through? She had to try.

Her dainty, fifteen-year-old fingers adeptly navigated the tiny keyboard on her watch's display as she pounded out an abbreviated status report she prayed would reach her mother.

> *Mom! R U OK? We R in Hamburg. With asshole Fynn and some creepy guy. Hotel Hansehof. 10 min from fish market. Haven't found my phone yet but texting from my watch. Tell me U R OK!!*

*What's the plan??? ♥ Stef*

Steffi hit Send, along with a Hail Mary prayer that the message would be received.

Another fart—this one louder—provided the perfect walk-on music for its composer as Ekkehard emerged from the bathroom, shuffling on his naked stumps, and wrapped only in a modest towel at the waist.

The sight was circus-worthy, and a shiver ran up Steffi's spine as she averted her eyes.

"Guten Morgen," he said, the corners of his mouth curling into what could only be interpreted as a pervy smile. "You are hungry?"

## MOISLINGER ALLEE/B207
## LEAVING LÜBECK
## FRIDAY, DECEMBER 19
## 07:25, CET

Reagan squinted against the morning sun as she took the third exit from the roundabout and onto Moislinger Allee.

She hated roundabouts—always had—but this route was a necessary evil since she'd decided to take her chances on a lesser travelled road to avoid highways, in hopes there might be fewer chances of playing bumper cars with others as she limped toward Hamburg.

Without Steffi as her copilot and chief mirror monitor, Reagan aimed to keep to the slower lanes for the trip, to the degree possible, which she knew would add a good half hour to her journey. Still, having left early, she hoped to be there a little after 09:00. Enough time to grab a brötchen, brush her teeth, and make herself look a little less homeless for her meeting.

As Reagan settled onto the new piece of road, she moved to the rightmost lane and throttled back, leaving ample room between her and the car ahead.

Her phone chimed an alert, as did her smartwatch. She dared not take her eyes off the road, so she stabbed the button on her phone, commanding it to read the message audibly.

*"One new message, received 07:20, from caller Steffi. New message:*

*Mom! Are you okay? We are in Hamburg. With asshole Fynn and some creepy guy. Hotel Hansehof. 10 min from fish market. Haven't found my phone yet but texting from my watch. Tell me you are okay! What's the plan? Heart emoji, Stef."*

"Jeezus! God!!" Reagan cried out as she listened to the robotic voice read Steffi's urgent message. As her hand went to her mouth, her right front wheel nearly drifted into a rail, and she had to jerk the wheel back to stay in her lane.

*"Would you like to reply?"* the voice prompted.

Reagan's thoughts were going a kilometer a minute, and she decided it best not to chance a return call. She knew what these two monsters were capable of, and she couldn't put Steffi at further risk by acknowledging the receipt of new intel.

"No!" Reagan barked in reply.

"All right, then," the AI helper responded.

*Hotel Hansehof. 10 minutes from the fish market.*

She didn't yet have a plan, but she had an hour and a half to work on one. Against better judgment, Reagan pressed her foot a little more firmly on the accelerator.

# CHAPTER FIFTY-SIX

## HOTEL HANSEHOF
## FRIDAY, 07:30 CET

STEFFI SAT IN the leatherette chair near the window, her eyes shifting around as she tried her best not to stare at the morbid goings-on.

The creepy man sat on the edge of the queen bed, wearing only a skimpy pair of speedo underwear as he massaged lotion onto the smooth ends of what remained of his legs. He had his back to Steffi, and she started weighing the chances of bolting past him and out the door.

She wondered if she could dig down deep and power herself through her ankle pain and to safety before this guy started motoring down the hall after her like a rabid corgi. She looked at her ankle. The swelling was reduced and the pain moderate. It might be her best chance. Her thoughts were interrupted by the sound of a card key opening the door.

Fynn stepped in, carrying a white paper bag and stopped dead in his tracks as he took in the scene. "Jesus! What the–?!! Put on some damn clothes. That's my daughter!"

"*Stepdaughter*!" Steffi interjected, only too happy to correct him.

Fynn nodded his agreement and set the bag of pastries on the side table, while Ekkehard grabbed his special Velcro-seamed trousers and slid them on. Curiosity got the better of Steffi as she couldn't help but watch the process involved with attaching his liners, followed by the blades.

Fynn's gaze turned to Steffi, and she stared back at him with a combination of contempt and disgust. The cat was out of the bag. The man had been the closest thing to a father figure for her entire life and now, she realized, it was *all* a lie.

Fynn approached Steffi, picking up the pastry bag and holding it out to her as a pathetic peace offering. He seemed to be considering an explanation, if not an apology, but she wasn't interested. She turned toward the window.

"Stef...."

"Don't."

"You must think I'm—"

"I must think you're... what?" She could feel her pulse quicken as she turned to face him. "An a-hole?! Yep!! A lying, evil, sorry excuse for a human being? Absolutely... I *must* think that, and for effing good reason. What the hell, Fynn?"

"I'm—"

Steffi's mocking laugh cut him off. She shook her head, finding it absolutely incredulous that this imposter had pretended to be a loving husband to her mother, and a supportive stepfather to herself, while all this time living under the same roof and deceiving them both.

"Does my mom even know you're... frigging gay?"

"You watch your mouth."

His admonishment held no weight. She brushed it off

and held her ground, surprising herself in the process as she tapped into a pocket of strength she didn't know she had. Her cheeks flushed as she continued.

"Or what, Fynn? Oh, and tell me, does Mom know you have an apparent fetish for circus people?" she blurted, gesturing to the other man standing by the bed. "Sorry… no insult intended," she added, addressing Ekkehard.

Fynn snarled, his teeth gnashing as he wadded up the treat bag and threw it at her, bouncing it off her chest. She had never seen this side of her stepfather and her eyes widened.

"I'm done playing nice with you… you… ungrateful, disrespectful little snot!" he hissed. "After all I've done for you and your mother!"

"Oh, I'm sorry," she began, bravely tapping into sarcasm. "I guess I should be effing *grateful* for being… kidnapped… by you and your goon lover, and for whatever else you've got up your sleeve here. Because I will never, ever, hold even the smallest measure of *respect* for you, you fucktard! You're a–!"

The roundhouse slap came out of nowhere, and with its velocity delivered a sharp, stinging outline of his palm on Steffi's cheek. It shocked both of them. Steffi's eyes went wide, welling with tears of pain and shock. "Enough!!" he barked.

Ekkehard had been following the exchange, his eyes going back and forth between the players like he was watching match point at center court. His gaze landed on Fynn and stayed there.

Steffi stared back at Fynn defiantly. She held back the urge to cry, refusing to give him the satisfaction of a perceived victory.

"We leave in ten minutes," Fynn said, addressing them both as he turned away. Steffi held her tongue as she snatched up her clothes and coat and carried them into the bathroom, slammed the door, and locked it behind her.

Steffi stood at the sink, staring in the mirror as she splashed water on her face and patted it dry. Her cheek was still reddened from Fynn's slap, and she found herself grappling with competing emotions of anger and fear.

She glanced at her smartwatch and noticed she hadn't received a reply to her text message. Her mind raced as she slipped on yesterday's clothes. She made no attempt at enhancing her appearance. She opted for the *kidnapped young girl* look.

Outside the door, she could make out the muffled voices of Fynn and his accomplice conversing in German. She didn't understand a word of it.

In the absence of a proper toothbrush, she ran her finger around her teeth and rinsed her mouth with water. As she pulled on her warm coat, she slipped her hands into the outer pockets. A package of gum, a few euros, and–her new favorite Christmas gift: her translator earbuds!

*Please tell me they didn't take my–!* Her hands frantically plumbed the depths of her inside zipper pocket where she found her– *phone!! Yes!*

Steffi turned on the sink's faucet and let it run as she sat on the toilet and relieved herself, flushing it twice to help mask any clues as she powered up the device. She muted the phone's volume and any alert tones.

As the screen populated with icons she took notice of its remaining battery life: 62%. It would have to do.

Steffi stuffed the buds into her ears, teased her hair down over them, and turned off the faucet. She zipped her jacket and walked back into the room, all business, and avoiding any eye contact.

"Los geht's," Fynn said, handing Ekkehard his coat and grabbing his own.

*Let's go.* Steffi harbored a secret smile. She'd understood him.

# CHAPTER FIFTY-SEVEN

## FISCHMARKT HAMBURG ALTONA
## FRIDAY
## 08:35, CET

FYNN EXITED HIS market stall and locked up behind himself. He had inspected the new industrial refrigerator unit the technician had installed, finding its larger capacity and cooling efficiency an upgrade. He was a bit peeved, however, that the older cooler's condenser failure had proved to be unrepairable after all, resulting in the need for the expense. His invoice had been ridiculous.

Fynn wiped the sweat from his brow, having had to load the old unit onto a dolly himself and wheel it around to the back of the building, near the trash receptacles. It would be taken away by a recycling company tomorrow, thankfully, because it might prove to be smelly.

Like a starved wolf, Fynn sunk his teeth into the stale brötchen, tearing off a large piece and tossing the remainder into the street. A bevy of screeching gulls immediately staked claims to it and a noisy fight ensued.

As he chewed on his worry, anger, and an unsavory break-fast, he pulled out his phone and checked in with his inbox. There were several new emails from clients, mostly markets, each confirming their desired order for Sunday. He thumbed in replies to each, assuring them their deliveries would be timely and guaranteeing their seafood to be fresh-caught and of the highest quality.

He turned his attention to two more new emails, these from his newly formed import partnerships. Both compa-nies confirmed delivery of his shipments, arriving Saturday at 09:00 and 09:30 respectively. Based on the customers' reac-tions the previous week, Fynn had tripled his orders for all of the Alaskan products, while quadrupling the order for Maine lobsters.

Each vendor had attached their corresponding invoice, each of which also stated, in very clear terms and bold font, that payment in full was due upon delivery.

Fynn spit the remaining wad of soggy, stale breadstuff onto the street and wiped his mouth. He took a deep breath and held it an extra moment, hoping to release at least some of his considerable stress as he exhaled. He shook a cigarette from its pack and lit it, taking an extraordinarily deep drag. He had everything riding on these shipments and there would be no room for error.

He consulted his watch, imagining–*willing*–Reagan's prompt arrival at the bank. He pocketed his phone, pulled out the other–Hei Li's–and thumbed in a message:

> *For Steffi's sake, don't fuck this up, Ray.*

## LANDUNGSBRÜCKEN
## ST. PAULI PIERS, HAMBURG
## FRIDAY, 09:15 CET

Fynn's walk back to the car had been a brisk one, elevating both his pulse rate and the clarity of his thinking during the three-kilometer stretch along the seaboard.

As he reached the St. Pauli Hafenstrasse, the clock atop the stone tower became readable, reminding him of the impending rendezvous time at the top of the hour. He took another bite of the particularly feeble fischbrötchen he picked up along the way, tossing the rest against the curb for the scrappy seabirds to sort out.

Hamburg's 700-foot-long floating jetty, the Landungs-brücken, was set on pontoons constructed in 1839. Though it had originally been built for coal storage, the jetties now served as points of departure for shuttle ferries, harbor cruises, and steamships.

Fynn watched as a group of passengers disembarked an arriving ferry, his nostrils flaring as he took in the smells of the sea. The vehicle was parked just ahead, and he could see two recognizable silhouettes inside as he approached.

He yanked open the door and climbed in, shooting a look first at the backseat passenger and then the front, before shifting his gaze to the rearview mirror and Steffi.

"Well, did everybody have a nice visit while I was gone?"

Steffi looked away, directing her attention out the window.

Her scowl answered his question. Fynn picked up the crumpled pastry bag sitting on his armrest. Judging by its weight, he knew it wasn't empty. "You didn't eat your breakfast, Stef."

"Not hungry," she muttered, her grumbling stomach exposing her lie.

Fynn started the car and turned to Ekkehard. "Any problems while I was gone?"

Ekkehard shook his head in reply.

Fynn clicked his seatbelt and backed out of their spot. "Okay then. Los geht's!"

Steffi's ears picked up on the translation a fraction of a second later. *Let's go!* Whether or not she would be offered any further nuggets in German remained to be seen, but she hoped so.

## CAFÉ BITTE
## HAMBURG FINANCIAL DISTRICT
## FRIDAY, 09:40 CET

The drive had been a white-knuckle one, as Reagan's limited visibility had forced her to surrender to the faster drivers, which meant all of them. Keeping to the right-most lanes, she had avoided lane changes whenever possible.

Still, she had made good time and made good use of her early arrival by transferring her iPad and a few other essentials from her suitcase to her backpack. While she was at it, she liberated her toiletry bag and availed herself of the restroom in a café where she'd purchased an apfel pastry and a tall coffee with an added shot.

As she brushed her teeth and tried to tame the bird's nest that was her hair, she stared at her reflection. Her expression was earnest, her tired eyes burning, and she could almost swear she saw straight through them, to the raging bonfire of black, dead cells piled up inside.

A quick glance at her smartwatch caused her pulse to quicken. It confirmed two things: the bank opened in fifteen minutes, and she hadn't missed any messages from Steffi.

Reagan chucked the uneaten pastry into the trash, tossed back the rest of her coffee, and threw caution to the wind as she exited to the car. *Mama's coming, baby!*

# CHAPTER FIFTY-EIGHT

FYNN'S FINGERS DRUMMED nervously against the leather-wrapped steering wheel as he made his way toward the financial district. Nobody had said a word since they'd left the Landungsbrücken, and he knew Miss Loquacious in the backseat didn't know any German, so he switched to it as he turned to Ekkehard.

"Wir sind in zehn minuten da. Sie sollte besser pünktlich sein. Andernfalls müssen wir unserem Gast möglicherweise wehtun," he said, his eyes checking in with the rearview as he made reference.

There was a momentary delay and as Steffi's earbuds delivered the translation, she concentrated on its message—and the urgency of impending danger. Her eyes involuntarily went wider, and she tried to conceal them from her captors.

*We'll be there in ten minutes. She'd better be on time. If not, we may need to hurt our guest.*

Steffi lowered her chin as she feigned nodding off, all the while shielding her interaction with her smartwatch behind the driver's seat as she urgently input an abbreviated text to her mother.

*≥ we r driving... 10 min from where u r 2 meet.*

*heard fynn say u better be on time or they will have to "hurt" me!*

*wtf?! getting scared! R U OK?! My ringer's off - u can msg me! <3*

Reagan was five minutes out as the gleaming towers of downtown came into view. Her smartwatch vibrated. So did her phone. The morning traffic was thick, the drivers aggressive, and any attempt to glance at either device would surely risk a collision. She had to press on and check the message later.

## LÜBECK BLANKENSEE AIRPORT
## FRIDAY, DECEMBER 19
## 09:55, CET

The Pilatus PC-12 NG turboprop finished taxiing, cutting its single engine as it reached the outer hanger. The flight time from Paris Orly airport had taken just shy of two hours, which was a short hop for the pilot and two client-passengers. But for the multitude of crustacean passengers in the cargo hold, the trip from the U.S. had been an eternity.

The circuitous journey across the pond from Maine to

Germany had begun by international charter jet to Paris. It had been a bit clandestine in order to avoid import manifests, tariffs, and customs inspections. Cash payments to the right people in the U.S., Paris, and Germany had greased the wheels for smooth passage, and the declared cargo consisted of musical instruments as far as anyone knew—or cared.

This aircraft's flight represented only the second such delivery of live lobsters they had made for this new client—the first being a week before—and he had promised not only payment in full on delivery, but a generous cash bonus for a safe and timely transport to his fish market.

This shipment was much larger than the previous week's, and it wasn't going to unload itself. The two burly passengers were all business as they exited the aircraft and met the pilot on the port side as he opened the four-foot by four-foot cargo door, aft of the wing. No words or smiles.

By all appearances the two men could have been twins, or at least gym buddies. Ingo and Ulf wore matching black, V-neck tees that stretched against their muscular torsos, and they both had necks like Fred Flintstone. The taller of the two, Ingo, wore a tightly tailored sport jacket that concealed his Glock but not his guns.

The cargo ramp was positioned and, with great effort, the first of two heavy, extra-large Anvil Road cases was wheeled down to the tarmac and a waiting cargo truck. Temperature gauges were checked before the cases were wheeled up onto the motorized lift of the small cube truck for the anticipated hour-plus drive to Hamburg.

Each case had been retrofitted with customized cooling units as well as a ventilation system to assure the inner Styrofoam boxes were protected during the journey. Wet packing materials and frozen gel packs helped maintain the cool, damp environment for the hundreds of crustaceans, each packed tail down and claws up.

It was almost like riding in coach.

To the casual observer, this was a touring rock band unloading their gear for their next show. For appearances, the imaginary band's name had been playfully stenciled on the sides of both cases:

## *BARACK LOBSTER*

# CHAPTER FIFTY-NINE

## COMMERZBANK
## JUNGFERNSTIEG, HAMBURG
## FRIDAY, 09:58, CET

"**D**A IST SIE hier," Ekkehard said, pointing through the windshield to the red SUV that had entered the far side of the parking lot.

*There, she's here.* Steffi both understood and had a visual on her mother's rental car. Her pulse quickened and her hands became clammy as she watched her maneuver the MG into a space near the bank's entrance and exit the vehicle. Reagan slung her backpack over her left shoulder and entered the building.

Fynn checked his watch and smiled. "Braves Mädchen," he muttered. *Good girl.* He switched to English for Steffi's benefit and made eye contact via the rearview. "Now we wait."

Reagan crossed the lobby to the desk with the placard marked Neue Konten. *New Accounts.* The banker was finishing up with another customer, so Reagan took a seat nearby and checked her watch. Her eyes went wide.

≥ *we r driving... 10 min from where u r 2 meet.*

*heard fynn say u better be on time or they will have to "hurt" me!*

*wtf?! getting scared! R U OK?! My ringer's off - u can msg me! <3*

Sweat trickled down Reagan's pits as she read Steffi's missive a second time through. She looked up, scanning the lobby as if through a viewfinder, her limited field of vision searching the faces for Fynn, for the tall man, for Steffi. *They must be waiting outside. Shit.*

Another message came through, vibrating both of her devices:

> *we are in the lot. saw u go in. be careful mom!!!*

Reagan's throat went dry. She started to thumb in a reply when she was interrupted.

"Danke... thank you for waiting. I can see you now," the woman said, her English impeccable. She motioned her over.

Reagan stood, her legs shaky, as she approached the desk. Her attempt at a smile failed.

"Guten Morgen. How may I help you? Did you wish to open a new–?"

"I need to speak with my accounts manager, Otto Becker, please," Reagan blurted, not meaning to appear rude. "I'm sorry, he's expecting me."

"Certainly," the woman said, picking up her phone. "Who may I say is here to see him?"

"Dunkel. Reagan Dunkel."

The woman nodded, then spoke quietly into the receiver. "A Frau Dunkel is here to see you. Reagan Dunkel. Yes... danke." She hung up the phone and smiled. "His office is on the second floor. If you'll follow me, bitte."

Steffi glanced at her phone; the messaging app indicated her text had just been read. She thumbed in a pithy follow-up–the praying hands emoji–hoping to God her mom had a plan.

# CHAPTER SIXTY

OTTO BECKER WAS a short man, only five foot five inches tall and slight of build. He was a relatively youthful thirty-eight years old, and his ambition had resulted in not only an early promotion to Senior Accounts Manager but also an expensive divorce and premature hair loss.

The canned ceiling lighting reflected off his shiny, bald head, and he steepled his fingers as he watched Reagan through his thick lenses while she signed the pile of documents before her, using his favorite pen.

Reagan's right foot rocked nervously as she added her signature to the last of the documents. She clicked the ballpoint closed and handed it back to him. "Whew...."

"Yes, many documents," he said, taking the pen and placing it squarely in front of him on the desktop. It took him several attempts to align the pen perfectly in the center of the desk, as if his anal retentiveness might result in some Feng shui harmony and balance in his little banking world.

Reagan couldn't help but watch the minute back-and-forth

corrections as he endeavored to return his writing utensil to its designated place.

"There," he muttered to himself before looking back up at his client. "Everything is in order, as you requested, Frau Dunkel. I must say, based on the circumstances, and the recent—what should we call them—*anomalies* with your account, I believe you've made the right decisions today."

"I appreciate your help, Herr Becker," she replied, stuffing the portfolio containing her copies into her backpack, behind the iPad.

"Bitte... and it's Otto," he said with a bashful smile as he held out his hand.

Reagan stood, noting what felt like an attraction vibe, but she couldn't be certain. He was nice enough and seemed harmless. She smiled, shook his clammy, outstretched hand, and stealthily wiped hers on her pants leg as she turned to leave.

"Would you like me to... show you out?"

"Danke. I think I know the way. Auf Wiedersehen, Otto."

Reagan's mind was racing, and she'd lost all sense of time. She opted for the stairs rather than taking the lift. With each step her pulse quickened as she neared the lobby, fully dreading the necessary encounter to come.

As she crossed the lobby she scanned the faces, not entirely sure whether or not she would be ambushed. Approaching the exit doors, she looked at her watch: 11:15. Her meeting had taken much longer than anticipated. *Over an hour?! Shit!*

She retrieved her phone and took the empty seat in the waiting area next to the New Accounts gal's desk. *A message from Steffi!* It was brief and, knowing her daughter to be the world's fastest texter, Reagan had long ago learned to decipher her abbreviations and overlook errant spelling.

The praying hands emoji said it all. Reagan began thumbing in a response:

> *Are you okay?*

Steffi had been chomping at the bit for any kind of communication, and her reply came within seconds:

> *Mom!!! yes but i don't know for how long... fynn hit me earlier. U r married to an asshole and... spoiler... he's gay AF! R U ok?!*

Reagan's brow furrowed as she punched in a reply:

> *I'm ok. Hit you?!! Is there somebody else with you right now or just Fynn?*

*And ... what do you mean... gay? What kind of car are you in?*

> *we R in a stupid sobb i think... black. back of the parking lot. we saw u go in.*

*me, fynn, and his transformer luvver with the messed up face tattoo. plan???*

*effing scared now!*

Reagan's face grew longer as she processed the threat assessment . .... *messed up face tattoo! The Tall Man!!* Rapid-fire images flashed through her mind: her parents... the train station... the man in the wheelchair... Ames's confirmation of her attacker... and this same murderous man now sitting in the car with her daughter, just outside.

Reagan's digits flew across the tiny keyboard. She didn't have a terrific plan, so she'd have to punt.

> *Steffi... I'm walking out of the bank in a minute and will drive away.*

*I know Fynn will follow my car because I have something he wants.*

*Plans are shaky but please trust me, honey! I won't let them harm you...*

*I love you more than ANYTHING!!*

Reagan closed her eyes as she waited for a response. It came fifteen seconds later:

> *K... b careful! ILYSMF*

Reagan stood, pocketed the phone, and steeled herself. She had her key fob at the ready as she exited through the automatic doors. She paused for a couple of seconds, pretending to look at her watch, while actually getting a stealthy visual on the location of Fynn's Saab.

She jumped into her chariot and made the tires squeal as she made a hasty dash toward the exit, badly scraping two parked Mercedes sedans, while losing her own driver's side mirror in the process. *Shit! Sorry! Crap!!*

She tamped down her instinct to stop and leave apology notes for each as she abandoned all concerns for her own vehicle and made her way out onto the busy boulevard. *It's a rental!*

"There she is!!" Ekkehard cried out, pointing, as if he'd just spotted Moby Dick.

"Dammit, Ray!!" Fynn hissed as he fired up the ignition. He stomped the gas pedal, and Steffi was thrust against her seat as the Saab screeched from its lurch, in hot pursuit.

*Go, Mom!!!*

# CHAPTER SIXTY-ONE

## FISCHMARKT ADJACENT
## FRIDAY
## 11:40, CET

INGO RUBBED HIS temples and looked over at his driver, wondering how in God's name anyone could call the pounding crap blaring from the stereo *music*. Ingo's migraine had kicked in and his tolerance for Ulf's hip hop had just come to an end. He reached over and switched it off.

"Hey..." Ulf grunted his complaint.

"Hey... enough of that dance party shit. Take the next left onto Rödingsmarkt. Less traffic. Almost there."

"Can we, uh, make a stop before we get there?" Ulf asked as he made the turn.

"Why the hell would we want to do that? We only have a few minutes to go."

"I..."

"I... what?"

"I need... to go potty."

Ingo couldn't believe his ears. "You need to... go... *potty*. What are we, five years old?! Are we in *Kinder* now?" Ingo shook his head. The throbbing wasn't helping. "Unbelievable."

"Can we? It's kind of an emergency."

"No chance, man. You can do whatever you need to *after* we make our delivery. I'm not risking our early bonus. Potty...."

Reagan weaved through traffic, blaring her horn as she barreled the hundred meters down Graskellerbrücke before hanging a right on Rödingsmarkt. The Saab was a few car lengths behind, but Fynn still had her in his sights.

"She's heading to the Fischmarkt!" Fynn blurted, mostly for his own benefit, as he negotiated the turn, narrowly avoiding a head-on crash with a cargo van.

"Dummkopf!!" Ulf cried out as he turned the wheel sharply to avoid the idiot who had swung into his lane. A series of loud thuds came from the cargo area as the heavy Anvil cases of seafood complained against their restraints and slammed the walls.

"Scheisse!!" Ingo screamed, waving his fist at the Audi. "Moron probably has to go potty," he muttered for Ulf's benefit, shooting him a glance.

Reagan squinted against the bright sun as she flew down Rödingsmarkt, continuing onto Baumwall/Binnenhafenbrücke and past the Baumwall subway station.

Her father had been a fan of car chases in movies, and she flashed back to watching *Bullitt* with him on more than one occasion. Now she was living it–and as a legally-blind person in a rental car–and everything was on the line.

She could see the familiar banks of the River Elbe now and, as she lowered her window, the distinct smells and a thousand memories wafted in.

She was rapidly approaching the Fischmarkt. If her eyes were to completely give out now, she could probably navigate by her olfactory nerve.

*Game time, Reagan!*

# CHAPTER SIXTY-TWO

STEFFI'S HEART WAS pounding; she felt utterly helpless as she bounced around in the Saab's back seat, praying for her mom and hoping she had some kind of plan.

She risked breaking the long-held silence as they approached the river. "What the hell is it you want anyway, Fynn? What are you going to do?" she challenged, her eyes piercing the rearview.

"Shut up," Fynn hissed, shooting a menacing look back at her in the mirror before breaking away. As he completed a highspeed turn they could see Reagan's MG, a couple hundred yards ahead. "Not one word from you," he growled, punctuating his threat with a stern glance over his shoulder.

As he returned his attention to the street ahead, something out of the corner of his eye caught his attention. It was a small cargo truck, and it looked like the same one they had nearly collided with minutes before, motoring aggressively along his right side.

"What the hell—?"

This got Ekkehard's attention as well, and as he looked over at them, he waved a one-finger salute to the driver.

"Dummkopf!" Ulf yelled back, returning the gesture with conviction.

Fynn didn't have time for this nonsense; he stomped hard on the accelerator, leaving the truck in his wake as he closed the distance between him and the MG. A tight smile began to form and Fynn muttered to himself, "You have nowhere to run, Ray."

# CHAPTER SIXTY-THREE

REAGAN HAD TO slow considerably as she navigated the final turn, taking her to a place very familiar for her: the Altonaer Fischmarkt.

It was impossible to miss, even for the visually challenged, as there happened to be a fully functional U-434 submarine docked there, its black hull half visible above the waterline, just outside in Hamburg's harbor.

With severely strained eyes, Reagan scanned the area, looking for an advantageous place to park. She didn't trust Fynn at all, and she was hoping for a place with a crowd—even if it was a small one.

Reagan noticed a half-dozen tourists assembled outside the attraction awaiting their tiny group's guided tour of the cold war-era diesel submarine, and her mind briefly flashed back to an obligatory tour of the cramped quarters with her father twenty years before. He'd been obsessed with the movie *Das Boot*. A lovely tour for contortionists, the U-434 tour had ruined her for small spaces.

With no visible parking there, Reagan continued on, pulling around the back of the Fischmarkt, by the rear doors and alleyway adjacent to the space she and her family had operated for decades. She was familiar with it. So was Fynn.

Even though the market was closed, there was no getting away from the residual smell from the sheer volumes of seafood exchanged here. A hundred gulls couldn't be wrong.

Reagan's nostrils flared and her gag reflex challenged her.

About fifty yards away, a couple of laborers were busy fixing a drainage pipe. *So much for a crowd.*

Reagan didn't bother killing the ignition. She exited the vehicle and, after scanning the lot, grabbed her backpack from the passenger seat. She extracted two items from it: her iPad and a thick, legal-sized manila envelope.

She walked around to the other side of the vehicle, choosing to use it as a barrier between her and any incoming trouble. She watched the way she had come in.

That's where Fynn would be coming from.

She closed her eyes for a moment and, against better judgment, took a deep breath in through her nose. It was like smelling salts to her, and the effect hit her like a jolt of electricity.

Reagan's eyes popped open wide just as she heard the Saab racing toward her. Her daughter was in that car, helpless and terrified, and Reagan knew she couldn't make any mistakes. She steeled her spine and stood her ground as Fynn pulled up ten feet away. The driver's side of the car was facing her, and he powered down his window.

He turned off the ignition and looked at Reagan, a smug smile on his face, which she found sickening.

"Hi, honey. Wow, it's great to see you," Fynn said, dripping sarcasm infused with danger. The sound of his voice made her cringe.

Reagan looked away, turning her gaze to the back seat where she could confirm the presence of Steffi. She brought her right hand to her chest as a sign of strength and love to her daughter, then turned her attention to the man seated up front.

"Mom!" Steffi cried out.

"Not now!" Fynn barked. "Not… yet."

"Are you okay, Steffi?" Reagan called out to her, ignoring Fynn. She turned back to look at Fynn, her expression drilling him with her scorn. "You effing asshole. Whatever the hell you think you want—and I've got a very good idea what that is now—it has *nothing* to do with Steffi. Leave our—" She paused to correct herself. "Leave *my* daughter out of this!"

Fynn climbed out of the Saab and shot a glance back at Steffi before reengaging with Reagan. "Your daughter—Steffi— is fine. And she'll remain fine as long as you've done what I asked you to do."

"You'll get nothing until I get Steffi. You give her back to me, unharmed, and let us go. Only then will you get what's yours," Reagan replied firmly. "That's the deal."

Fynn stared back at his wife, long and hard. Reagan held his stare, refusing to blink first. "As you wish, Ray," he finally said, looking over his shoulder and giving his partner a nod.

Reagan held her breath as she watched the Saab's front passenger door open and a lanky, birthmark-challenged monster climb out. He looked at her, reading her reaction to him, and then he smiled a hideous smile.

A shiver shot down her spine like so much lightning. She tamped it down to the best of her ability, not wanting to appear outwardly shaken or surrender what little power she still possessed. Reagan remained expressionless, although she was screaming inside.

This man—this soulless killer—was far uglier and more grotesque than she had realized from the photos she had studied. Knowing what he had been involved with, what he had done to her parents, and to her best friend, made him all the more repulsive and despicable.

She'd expected someone much taller, however.

Ekkehard turned his back to Reagan, opened the rear door, and nodded for the young captive to come out. Several seconds went by before Steffi slid herself across the seat and emerged, her red eyes puffy and her lip visibly quaking as she looked at her mother.

Reagan tamped down her hatred for the two men just long enough to exude the confidence she herself didn't feel. The sight of Steffi looking so vulnerable clawed at her motherly instincts; it made her want to run to her daughter, but she knew it wasn't an option.

Instead, she made an attempt at a half-smile for Steffi. "Are you okay, baby?"

Steffi pushed the hair away from her eyes. Her expression telegraphed her fear.

"Have they hurt you?" Reagan probed further, gesturing to the two men. "Please tell me if they have."

Steffi suddenly looked five years old; she shook her head. "What do they want, Mom?" she asked weakly.

"Let's see, what do they want?" she said, turning to Fynn. "Maybe we should ask your wonderful *stepfather* what it is he wants," Reagan continued, glaring at the man she had once loved, and once known, until very recently.

Fynn stared back. This wasn't on the agenda.

"C'mon, why don't you tell us, Fynn. You've obviously gone to a great deal of trouble. Tell us—tell your *family*, assembled here—just what is it that you feel you're lacking in your little life. I mean, obviously it's becoming abundantly clear that your family no longer means anything to you."

Fynn's jaw clenched, and his hands began to ball up into fists at his side. Still, he said nothing. But Reagan wasn't done.

"And, it appears, you've let *greed*—hell, you've let sheer *evil*—take over, and… well, we're now realizing this has been a long time in the making. Hasn't it, Fynn? Tell me, am I getting warm?"

"Enough!" Fynn hissed. He took a step toward Reagan.

During her cross-examination, Reagan had stealthily powered up her iPad. She punched in her password and clicked on the lone file folder's icon. "If it pleases the court," she began, "I'd like to present Exhibit A…."

"Stop the shit, Ray! I've got—" Fynn barked, not at all amused.

Reagan held up her hand; she wasn't about to be dismissed. She'd come too far.

"Don't worry… this won't take long," she replied as she found the desired file and, with it, her nerve.

"What the hell do you think you're trying to accomplish? You don't hold any cards here. Just hand over the bank doc—"

"Here we go," she muttered for his benefit, cutting him off. "How about we take a little trip down Memory Lane, shall we?" Reagan paused as she spun the screen to face Fynn. He took another step forward, his hand outstretched as if to grab the device.

"Nuh-uh," she said, pulling the iPad back toward her. "You can see it just fine from right there."

Fynn stopped, his mouth forming a tight line as he huffed out a sigh. He looked at his watch, then back at Reagan. "Make this quick, Ray. You're pissing me off more than a little now."

She let the first image populate, full screen, and held it out. Fynn strained his eyes, his head tilting like a confused dog as he took in the black-and-white photo. It took him a few moments. His brow furrowed. His eyes met Reagan's.

"I know. It's been a little while... a dozen years, actually. The *train* station. I was there. You were there. Steffi was there, though she was only three," Reagan said, pausing to engage the other man. "And, you were there, too, scarecrow!" she said with mocking excitement.

Ekkehard's shoulders straightened as he and Fynn exchanged glances.

"Oh, and *my parents* were there!" Reagan declared, watching for Fynn's reaction as she ran through a series of sequential images taken at the platform that day, pausing for several seconds in between. "Jogging any memories yet, guys?"

"Give me that damned thing!" Fynn yelled. "This is bullshit, and you know it!"

"Is it? Hm... the police may have a different opinion."

"What are you talking about?!"

"Oh, they'll be receiving a copy of this little slideshow–with extensive notes–if anything were to happen to Steffi or me, I promise you. So, I suggest you just shut the fuck up for a second." Reagan held her ground and advanced to the next image.

Steffi was listening very intently now. This was a side of her mother she had never witnessed before, and a whole new respect for her badass mom was rapidly forming.

"Our friend here," Reagan began, pausing to gesture at the other man, "oh, I'm sorry, we haven't been properly introduced, but we can clearly see him in these next images, posing as a decrepit man in the wheelchair here."

She advanced to the next photo, then the next, before she continued.

"And, after this supposed stranger makes eye contact with *you*, Fynn, you walk away from my departing train's platform, guiding my dear, unsuspecting parents as you go, and..." She clicked to the next photo. "... wheelchair man has suddenly been *healed*, having left his burdensome chair behind, and *walked* away with *you*! It's a damned *miracle*, ain't it? Praise *Jeezus!*" she cried out, sounding not unlike a televangelist.

She paused for effect and continued, her voice getting stronger, her tone more prosecutorial. "And, at your direction, he pushed my dear parents–your employers–and the people who stood in your way to inherit their family business–to their *deaths* on the train tracks, *Fynn Dunkel.*"

If there had been a jury present, they would have gasped. As it was, Steffi's eyes went wide, her expression slack-jawed, while a couple of pipefitters stood there with their hands on their hips as they listened to the blistering testimony from fifty yards away.

Ekkehard had heard enough as well. He walked around to the front of the car as if to rush Reagan, but Fynn held up his hand in a gesture to stop. "Nein!" Fynn barked, halting him.

This presented Reagan with her first opportunity to size up the man. Ekkehard stared angrily at her, and she studied his face closely, confirming his unmistakable port wine stain before letting her gaze travel down to his feet. Or lack thereof.

Only now did she understand why he hadn't appeared

taller. She stared at his freakish blades and bit her lip. "Oh, look! Flipper has decided to join us!" she blurted, immediately regretting the insult as he took another aggressive step toward her.

"*Stoppen*!!" Fynn yelled out, gesturing wildly. "Go! Back to the car and stay there!!"

Ekkehard gritted his teeth, fuming and embarrassed. He looked back at Fynn.

"Now," Fynn commanded, as if scolding a toddler.

Ekkehard gestured to Steffi. "What about–?"

"She can stay here, for now," Fynn said.

Ekkehard's shoulders drooped slightly as he walked away, deflated. He plopped into the passenger seat and slammed the car door like a petulant child.

Fynn shook his head and turned back to Reagan. "This," he said, dismissively, as he gestured to her tablet, "this means nothing. You have... nothing, Ray. And I don't believe your *police* threat for one second. I could always read you. You aren't a good liar, Reagan. You never have been."

Reagan looked back at him, giving him nothing as her mind raced in a million directions.

She listened to the sounds of arguing gulls and took notice as it became mixed with a new sound in the distance, that of another vehicle. Fynn's voice brought her back to the moment.

"Just the same," he said, reaching out toward her. "I'll be taking that tablet. Nice try."

Reagan shrugged, handing him the device.

"And I'll be taking those documents as well, please. I trust they're in order, Ray."

"Oh, they are... trust me. But while we're here, you might

want to take a look at them," she said, handing over the envelope. "Just in case."

Fynn's brow scrunched slightly as he took the envelope and broke open its adhesive seal. He pulled out the impressive looking folio and immediately recognized the bank's logo on the letterhead of the cover page.

Reagan studied Fynn's face closely as he began scanning the pages. As he got deeper into the documents, his features began telegraphing a gamut of emotions, beginning with delight, which morphed to confusion, then shock, before erupting into volcanic rage.

"What the fucking *fuck* is this shit, Reagan?!! This isn't–! Where's the document relinquishing ownership to me? The release of the freeze on the accounts and–?!! Wait, what the hell is *this* one? Who–or what–is *Kaiser Holdings Limited?*"

"Oh, that one… um, that's the corporation that bought us out."

"Excuse me?" Fynn said, looking up from the wad of contracts. "You'd better be kidding me, Ray. Really, who are they?"

"They are the new owners of our Fischmarkt, Fynn. Well, of *my* Fischmarkt. The transaction is legal, cleared, and final. I got a very good price. More than I was originally asking, to be honest. Too bad you got greedy and tried to take away *my* business, asshole. You could have been a part of this, but you have nothing now."

Fynn's confusion was giving way to dangerous escalation. "Reagan, tell me you didn't."

She shrugged back. "So, anyway, those are your copies. I have others. Oh, and I almost forgot. Check out the last three pages there."

His hands shaking, Fynn rifled through the papers,

arriving at the final three. His eyes scanned the documents, the official stamps, the signatures… on the divorce petition. He slowly looked up and met Reagan's eyes.

"You've been *served*, motherfucker! I'll see you in court!" Reagan punctuated her statement with a sharp kick to Fynn's crotch. He groaned loudly as his legs buckled beneath him, the papers dropping to the ground as he collapsed.

The unmistakable roar of an approaching diesel truck had completely drowned out the gulls now, and Reagan could see it barreling toward them.

Ekkehard was a little slow on the uptake, but he now saw the vehicle. It looked familiar. He awkwardly liberated himself from the Saab's seatbelt and began climbing out.

"Steffi!!" Reagan yelled above the diesel roar, gesturing for her daughter frantically. Steffi did a doubletake from the approaching truck to her mother then sprinted to the MG, climbing into the driver's seat without hesitation. Steffi revved the engine as Reagan grabbed her tablet from the ground and jumped into the passenger side. A second later, the MG launched with a squeal of burning rubber in its wake.

Ekkehard made his way over to Fynn and began helping him to his feet.

"Leave me! Go get *them*, you fool!" Fynn hissed, pointing to the MG as it rocketed away. Ekkehard's hesitation was but a flicker as he scooped up the car key that had fallen from Fynn's pocket, jumped in the Saab, and joined in pursuit.

Fynn, still shaky, turned and watched as the cube truck pulled up ten feet away, coming to a noisy and abrupt stop. It had parked sideways, blocking any views to the alley, and two very pissed-off guys hopped out.

# CHAPTER SIXTY-FOUR

STEFFI'S HANDS GRIPPED the steering wheel like she was strangling an anaconda, while Reagan stroked the back of her daughter's head.

"You okay, baby?" she asked, still shaking. "Gawd, I was so worried about—"

"Mom!!!" Steffi cried, her eyes momentarily darting to the rearview. She could now see the Saab a hundred yards back and gaining. Panicked, she glanced over at her passenger. "Where the hell are we even going?!! The Saab's effing chasing us!!"

Reagan spun around, straining to get a look out the back window.

"And what happened to the driver's mirror? It's freakin' *gone!*"

"That's the last of our worries, honey!" Reagan answered, facing front again. It took her a second to get a bead on their location. "Okay... coming up... take the next right... *here*! Right on Klopstockstrasse!"

Steffi let out a gasp as she cranked the wheel, barely

negotiating the turn, and to a chorus of angry horn beeps. Catching her breath, she dared ask, "*Now* what?"

"Whew... okay... we're good," Reagan replied, trying to sound reassuring in the midst of her own panic. "Uh... in about, maybe, three kilometers, we'll be looking for Willy-Brandt-Strasse. It'll be another right turn. We'll both watch for signs."

Steffi's eyes went back to the rearview. The Saab was still about a hundred yards behind. Her eyes scanned every sign that presented itself; she wasn't feeling entirely confident in her copilot's ability to see them.

"There!" Reagan barked, pointing to a sign ahead. "One hundred meters. Willy–"

"–effing Brandt, I know!" Steffi interrupted with a glance at the speedometer.

Moments later, the turnoff presented itself with two right-turn lanes. Steffi braked just enough to navigate into the right-most lane, the MG leaning as they made their way onto Willy-Brandt.

"Good job."

Steffi exhaled through her ballooned cheeks as the lane straightened out again.

"The Saab's tracking us, Mom! We can't outrun him. How much further? Or do you even know... ?"

Reagan's thoughts were racing. There hadn't been a car chase in the plan, and the maniac in the Saab was gaining. She made a snap decision, and a frightening one, as she blurted it out.

"Coming up in a few minutes! It'll be a gigantic, stone building, with a big clock tower–actually two towers–even I'll be able to see it! It'll be visible on the right; you can't miss it!"

"Okay…."

"I love you, Steffi," Reagan said, turning toward her.

"Love you, too, Mom," Steffi replied, her eyes straight ahead as she weaved through traffic.

Up ahead, in the distance, the clock tower became their beacon.

Ekkehard was closing in now, having made an aggressive maneuver around a commercial vehicle to fall to within seventy-five yards of the MG.

Traffic was heavy, with several vehicles still between him and his prey and, up ahead, he caught a glimpse of where they were all heading. He swallowed hard as thoughts of his own worst nightmare started flooding in.

"Oh, Gott… das Hauptbahnhof," he muttered.

# CHAPTER SIXTY-FIVE

## *HAMBURG HAUPTBAHNHOF*
## HAMBURG CENTRAL STATION
## FRIDAY
## 12:25, CET

AS THEY NEARED the station, a dumb man in a Smart car came out of nowhere, jogging sharply right and coming into the path of the MG, forcing Steffi to crank the wheel to avoid it.

"What the–?! You effing idiot!!!" Steffi yelled, laying into the horn and gesturing with her finger as she struggled to maneuver away from the rapidly approaching imbedded metal bollards that lined the building's sidewalks.

"Watch out for the–!" Reagan yelled, narrowly pulling her arm in through the window as Steffi braked hard, the MG's entire right side making glancing contact with several of the unforgiving metal poles.

"Ahhhhhhhhh!!!!" Steffi screamed as the car noisily scraped along, leaving red paint and assorted pieces of trim in its wake, while sending several pedestrians running for cover.

The MG came to an abrupt stop, with several car horns blaring at them. Steffi looked over at her mom and started sobbing. "Mommmm!!"

Reagan resumed breathing and cupped her daughter's head in her hand. "Steffi! Are you okay?"

Steffi looked back at her through a river of tears. Reagan repeated herself, brushing the hair from Steffi's eyes. "Answer me, baby! *Are. You. All. Right*?!"

Steffi managed a nod. "But… the *car*! I ruined it!!"

"No, you didn't! Don't worry about it!! It's a rental!!"

"But–"

"No buts, Stef!!! There's no time for buts! Listen! We need to get out… right here… *right now*!! Do you understand?"

Steffi stared back, her eyes wide, the neurons not fully firing.

"*Stefanie Alice Dunkel*!!" Reagan hollered emphatically, using the rarely used full name for emphasis. "C'mon, baby!!"

Steffi hadn't heard her name used that way since she was in the sixth grade, the time she'd caught the bedroom curtains on fire with her curling iron. Her eyes locked in with her mother's, and she nodded her understanding and popped open the driver's door.

The passenger door took a little more effort as Reagan forced it open, grabbed her backpack, and spilled out onto the cement area outside the station. Steffi came alongside her and looked back at the unfortunate MG as Reagan grabbed her hand and initiated a sprint inside.

# CHAPTER SIXTY-SIX

EKKEHARD LOOKED UP and saw the clock tower. He craned his neck out the window, trying to figure out the cause of the chaotic honking just ahead.

A moment later, as traffic resumed its crawl, he got his answer with the sight of the wounded MG leaning up against the bollards. As he got closer, he could see the vehicle had been vacated.

"Scheisse!" he yelled, jerking his head left, then right, in search of a place to pull over, but he knew there wouldn't be one. Unless....

Ekkehard didn't bother using his turn indicator as he cranked the wheel and braked hard. His hasty maneuver elicited an even larger chorus of horns as he came to a diagonal stop just ahead of the crippled MG, the Saab's ass end sticking out into the traffic lane and causing an Audi to skid to a stop behind it.

"Arschlock!" the driver screamed, pumping his fist threateningly.

Ekkehard grabbed Fynn's Walther from the glovebox and exited the Saab, the gun visible and pointing directly at the

Audi's driver. The man immediately held up both hands, gesturing surrender to the crazed man with the shitty face tattoo, as Ekkehard pivoted on his blades with the grace of an Olympic figure skater and bolted for the train station entrance.

Serving well over a half-million travelers per day, Hamburg's Hauptbahnhof saw about 720 local and national trains come and go daily. It had the distinction of being not only the busiest passenger railway station in Germany, but also the second busiest in all of Europe.

Reagan gripped Steffi's hand tightly as they made their way through the crowd, crossed the lobby of the main western entrance, and scurried up the stairs. As they reached the top, Reagan paused to catch her breath and get reoriented.

"Where are we going? This place is huge! Are we catching a train?"

"A train?" Reagan half-replied, lost in thought. The sights and sounds of this place were filling her head, a million memories loudly queueing. "No...."

"Then where, Mom? What's the plan? That guy might be—" Steffi said, pausing as she noticed her mother's expression. Reagan's jaw was slacked, her strained gaze having locked onto something down in the lobby they had just crossed.

"Shit! It's *him!*"

Ekkehard fought his way through the crowd, shoving a young woman aside as he came to a stop, mid-lobby. He looked up to the next level, his eyes narrowing, searching the sea of people for his prey. He knew they couldn't have gotten far. Just then, a quick blur of motion got his attention: two people dashing away.

"This way!!" Reagan commanded in a hushed voice, her grip vicelike as she pulled Steffi in the direction of the *Nordsteg*–the north footbridge–leading up to the rows of food and drink outlets.

Ekkehard shoved the Walther pistol into the back of his waistband and began quickly ascending the stairs, careful not to catch his blades on the steps.

As they reached the top of the steps leading to the footbridge, Reagan paused, squinting as she tried to make sense of the spectrum of colorful electric marquees. Even though the station was well illuminated, thanks to its glass-paneled domed ceiling, the barrage of colors was problematic for her and seemingly like a scene from the movie *Blade Runner*. The signs were all fighting for attention, and the one that finally jumped out at her was the one with the simplest logo. It was the place she remembered her father having a particular fondness for that fateful morning, all those years ago: "The yellow M."

"Mom?"

"McDonald's," Reagan said, turning to her, her expression earnest as she pointed to it.

"Are you kidding me right now? Seriously?! You're–?"

"We're not stopping for nuggets, if that's what you're wondering. C'mon!"

Ekkehard had seen them come this way and he figured the Nordsteg would be where they were heading, as there would be more places to hide and more people to blend in with.

Reaching the base of the stairs, there were two options going up, both heavily populated.

Though the escalator would have been easier for him, it would be slow-going. Ekkehard hated stairs when he was wearing his blades, but time was of the essence, so he started hoofing his way up, weaving through the crowd toward the footbridge and not caring who he was mowing over.

Along the storefronts lining the footbridge, scores of passengers were milling around, some standing along the railings as they scarfed every manner of fast food, others milling around the eateries and beer bars as they waited for their departures.

In addition to the throngs of travelers, there were an abundance of down-on-their-luck homeless people and marginalized groups hanging around, not eating but wishing they were.

Reagan couldn't help but notice how much the general population had changed since she'd left, as the crowds appeared to be largely comprised of foreigners. She remembered reading about the influx of Turkish and Syrians, but seeing them all now, she hardly recognized the place.

As Reagan and Steffi approached the McDonald's, Steffi shot a look over her shoulder toward the stairway, where she could see their pursuer making strides in their direction.

"Mom! He's coming our way!!"

"Shit. Okay, now..." Reagan replied, as she hustled them both to the entrance and brought them both to a squat amongst the customers. "Listen closely, honey," she said, trying to scan the small space as she peered through the forest of legs. Her eyes darted around like ball bearings inside a pinball game.

"*Listening*," Steffi replied, her attention laser focused now.

"I need you to stay here," Reagan said, pulling up her daughter's hood as if seeing her off for *Kinder*.

"Wait. What do you mean? What about *you*? I'm not going *anywhere* without–"

"Stef! You said you were listening. Now, you asked what the plan was and… well, this is the best–and only–one I have at the moment. We need to split up so I can draw that man away and–"

"No *way*, Mom!!" Steffi countered emphatically, her features telegraphing a mix of both her intense anger and little-girl fear. "You don't get to just *leave* me here in… a sketchy Micky Dee's, in the middle of an effing train station– in a *foreign* fucking *country*–while you dash off and risk your life playing a superhero!"

There was no time to argue.

"I'll come back for you! I *promise*, Stefanie!! Please… go hide in the bathroom back there. Stay put; I'll find you!" Reagan instructed, hating herself for resorting to the tough love the moment demanded.

Steffi rubbed the tears from her eyes, and when she reopened them, her mother was gone.

# CHAPTER SIXTY-SEVEN

REAGAN DASHED ALONG the row of food outlets, her backpack bouncing wildly on her shoulder as she snuck occasional peeks behind her.

She watched as Ekkehard reached the landing and stopped, scanning the area. Reagan had noticed that negotiating the stairs had been a challenge for him. She hoped to exploit that. She turned to run but paused when she heard a loud shout coming from the other end of the footbridge.

"Hey! Ich sehe Sie!!" Ekkehard yelled again, waving his arm at Reagan. Several people stared at the strange man who was now running in her direction. Strange people were rather commonplace in a station this size, but strange people with a Rorschach inkblot on their face and metal blades for feet were quite another thing. Most moved aside as he dug in, sprinting after Reagan.

Reagan had not only heard Ekkehard, but she'd also understood him: *I see you!!* She now knew him to be as relentless as he was dangerous. She ducked into the middle of a line of customers waiting to purchase pastries, eliciting several complaints with variations on "Hör auf zu drángeln!" *Stop cutting the line! Stop pushing!*

"Entschuldigung! Es tut mir leid!" she said, apologizing profusely as she imbedded herself further into the pack. From her place in line, she turned around just in time to see Ekkehard sprint past the shop as he continued down the footbridge.

Reagan again apologized to several people as she slid out of line, scanning the landing, and making a dash for it in the opposite direction.

As she maneuvered to pass a slow-moving group, she bumped into two disheveled men, obviously homeless, who both stared at her and smiled lasciviously. They probably possessed a dozen teeth between them. Reagan apologized and was about to briskly walk away when one of the men grabbed her by the crook of her arm.

She spun around defensively, prepared to fight him off, if necessary, but he just smiled, then pointed to his mouth. *He's hungry. They both are.*

Reagan dug her hand deep into her jacket pocket and pulled out a wad of euros, stuffing several into each of their palms. "Für Sie, hier ist etwas Geld," she said to them. *For you.* The men each expressed their thanks through gestures of appreciation and as she turned to leave, her eyes went wide with fear. Not of them, but of someone–or something–coming from behind them.

Reagan immediately sprinted away and as the two men turned around, they saw the source of her concern, rapidly approaching, and causing the shorter of the two to men to lose bladder control.

"Aus dem Weg, ihr Penner!" the running man yelled,

waving frantically at them as he threatened to run them over. *Out of my way, bums!* The men didn't take kindly to the insult, plus they didn't want harm to come to the young woman who had just shown them kindness.

They separated slightly as if to allow him to pass between them and as Ekkehard was about to pass, the man with the wet trousers looked down at the blades and, with a nearly toothless grin, returned the insult.

"Suchen Sie die Eislaufbahn?" *Are you looking for the skating rink?*

This got a few laughs and snickers from the passersby. That is, until Ekkehard spun around, holding the Walther pistol for all to see.

This squelched any further attempts at humor. Ekkehard squeezed off a *fuck-you-all* warning shot into the air, the round penetrating the glass domed ceiling several stories above. He slid the pistol back into his rear waistband.

The crowd dissipated, as if Charlton Heston's Moses had just magically parted the Red Sea, allowing Ekkehard to sprint through and disappear into the fold.

The gunshot's report echoed through the terminal and a handful of security officers scrambled to discern the source.

It had definitely gotten Reagan's attention, too, as well as everyone else's. She hadn't realized Ekkehard was armed until now, which ratcheted up the threat level to DEFCON: *FUCK.*

The McDonald's restroom door creaked open and a gender-neutral goth teen emerged, eyes wide at the sound of a shot. Before they could even ask what happened, Steffi slipped inside, slammed the door and locked it behind her. *Definitely a gunshot! Shit!!*

She shuffled around nervously in the tiny space, not wanting to touch a single surface in this restroom from Hell. She kicked a spent syringe to the corner under the filthy sink and looked at herself in the graffiti-etched metal mirror as she tried to restore a rhythm to her breathing. Somebody pounded on the door, obviously feeling a similar panic in response to the shot.

"Occupied!!" Steffi yelled, having no clue of how to say it in German.

Her mom was out there, drawing fire from a maniacal killer, and here she was, feeling completely helpless, useless, and scared shitless. *God, protect my mom!*

# CHAPTER SIXTY-EIGHT

REAGAN MADE A mad scramble for the stairs leading down to the train platforms, trying her best to serpentine between everyone else as she did. As she reached the platform, she spun her head left and right, willing her compromised eyes to glean the details she needed to get away from the monster.

She spotted a large, clearly marked sign off to her left, indicating train Platform 6, and she sprinted toward the group of passengers awaiting their inbound locomotive.

The air was thick with the competing sounds of wheels clacking along rails, the high-pitched shrieking of brakes, and the public address system announcing departures and platform changes. The noises all fought for space in Reagan's chaotic brain as she tried not to have a full-on panic attack.

The memories flooded back faster than she could manage them, and all she could think about was how much she had lost here that day twelve years ago. To her surprise, her mind allowed her one other thought as well: *Ekkehard lost something here that day as well. His friggin' legs!*

Reagan shook away the thoughts as she reached the group,

laboring to catch her breath, ducking behind those gathered as she snuck a look back in the direction from where she had come. She could see Ekkehard pushing his way through the crowd as he negotiated the stairway down, and it was obvious he was being mindful of his steps.

Reagan's pulse quickened, and she realized she may have painted herself into a corner. A bright light and a distant rattle of the tracks got her attention—and that of all around her—as an incoming train was approaching. Some of the awaiting passengers began to shift their positions, jockeying for what they hoped would be the best locations for boarding.

Reagan shuffled closer with the crowd surrounding her, sneaking another peek toward the stairs in the process. Ekkehard was just stepping off the bottom stair and had reached the platform level. She could see he was scanning the area for any sight of her. *Scheisse!*

Two levels up, at the other end of the station, two officers were scrambling through the crowd on the Waldenhalle footbridge, ordering people to take cover as they scanned the area for any sight of a shooter.

As the train slowly approached, the public address system announced the impending arrival at Platform 6. This got Ekkehard's attention and, lacking anything else to go on, he began briskly walking toward it.

The Platform 6 crowd shifted again as one, moving a bit closer to the painted safety lines. The locomotive was drawing nearer, and so was Ekkehard.

*Think, Reagan!!*

Ekkehard was armed, and all she was armed with was an

iPad, some papers, and–a desperate thought came to her as she swung the backpack from her shoulder and kneeled, imploring her shaking fingers to open the main zipper compartment.

Ekkehard had to be close now, Reagan figured, and it was all she could do not to audibly gasp. She thrust her hands into the pack, shifting her papers and iPad aside, as she searched for the one item she hoped she might have stuffed in there.

From her kneeling position, she could hear the shrill brakes and the slowing clack of the wheels on the track as the train approached. She was staring at kneecaps and shoes as the crowd around her again began shifting slightly forward.

Reagan's fingers felt something familiar as she wrapped them around the item of her desire. Just as she liberated it from the pack, a new pair of shoes entered her field of vision.

And they weren't shoes.

Ekkehard was now part of the group, his blades a mere half meter away from where she was squatting. Reagan tried not to hyperventilate as she looked at them, knowing the killer was essentially standing directly over her.

All Reagan could do was freeze as she listened to the train rolling closer. She only had one shot, she knew, as she carefully began unfolding the four hinged sections of the long white cane she had hoped she would never need.

With perfect German diction, the voice once again announced the arriving train at Platform 6 as Reagan extended the cane to its full, fifty-one-inch length, mindful not to bump anybody. She couldn't rely on a visual, but her remaining senses told her the train was only meters away now, the sounds and vibrations at ground level confirming it.

Ekkehard's blades suddenly moved, and Reagan just managed to get her fingers out of the way before her digits could be pulverized beneath them. His blades pivoted to the right almost ninety degrees, then pivoted similarly to his left before recentering next to her.

He was scanning the area for her, knowing she couldn't have gotten far.

It was now or never. Reagan carefully threaded the aluminum-alloyed cane into position, about six inches above ground level and just inches ahead of both blades. She gingerly guided the hard, white molded tip until it lodged firmly against the side of a cement trash receptacle. She was far from being a religious person, yet she prayed it would hold.

As the train slowly approached, the crowd began surging slightly, moving to the sides now, in two different directions, as they began heading closer to the likely door positions.

Reagan stared at the blades and was beginning to think all hope was lost as her protective human cocoon was dissipating, about to leave her visible and vulnerable.

Ekkehard scanned the area once more, his eyes darting between the platforms, the footbridges of the Nordsteg and, at the other end of the station, the Waldenhalle. Seeing no sign of his quarry, he had to investigate this train as it presented a likely escape opportunity for her.

He wasn't going to fail Fynn a second time.

Ekkehard made his move. Lunging forward, his right blade caught the cane first, with his left hooking it a half-second later. The cane gave some, its hollow aluminum sections holding together and struggling against the strong elastic bands woven through them. The molded tip kept its end of the bargain as Reagan maintained her death grip on the leather-wrapped handle.

Ekkehard's eyes went wide with surprise and panic as his momentum had now hurled him forward, his carbon fiber feet trapped against an unseen barrier and rendered useless to help catch him. *Have a nice trip!*

Ekkehard's arms shot out in front of him, in Superman fashion, in a desperate attempt to break his fall, but he had tumbled too fast, and too far, his upper body having broached the painted safety line and his arms extending across the near rail as the slow-moving locomotive rolled into its final position.

His scream was high-pitched and primal; its volume piercing and nearly pitch-perfect in concert with the squealing brakes.

# CHAPTER SIXTY-NINE

THE COLLECTIVE SCREAMS of horrified passengers had helped direct the station's security officers to Platform 6, and with that, to their gunman.

The security staff had moved the platform passengers back, away from the scene, and had erected a barrier of yellow tape, while a few looky-loos onboard watched the ensuing chaos from their window seats.

Reagan was sequestered off to the side, standing against a cement pillar, as two officers took her statement. They had already collected and bagged the firearm found trackside, and medical personnel had whisked Ekkehard away, to University Medical Center Hamburg.

Recounting the circumstances, and what she had seen, was brutal. Reagan had stood from her crouch just in time to witness Ekkehard's fall onto the rails, and even though he had deserved his karma, the excruciating visual would be seared into her memory forever, as it made the thoughts of her parents' demise all the more graphic and painful to imagine.

Reagan held up a hand to the officers and quickly turned away, signaling she had to vomit a second time. As she dry-heaved what bile remained in her empty stomach, the two officers glanced at each other and nodded.

"I'm sorry," Reagan muttered, wiping her mouth with the tissues she'd been given.

"Es ist okay," the junior officer replied before switching to English in response to what he'd heard her utter. "It is no problem. You are okay?"

Reagan nodded. "Was there anything else you needed from me?" She shot a glance up toward the Nordsteg footbridge. "My daughter... I told her to hide up there, and I really need to go find her."

"Of course. No, I think we have everything we need for the moment," the senior officer replied. "You will you be staying in Hamburg for... ?"

"Not sure how long. Sorry, I didn't mean to interrupt. This was supposed to be a nice vacation for my daughter and me, but we've had... uh, some unexpected changes to the plans."

The officer nodded his understanding, jotting a note into his pad. "We can reach you at the phone number you provided if we have any further questions?"

"Yes... yes, you can," Reagan replied, shouldering her backpack. "Danke schön."

"Bitte schön."

The PA system was announcing an "Alles klar," as well as a few platform changes, which made it difficult for Reagan to hear as she jogged up the steps to the Nordsteg footbridge, the phone pressed hard against her ear. She stuffed a finger in her other ear as she tried Steffi's phone for a third time.

"Come on, honey," Reagan muttered, willing her daughter

to answer. The call went straight to a full mailbox, and her texts remained unanswered.

As Reagan reached the landing, she frantically waded through passersby, like a salmon swimming upstream, as she headed for the big, yellow M.

Upon reaching the entrance, Reagan spun around, every which way, her eyes struggling to scan what seemed like a myriad of faces. Not seeing her daughter, she again pulled out her phone.

Reagan furrowed her brow as she redialed, the phone ringing twice before she heard subsequent rings, much louder, coming from behind her. She felt a tap on her shoulder and as she turned around, Steffi flew into her arms, sobbing. Mother and daughter latched onto each other, shaking as if riding out a seismic event and neither let go for a full ten minutes.

# CHAPTER SEVENTY

REAGAN AND STEFFI poured out of the station through the main western exit, still holding hands as they stepped out into partially cloudy skies.

Reagan squinted, pausing to look at her watch, then comparing it against the clock in the tower. They were both in agreement that it was 3:17–or 15:17, CET.

"Time flies when you're having fun," Reagan said, turning to Steffi as they crossed the busy pedestrian area. Steffi shook her head, not quite on board with her mother's attempt at levity. The only response she could muster was an exhausted, "Yeah."

They proceeded toward the street, where they had hastily "parked" the MG.

"Mom!"

"Yeah, honey?"

"Look. The rental. They have it loaded up onto a tow truck!"

"Shit," Reagan said under her breath as they both quickened their pace to close the distance.

A police officer was supervising the tow truck operator

as the load was leveled and secured, while multitasking by directing traffic around the rig. The Saab was no longer there.

"Hallo!" Reagan called out as they approached.

"Yes?" the officer replied, a bit distracted as he waved a delivery van around the rig.

Reagan flashed a quick smile as she walked up. "Sprechen Sie Englisch?" she asked. She thought she'd heard him reply as such. "Sorry, for my daughter... ?" she added, gesturing to Steffi, again with the smile.

"Yes, yes... how can I help you?"

"Uh, that car there?" she replied, pointing to the battered MG. "That's my car... well, it's my *rental* car."

The officer looked over at her, sizing up the situation. "That vehicle. It is yours?"

Reagan nodded emphatically, her wheels turning as she worked on her story in real time.

"Yes, we are visiting–on Christmas vacation, from America. Our car–this rental here–it was stolen earlier today. Our luggage, everything, was in the cargo area. All of our stuff...."

"You say somebody stole this car. And you reported this to the–?"

"We tried. I mean, I was going to, but by the time we noticed it was gone, my phone battery was dead, and my charger was in the car. With all our stuff. The car was parked over at the Fischmarkt, around noon, and–that's where it was taken from."

The officer whistled, getting the attention of the truck operator, signaling for him to take over with the traffic direction while he took the woman's statement.

"Gawd, it looks so horrible–the rental; it's all scratched

up and dented!" Reagan said, tapping into her drama skills to sell her concern.

The officer looked askance as he listened to her account. He glanced at her daughter.

Steffi kept a straight face, impressed by her mother's performance, while remaining thankful she hadn't thrown her under the bus as the one who had been driving at the time. She knew that not being licensed, on either side of the pond–while destroying a rental car–wouldn't bode well for her record.

He turned back to Reagan as he pulled out his pen. "I will take your information, Frau–"

"Dunkel, Reagan Dunkel."

As the officer began jotting this into his notes, he took pause, looking up at her with a look of concern. "You said your name is Dunkel?"

"That's right. D-U-N-K-E-L."

"If you'll excuse me just a moment, I need to make a quick call. Please stay right here."

"I will," Reagan replied. As the officer walked several feet away, he placed a call with his radio, just out of earshot. Reagan turned to Steffi. "How am I doing?"

"Gawd, Mom," Steffi replied quietly, stifling a grin. "Academy Award," she whispered.

A minute went by before the officer returned. "Frau Dunkel, just so you know, we will be towing the vehicle to our impound yard. I will be happy to give you and your–"

"Daughter. Steffi."

"Hi," Steffi said, adding a small wave.

"Yes. Well, I will be happy to give you and your daughter a ride, at which time you can reclaim your belongings from the car, and we can arrange for transportation to wherever you are staying."

"That would be great. Danke."

"Bitte. This way, please."

# CHAPTER SEVENTY-ONE

THE THREE OF them rode in silence, the officer and his American passengers, for the roughly twenty-minute drive.

Reagan was seeing some *very* familiar landmarks now, including the Hamburg Police Headquarters building, which they had just passed as they continued in the direction of the Fischmarkt.

"Excuse me?"

The officer checked in with the rearview as he answered. "Yes?"

"We're going to the Police impound to get our things, right?"

"We will be, yes. But we have another stop we have to make first, then we will retrieve your belongings," the officer replied, returning his eyes to the road ahead as he made a turn toward the docks.

Steffi looked over at her mother, getting a shrug in return.

The patrol car pulled into the Fischmarkt lot and proceeded down the side alley toward the rear of the main building, where another two police vehicles were parked, as well as a white panel van.

Steffi squeezed her mom's hand.

"I'm sorry, what are we doing here?" Reagan asked.

"You said the vehicle was stolen from the Fischmarkt, yes?"

"Yes, but...."

The officer pulled alongside the other official vehicles, and he cut the engine. "Wait here, please," he instructed as he got out and walked over his colleagues, who were gathered fifty yards away. As he approached, he could read their grim expressions.

Reagan and Steffi watched as he met up with another officer who looked back toward them, gesturing. "Gawd, what the hell?" Reagan muttered.

"What do think they want, Mom? Don't they believe your story?"

"Not sure," Reagan replied quietly.

"He's coming back."

"I can see that, sweetie. Let's just see what's going on, then we can get our suitcases and find a hotel. It'll be dark before long, and...."

The officer stepped up alongside the rear door on Reagan's side and opened it.

"If you'd please follow me, Frau Dunkel, we have a few questions."

"Sure, but...."

"Am I coming?" Steffi asked, having tried her door handle and finding it locked.

The officer leaned in, looking at her as he responded. "Bitte warten Sie hier."

"Be right back, Stef," Reagan said, hoping she was right about that.

Steffi watched through the window as her mother followed the officer over to the rest of the group.

"Frau Dunkel," the officer said, introducing her to the

others. "And… forgive me, I neglected to introduce myself earlier. I am Officer Rauff."

"Officer Rauff," Reagan said, nodding to him. She searched the faces of the others.

A few polite, professional acknowledgements were exchanged, with brief attempts at half-smiles, with each officer's expression snapping back to frowns reflecting the gravity of the moment.

"If this is about my stolen car, I've already explained–"

"Thank you, Frau Dunkel. We are here… for a different matter, I'm afraid," the lead officer said, done mincing words. He watched her closely as he continued. "Do you know a man by the name of Fynn? Same last name as yours?"

Reagan's eyes narrowed, her face tightening at the mere mention of his name. Her pulse quickened as she hesitated with her answer. "I do, yes."

Several seconds went by without elaboration. Officer Raupp broke the silence. "And may I ask, what is your relationship to Fynn Dunkel?"

"My husband… estranged husband," she said, correcting herself. "We have been married for–I'm sorry; why are you asking me this? Is he in some kind of trouble? Has something happened to him?"

Reagan searched their faces, trying to get a read on things. Most of them looked away, but not Officer Raupp. "I'm sorry; yes, it seems something has happened, and we're trying to learn more about what occurred. And why."

"Please. Just tell me what I need to know. It's already been a *very* difficult day for my daughter and me. Where is he? Where's Fynn?"

Raupp had already been made privy to the earlier incident

at the Hauptbahnhof, with her name being cross-referenced as the would-be victim of the gunman found at Platform 6. He could appreciate how *difficult* her day had been already, and he knew that it was about to become more so.

"If you would please come with me," he said, as sensitively as he could under the circumstances. He gestured to a spot down the alley, about thirty yards away, where another man was standing.

Reagan looked back toward the car, then up to Officer Raupp, reluctantly nodding her agreement.

Officer Raupp led the way with Reagan a half step behind him. Her mind was racing in a thousand directions as she tried to imagine the different scenarios, each worse than the last.

Raupp's thoughts were churning as well. He wasn't pleased about the decision to bring the woman here, as this wasn't exactly typical protocol. A broken watermain had completely flooded the morgue earlier that afternoon, however, and put a wrinkle in the procedures. The new Polizeipräesident–duly distracted by both the flooding and the incident at the Hauptbahnhof–had made the hasty decision under duress. Even though Raupp didn't have much respect for the interim chief, he had orders to follow and a pension to protect.

As they reached the other man, Reagan could now see he was standing next to a large refrigeration unit, very similar to the ones she had used for years at their Fischmarkt booth.

The lid was closed and, in addition to the cries of distant gulls, she could now hear what sounded like a bevy of flies. She stopped in her tracks, her heart skipping a beat as she looked over at Officer Raupp for any clue. His mouth tightened into a line, which didn't bode well, and he nodded to the other man, who slowly lifted the lid to the reefer unit.

The sound of buzzing flies became more pronounced, the volume increasing exponentially with the opening of the box. The attending officer stepped aside as Reagan took a deep breath, holding it in as she slowly approached. She couldn't see inside the reefer yet, but as she reached the officer, he offered her a handkerchief. It was similar to the one he held against his nose and mouth.

Reagan stopped about a foot from the unit and avoided looking in. She closed her eyes. The buzzing sounded akin to a colony of pissed-off honeybees as she waved away what had to be a hundred flies. The sound dissipated for a couple of seconds, but it immediately returned.

*What have you gotten yourself into, Fynn?* She wanted to scream, to run away, to pretend none of this nightmare was happening. But it wasn't an option. She steeled herself, let out her breath, and opened her eyes.

Even with the car's windows rolled up, Steffi could hear her mother's primal scream from a hundred yards away. She had never heard anything remotely like it, and she pounded her fists against the glass as she added her own screams to the mix.

Reagan's legs quaked, her knees buckling as she collapsed into Officer Raupp's arms.

The sight had been worse than anything her dark and fertile imagination could have anticipated. Her reaction told Officer Raupp and the others they had received further corroboration of their positive ID for Fynn Dunkel.

The refrigeration unit wasn't powered, having not been

since it had failed—with Fynn wheeling it there for disposal—days before. Inside the musty box lay the body of Fynn Dunkel, his face bloodied and bruised, his eyes wide open, and with a perfect, clean bullet hole in his forehead.

Fynn's torso lay there, folded awkwardly inside the refrigerator. It was clear that there had been no effort to make him comfortable, and he was submerged up to his shoulders in warmish, pink water that had probably been long-melted ice, mixed with blood.

To add insult to lethal injury, his killer—or killers—had sent a message to others who might feel inclined to try and rip them off. They'd left him this way, surrounded with many dozens of lifeless lobsters packed around him. It was the lobster tail protruding from his mouth that had been the crowning touch.

Reagan screamed again as she fell to her knees.

Her shoulders heaved as she wailed. She would do anything to unsee what she had just witnessed. The man she had been married to, and with whom she had shared a dozen years of her life, lay dead. Fynn had deceived her, betrayed her trust, and waged violence against the people she loved. He had given her every reason to truly hate him.

Even so, she hated seeing him like this even more.

# CHAPTER SEVENTY-TWO

O FFICER RAUPP TOSSED back a tiny gulp of water, crumpling the laughably tiny paper cup and tossing it in the receptacle next to the dispenser. With two fingers, he pinched the skin between his eyebrows, as if to do away with the decades-old, deep frown lines that had formed there.

As he rounded the corner, Raupp could see Frau Dunkel and her daughter still seated at the table where he'd left them thirty minutes before. They hadn't moved, yet their slumping posture suggested they were fading fast. And from what he had learned today, he couldn't blame them.

The stories had checked out, with the possible exception of the stolen rental, but with everything they had gone through, he wasn't going to pursue that one further. Reagan Dunkel's statement was what would go in the report, and a copy of his police report was what her insurance company and the rental company would receive. *Merry Christmas, Frau Dunkel.*

The perps who had killed Fynn Dunkel were now in custody, in Lübeck, having been picked up before they could fly back to France. Fischmarkt security cameras had recorded the murder as well as provided ironclad descriptors of the cube truck and the assailants.

Raupp opened the door to the small room they used for questioning suspects, and as neither of the women were considered suspects, he'd been given the green light to release them.

Reagan and Steffi looked up as he came in wheeling their two suitcases. He stood the luggage next to the door and took a seat across from Reagan and Steffi. A tired half-smile slowly found its way to his face.

"Frau Dunkel and Stefanie, I know this has been a very hard series of days for you both. Again, I am sorry for what you had to learn today, and you have my condolences."

"Thank you," Reagan managed, not quite sure how to feel about any of it.

"And you will be glad to know that you are free to go. The men who… the perpetrators who assaulted your–" Raupp stopped shy of being indelicate with describing their marital status, or that of the young girl's deceased stepparent. He rephrased the best he could, especially since English was his second language. "Lübeck Police has taken custody of those accused of taking Fynn's life. We are in possession of security video which confirms this, so… I can take you to your hotel now."

Reagan chewed on this new dollop of information, adding

it to the mix as she began processing it with all of the other developments that had come to light over the past week. This was going to take some time and, try as she might, she wouldn't be making sense of it anytime soon.

As they sat there, part of her wanted to ask for more information about the men in custody, but she knew it really didn't matter.

She knew Fynn had made some very questionable associations in his lofty and ill-advised quest to be the big player on the fresh seafood scene here. She knew now, too, that the wheels had been put in motion long before, and she had been played like a violin. And she abhorred violins.

Reagan's thoughts returned to the here and now and she blinked several times. "I'm sorry; did you say our *hotel*? We haven't made any arrangements yet and—"

"We've taken the liberty of booking one, and they are expecting you, so…."

# CHAPTER SEVENTY-THREE

## THE EAST HOTEL HAMBURG
## FRIDAY, DECEMBER 19
## 20:15, CET

OFFICER RAUPP HAD delivered!

As Reagan soaked in the luxury of the marble bathroom's restorative tub, she wished there was a category for "Best German Cops" on *Yelp!* because she would definitely leave him a five-star review if she could.

The east Hotel was exceptional, by Reagan's standards, and she couldn't help thinking that might account for their trademark use of the lowercase *e* in the name. Being the penny pincher she was, it was probably not one she would have considered popping for. The location was great, and she was sure she wouldn't have scored half as decent a room at this hour without a reservation.

*Hamburg P.D. must get a special rate. Maybe I should join the force.*

Reagan was grateful to Officer Raupp for this, and even

more so for his not probing further into who was driving the rental car when it collided with the pillars that morning. He had done Steffi and her a favor, she knew, and she made a mental note to submit a copy of the police report to the rental agency in the morning.

She reached over and plucked the crystal wine glass from its place on the edge of the tub, gesturing with it as if in a silent toast as she tossed back the rest of her very dry, exquisite, now-favorite German Riesling. She set down the empty glass next to the now-empty bottle and, using her toe, flipped the lever to empty the tub.

Reagan had the bathroom light extinguished, the only illumination coming from a sliver of dancing blue light escaping from the muted flatscreen TV in the bedroom. Steffi was already lights-out, having survived the most intense couple of days in her young life.

Reagan closed the door and switched on the bathroom light. As she patted herself dry with the fluffy hotel towel, she studied the bathwater while it slowly spiraled down the drain. She shook her head. *If only the horrors of the past week could be flushed away as easily.*

In the absence of her customary nightlight, she left the bathroom light on, and its door open a crack, as she slipped into her jammies. She gently climbed into the plush, pillowtop king bed, mindful not to disturb her sleeping beauty.

She glanced over at the TV and noticed the local news was recapping its story of the gunman who had lost both arms at the Hauptbahnhof. *Fuck around and find out, Ekkehard.*

Reagan grabbed the remote and switched off the TV, sending their world into pitch black. She scooted closer, entering into a spooning position with the one thing in her life that still mattered.

She gently kissed Steffi's head, held her like she would never ever let go, and whispered softly, "Sweet dreams, baby. Tomorrow will be a better day... promise."

## SATURDAY, DECEMBER 20
## 09:40, CET

The sound of a toilet flushing registered with Reagan as her head found its way from beneath the thick down pillow, and she emerged from the depths of a coma-like slumber. A glance at the clock radio told her she had been out for nearly twelve hours. Or had there been a power outage?

"What the–? Honey?" she groaned.

Steffi emerged from the bathroom, her hair in a towel turban and a toothbrush wedged in her mouth. "Mornin', Mom," Steffi managed, running the brush across her bottom row. "I let you sleep. Took a shower... the shower here's effing awesome, by the way. Like standing in the rain!"

"Mm... that sounds pretty awesome right about now," Reagan replied, struggling to sit up. "Whew. Check my math, but I think I slept for twelve hours. I don't think I've done that since I was, like... *your* age," she said, reflecting on the last part. "How 'bout you? You sleep okay?"

Steffi pivoted to spit her foam into the sink and ran the water, answering from the bathroom. "Yeah, mostly. Had some shitty dreams though," she said, wiping her mouth as she emerged. "I wish we could, like, have a do-over for the last couple of days." Steffi's unintentional pout made her look several years younger than her age, which didn't go unnoticed.

"I know, honey. Believe me, so do I. Come here," Reagan said, patting the bed and inviting her over for a hug. Steffi responded without hesitation, and they held the embrace for several minutes before another word was uttered.

"So, can today be, like, a free day... without... car chases and psychos?" Steffi asked.

Reagan cradled Steffi's face in her hands and looked into her moist, innocent eyes that looked like they could flood with tears at any moment.

"Absolutely. Today, tomorrow, and the next day–and the day after that. All free days from now on, baby. I promise," Reagan replied, her earnest expression confirming such.

"Good," Steffi replied, her stomach grumbling. "Now, go take a shower, Mom. The card on the desk says breakfast is served till noon on Saturday, and I'm effing starved."

At thirty-five euros per person, the most important meal of the day turned out to be the most expensive meal of the trip so far, but Reagan didn't hesitate. After slaying their drag-ons, they'd earned this, she figured, plus Steffi's was five euro cheaper because she was under sixteen.

They had definitely gotten their money's worth, with each of them enjoying the sumptuous offerings of croissants, fresh regional breads, and Danish pastries. The local cheeses, sausages, muesli, plus assorted yoghurts, fresh fruits, and homemade jams fit the bill.

Reagan snapped a happy selfie of the two of them each holding a roll dripping in local "breakfast honey," a specialty item that was harvested from the rooftop's 50,000-bee beehives.

She set down the phone and enjoyed her first bite of the east Kiez honey, purring like a kitten as she experienced the delicacy.

"Oh. My. Gawd... mm... you won't get honey like this in Bot Hell."

Steffi was half done with hers as she mumbled her reply. "Seriously. *This* is insane."

# CHAPTER SEVENTY-FOUR

THE GIRLS SPENT the next three hours poking around the local shops, strolling along the St. Pauli Piers, and adding to their growing collection of selfies. Steffi struck several poses in front of the submarine, and Reagan was happy to see her smile returning.

Not wanting to kill the buzz, they avoided the Fischmarkt completely.

"I've got an idea," Reagan said as she shifted her backpack to the other shoulder and looked at her watch. The afternoon was ripe, the sun heading lower in the sky. She didn't want to be out after dark, and she didn't want her daughter to see any hookers, who might be trolling early on a Saturday night.

"You're gonna like it," she said, selling it with a grin and a twinkle in her eye.

Steffi smiled back. The last time she'd heard her mother say that was when she'd surprised her at the mall with the green light to get her ears pierced, in fourth grade. "O-kay...."

"Trust me?"

"If it involves breakfast honey, I'm totally down."

"Not exactly, but... come on," Reagan said, grinning.

They hooked arms and strolled away in the direction of the hotel, looking like two BFFs cruising the mall.

It was an evening of firsts, as neither of them had ever experienced a spa treatment of any type, and deep-tissue massages were on the program.

Reagan and Steffi had no idea what they had been missing, and how much they had needed this. The hotel's resident massage team kneaded them in return, for sixty minutes each, on side-by-side tables, with a ticklish Steffi giggling through half of it. Reagan silently cried through much of hers. The release was deep and nothing short of medicinal.

The spa's sauna session followed, giving way to long showers in the dreamy, rainlike stream, before heading to the hotel's restaurant for the third first.

As they waited for their food, Reagan awkwardly practiced holding her set of ornate, plastic chopsticks while Steffi gave her pointers, maneuvering her own pair effortlessly like a heavy metal drummer showing off with his stick twirls.

"Since when do you know how to use these? It's not like we go out for Chinese often."

"Panda Express," Steffi said, shrugging like it was nothing. "The food court, Mom. Self-taught."

"Ahh. Guess I've got to get out more."

"Ya think?" Steffi replied with a chuckle, looking up as their server arrived.

"Here we are," the young man said as he rested the edge of the large serving tray on the table while selecting plates from it and announcing their contents. Steffi's eyes went wide, her smile ear to ear. Reagan's expression was something more akin to abject horror.

"One Dragon Roll... one East Meets West Roll... one spicy tuna roll... two maguro sushi... two yellowtail sashimi... two salmon sashimi... and one salmon skin roll," the twenty-something redhead said. His German accent was moderate, his diction perfect, and his mile-wide smile blinding.

"May I get you anything else?" he asked, blushing slightly as he saw Steffi staring.

"Wow, um, no I don't think so, thank you," Reagan said politely. As the server walked away, Reagan whispered to Steffi. "Well, maybe a barf bag."

"Oh, Mom. C'mon, it was your idea. This sushi looks amazing... and he's kind of cute," Steffi replied, giggling as she indicated the server. She turned back to her mother and smiled. "Seriously, I'm proud of you, Mom—especially knowing how much you hate fish—so, thanks for taking one for the team," she said, adding an appreciative smile. She picked up her sticks. "Watch and learn."

Reagan marveled as her daughter expertly wielded her implements, extracted a thick slab of the multicolored Dragon Roll and dabbed it into her tiny dish of black sauce and green mystery paste.

With an economy of motion, Steffi stuffed the entire piece into her mouth, chewed, and immediately began humming her approval. Reagan found it amazing that it had been a one-bite deal, especially considering it looked to be about the size of the Hostess Ding Dongs she used to put in her school lunch. Or a hockey puck.

Reagan snapped a photo to commemorate Steffi's bliss. "Glad you're enjoying it, babe."

Steffi wiped her mouth and gestured to the plates spread before them. "So effing good. Okay, Mom. Here, your turn," she said, grabbing the phone from her.

"I dunno… I mean, it's fish. *Raw* fish."

Steffi pointed to the maguro tuna, then readied the camera. "Go ahead, try the red one!"

"The red one… gawd, what is it?"

"Think of it as friggin' candy, Mom!" Steffi said, a big grin on her face.

*Do the thing you fear, Reagan.* She readied her chopsticks and, on her second try, successfully picked up the tuna-topped vinegared rice bite, dipping it into the soy sauce before bringing it up to her nose. It didn't smell much like fish, she thought as she smiled for the camera and declared, "Making memories with my girl!" before stuffing the whole thing in her mouth and closing her eyes. *Think of it as candy, Reagan.*

Steffi watched intently as her mother reacted to the texture and the flavors of this Japanese morsel, while also hoping she didn't throw it all up. Reagan bobbed her head slightly, in what seemed like a nod of approval. She was not only accepting her first bite of sushi but also appreciating it. This butter-like delicacy was actually delicious. She swallowed.

"Friggin' candy," Reagan said, wearing a proud grin as if she'd just won a competitive eating trophy.

They played two rounds of Braille Uno up in the room while enjoying the guilty pleasure of the chocolatey-marshmallow dessert confections Reagan had found in one of the local stores earlier. A childhood favorite.

"These are really called *Super Dickmanns*?" Steffi asked with a naughty laugh as she polished off her third one. "I mean, was the name, *Super Penis Cakes* already taken?" she blurted, snorting loudly as she fell backwards onto her pillow.

This got Reagan roaring as well, and between fits of laughter and a buttload of silly selfies, they polished off the entire nine pack while watching the classic German holiday sketch comedy, *Dinner for One*.

Neither of them had ever laughed so hard in their entire lives and, for this, Reagan gazed up toward the dark ceiling and beamed a smile. She stopped short of sending up anything resembling a shout-out of thanks for the gift of laughter, and of survival, because that might be construed as a nod to a higher power.

But she did appreciate it.

And if she realized it or not, when it came to gratitude, the thawing process had begun.

# CHAPTER SEVENTY-FIVE

## SUNDAY, DECEMBER 21
## O' DARK THIRTY

R EAGAN WAS DEEP in REM sleep as she navigated the trenches of her recurring nightmare, tossing and turning in her hand-to-hand combat against the legions of retinal cell killers, when something began vibrating beneath the pillow she was faceplanted into.

The invaders were thrashing with their swords, mercilessly chopping away at her defenseless cone cells, when she got her first inkling of outside stimulus.

In her dream, she was vastly outnumbered as she ran down the dark alleyways, moving toward the vibration in an effort to escape the cruel and relentless slaughter. The sound was getting louder as she got closer, when all of a sudden—

Reagan's eyes sprung open and she blinked wildly, struggling to get her bearings in the darkened room. She was breathing fast, and her pulse was elevated, her brow dripping with perspiration.

*Where am I? Germany! What day is it? Fuck if I know! What the hell's vibrating?*

As she rolled over onto her back, her arm emerged from beneath the pillow and the source revealed itself.

She struggled to focus on the watch's illuminated display as it continued vibrating. It was an incoming call, but she couldn't make out the number. She swung her feet over her side of the bed and grabbed her phone, heading toward the narrow shaft of light coming from the bathroom.

She closed the door behind her and took a seat atop the closed toilet lid, with one hand rubbing her eyes in hopes of jumpstarting them as she studied the watch display on her other, comparing it against that of her phone.

*Unknown Caller.*

The vibration stopped and she scrutinized the display, checking the tiny time icon, which told her it was 01:33. *One-thirty in the morning! What the–? Who the hell would be calling me?*

Her initial thought was that Officer Raupp might be calling, or maybe the one who'd questioned her at the train station. But there was no indication of a message having been left.

Reagan went to the sink and splashed cool water on her face, patting it dry with a hand towel before returning to her throne and checking the *Recents* folder on her phone, then dialing the top number. It only rang twice before somebody answered.

"Oh, my God. I am so sorry for calling you in the middle of the night, Reagan!" the apologetic voice said. Reagan knew at once who it was, and with recognition came relief.

"Hei Li!" Reagan whispered loudly, fully awake now, but

trying not to waken Steffi. "*Hei Li*… gawd! Don't worry about the time, silly. I'm so glad you called. Are you okay?!"

"I'm calling you from my new phone. The other one–"

"I know about the other one," Reagan interjected, rubbing her eyes. "When I got some calls from it, and they weren't from you, I really started to worry. Oh, Hei Li, it's great to hear your voice, and I wasn't sure how to get ahold of you. It's been a crazy–"

"That's why I'm calling. When you and I talked, Fynn overheard about you being here. About your plans to go to Lübeck. It's my fault, and I feel bad."

"Listen to me, Hei Li—"

"Fynn fired me. Threatened to hurt me and my family if I said anything."

"It's not your fault, okay? There were some things about Fynn you and I didn't know. He became a complete stranger to me. He had a lot of secrets. *Dark* secrets… I had no idea."

Reagan listened to the dead air for several seconds, during which she thought she heard a sniffle coming through the line. "You heard… ?"

"Saw it on the news. I still can't believe it. *Any* of it. I mean, it's terrible what happened to Fynn. I'm sorry."

Reagan ran her fingers through her hair as she considered her reply. Her emotions were still raw, and despite everything that had happened, she couldn't help feeling *some* level of mourning for the person she'd once loved and created a life with. She opted not to launch into the negatives, as they wouldn't help anything.

"Thank you, Hei Li. It's been a lot to process. I guess sometimes in life we may think we know somebody well, when… perhaps… we really don't know them at all.…" Reagan said, her voice trailing off.

"Still, I'm sorry. For *you*, Reagan. And for Steffi. Losing her father that way, and–"

"*Stepfather.*"

"Oh, and when the TV showed what happened at the Hauptbahnhof, I knew it had to be the other guy… the ugly one. I've been praying for you two, and–"

"Yeah, thank you. It was a scary time," Reagan blurted, a little uncomfortable with the prayer talk. "Kharma, I guess."

"Mm. That must have been quite the ordeal, for you both. Especially Steffi, I'll bet.

"Yes, you could say that."

"How's she doing with all of this?"

Reagan almost let out a laugh. Not because anything was remotely funny, but because of the sheer insanity of everything that had been playing out these past few days. She gathered herself and replied softly.

"Steffi is… Stef is… a frigging *warrior*, Hei Li. She's young–coming up on sixteen–yet she's seen things this week that *nobody* should ever have to experience in their entire lifetime. Truthfully, she has risen to the moment and, in real time, shown me just how incredible she is. I mean, we're both processing this crap–and will be for quite some time, I'm sure–but, well, let's just say I couldn't be any prouder of my daughter than I am right now."

"Yes, I'm sure you have every reason to be."

Reagan stifled a yawn. "And about your job, Hei Li—"

"I'll find something."

"You didn't let me finish."

"Sorry."

"No problem. Now, have you heard about the Kaiser Holdings purchase?"

"Of the Fischmarkt?"

"Of the Fischmarkt, yes."

"I remember hearing something about you were thinking of maybe selling it."

"Yes, well, it wasn't a maybe, but Fynn had a few other ideas. But as the owner, *I* sold it, to Kaiser Holdings. They are good people, Hei Li. And, in negotiating the deal, I strongly recommended that they keep you on."

"Keep me? In my job, you mean? *Working* for them?"

"Yes. And I told them how much they should be offering to pay you, which would be substantially more than you've been making, and with the promotion to Supervising Manager."

A happy squeal came through Reagan's earpiece. Several seconds went by before Hei Li could form her words, but the reaction was music to Reagan's ears.

"I don't know what to say... whew! I'm–I–just–can't believe this! Thank you so much!"

"You totally deserve it, Hei Li. And I'm sure they'll be expecting you to get things set up about three hours from now, so I'd better get off the phone. My suggestion would be to sell those new lobster tanks to a restaurant, or maybe a pet store... you won't be needing them. Just concentrate on what you know, and what our family's done best all these years. You know the market–and our customers–like the back of your hand, Hei Li. You'll be very successful, I know it, and you haven't seen the last of me. Okay?"

"Promise?"

"Promise."

"When do you fly back home? Will I get to see you before you do?"

"Not sure. Hope so. Depends. That's something I need to discuss with Steffi after breakfast. I'll go with whatever she decides–whatever she needs–and wherever she wants to spend Christmas."

"Sounds good. Merry Christmas, Reagan. God bless you."

"Merry Christmas, Hei Li."

Reagan turned off her electronics and slipped back into bed, mindful not to wake Steffi as she slid over to spoon with her.

Steffi was awake now, but she didn't let on. Her eyes were open and still wet from the tears that had cascaded down her cheeks, having eavesdropped on her mother's praises from the other side of the bathroom door, before scampering back to bed.

Other than the usual complaints like being told what not to wear, or that her grades were lacking, Steffi wasn't accustomed to a lot of parental feedback–let alone kudos.

Steffi closed her eyes, taking comfort in her mother's assessment of her, and how extra nice the arm lovingly draped across her felt. A smile found her face as she drifted back to sleep.

# CHAPTER SEVENTY-SIX

S TEFFI LOOKED OVER the top of her mug of hot chocolate and watched as her mother slathered an inordinate amount of breakfast honey across the surface of her croissant.

The excess was dripping between her fingers, but Reagan wasn't the least bit concerned; she was totally in the blissful moment as she reveled in the perfection that only 50,000 rooftop bees could create.

Reagan licked her fingers clean and looked up, surprised to see she was being watched. "What?"

"Nothing," Steffi said, her eyes smiling from behind the mug. "Just nice to see you... enjoying something. You should find stuff at home that brings you joy, Mom. It looks good on you."

"Well, I guess I'll take that as a compliment. And that's some pretty sage advice, young lady. How about you? How's your enjoyment level at the moment?"

Steffi set down her mug, leaving behind a chocolatey mustache, which she licked off. "All things considered?"

"All things considered," Reagan replied, directing all of her attention where it should be. "How's Stefanie?"

"I dunno..." Steffi replied, looking away, her eyes traveling around the otherwise empty restaurant as if searching for the perfect answer. It was just the two of them enjoying a late breakfast, and when her gaze returned to her mother, she saw her studying her intently.

"What?"

"Have I told you lately just how incredible you are?"

"Mom..." Steffi replied, her eyes scanning the room again to see if some eavesdropping group might have just suddenly materialized at the next table. It wasn't just embarrassment she was feeling, though, as her concern had to do more with not wanting to start bawling at the table.

Her carefully cultivated, mid-teen shields were down at the moment, and her vulnerability made her feel fragile.

"I don't mean to embarrass you, honey. I just–"

"I don't want you to be upset with me," Steffi said, looking down at her plate as she pushed it to the side.

"Why could I possibly be upset with you, Stef?"

"It's just... I mean, you asked. How I'm doing."

"All things considered, yes. You can tell me. I'd like you to tell me, Steffi. How are you doing? Please, you can be completely honest with me. I'm your mother. I love you, more than anything in the world. There's no wrong answer, and–"

Reagan stopped herself when she saw her daughter's lip starting to quiver. She rested her hands on Steffi's and gave her the time to formulate her feelings.

Steffi's fingers melded with her mother's, and two unscheduled tears trickled down her cheeks as she replied.

"Germany's great, and everything, but—*all things considered*—I think… I want to go home."

Reagan smiled back encouragingly, squeezing Steffi's hands softly.

"Final answer?"

After a second's hesitation, Steffi nodded.

"Then that's what we'll do."

# CHAPTER SEVENTY-SEVEN

AFTER JOTTING THE last of her notes onto the hotel's notepad, Reagan thanked the airline rep profusely and hung up. She made a quick call to the hotel concierge, advising them of an email printout she would be expecting and asked them to save it for her to retrieve later. She also advised the clerk that they would be checking out in the morning. Early.

Reagan ground her palms into her exhausted eyes, harder than was healthy. They were ruined anyway, she figured. She took a sip of her now-cold room service tea and returned her molten-hot credit card to her wallet. Looking at her watch, she was surprised to find it was already past 14:00.

The last-minute flight changes had been difficult to arrange, not to mention exceedingly expensive, but she considered herself lucky to have scored two First Class seats, and she didn't hesitate to purchase them. She wasn't going to get *stupid* with her money, ever, but the days of being frugal just to be frugal were over. That had changed.

Reagan looked over at Steffi, who was curled up atop the bed. She'd let her sleep a while longer, she decided, as there was plenty of time before dinner, whatever that would consist of–and it wouldn't be sushi.

She carried her cellphone to the bathroom and closed the door. Taking a seat on the toilet's lid, she began checking for any messages she might have missed in all the chaotic goings-on that had required her immediate focus.

There was one new one. And it was from her bestie!

*Ames! Gawd, I've been such a horrible friend!* The self-loathing reprimand was coming from a place of guilt, and not at all based in reality. Still, the thought distortion reared its ugly head as she opened the message.

> *Twinner! What's going on, girl? I'm back home as of yesterday. They kept me for an extra day because of a new development. Kinda sucks, but it's not the end of the world. The left arm's in a cast, which is no biggie since I'm righthanded. Ribs will be a little sore for a while, they tell me, but I can deal with it. Slightly bummed about the left eye though. I was rather fond of that, mainly because it matched the right one perfectly, but they couldn't save it... it had to go. They tell me they can match the color pretty well, so, no Popeye jokes when you see me, okay? Promise.*

Reagan's hand shot to her mouth, and she immediately began sobbing as the phone slipped through her fingers and tumbling onto the bathmat. "Jesus! God! No!"

She sat there, her face buried in her hands for several minutes as she absorbed the horrible news, all of which hit like a hundred body blows. Her head felt heavy as she labored to lift it from its cradle. Willing her eyes to open, she struggled to focus through the waterfall of tears, rubbing fingers against the blur in an effort to squeegee away the news, the tears, the pain.

Reagan picked up the phone at her feet and opened the message again, picking up where she'd left off:

> *no Popeye jokes when you see me, okay? Promise.*

*Jerry's taking good care of me. All I want is tomato soup and grilled cheese sandwiches, and he's been a godsend. Oh, and speaking of Jerry, he spent most of yesterday supervising a couple of guys who got your house fixed up the way it was before Lurch broke it. So, whenever you get home, it'll be like nothing ever happened. Almost. Anyway, Merry Christmas, Twinner! Let me know how you and your precious girl are doing!*

*I'll keep an eye out for you! LOL*

*~ Ames*

It was all Reagan could do not to roar like a banshee as she jumped to her feet and caught herself, her right arm cocked and raised as she double clutched, stopping just short of violently hurling her phone against the bathroom mirror.

She couldn't believe it. Any of it. And she found it especially hard to get her head around the fact that Ames could crack *jokes* about her situation. "You're horrible!" is what her kneejerk reply would be if she were with her bestie in person, but this gut punch had rendered her unable to come up with any kind of emotionally intelligent reply. For now, anyway.

She hoped she'd be better equipped to handle a proper response tomorrow, once she'd had time to sensitively craft one. In the meantime, she'd surf the anger wave and direct her considerable venom where it belonged, sending out a curse for the ages.

*Damn you to hell, Ekkehard!*

## UNIVERSITY MEDICAL CENTER
## HAMBURG-EPPENDORF
## ROOM 666
## SUNDAY, DECEMBER 21
## 15:30, CET

The attending nurse tamped down her frustration, doing her best to maintain a professional demeanor as she finished taking the vitals of her most difficult patient, and then entered them into the notes. Of the 1,738 beds in this facility, she dreaded this guy the most.

The man lay there, ignoring her as he always did, staring out the window as she checked the dressings on his arms' stumps. Both arms had required more aggressive amputation, with margins well above the elbows, due to the bone crushing trauma they had received, and it was unlikely he'd ever be rocking a tank top.

The nurse spoke loud enough to be heard above the din of the TV, which he shared with another patient in their double room. "Ich komme in einer Stunde wieder, um noach Ihnen zu sehen, Herr Hase," she said, promising to check on him again in an hour's time.

Getting no response, she turned to go, leaving the roommates to themselves.

Ekkehard turned his gaze away from the window, settling instead on the obnoxious overhead TV his roommate insisted be on, seemingly at all hours of the day. It was stuck on the omnipresent local news channel, which seemed impossible to escape.

Ekkehard bristled, his features becoming grimmer as he watched yet another repeat of two sensational news stories, one of which took place at the train station, the other being the discovery of a body adjacent to the Fischmarkt.

Ekkehard shot a look over at the man occupying the other bed. The man wasn't even watching it; his mouth hung open as he snored. Ekkehard had heard the man conversing in English to a visitor earlier, so he addressed him accordingly.

"Hey! Asshole! How about turning that shit off!"

A loud snort escaping the man as his mouth slammed shut. Fuming, he turned toward Ekkehard and shot him a scowl, mixed with a cruel aside as he rolled back over and turned away from him.

"Do it yourself. The remote's right there on the table!"

# CHAPTER SEVENTY-EIGHT

REAGAN STEPPED OUT of the elevator, and as she crossed the lobby, a glance out the window told her it would be getting dark soon. She checked in with her watch, which confirmed this. She had enjoyed an unscheduled three-hour nap.

The desk agent smiled as Reagan approached, and she addressed the American visitor in English.

"Hello. I have your copies from the printer, Frau Dunkel," she said, handing them to her. "And you said you will be checking out tomorrow?"

"Yes, thank you. And quite early, I'm afraid," Reagan replied, noting the name Frau Lemmer on her tag.

"I see. We hope you have enjoyed your stay with us."

"The hotel? Yes, it's been very nice. Thank you, Frau Lemmer."

"Good... have you and your daughter had a relaxing vacation time in Germany?" the twenty-something blonde asked, playing Twenty Questions while beaming her best PR smile.

*You mean, aside from my daughter's kidnapping, a few car chases, a death in the family, and narrowly escaping crazed killers?*

The girl was still smiling in anticipation of her answer, so Reagan went with, "Perfect."

"I'm so glad to hear it. May I help you with anything else?"

"Um, one thing, yes. I'd rather not go out after dark, so might you recommend a good local place that offers delivery?" Reagan asked. "We've already done the sushi bar."

The girl produced a take-out menu emblazoned with a bold logo on the front: *Mr. Kebab*

"Do you like Turkish food?"

Reagan emerged from the rainforest-like shower, having followed on the heels of Steffi's lengthy one and was happy that the hotel seemed to have an abundant hot water supply.

They had opted for showers tonight versus in the morning because the 02:30 checkout would be brutal.

A knock on the door signaled dinner had arrived, and Reagan hoped the until-now-untried, but highly recommended Döner kebab sandwiches would be worthy of the hype. She slipped into the hotel robe, grabbed a fistful of euros from the zipper pocket of her backpack, and exchanged most of them with the delivery guy who, in turn, handed her two white paper bags.

"Danke," she said, closing the door and relocking it with the deadbolt.

The hairdryer was whirring loudly from the bathroom, so Reagan raised her voice to be heard over it. "Hungry?!"

The dryer immediately powered off and Steffi, following her nose, leaned out the door.

"Whatever that is, I'm totally down with it!"

Dinner had paired perfectly with the remaining Super Dickmann's, and they polished them off over a very competitive
round of Braille Uno.

"Draw four!" Steffi chirped. She laughed as her mother
scooped up more cards and added them to her already massive card fan.

Reagan pouted playfully, knowing she didn't have a prayer
of winning with Steffi only holding two cards. They weren't
utilizing the main tactile feature of the Braille cards, as neither
was quite ready to embrace the buzzkill that would come with
learning the system.

Not yet anyway. If nothing else, the raised bumps did
enhance the cardholders' grip.

Reagan laid down her cards in an act of surrender and
held out her hand to shake with the victor. "Good game,
babe. I've had it."

"Thanks, Mom. Maybe you'd enjoy the game more if you
had, like, a music stand or something to hold all your cards,"
Steffi quipped.

"You're a cruel one," Reagan replied with a wink as she
collected the cards and returned them to their sleeve.

"Think they sell those Dickmann things at the airport?
Gotta bring some of those home; they're the bomb."

"They are amazing. We'll look for 'em. Good idea,"
Reagan said, secretly wishing she could bring home a pallet
of them for her injured bestie. "Did you set out what you're
wearing on the plane?"

"Yeah," Steffi replied softly, looking away, her mind apparently elsewhere.

"You okay?"

"Hm? Um, yeah...."

"What're you thinking about, honey?"

A few moments went by before Steffi could frame her response. She turned to her mother and asked the unspoken question.

"So, I guess this means you and Fynn are divorced now, huh?"

# CHAPTER SEVENTY-NINE

**LUFTHANSA FLIGHT LH 415**
**OUTBOUND HAMBURG**
**MONDAY, DECEMBER 22**
**05:40, CET**

STEFFI'S EYES WERE still puffy. Both she and her mom had nearly slept through the 01:30 alarm, only to be saved ten minutes later by their back-up, a wake-up phone call from the front desk.

She picked up the tiny neck pillow, plopped into her first-class window seat, and fastened her seat belt as she watched her mother in the aisle, struggling to squeeze the large shopping bag into the overhead compartment. It was no easy trick, considering all the boxes of Super Dickmann's they'd scored at the duty-free shop an hour before.

Reagan swore under her breath as she finally managed to close the compartment, offering an apologetic smile to the line of passengers loading behind her as she poured herself into her seat.

After getting her personal items squared away and within easy reach, she looked over at Steffi and patted her leg. "Made it! Good job… phew."

"How long till we're home, Mom?"

"It'll be a long day, baby. An hour's flight to Frankfurt, then our layover is…" she paused to verify with her itinerary, "… about three hours there, then we catch our connecting flight–which will be nonstop, thankfully–to Seattle."

"How long's the nonstop flight? Couple of hours?"

"Mm… a little longer than that. Not quite eleven hours…."

"Holy crap!"

"Shh, watch your language, honey," Reagan reminded her. "Hopefully we'll both sleep."

"Yeah," Steffi muttered, shaking her head as she pondered what would surely be the longest day of her life. She turned back to her mom and asked in all earnest, "Could you please grab me a couple of the Dickmann's?"

"I'm going to pretend you didn't just ask me that."

The three-hour-and-ten-minute layover seemed like an eternity. If nothing else, it had provided a lengthy window of time to grab a meal. And maybe a history lesson.

"So," Steffi said, taking a pause as she regarded the half-eaten hotdog in her hands. "It just clicked for me: *Frankfurt*-er!"

Reagan finished chewing her cheeseburger before replying. "Yep. Pretty sure they originated here." She popped the last of her fries into her mouth. "And I'll give you three guesses where *this* became famous," she added, gesturing to her burger.

"No way! *Hamburg*-er!"

"Ding! Ding! Ding! Here's your prize!" Reagan said, chuckling as she pulled a couple of the Dickmann's from the carryon bag.

"Wow."

"Yep. Germany's got it going on. I'd hoped to introduce you to much more this trip, but hopefully next time."

"Yeah," Steffi replied, her thoughts elsewhere now.

*If there is a next time* is what both of their thought bubbles would probably indicate.

Steffi stared out the window as the Airbus A340 continued its climb. Reagan strained to see past her as the last glimpses of Frankfurt–and Germany altogether–gave way to the puffy clouds they were now entering and would be surrounded by.

Reagan turned her gaze forward, her limited vision now focused on the Fasten Seat Belt sign. She took its advice, checking her buckle and that of her daughter's, before reclining her seat slightly.

She had the next eleven hours to unpack the events of the last few days, as well as the myriad of emotions that continued to flood in. The adrenaline that had been fueling them had waned, giving way to utter exhaustion. Sleep would soon follow.

The reality was kicking in as Reagan recognized she would

likely never see her homeland again. A tear trickled down each cheek, and she wiped them away before Steffi could notice.

*Auf Wiedersehen, Deutschland.*

# CHAPTER EIGHTY

## HOME
## BOTHELL, WASHINGTON
## MONDAY, DECEMBER 22
## 3:15 PM, PACIFIC

THE UBER DRIVER parked his Chevy Volt in the empty driveway and hopped out to assist with the luggage.

"We're here, honey. Come on," Reagan said, turning to the rear seat and nudging Steffi, who had slept the entire way from the airport, faceplanted against the suitcase on the seat next to her.

"Mm..." she mumbled as she got her bearings. "Wait... we're home?"

"We are home, darlin'," Reagan confirmed as she climbed out. "C'mon."

The driver pulled Reagan's suitcase from the trunk, as well as her small carryon and the big, twine-handled giftbag containing the Super Dickmann's. He brought the luggage up to the porch and circled back for Steffi's.

Reagan rummaged through her zippered folio, pushing past the passport and travel documents until she found her travel wallet, from which she pulled out a hundred-dollar bill.

As the driver returned with the last case, Reagan smiled and handed him the cash.

"Let me get you some–" he started to say as he fished for his wallet.

"No need. Merry Christmas," she replied. "And thanks."

"Seriously? Wow… thank you so much, and welcome home from… wherever you're returning from. Merry Christmas." He beamed an appreciative smile and jogged back to his car, waving as he took off down the street.

Steffi made it up to the porch and almost distended her jaw as she yawned. "Whew."

"I feel ya, hon. It's called jetlag," Reagan said, her eyes scanning the front door, her mind visualizing the intrusion and the chaotic attack that had taken place inside just a week before. She flashed back on what Ames had told her about having the place fixed back up. *That's a bestie for you.*

Reagan shook her head, counted to five, and inserted her key. The door creaked open, and they dragged their luggage inside, parking it by the entrance. The fine hairs on Reagan's arms stood on end as she approached the living room, her adrenaline cuing up for the vibes and energy of the then-tall man having been inside her home. In search of her.

The Christmas tree was intact. It was only slightly off axis and seemed to be more or less the way she had left it. A couple of small, framed photos on the mantle had been moved.

It was when she turned the corner and entered the kitchen

that her imagination went into overload. The photos on the fridge had been rearranged completely, and affixed to the surface randomly, though not by their assigned magnets.

In the center of the collection was the photo of Fynn in his younger days, smiling at the camera with a grin that not only hinted at mischief, but also a bevy of secrets–and an underlying danger Reagan only now understood fully. She shook her head as she stared at it for a long moment, a cocktail of emotions vying for her attention, none of them pity.

"Mom, where's the iMac?" Steffi asked, staring at the empty table.

Reagan winced as a barrage of rapid-fire images and sounds came flooding in and her imagination reconstructed the violent scene that had taken place where they stood. Images of the tall man tossing Amethyst around the kitchen like a rag doll, Ames's screams as she struggled against her attacker before being sent crashing face first into the computer's screen and collapsing on the floor; Ames left for dead.

Her blood went to full boil in a scant few seconds as she considered the savagery that had been waged against her bestie. Her bestie who, for the rest of her days, would now have one functioning eye. *An eye for... two arms.*

And, just as quickly, the thoughts disappeared as Reagan turned to Steffi. She spared her daughter the imagery and instead went with a simpler explanation; a white lie: "Our friend, Ames, said there was a problem with the iMac; we might need a new one, so I'll check into it."

"'Kay. I'm gonna go take a shower," Steffi said, as she shuffled down the hall.

"Okay." Reagan didn't even bother calling out her customary hot water advisory.

She turned her attention to the computer table, noticing it was brand new, but identical to the IKEA one that had been destroyed in the mayhem. As her eyes began to moisten, a tight-lined grin spread across her face.

*Thanks, Twinner.*

Hot showers gave way to unscheduled naps and, after three hours, Steffi's rumbling stomach served as her alarm clock.

She let her mom sleep while she rifled through the slim pickings in the pantry. The fridge offered little more, but at least there was an unopened quart of milk and a stick of butter. And an opened package of not quite gray hotdogs. She gave them the smell test and shrugged, figuring they had ample nitrates to last a millennia.

She set about boiling some water and putting out two paper plates. She dumped the sleeve of day-glow orange powder onto the cooked, drained mac 'n' cheese noodles and stirred in the dairy components. After slicing up two wieners, she dumped them into the mix and surveyed her work. *Dinner for survivors.*

She went down the hall to wake her mom.

Reagan took a sip of her dry Riesling, noting it didn't pair half badly with the bomb shelter cuisine. Steffi polished off her blue Gatorade and collected the empty paper plates as she got up.

"I'll do the dishes," she said with a chuckle.

"Thanks for dinner, honey. Best meal I've ever had," Reagan replied, winking. "Chef Stef to the rescue."

Steffi returned to the table with a box of Dickmann's and plopped back into her seat.

"Now you're talkin'," Reagan said.

"Okay if I bring one of the other boxes to Vickie's tomorrow?"

"Sure thing," Reagan said, mindful of how excited Steffi had been with her marzipan gift purchase for Vickie. The one she'd left in the snow. "What time are you going over there?"

"I dunno. I'll call her in the morning, see when they can pick me up," she said, popping the super dessert into her mouth. "What are you doing tomorrow?"

"Mm, probably computer shopping online," Reagan said, holding up her phone. "That and call the body shop to check on the car, couple loads of laundry, tend to my Hoyas...."

*Change beneficiary... Fynn's stuff to Salvation Army... file for name change....*

"Good times... *J.K.* Let me know if you need any help."

"I will. Thanks, hon. You tired?"

"Yeah, kind of, but the nap helped. Why?"

"Feel like watching *A Charlie Brown Christmas*?"

"I'll make the popcorn!"

# CHAPTER EIGHTY-ONE

## TUESDAY, DECEMBER 23
## 11:15 AM

I T HAD ALREADY been a productive morning for Reagan, which was amazing considering how jacked up their body clocks were.

She had showered three hours before and had already attended to the hundred-plus Hoya plants occupying the numerous plant stands along the bay windows.

Breakfast had been a couple of Dickmann's with her coffee.

She found it hard to believe they had just gotten home the day before. They had both fallen asleep during the video last night, having missed the Charlie Brown choir singing "Hark the Herald Angels Sing" at the end. It was Steffi's favorite part, but it wasn't like they hadn't watched it before a hundred times. The old VHS copy was still holding up, so they could cue it up again later. Maybe even make it a Grinch double feature, depending on when Steffi got back from Vickie's.

Reagan finished folding the second load coming from the

dryer, having already spoken with the body shop and being told her vehicle was finished and could be delivered tomorrow.

Shopping for anything important—or insanely expensive, as in this case—via her phone was brutal because the screen was so tiny, but it was the only game in town until she got a new computer, and her rectangular magnifying glass helped a little.

Reagan had purchased a new Mac—though she'd opted for the Apple Mac Studio M4 Max, because the new all-in-one iMacs were no longer available with the twenty-seven inch screens, only twenty-four inch, which wasn't going to cut it as her eyesight progressively got worse. She also had to think longer term, too, for Steffi, which helped justify the fortune she was paying.

Her diminished vision had forced her hand, and she felt compelled to pony up another five grand for Apple's latest and greatest separate display: a massive thirty-two inch one.

"XDR 16:9 6K HDR IPS LCD monitor?" she muttered, trying to decipher the specifications. She didn't even know what half of those descriptors stood for, but at that price it had to be a BFD. All she knew was that it was their biggest and best, and the keyword that sold her was it was dubbed the "Retina" display, which had to be better than a retinitis display.

Reagan had opted for next day delivery and arranged for the geeks to set things up.

Next item on her list had been to schedule a Salvation Army pick-up of donation items. All of it Fynn's. They weren't coming until next week, so she had plenty of time to stuff his clothing—an entire closet, plus two dressers' worth—into trash bags. He had always had more clothes and shoes than she did and having just learned of his double life, that started to make sense why.

Though she wouldn't be accomplishing it today, she had made the decision during the long, Paris-to-Seattle flight that she was going to change her last name. She had never liked taking the name of Dunkel; besides, it meant *dark* in German, and it was now forever tainted.

No, after New Year's she would file for the change back to her maiden name: Licht, which meant *light*.

The irony wasn't lost on her.

# CHAPTER EIGHTY-TWO

## WEDNESDAY, DECEMBER 24
## 1:40 PM

STEFFI HAD STAYED the night at Vickie's, and they were spending today being chaperoned by her mom to the mall and "maybe a movie." That was perfect, as far as Reagan was concerned, because she had a full dance card.

The big box store had been less than helpful with their stated delivery window for the computer, promising their arrival sometime between 9:00 a.m. and 3:00 p.m. This left a ginormous hole in her day, but she had plenty of ways to fill it.

Thankfully, the body shop had been much more respectful of her time, delivering the *Fuckus* via a large tow trailer by 10:15. It was now tucked safely back in the garage. The shop had done a stellar job of erasing any signs of the car's injuries, and with the new paint and detailing, it looked better than it had in years. Maybe ever.

Reagan tossed the last of eight large trash bags full of Fynn's clothing into the corner of the garage, next to two sizeable moving boxes full of assorted footwear. It felt akin to moving Imelda Marcos. There hadn't been a moment's pause for any emotional attachment, nor memories, as she surgically removed any trace of his existence.

Another box–this one destined for the landfill–contained any and all photos of him, including the ones off the fridge, as well as his yearbooks and anything he had considered keepsakes.

*Buh-bye!*

Reagan closed the garage door and returned to the kitchen where she absconded with one of Steffi's precious blue Gatorade bottles. The blue matched her mood and, besides, she had to see what all the fuss was about. Chugging, she powered it down in a series of non-stop gulps before coming up for air. *Not half bad!*

The squeal of vehicle brakes outside got her attention. The geeks were here!

Turns out there had only been one geek, but he knew his way around computers, that was for sure. Reagan had marveled at the speed with which the young, twenty-something tech had gotten things hooked up and the system running. Even her internet. And he was gone within thirty-five minutes.

While she waited for her new system to absorb the contents of her backup external hard drive, she took the time to adjust the settings on her new, air traffic control-worthy monitor, bumping up the fonts and cursor size, while setting up new easier-to-read folders.

She couldn't wait to see her and Steffi's phone photos on this thing. There would surely be a new desktop photo in the bunch.

The status bar showed it would be a while for the file transfers, so she poured herself a glass of the premixed, bottled Holiday Nog and dug out her pristine, 1964-era LP copy of *The Beach Boys' Christmas Album*. As side one cued up on the turntable, the cutesy Brian Wilson-penned "Little Saint Nick" filled the room. Like most of the tracks, it was a quick, two-minute burner.

Reagan took a swig of her cocktail and chuckled as she studied the front cover photo of five grown men, all decked out in their likely Sears sweaters, as they placed red ornaments on the Christmas tree. The album had been one of her father's and, as side one gave way to side two, she began to feel a warm glow, the effect coming from either the memories or the brandy.

Steffi would be home any minute, which Reagan hoped would coincide with the delivery of the large combo pizza that was en route.

Reagan swapped out the LP halfway through, having tired of it, choosing instead another Christmas favorite by an artist who was rocking the Christmas sweater way better than the Boys, and was sitting by an open fire, no less.

The Holiday Nog was proving quite tasty, festive, and buzz-inducing. Reagan carried her second tumbler of it with her as she stepped out onto the tiny patio. Her stomach growled. Nat King Cole sung of his love for chestnuts while visions of pepperoni danced in her own head.

The doorbell got Reagan's attention and, as she swung the door open, she was greeted by two smiling faces: Steffi's and the pizza guy's.

# CHAPTER EIGHTY-THREE

## WEDNESDAY, 9:35 PM

SPOILER: THE GRINCH'S heart was undersized, times two.

Reagan paused the tape which, at this point, was barely watchable from the number of passes it had made across the VCR's heads over the decades. She looked over at Steffi, who seemed to be sinking further into the couch cushions.

"You done?" she asked, already knowing the answer as she powered down the electronics and set the remote atop the empty pizza box between them.

"Yeah," Steffi replied softly. "Tired."

With the TV now off, the room had plunged into an uncomfortable level of darkness. Reagan got up and slowly felt her way along the familiar wall and, reaching the hallway, switched on the runway lights before returning to the couch.

"I know. Same here," Reagan said, pivoting to face her daughter. "You know, we have to listen to our bodies when we're this exhausted; they're trying to tell us something."

As if on cue, Steffi released an impressive fart she didn't

realize she'd been holding. She was as surprised by it as her mother was, and they both let out huge belly laughs.

"Oh my God! Sorry, my body was trying to tell me something!" Steffi squealed as she threw her head back.

Reagan shook her head, appreciating the moment's much needed levity. "Not exactly what I meant, but...."

"Sorry," Steffi giggled, taking a moment to collect herself. "Ahem. You were saying?"

"Well... I know it's only been a couple of days, but we haven't really talked about *stuff* since we got home."

"What stuff?"

"You know... I mean, we've both been through a *lot* of crazy, *crazy* stuff this past week and we need to check in with each other, y'know? We need to process it, heal from it."

"I guess."

"Which means, if you want to talk with me about whatever's on your mind–*anything*–let me know. Okay? Don't hesitate."

"'Kay."

"Promise?"

"Promise."

"Okay. So, how are you doing right now? Are you okay?"

"Mostly, yeah, I guess," Steffi replied, unable to suppress her yawn.

The effect was contagious and immediately triggered a similar yawn in Reagan. "Gawd... wow... see? We're not even close to being caught up with our sleep yet, so...."

"I didn't sleep much at Vickie's. She was kind of hyper and talking half the night."

"Oh? About what?"

"Just… how she's getting her license in January. And her mom got her a car."

"For Christmas?"

"Yeah," Steffi answered softly, sounding slightly dejected, which didn't go unnoticed.

Reagan took a moment to weigh her response. "Well, that must be nice. I didn't get my first car until I was twenty. A used Volkswagen bug. Bought it with my own money from the–"

She stopped herself, reluctant to utter the word associated with her parents' business.

She bit her lip. She had planned it to be a Christmas morning surprise but now seemed a better time for the reveal, and she blurted it out.

"Hey, honey. Do me a favor and bring your stocking over here."

"My stocking?

"Yeah."

"Mom, it's not Christmas morning yet."

"I know. The stocking won't get filled until Santa brings his stuff, but–"

Steffi's look stopped her. "Mom. I'm not five," she said, shaking her head.

"I know. Sorry, old habits die hard. It's just… you'll always be my little girl."

"I know. It's okay."

"So, please bring me your mostly empty stocking and don't peek inside. Okay?"

"'Kay," Steffi replied, dutifully making the seemingly long pilgrimage to the living room mantle. She returned with her stocking, the one with the felt snowman applique on it, and set it in her mom's lap.

"I was going to wait with this, but... well... reach down into the bottom. There might be something deep down, in the toe there," Reagan said, a smile beginning to form.

Steffi did as instructed. Her arm sunk inside, up to her elbow, before her fingers hit paydirt. She scrunched her brow as she looked back at her mom and slowly retrieved the mystery item.

"What is it, babe?" Reagan asked, her eyes wide. She hoped she'd get the desired response.

Steffi held the tiny, wrapped box up for closer inspection. "A pack of cigarettes! Yay!"

"Um, I don't think so... and don't *ever* let me catch you smoking, or you'll be grounded until you're forty-five!" Reagan replied, which got them both chuckling.

Steffi ripped into the paper, revealing the nondescript black gift box. She looked at her mom as if seeking permission to proceed.

"Go ahead, open it."

Steffi lifted the box's lid, followed by the rectangular piece of cotton, and raised her free hand to her mouth. Her eyes went wide at the sight of a volleyball keychain and attached to it a familiar looking Ford key. She blinked several times before looking at her mom. "Nuh-uh...."

Reagan's enthusiastic nod was all the confirmation she needed.

Steffi sprang from her seat and melted into her mother's arms. "Is this for reals?!"

"It's definitely for reals, honey. I got her all fixed up, painted, and she has four new tires. It's in the garage! Besides..." Reagan said, pausing as she absorbed the enormity of the moment, and the end of her independence. "It's time to pass the torch. My driving days are over."

# CHAPTER EIGHTY-FOUR

## THURSDAY, DECEMBER 25
## CHRISTMAS MORNING
## 7:13 AM

HAVING HAD THEIR main gift exchange previously, Christmas morning involved going through the Santa bounty in their stockings.

Reagan's had been filled mostly with candy and a couple of lottery tickets, while Steffi's stocking continued the new car theme, with a volleyball-shaped air freshener, three emergency road flares, and assorted Ford accessories. Even so, stockings had taken all of five minutes.

Reagan scooped the last thick slice of French toast from the skillet and added it to the stack already plated. She placed it on the table, adjacent to the platter of bacon, the Mrs. Butterworth's bottle, and the glasses of mango juice.

She poured herself a second large mug of coffee and added a generous splash of Bailey's to this one. She yawned as she stepped out onto the back deck. The throaty motor of a hummingbird buzzing nearby got her attention. As she turned in hopes of a visual, the tiny creature zoomed off in a blur, having been spooked by the roar of the neighbor's lawnmower coming to life.

Reagan's mental cobwebs were thick this morning, her reaction times suffering, and her resistance futile. Sleep had been fitful at best, even with her spooning partner next to her. Taking full advantage of her own weakened condition, her subconscious had decided to torture her with yet another round, and a new scenario, just in case she had forgotten the fact that she was going *fucking blind.*

As she stood against the patio railing, Reagan closed her eyes, powerless against the thought distortions as the previous night's imagery forced its way back in. This reimagined nightmare was a variation on the Pacman one, but the theme was the always the same: cone cell annihilation.

This twisted remake involved healthy cone cells represented as dominoes, killed off one by one, in sequence, and as they individually died, their dead husks toppled into the next healthy cell, killing it. There were millions of them, perfectly spaced and arranged in intricate patterns, crashing down and with no way to stop them.

In the dream, Reagan desperately tried to outrun them before being squashed and utterly defeated, but to no avail. She had been jarred awake, sweating profusely, just as the final domino was about to fall with her in its crosshairs.

This signaled the end of the movie, and as she stood at the railing, a desperate gasp now escaped her.

"Mom?"

"Jeezus!" Reagan spun around, her face ghostlike, as she

was yanked back into the present like a puppet on its strings. The coffee mug slipped through her fingers, crashed down to the ground and shattered into several pieces as the caramelly libation splashed up, soiling her slippers and spritzing her calves and the hem of her favorite white robe.

"Sorry, Mom! Geez—I didn't mean to—! Are you *okay?*" Steffi blurted at the sight of her mother's coloring. "Here, let me get something," she said, dashing toward the kitchen and unspooling way too many paper towels for the job.

Reagan stared down at the spatter on her slippers. They were probably ruined. Her favorite mug definitely was. And it had been the last of the Bailey's.

"Okay… watch out for the sharp pieces, Mom. Just… yeah. Leave your slippers on the mat and go back inside. I've got this," Steffi declared as she got to work.

Steffi mopped up the lake of syrup with her remaining bites and set down her fork. She washed it all down with her last gulp of juice and pushed her plate away.

"Thanks for breakfast, Mom."

"You're welcome, honey. Thanks again for cleaning up my mess out there. All thumbs."

"No worries," Steffi replied, just as the washing machine signaled that the robe and slippers load was done. "Want me to put the stuff in the dryer?" she asked, standing and taking her plate to the counter.

"Yes, please. Danke."

"Bitte."

As Steffi made her way to the laundry room, Reagan wiped a spot of syrup that had dripped onto her *I Don't Give a Schnitzel* tee-shirt, something she would add to the next load.

"Plans for today?" she called out.

"I dunno... probably just organize my car and stuff. Need to go on the computer later," Steffi replied as she emerged from the laundry room and rinsed the dishes. "How about you, Mom?"

"Might take a nap later, but I've got to call Ames, see how she's..." Reagan paused as her phone vibrated.

*Well, speak of the devil!* She gestured an *excuse me* to Steffi, then answered.

"Twinner!"

# CHAPTER EIGHTY-FIVE

I T TOOK A moment for the connection to lock in, but when it did, the screen revealed the incoming call to be a video one. Reagan propped the phone against the syrup bottle as Ames's face filled the screen.

It was the eye patch that got her, and she tried not to reveal her shock at seeing Ames this way.

"Hey, Bestie!"

"Hey, Ray Gun," Ames replied, smiling. Her dressings had been removed, as had most of the stitches. Purple bruises had mostly morphed to yellowish tones. She wore freshly applied lipstick, and her right eye was sporting some mascara and lashes.

Still, it was all about the patch on her left.

"Welcome home, sweetie. Merry Christmas!"

Reagan returned a smile, to the best of her ability. "Hey, beautiful. Merry Christmas to you! Your ears must've been ringing because I was just telling Stef I was gonna call you. How are you feeling?"

"I ain't gonna lie. Still feel beat up from the feet up, but I'm getting there. You should see the other guy!" she chirped, breaking into a fit of laughter that was immediately curtailed by sore ribs. "Ooch... it only hurts when I laugh. Anyway, I'm back home and being spoiled by my man. Life is good."

*Life is good?! Yes, you* should *see the other guy...*

Reagan nodded, her smile still tight as she tried to get herself together emotionally. She tried to focus on Ames's smile rather than the patch. At least it was purple–and sparkly; Ames wouldn't have it any other way, she knew.

"You look good, Ames. Better. Gawd, I'm sorry I haven't called you since I've been home. Some friend I am, right?"

"Stop. You just got back, and–not to minimize it–I know you've had a few things on your plate. I'm just glad you're back safe, Twinner. I can deal with a lot of things, but the thought of not having you in my life isn't one of 'em."

Reagan wiped away the tear that was threatening to form. "Same goes for me, Ames. You know that, right?"

Ames nodded, rubbing at her fresh mascara and ruining it. "With all my heart, Ray Gun."

They both took the moment to collect themselves, nodding and smiling, their considerable love expressed nonverbally. Ames was the first to speak.

"The place look okay? I mean, aside from the computer and all?"

"Gawd, Twinner, you are amazing... I can never thank you enough. I got a new computer, so, otherwise, things look like nothing ever happened."

"That was the idea. Good."

"More than good."

"Mm... how about you? *You* okay?"

"Yeah. Mostly. Yeah. I mean–*fuck*–it's been...." Reagan managed, looking away briefly.

"The stuff with Fynn? Did you manage to find–?"

"You could say that, yeah," Reagan interjected, deciding now wasn't the best time to elaborate. "Sorry to interrupt. We… did… hook up. And it's over," Reagan said, catching how incredulous it all sounded. "I can fill you in later on all that, but let's just say he won't be coming back."

"Mm… I'm sorry. I mean, I *guess* I'm sorry… should I be?"

Reagan shook her head. "Nope. Thanks, but nope. I'll be fine. He made his bed and…."

Ames let the silence hang there for a moment. "How's Stef taking all this?"

Reagan shook her head slowly, hardly knowing where to begin. "Steffi… whew!" she said, catching her breath. "It's still early, but Steffi seems to be handling everything amazingly. I think I'll schedule a therapy session for her, though, just in case. Probably sessions for both of us. Gawd…."

"Wow, that intense, huh?"

"If you had any idea of the craziness my girl got subjected to this past couple of weeks… Let's just say we were thrust into an effing action movie with no script, and we did our own stunts… gawd, we're literally lucky to be alive; I'll just leave it at that for right now."

"Baby, it sure sounds like it. I won't press you for the details now. But you *know* I will later!" Ames replied, laughing again before clutching her ribs. "Damn!"

"I can tell you this, though. You can sleep well knowing, with absolute certainty, that the monster who roughed you up will *never* be able to lay a finger on anyone again. We saw to that."

"Bless."

"Yeah… so, we need to get together in the new year, once you're feeling up to it, Ames."

"Well, funny you should mention that."

# CHAPTER EIGHTY-SIX

BEFORE HANGING UP, Amethyst had extended a very warm invitation for Reagan and Steffi to join her and Jerry for Christmas dinner at their place. Reagan had acknowledged the sweetness of the offer but also mentioned they didn't want to be a burden. Besides, she was no longer driving.

Ames had been prepared for any debate contingency and refused to take no for an answer. Jerry would even take care of transportation, if need be, she said. So, it was decided!

After the call, Reagan immediately informed Steffi of the evening plans, and she was excited to be invited.

The conversation with Ames had been much needed, but also perfectly timed, as it had reminded her of an important addition to her extensive to-do list. And there was no time like the present.

Reagan spent the next hour researching therapists, reading reviews about them, and making inquiries online as to whether or not they were taking new patients. *Patients?* That word had given her pause, but she figured that's what they would be.

She had narrowed her search to her top five choices, hoping one of them might have an opening for the two of them sometime after the holidays, but she wasn't too optimistic. She put a big check mark on her list, next to *Therapist.*

Reagan continued to the next item, researching the Department of Licensing website to see what was involved with scheduling a driver's test for Steffi, after her sixteenth birthday the following month. She made a note to call them next week, after the holidays. *DOL: Check!*

While she was at it, Reagan dug the Ford's pink slip out of the file cabinet and went through the procedures for transferring ownership to her daughter. She also emailed her insurance agent and advised him of the upcoming changes to the policy. *Check! Check!*

She even downloaded the requisite forms to initiate her request for name change. As she waited for the printer to finish doing its thing, her finger hovered over the wireless mouse. After a moment's hesitation, she clicked it again, adding a second set to the printer's queue.

*Just in case... Check!!*

After wading through an ocean of emails, she attended to the task she most dreaded and had saved for last: an appointment with the Retina Clinic. January 10–a Saturday morning, when Steffi could drive her. *Oy. Check!*

Aided by her handheld magnifying glass, Reagan made annotations of the upcoming appointments into the tiny squares of the kitchen calendar, taking pause to acknowledge the year was nearly toast.

*Happy New Year? Is that even a possibility? Let's get through Christmas first, Ray!*

Reagan looked at the clock and was pleased to see she'd

accomplished most of her list and it was only 10:25. She informed her daughter she was done with the computer in case she needed to use it.

Steffi had decided she could organize her car tomorrow, choosing instead to avail herself to the bitchin' new computer so she could work on a little project she hoped to surprise her mom with. She adjusted the big monitor's angle so that there could be no peeking.

Reagan stood at the kitchen counter and rubbed her tired eyes, grinding them beyond their tolerances, and nearly into the back of her skull. She looked out the window, jazzed to have chosen the perfect moment, as a young, ruby-throated hummingbird hovered on the other side of the glass, seemingly staring right at her for several seconds before zooming off. *Wow!*

Reagan smiled broadly, amazed at the timing and her good fortune. As she was about to turn away, another phenomenon caught her eye, as if begging for attention. It was a dark shape in the distant sky and was almost dismissed as a storm cloud until its mystical shapeshifting activity began warrantying further study.

She had heard of them, seen the photos—even a few videos, but always dreamt of one day witnessing one herself. And now she was observing one in real time: a murmuration!

Reagan caught her breath as her tunnel vision tried to focus on the hypnotic synchronicity of what had to be European Starlings, dancing their impossible dance and to a playlist only they could know. It was absolutely incredible to watch as the hundreds of feathered friends effortlessly zoomed back and forth, this way and that, expanding and contracting... and all without colliding into one another. She wondered if anyone else was watching this spectacle right now, or was it only being performed for her benefit? She liked to think it was the latter.

She continued to watch in slack jawed amazement for another several seconds before the beautiful black blob took a bow, dissipated, and vanished from view.

Tears rolled down Reagan's cheeks, and she found herself clapping her hands in appreciation of this gift. She closed her eyes and marked the moment, hoping to sear it into her memory forever.

Despite conscious efforts to avoid categorizing it as such, she knew she had just glimpsed a special kind of magic, and it could only have come from an invite to peek through the tent flap of *God's Greatest Hits*.

# CHAPTER EIGHTY-SEVEN

S TEFFI SAT AT the computer, multitasking with her bag of Flamin' Hot Cheetos, while Reagan used the magnifying glass to inspect her precious Hoya cuttings.

"Please make sure you don't get greasy hands on the electronics, honey."

"I won't," Steffi replied, wiping away the orange evidence from the new keyboard. "The new monitor's rad!"

"Yep, pretty rad," Reagan agreed, smiling at the descriptor.

"Hey, Mom. What's with these papers?"

"Which ones, honey?" she replied, busily wiping off the counters.

"These ones. Petition for... Name Change?"

*Oh, shit.* "Um...."

"Wait, are you actually thinking of changing your *name*? Why? I think Reagan's cool!"

Reagan hung up the towel and joined her daughter. She picked up the documents.

"Sorry, I haven't changed anything. Not yet, anyway. I wanted to have a talk with you about all this first."

Steffi looked up at her mother, clearly confused.

"And I agree, Reagan's cool. Actually, with all that's happened recently, I was considering the possibility of changing my *last* name—*Fynn's* last name—back to my maiden name: *Licht*. What would you think about that? I wouldn't do it without talking with you first."

Steffi took pause as she considered this. She leaned back in the chair and turned to her.

"Can I change mine, too? I think Dunkel's lame. It sounds like an effing donut shop."

# CHAPTER EIGHTY-EIGHT

WITH STEFFI STILL immersed in some apparently Top Secret activity on the computer, Reagan had decided to soak her sore parts, at length, in the hot bath.

Her butt didn't have the benefit of a pop-up Butterball turkey timer, but she was beginning to prune and was pretty sure she was done. Reagan enjoyed the last sip of her Limoncello and activated the drain. As she toweled off, she swore she could smell cookies baking.

She had been correct, and as she sauntered back into the kitchen, Reagan tightened the sash on her robe and beheld the Wonderland-in-progress as Steffi iced the last of the Christmas cookies. Santas, Christmas trees, candy canes, even a few stars. Steffi had really gone for it, and it was a nice surprise. Just seeing her girl rocking the elf hat nudged Reagan toward a festive mood.

"Look at you!" Reagan chirped, kissing her little elf on the cheek. "They're beautiful. Would it be okay if we bring some of these to Ames'? I told her we'd bring dessert?"

"Way ahead of you, madre!"

After cleaning up the kitchen mess, Steffi returned to the project at hand.

She kept an eye on things and made sure the volume of her earbuds was low enough to hear any requests. She glanced over occasionally from her vantage point in the computer chair as she put the finishing touches on her little project. She hoped her mom liked it.

Reagan sat on the patio in her favorite reclining chair, feet up, a water bottle in hand, and her eyes closed as she drank in the blissful silence. No lawnmowers, no neighbors sharing their hip-hop music. Just the buzz of hummers and the occasional cooing of a nesting pair of doves in the overhang.

It was a beautiful day, this early Christmas afternoon, with temperatures that seemed to have been plucked from May and inserted into December. Reagan wanted for nothing and had everything she needed in the moment, including a backup bottle of Arrowhead and two sugar cookies on the side table.

The sun was softly kissing Reagan's face, the roses were sharing their best perfume, and a refreshing breeze gently raked across her skin.

Her eyes might be closed, but her mind's eye wasn't. All of her senses were in play, she noted, and she could see it all with crystal clarity.

*Life is good.*

# CHAPTER EIGHTY-NINE

S HE HATED TO disturb her, as she'd never seen her mother look so absolutely content. Still, they would need to change clothes if they wanted to be on time. Plus, she had finished her little project.

"Mom?" she asked softly.

Reagan's eyes fluttered open, but the serene half-smile remained. "Hi, honey. Wow, I must've been out. It's just so glorious out... what time is it?"

"About a quarter to four. We'll need to get ready pretty soon. I see you finished your cookies."

"They were delicious," Reagan replied, extracting herself from the chair. "I'll put together a dessert plate we can bring with—"

"Done deal, Mom. I added some Dickmanns' to it, too. We're good."

"Aren't you something?"

"I am," Steffi said, smiling in agreement as she grabbed the empty cookie plate and gestured inside.

Reagan stepped into the living room and watched as Steffi

dragged a kitchen chair over to the workstation, parking it alongside the computer chair.

"So, Mom, why don't you bring your water bottle with you; I want to show you something. It won't take long," Steffi added, pointing toward the computer station.

"Something on the computer?"

"Yeah, you can sit here, in the computer throne where you'll be more comfortable."

"Okay," Reagan said, dutifully plopping into it and staring at the widescreen monitor as Steffi reached over and jostled the mouse to wake it from its factory screensaver.

"Here we go…"

"What are we–?"

"Just a moment," Steffi said, guiding the cursor toward the mystery icon. A quick check of the settings confirmed the speakers were on and things were ready for launch. "Oh…." She flipped on the runway lights for ambiance and switched off the kitchen lights to get rid of the glare. "Better. Ready?"

"I think so," Reagan said with a chuckle.

"Just a little something I…." Steffi paused, wiping away what might have been a tear. "Just… because I love you so much. More than ever, Mom," she said, her lip beginning to quiver. "Merry Christmas!"

Steffi clicked the mouse and grabbed a seat in the adjoining chair as the XDR 16:9 6K HDR IPS LCD-blah-blah monitor came to life, realizing its full potential as the video window filled the widescreen.

Bing Crosby's theme song coincided perfectly as an animated title card playfully announced, "It's Beginning to Look a Lot Like Christmas."

Reagan's hand squeezed Steffi's as the title card gave way to the first of several selfie images and landscapes documenting the positive aspects of their recent mother-daughter Germany trip.

Reagan's expressions ran the gamut, changing back and forth accordingly, as the musical slideshow played, with several new-to-her images from Steffi's phone having been incorporated into the mix with her own. Her smiles morphed to happy tears, then back again, her chuckles occasionally reduced to mere squeals of emotion as memories of the resplendent trip–and their precious time–played out.

Steffi had pulled all the stops, incorporating any number of fancy visual transitions and effects and, when Bing's song neared its end, she had mercilessly cross-faded to a song she knew would have a strong impact: "Santa Notte," by her mother's favorite artist, the multi-lingual and incomparable Caterina Valente.

Steffi rubbed her mother's hand as the new song faded up, tears forming in her own eyes as they were for her mom. Sung to the familiar melody of "Silent Night," the Italian lyrics were equally impactful–maybe even more so–as the highly charged song accompanied the many meaningful moments the two of them had captured together.

Reagan's shoulders were heaving slightly, her eyes wet with tears but locked into the presentation. A laugh escaped her when the photos of her eating sushi popped up, and when the final image faded away at the end of the song, Reagan broke down completely, the end graphic spelling out Steffi's sentiment: "Thanks for the Best Christmas Vacay Ever, Mom! I Love You!"

Steffi hugged her, adding her own happy sobs and tears to the mix, as the memories and the moment sunk in. The room was quiet, save a quiet cooing coming from the patio doves, and Steffi exited to grab a box of Kleenex for them to share.

Several minutes went by before anyone spoke, but one thing was clear: the magic memories of their Christmas vacation together were forever preserved. Anything negative, anything even approaching a bad memory of the horrific things they had both experienced—those memories would not populate their Christmas.

Not this year or any other.

Nothing, and no one, could ever take these magic moments away. Reagan knew she would never ever forget them.

"Thank you, baby."

# CHAPTER NINETY

## THURSDAY, DECEMBER 25
## CHRISTMAS
## 5:28 PM

REAGAN HAD CALLED the house earlier in the afternoon, thanking Jerry for his kind offer of transportation and telling him Steffi had felt strongly about driving.

It was already starting to get dark. Steffi slowly guided the Ford down the narrow street as they reached the cluster of townhouses. Parking was at a premium here, apparently, especially on Christmas.

"See anything?"

"You're asking the blind lady that?"

"Sorry. Poor choice of words. We may have to circle around and—*wait*... I see one!"

Steffi pulled alongside the one empty curb spot and took a moment to judge the feasibility of fitting between the Lincoln Navigator and Toyota Tacoma hogging the space.

"Didn't leave much room, did they?"

"Eh... watch and learn," Steffi muttered as she adroitly cut the wheel and parallel parked between the vehicles on her first try. She cut the ignition and turned to her mother, who was smiling proudly.

"You're going to ace that driving test, you'll see."

"Thanks."

"Mind grabbing the dessert tray from the backseat?"

"No worries."

Some of the townhouses on this block were modestly decorated for Christmas, to the extent allowed by the Homeowners' Association. Then there was Amethyst's and Jerry's, which dared to take the festivities to the next level with its garlands and oversized red bows adorning the railings to the porch, and a gorgeous, oversized wreath with colored lights on the front door.

The drapes were open, revealing a beautifully decorated, eight-foot-tall faux Christmas tree in the living room, splendid enough for the whole townhouse cluster to enjoy.

Steffi balanced the dessert tray with both hands while Reagan stepped up to the landing and pushed the doorbell button.

"Pretty," Reagan said, smiling at Steffi.

"Yeah."

A moment later, the door swung open wide, with Amethyst beaming her widest smile. She was rocking an all-red pantsuit, red heels, and her sparkly purple eyepatch.

"Twinner!! God, look at you!"

"Ames!" was all Reagan could get out before they swallowed each other in a warm bearhug. After a long moment smothered in her bestie's bosom, Reagan came up for air. "It is so good to see you, honey. You look amazing, as always."

"Aww, thanks, kiddo! You're a sight for a sore eye," Amethyst replied, risking the pun. They separated from the hug to get a better look at each other. Reagan shook her head, her smile a tight line as she took in the features of her best friend's face. Amethyst could sense Reagan's awkwardness as she seemed to be averting her eyes from the new sparkly accessory. "Kind of festive, huh?" she asked with a laugh, breaking the glacier.

Reagan's hand went up to her mouth as she tried not to giggle. She initiated a second hug and whispered in Ames's ear, "I love you. Thank you for inviting us to spend Christmas with you."

"Are you kidding? Jerry and I couldn't think of anybody else we'd rather spend it with," Ames replied, switching to a whisper as she said, "Besides, those Telluride cousins are weirdos."

This got another snicker from Reagan.

Ames shook her head, her arms spreading wide as she directed her attention to Steffi, standing one step behind her mom.

"Stef-a-*nee*!"

Steffi smiled broadly. She had always thought her mom's bestie to be cool. Even cooler now with the bitchin' patch. "Hey, Ames!"

"Come here, girl! Let me get a good look at your fine self!"

Steffi stepped up to the landing, handed her mom the dessert platter, and hugged Ames warmly. "Thanks for inviting us over."

"Don't mention it, sweetie. Here," Ames said, taking the dessert tray and stepping aside. "Come on inside. Jerry's out on the patio–with my Christmas present!"

"Did he get you a barbecue?" Steffi asked as she took a step inside.

"Uh, not quite!" Ames replied with a laugh.

Reagan followed Steffi, stopping in the middle of the living room, their mouths both hanging open as they took in the enormity of the Christmassy display. It was akin to stepping into a German Christmas store and, everywhere you looked, Amethyst's gift for decorating was evident.

The room was brightly lit, which helped Reagan as she directed her limited gaze to each zone, sweeping the room, and taking in each detail.

"I get a little obsessed around Christmastime," Ames admitted, smiling at her handiwork.

"It's absolutely gorgeous, Ames."

"So rad," Steffi agreed.

"I love this little Christmas village on the mantel," Reagan said, stepping in closer to admire the lights in the windows. "Reminds me of where I grew up."

"It's from over there! Jerry attended a conference in Munich and brought it back with him, years ago. It might be my favorite decoration."

"Well, everything's lovely," Reagan replied.

"Thanks. I'll just take this platter to the kitchen then, and—" Ames said, pausing as she got a closer look through the plastic wrap. "Mm... Christmas cookies! Nice. Wait... what are these other things, the dark ones?"

Steffi smiled at her mom knowingly, all too happy to provide the answer. "They're Super Dickmann's!" she said with a chuckle.

"*Dick* mans? Hm... I'm gonna have to try one of those!" she said, throwing her head back as she laughed and disappeared around the corner. "What can I get you two ladies?" she called out from the kitchen.

So as not to shout, Reagan and Steffi stepped into the kitchen where a veritable cocktail bar was on display atop the counter. "If that white wine's open, I'd love a glass of that, please."

"You've got it. How about you, Steffi? White Russian? Gin and Tonic?" the hostess asked kiddingly.

This got a hopeful smile from Stef.

"Don't give her any ideas, Ames!" Reagan interjected. "I confess to being the world's worst mom by introducing my princess to the wonderful world of egg nog the other night. She lived to tell about it, but barely," Reagan said, winking at her daughter.

"Maybe just some apple juice, thanks," Steffi replied.

"Apple juice we've got," Ames said as she prepared their beverages. "Jerry should be along any—"

"Tada!" came the booming bass voice, the greeting sounding like it had been delivered by the great Barry White making a stage entrance to a packed house.

It was the visual that caught Steffi off-guard, though, as it was a total mismatch. Jerry stepped into the kitchen, his outstretched pencil-thin arms swimming in the long-sleeved dress shirt, under an ugly Christmas-red sweater vest.

"Welcome, friends! Hi, Reagan!" he said, initiating a hug. She reciprocated, mindful not to break the stalky man in two.

"Hey, Jerry! Merry Christmas… it was so sweet of you and Ames to invite us over."

"Our pleasure, absolutely. And Steffi. Nice to see you, glad you could join us."

"Thanks, it's nice to be here."

Jerry stood about six-foot-four, by Reagan's estimation and, if she had to guess, about a hundred-seventy pounds. He had to be a foot taller than Ames. His full brown beard helped fill out what she guessed to be a very thin face underneath it.

Then there was the voice. Steffi bit her lip.

"I see everybody's got their beverages. I think I'll pour myself one of what Reagan's got there. Hon, what would you like?"

"I've got a glass of Zinfandel going already. Thanks," Ames replied.

"Okay then. So, the ham just came out of the oven twenty minutes ago and it's not going to carve itself," Jerry said, grabbing his apron, "so if you'll excuse me, maybe Ames can take you girls out back and show you her... Christmas present." He winked at Ames.

"Come, follow me. You might want to leave your drinks here."

Reagan and Steffi exchanged a shrug and set their glasses on the counter as they followed their hostess toward the patio slider.

Ames grabbed the wand that controlled the blinds and pulled them across the track, revealing little more than a pool of light coming from the porch fixture.

"Okay, get ready for the main event," she said with a smile as she put her hand on the glass slider's handle.

"Ready," Steffi replied.

"Yep. Ready," Reagan said.

Ames nodded and slowly slid the slider open. She was the first to step out and after a couple of steps, she stopped and switched to a higher pitch form of baby talk.

"Wow… look at you! Right where I left you! Who's a good girl? Huh? That's my good girl…."

Steffi and Reagan stepped out as well and when they saw who she was directing it to, their eyes went wide. Steffi's especially. There, sitting majestically and perfectly still, was the most beautiful dog either of them had either seen.

"Good girl, Sadie!" Ames said, pouring on the praise as the stunning, knee-high, tan and white Pitbull mix sat there proudly. She looked like a carving by Michelangelo.

Steffi was chomping at the bit and barely able to suppress a squeal.

"Guys, I'd like to introduce you to… Sadie!"

This kicked Sadie's tail wagging up to the next speed as Steffi took a tiny step forward, her smile a mile wide. "Oh, my God… Mom, look!"

Reagan's tight smile relaxed slightly as she took in the sight. This wasn't the run-of-the-mill hyper dog she was accustomed to enduring on her neighborhood walks; this was obviously a very special animal. Still, Reagan hung back and watched from her comfort zone.

Steffi came another step closer and looked at Ames. "Is it okay if I pet him?"

"*Her*… and yes. She's quite social," Ames replied, beaming proudly.

"Hi, baby… Hi, Sadie… ," Steffi said as she delicately stroked the appreciative pooch's fine coat, the dog's tail wagging at full speed. "Mom. You have to pet her!"

"I don't know…." Reagan said, her hands stuffed in her pockets. "Dogs have never seemed to like me much. I guess I'm just not much of a pet person."

Sadie turned toward the sound of her voice. She seemed to

be making a connection with Reagan, looking at her with her soulful eyes before walking over and sitting nicely at her feet.

Sadie offered her right paw in a gesture of "shake."

"Oh, my," Reagan said softly, not entirely sure what to do. "What's she–?"

"She's asking you to shake, Mom!"

"Really?"

"What a good girl, Sadie," Ames said, encouraging the interaction. "Can you shake hands with my bestie, Ray?" Ames turned to Reagan and smiled. She could sense her apprehension. "It's okay, Ray. She won't bite."

"Isn't she... she's a Pitbull, right?"

"Part Pittie, yeah, but don't believe bad things you may have heard about the breed. They often get a bad rap. It's all in the way they're raised, really, and how you train them. They can be the sweetest, most loving dogs of all, really." Ames said before pivoting back to Sadie. "You're living proof... isn't that right, sweet girl?"

Sadie smiled back then turned her thoughtful gaze back to Reagan.

*You survived sushi, Reagan. You can survive this.*

Reagan's right hand emerged from her pocket, and she slowly reached out, her palm facing upward, as Sadie set her paw gently on it. The pad of the dog's paw felt pillowy soft resting in Reagan's hand, and she bit her lip, almost ready to cry as she gave the paw a gentle shake before pulling her hand back. "I've never ever done that before," she said, looking at her bestie. "What a love...."

"Believe me, that was my reaction too. I didn't even know I wanted a dog until Jerry brought her home from the shelter. Sadie's so chill. I'm just hoping I'm not allergic. She has a great energy, and you can see her appreciation in her eyes." Ames switched to the dog-directed baby talk as she continued. "Isn't that right, sweetie? Who's my pretty princess?"

"Does she have a sister? A brother?" Steffi asked, wanting to adopt her clone on the spot if there was one.

"Not that I know of. I think she's one in a million, really. The shelters are full, and she'd likely have been scheduled for euthanasia if Jerry hadn't stepped in," Ames replied with a sigh.

"You're both very lucky, you and Sadie," Reagan said, unable to take her eyes off the dog. "What an amazing Christmas gift!"

"Yeah… okay, I'd better put her back in her crate so we can eat our dinner. Steffi, want to come along and help me with her?"

"Can I, Mom?" Steffi asked, her enthusiasm on full display.

"Of course, honey. I'll meet you guys inside," she replied with a wink.

"We'll just be a minute," Ames said, smiling at her bestie as she handed Steffi the leash.

"Come on, Sadie," Steffi said, a song in her voice.

A grin slowly found Reagan's face and she let out a sigh as she watched the pooch dutifully walk with them toward the side of the house. Before the three of them disappeared around the corner, Sadie paused momentarily, looking over her shoulder to check in with Reagan, who waved back.

*I love you, too, Sadie.*

# CHAPTER NINETY-ONE

R EAGAN FINISHED HER last bite of candied yams and dabbed her mouth with the fancy cloth napkin, hoping not to soil it. She hadn't used a cloth one since she was a kid, at her grandmother's.

"Hey, you guys… dinner was amazing. Really, *everything* was just perfect. Thank you."

"We're so happy we could share Christmas dinner with you. Glad you enjoyed it," Ames replied, taking a sip of her Zin. She turned to her husband. "Save those little ham scraps for Sadie."

Jerry pushed another large forkful into his mouth, nodded his acknowledgement and smiled as he chewed.

"Yes, it was really, really good," Steffi said, pushing her plate away, unaware that she was staring at Jerry's manic, bouncing Adam's apple. All she could think about was Ichabod Crane, or the Jack Sprat guy in that freaky nursery rhyme she'd read a million times.

"Well, I don't know about anybody else, but I saved myself for a Super Dickmann's!" Ames blurted with a laugh as Jerry almost did a projectile spit take.

The group congregated to the family room, where everyone had engaged the reclining buttons on the two leather couches.

"You need some more light, hon?" Ames asked as Steffi inspected the outer edge of the monstrous eighty-inch flatscreen.

"No, I think I found it," she replied, as she inserted the USB to HDMI adapter into the proper input. "Yep, we're good."

"Pass your mama that Kleenex box before you sit down, please," Reagan said.

"Dickmann anyone?" Ames asked, offering the nearly empty platter.

"Why not?" Jerry said, grabbing two. He obviously had zero concerns about calories.

Steffi handed her mom the box of tissues and sunk into the reclining seat next to hers.

"Ready?"

"How long is the video, sweetie?" Ames asked, noting the wall clock showed 7:15.

"It's like five minutes, I think. Maybe six." Steffi replied.

"Perfect. Go for it," she said with a smile.

As the screen came to life, Reagan sighed and coaxed a tissue from the box. The title card was just coming up, and the tears were already forming.

As the video faded to black, Steffi brought the room lights back up with the other remote. Other than the sound of sniffles, things were quiet.

Amethyst carefully dabbed a tissue at the area behind her patch. Her temporary eye prosthesis was only a "conformer," meant to hold space and avoid scar tissue until her doctor determined she'd be ready for her permanent prosthesis, likely in February. Even so, her tear ducts still worked fine.

"Lord, have mercy," she managed. "Steffi, that was absolutely beautiful. Whew...."

"Yes. It looks like you had a terrific vacation," Jerry said, smiling cluelessly.

Steffi and Reagan shared a knowing look and nodded. "It... was," Reagan conceded. She turned to Steffi. "Thank you again, sweetheart. That's the best gift I've ever received. Love you."

She and Steffi shared a brief hug. Ames glanced back up at the clock: 7:27.

"Okay, y'all. Grab your coats. Service starts at eight, and it's a ten-minute drive."

"Service?" Reagan asked, having no clue of the plan.

"Oh, I forgot to tell you: Church. You've heard of it," Ames replied, chuckling. She reached out her hand to help liberate her bestie from the recliner. "C'mon. It'll be good for you."

# CHAPTER NINETY-TWO

## THE AWAKENING CHURCH
## BELLEVUE, WASHINGTON
## CHRISTMAS, 7:52 PM

REAGAN WRUNG HER hands nervously as she sat next to Steffi in the backseat of Jerry's Volvo. There had been no mention of church being on the agenda and she felt almost blindsided. She checked the pocket of her coat, taking inventory of the emergency tissues she'd stuffed there during the video.

*Gawd.*

The parking lot was absolutely packed with cars for the Christmas service, and a line of parishioners were filing into the church building.

"I'll let you three out and go find a parking place... maybe in Kirkland," he joked as the ladies climbed out. "Save me a seat, I'll find you."

"'Kay," Amethyst said, slamming the door. "Just in time, you guys. This way!"

Ames spotted a friend and waved to her. The woman waved back, smiling awkwardly as she did a doubletake at the eyepatch. *Whatever.*

As they continued toward the chapel, Ames suddenly stopped in her tracks, gesturing to her companions before bringing her hand up to her nose. "Excuse me, ladies… I… I… have to–" she managed before rearing her head back and letting out a ferocious sneeze: "*AAH-CHOOO!!*"

"Gesundheit!" Reagan said.

"Bless you," Steffi agreed.

"Phew… thank you both," Ames replied, wiping her nose with a tissue.

"Hope you're not catching a cold, Twinner."

"Nah, don't think so. I just hope it's not an allergy…."

As they joined the queue at the entrance, Steffi thought back to what Ames had mentioned right before dinner. As the two of them were putting Sadie in her crate, Ames had reiterated her allergen concerns, hoping they wouldn't manifest, because that could result in the need to return Sadie to the shelter. That would be both heartbreaking and a death sentence.

And not an option.

*Or… maybe this might be performance art for Mom's benefit… ?* Ames and she had both witnessed the spark between the two. Either way, Steffi knew she would be praying hard once they got inside, because she'd be lying if she said she wasn't hoping for Sadie to come home with *them.*

With Reagan and Steffi in tow, Ames shimmied to the middle of an aisle near the back of the church. As they took their seats on the oak pew, she noted it was comfortable enough for three and would be tight once Jerry arrived. *Good thing he's skinny.*

The light was dim inside the chapel, with the sparce accent lights trained on the large wooden cross, the pulpit, and the steps leading up to it. Perfect potted poinsettias were placed at three-foot intervals along the bottom step.

Reagan fidgeted with the paper program, rolling it into a tube in her sweaty hands. She wouldn't be able to read it anyway.

As the last of the congregation found their seats, things got very quiet. Other than an occasional cough, the only sound Reagan was aware of was that of her heart pounding in her chest.

"Good evening, and welcome to our special Christmas service," the pastor said.

He looked pleasant enough, Reagan thought. Early forties with a nice, seemingly genuine smile. His arms were spread wide as he continued his welcome.

"It's a joy to have you all with us tonight as we celebrate the birth of our lord Jesus...."

*Jeezus.*

"It's a time of joy, of love, family... and memories of fond traditions. But this is also a time to reflect upon not only our memories, but also the life lessons we have had along the way."

Reagan's sweaty grip on the program tightened. Amethyst, sensing this, reached over and rested her hand lightly on her bestie's knee.

"God puts many challenges in front of us. He puts challenges in our path as a way for us to learn and to grow. For us to blossom. He is a loving God who grants us many joys, and He loves to celebrate our successes when we rise to the challenges He's placed before us."

Reagan's hand found its way into the pocket of her coat lying next to her, her fingers grasping what felt like four tissues, in the event the pastor decided to further riff on the theme of challenges.

*Challenges* she knew.

With the weird, spotty lighting in there, her tunnel vision could only really focus on two things: The big, well-lit, impossible-to-ignore cross, and the man now speaking. A light was trained on him perfectly. Everything else fell off into grainy shadow, with a hint of reddish blur coming from the poinsettia.

"For many, this past year has been one of challenges. Even the most blessed amongst us have experienced lows that we did not expect. This is true for me as well. This year will soon be behind us, and for some, that will not come a moment too soon."

*Amen.*

"If *you* are struggling, if *you* feel you are walking in the dark, walking on a hopeless path during this Christmas season, have hope. Cast your gaze upon Jesus and put your trust in Him."

A smattering of soft *amens* came from the congregation.

Reagan turned to Steffi to see how she was reacting and was surprised to be treated with a smile and a nod in response. On Reagan's other side, Ames squeezed her hand. She seemed to be trapped in a support sandwich.

"Remember that God loves you. God can bring hope into *any* situation you may face. And with the knowledge of that love, that's where we find *hope*."

The wad of tissue was now sitting on Reagan's lap, in the on-deck circle and at the ready.

"As we celebrate this season, let's remember this verse from Jeremiah 29:11: *'For I know the plans I have for you,'* declares the Lord. *'Plans to prosper you and not to harm you. Plans to give you hope and a future.'*"

The pastor raised his hands, his arms stretching wide, as he took this part of his message home before the hymn that would follow. "So, as we celebrate this joyous day, I invite each of you to open your eyes, and your heart, to the hope that Jesus Christ can give to your life… let us take this moment to send up our silent prayers as we pray for hope."

Many heads bowed, while others cast their faces to the ceiling and closed their eyes, lifting their hands palms-up into the air, swaying gently as if spring flowers in a breeze. The chapel went quiet for two minutes as people sent up their concerns, their hopes, their praises.

During this, Jerry managed to squeeze in next to Amethyst. He bowed his head.

Steffi bowed hers as well. Her heartfelt prayer was well underway.

Reagan's thoughts went to her concerns: not concerns for herself–she was now resigned to the utterly dark world she would be facing in the not-too-distant future–but for the challenges her daughter would likely face in the years to come as her inherited Retinitis Pigmentosa slowly came home to roost.

*Maybe they might develop a cure to spare my precious Stefanie the irreversible blindness I'm now facing. Surely the experiments with mice will reveal a cure, right, God? Or maybe some kind*

*of miracle injection, maybe? Something. She has time. Please...
there has to be—*

A larger smattering of *amens* rolled in as the two large
monitors lit up on either side of the chapel. The organist
began playing the opening bars of the hymn as the twelve-
person choir rose from their seats.

*But I wasn't done!*

Reagan's foot was rocking nervously. She knew this one,
which scared the bejesus out of her. She turned to her bestie
with a look that told her she was about ready to lose it.

Ames patted Reagan's knee gently, offering comfort as if
to a young child. Reagan searched her bestie's face, her expression exuding only love. This coming from somebody who had
just lost an eye! Ames leaned over and whispered into her ear,
"You've got this, Ray," just as the choir launched into it.

Steffi leaned over, resting her head against her mother's
other shoulder, which was now heaving uncontrollably.

Before she realized it, Reagan sensed herself being slowly
pulled into the deep end. The tug was quite gentle, yet she
surmised she was powerless to swim against it if she were to
try. It felt like her feet were no longer touching the bottom,
yet she was buoyant, floating along as the pastor's message
combined with the hymn's lyrics, safely washing over her in
a soft, comforting wave.

Reagan could only go with it.

She recognized the challenges she faced were indeed many.
As much as she hated not being in control, she slowly began
to relinquish it, surrendering to the power of the message.

As Reagan held her bestie's hand, she felt a gentle squeeze
of encouragement coming from her. Tears rolled down her

cheeks as she listened to the unfamiliar, yet truly beautiful, singing voice of her teenaged daughter.

Reagan closed her eyes and let go, lost in the spiritual undertow, as she found herself giving it all to God. As the congregation continued to sing, a great weight seemed to be lifting from her, and an appreciative smile slowly spread across her face.

*A-mazing grace! How sweet the sound,*

*That saved a wretch like me!*

*I once was lost, but now I'm found,*

*Was blind, but now I see...*

# ABOUT THE AUTHOR

Jafe Danbury hails from the trenches of the Hollywood production scene, where he spent decades as a camera operator, director of photography, and director. He has also worked as a teacher and is a decorated U.S. Navy veteran.

He enjoys noodling on the guitar, long road trips, likes his bacon crispy, and loves a good dive bar—especially if it happens to have a twenty-two foot shuffleboard table. He prefers a leisurely walk to running, unless being chased by a clown with a chainsaw.

Jafe and his lovely bride currently reside in central

California and are working on their exit plan. Their children currently consist of several rescue dogs and a wacky umbrella cockatoo, but their house has a revolving door when it comes to rescue critters and may include the occasional owl, abandoned sparrow, or wayward kitten.

***Before the Lights Go Out*** is his fifth novel.

## ALSO BY JAFE DANBURY:

*The Other Cheek*

*Leaving Phoenix*

X

*So Much Forever*

# AUTHOR'S NOTE

As with all of my book projects, I tend to do a deep dive when it comes to the research involved, as I endeavor to get things right in telling the stories.

The idea for *Before the Lights Go Out* came to me quite by accident. I remember first learning of the untreatable genetic condition known as Retinitis Pigmentosa (RP) back in October of 2022, when I read an excellent online news story written by Meghan Holohan, Health Editor at Today.com.

The story profiled a Canadian couple, Edith Lemay and Sebastien Pelletier, who had been given a nightmarish prognosis when they had their three young children evaluated for their severely diminished night vision. All three kids were struggling to see in dimly lit conditions, with their youngest bumping into walls and furniture.

When their ophthalmologist diagnosed all three children with a debilitating genetic disease that would eventually render them completely blind, it hit the parents like a ton of bricks.

Disbelief and shock gave way to denial, anger, and sadness.

With no known cures for RP on the horizon, the family was faced with a very harsh reality. Rather than wallow in despair over a prognosis they had no control over, the couple decided to take action and focus on what's good.

At the suggestion of a counselor, they decided to "offer them experiences."

They began traveling, with the goal being to show their children how beautiful the world is, and to fill their visual memory with as many beautiful things as possible. Bucket lists were filling for each along the way!

The family's heartbreaking prognosis became a heartwarming story, and it stuck with me.

It was a short time later that I began to wonder if there might be a way I could take that kernel of a premise and perhaps put a dramatic, even thrilling, twist on it. I decided I wanted to try it, so I set about reading all the literature I could find about RP.

I digested several heart wrenching books written by people who were diagnosed with the disease and how it affected their daily lives. I read many scientific articles and technical journals about it. RP is a cruel companion; it can be a slow-motion trainwreck for those who are diagnosed with it, and as I write this there is still no known cure. My heart breaks for anyone who is afflicted.

Still, there are several experimental studies being conducted, and—like most diseases—there's hope that science will eventually come out with a treatment for it. Hopefully sooner than later.

This story is just that... a story. But I tried to shine a light on some of the challenges one faces and make it an entertaining read at the same time. I took some dramatic license, here and there, and any errors are my own.

At the end of the day, like all of my stories, it's a story of hope and even redemption. It's what I try to instill in my writing, even when it takes some very dark paths in the telling. I like to think that we all hold out hope when things are at their darkest and, ideally, find it... before the lights go out.

That's my wish for Edith Lemay and Sebastien Pelletier, and their children as well.

While I'm at it, I'd like to thank several people. Firstly, my editorial guru, Lisl, who has taken me on once again for this, our fifth book project together! Many thanks, "Coach!" As always, your awesome sauce is evident.

To my beautiful wife, Martina, who had to deal with me hunkering down in my little writing dungeon for the better part of a year to craft this: "Danke!"

I'd also like to thank a longtime friend and fellow veteran of Hollywood, the multitalented Fred Martin, who graciously supplied me with the moody source image that would eventually become the background for the street scene on the front cover of this book. Thank you, sir, for your artistry and generosity.

And I'd like to give a shout out to my own awesome optometrist, Dr. Colvert Gonzales, O.D., at Hattori Vision Center, in Monterey, California. "Dr. Covie" is an amazing optometrist, in that he is not only a consummate professional, and amazing at what he does, but he also always takes the time–and seems to relish any opportunity–to fully explain everything in a clear, easy to understand manner. I always come away from my visits with a greater understanding about how the eyeball works, and for that I'm appreciative.

I hope he approves of the way I told this story.

And I hope you do too. If so, I'd be deeply grateful if you might favor me with a review on Amazon, Goodreads, and/

or Barnes & Noble. It's your feedback that keeps me going! Thank you in advance, truly.

Thank you for taking the journey with me, and blessings to you all! Oh, and I almost forgot: **You can listen to Reagan's complete 2-hour, 34-song playlist on Spotify!**

*"Before The Lights Go Out" (JafeToonz)*

Here's the link to it… enjoy!! ~ Jafe Danbury

https://open.spotify.com/playlist/0B1hWAh8N0V1pzUmrluBxJ

JafeDanbury.com

Linktr.ee/JafeDanbury

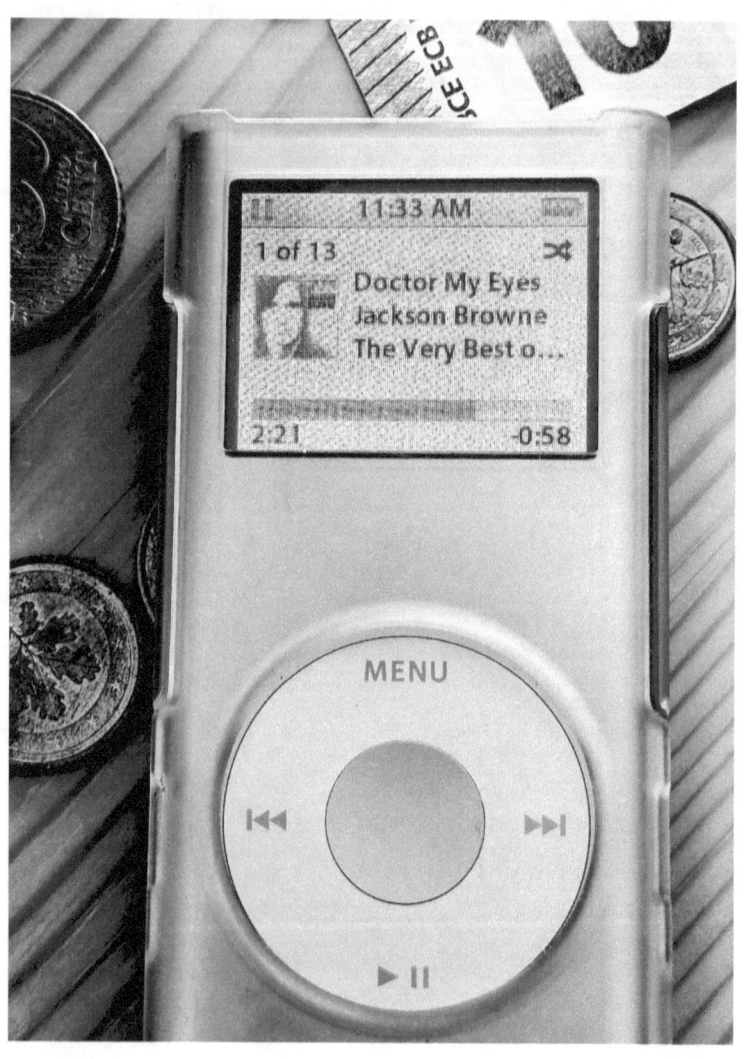

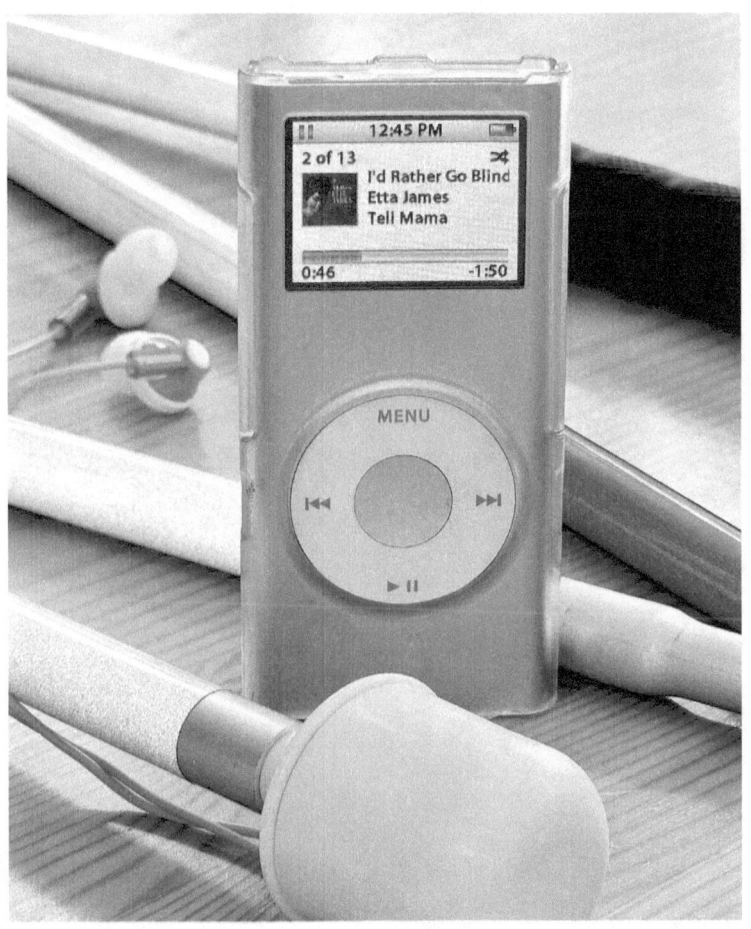

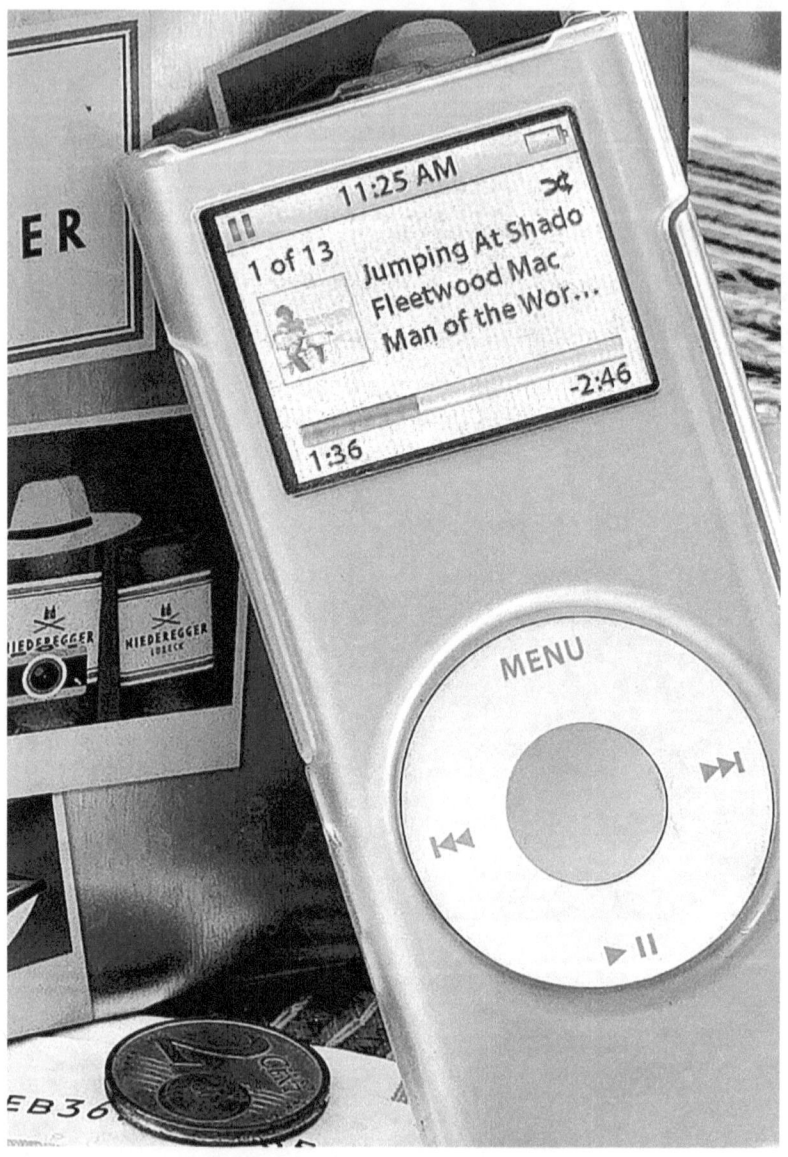